FATE UNTOLD

NZ KHOTIMSKY

ISBN: 979-8-9861496-0-8 (Paperback)

To everyone who believed in me

Trigger Warning

This story contains sensitive material including but not limited to sexual content, profanity, sexual abuse, abusive relationships, death, blood, trauma, murder, violence, and more.

Part 1

ONE

*D*ying was like the final period at the end of a novel. But what happened after the last page? An eternity of whatever comes next? Or the finality of a closed book? I glanced out the window, the town blurring in the background as my thoughts continued to hold me captive in my head.

Vita loved adventure, and I knew no matter where she was, she was living big.

No, not big— Grand.

But one thing I knew for sure; she wasn't dead. She couldn't be.

"She's lost in her head again, poor thing." My mother eyeballed me in the rearview mirror. She spoke of me in third person as if that would eliminate any chance of me hearing her.

A sharp speed bump caused my head to be thrown forward, and my finger slid through the foggy pattern I created on the cold backseat window with my idle breath. I sighed and resumed my craft while trying to tune out my parents in the front.

"Lisa, dear, be sensitive. These are trying times. Poor girl just lost her *sister*," my father said from the passenger seat, saying "sister" in a whisper. He spoke softly, a poor effort to conceal his less-than-comforting words.

My parents exchanged a quick glance as my mother stopped at a red light. I wondered if they thought about death together. They always operated as a unit and breathed as a unit. Would they take their last breath at the same time? Would they hold hands?

They weren't wrong— my sister was indeed *lost*. She'd been lost since August, three months now. Gone while the leaves turned brown and fell off. Gone as the snow had already touched the ground. But not dead.

Time passed at a glacial rate as the red light took ages to change, and my mother buried her face in her hands. "I won't be able to drive all the way home. David, can we switch?" My mother racked back a sob. "To have a funeral for our oldest child—" She gulped some air. "Good heavens." My father reached over and rubbed her back, his other hand pinching his eyebrows together.

It was hardly a funeral. A funeral would indicate that the dead person in question was present in some shape or form. In a casket.

A grain from an urn. A seed. One of those necklaces people made from ashes— Anything.

Vita wasn't there. My sister was lost, but she was hardly dead. How could she be when her body was never located? She disappeared without a trace. The police searched for months and gave up, but that doesn't mean she was dead. It was probably some elaborate off the grid detox she saw on the internet. That sounded more like Vita.

A month after my sister disappeared, the police told my parents that the chances of finding her alive were minimal and unrealistic. I can still remember the monotony in their voices as their generic terms staled the mood. They couldn't have sounded more disinterested if they tried.

After the second month, the cops called off all the searches but were still accepting phone calls from anyone who might've had any clues to contribute. Once we hit the third month, they already forgot her name and moved onto the next big case in our small town, slapping a cold case stamp on her folder and stashing it away in some dusty cabinet in the basement. Vita's five minutes of fame were recalled, replaced, and redistributed.

My parents were beyond devastated as the last of their hope flickered out, and they spiraled into the dark cloud that continued to hover over their heads. They said so themselves in their hushed conversations thinking I couldn't hear.

Vita is gone forever. She was taken too soon. She's in a better place.

What my parents failed to realize was that Vita wasn't actually dead – she was just lost. I would know if she were dead. I'd have felt it. Any time Vita was sick in our childhood, I felt it in my bones. The day she broke her clavicle in sixth grade, I felt it in class. The day she got mono freshman year of high school; I was on edge during my seventh-grade field trip.

My parents were too quick to give up. Perhaps it was their coping mechanism. I couldn't fault them. Sometimes, it was easier to give up rather than watch your waning hope grow thin until it leaves you in a state of perpetual mental purgatory.

But to call what we just came from a funeral was insulting to Vita. If she were attending, she'd have been smiling and rolling her eyes at the theatrics of an empty casket that was buried in an empty plot in a thriving cemetery in a prime real estate section. I can't even remember what the funeral director said. That's how unoriginal it was. Meanwhile, my parents held each other and shivered from their tears as if he was professing something profound.

During his obviously rehearsed speech that he probably said for every funeral, all I was thinking about was the grave they chose for her. Her quaint grave was right beside a looming weeping willow tree, the lazy branches brushing against her headstone every so often with a welcoming touch.

If Vita were actually dead, she'd have a monument that soared well above that weeping willow. She might even be a statue herself. She loved taking pictures of herself, not because she was shallow – but because she appreciated the art in photography. Vividly remembering our memories and conversations just by reminiscing through the photos, having an otherworldly sense of self.

After Vita disappeared, I studied the last photos I had of her on my phone. No one else could capture a moment frozen in time like I could, she'd always say. Thus my entire camera roll was full of my memories with Vita. Countless moments when all I wanted to do was get away from life and she had a way of making it feel worthwhile.

Someone like Vita doesn't just disappear inexplicably. There was obviously more to the stor—

"Alluna, dear, we're home," my mother said through a hitched breath.

I blinked myself back into a reality I didn't want to be a part of.

My parents were giving me sad smiles. My mother's strong angular eyebrows and narrow jaw reminded me of my sister, whose features were sharper than mine.

"Go wash up for dinner," my mother said as she wiped her bleary eyes and tried to compose herself with an action-oriented task. It helped her most days to focus on cooking or cleaning. Drowning herself in work kept her hands busy. Typing away and answering phone calls during her remote job as a paralegal distracted her from her daughter's disappearance.

My father wasn't a man of many words, I could hardly ascertain his thoughts from his head. He trailed behind my mother like a lingering wisp of smoke.

No matter how much everyone else tried to resume their life, Vita's absence hung over them. I couldn't - and wouldn't shake the feeling that she was still out there somewhere.

For lack of any rational reason, I gravitated toward Vita's bedroom every day, pretending she was there sleeping next to me. It made me feel closer after she left me with no explanation. My room was full of dark jeweled tones, year-round foliage, mini pumpkins decorating each corner, and earthy scents. I could never make my room sparkle the way Vita did. Hers was an explosion of springtime, full of shimmering pastels. It always made me feel like I was stepping into a different world. A more exciting one, at least.

I lied on her bed, counting the repeated patterns on her flowery wallpaper. My eyes fell to her laptop case. Particularly, the piece of paper sticking out. Initially, it didn't strike me as anything out of the ordinary.

Until I realized that it was uncommon for someone like Vita to have random pages in her room. She was practically digital and hadn't had a looseleaf paper full of notes since elementary school. She'd convinced our parents to get her an iPad in sixth grade and was the talk of the school with her bedazzled case.

Unable to fathom what this paper was and why I hadn't found it before, I pulled it out, my eyes bulging at the words before me.

How to do New York City (from the next resident expert) was the title written at the top in Vita's handwriting.

As I gingerly held the bucket list in my hands, I was suddenly struck with something caught between the intersection of Epiphany Lane and Inspiration Road. Whatever struck me might as well have been a fully loaded proverbial pistol with the big bang that lit up the synapses in my brain.

There were at least a dozen locations on the list, some that I recognized straight out of Gossip Girl and Sex and the City— our two absolute favorite shows.

I couldn't believe Vita had never told me about this list. It was full of glorious filming locations, adorable photo ops, and stores that we talked about for days. We used to daydream about strutting through 5th Ave in our Jimmy Choos, shopping bags in hand, making a pit stop in Central Park with our overpriced lattes, prattling about rich people problems. How could the caterer have served croquembouche hor d'oeuvres when we clearly requested Chantilly cream? And the maid—the nerve of that maid—who dared bring us a cashmere blanket when we ordered silk? Men at our fingertips who wanted to shower us with lavish gifts and everflowing adoration at our very presence while we graced the streets with class dripping from our pearls. The real New York City dream.

Bringing the paper back to her bed, I held the list close to my heart and imagined Vita was beside me. She would've told me that the list was a surprise itinerary for us when we finally went together. She would've said that once we returned home, we would be changed individuals. She would've said that it was our step into the vast pool of metropolitan life in the city that never sleeps. Our first bite into the forbidden Big Apple.

I could hardly believe I discovered this list, not that Vita had gone to great lengths to conceal it. All I had to do was enter her room, as I did every day, and see the paper right before my very eyes. How could I have been so blind?

After months of nothing new from Vita, I was now in possession of a precious treasure. Something that could've been created as recently as the day she left. There were no dates indicating when the paper was written. She could've left it there for me in her laptop case—hidden in plain sight—so I could put the puzzle pieces of her disappearance together. Connect the dots with these bucket list hot spots. Maybe she took the trip without me? New York certainly seemed like a hotspot for people to go soul-searching and find themselves. But there was no way she would've gone without telling me.

I could feel the neurons in my brain firing explosively as I carefully folded the paper, tucked it in my pocket, and opened her laptop. I was googling the first location faster than my mind could process and pulling up photos.

Dumbo near the Brooklyn Bridge. A quaint little area with cobblestone streets, high-end boutiques and unbelievable views. The images of the skyline at sunset splayed across my screen, the fiery orange skies with red tangs intermingling with the skyscrapers that seemed to caress the clouds above. At a total loss for words, I imagined seeing this sight in person and failed to comprehend the real-life beauty that I'd find.

Just as I was about to click on another website, a news article caught my attention.

Another NYC Disappearance Takes The City By Surprise

Was I hallucinating? Clicking onto the link, I navigated my way into the heart of the article.

...third disappearance in three months, all young women, early twenties, vanishing into thin air, police perplexed...

I slammed the laptop shut. No matter how coincidental everything seemed, I couldn't just connect my sister's disappearance to New York City. People disappeared all the time, all over the world. Just because New York City was Vita's dream didn't mean it meant anything. I didn't have to go and connect random dots across the globe. I wouldn't. The only place I should've gone was downstairs for dinner.

Just as I stood and straightened out the pastel blue skirt I wore to Vita's fake funeral as a personal homage to someone who could never stand the color black, especially for a funeral, my mother called me to dinner.

"David, you left the onion puree uncovered in the fridge." My mother took her seat beside my father. I waited for her to take her first bite before helping myself to the roast she'd prepared for supper.

"Now the whole fridge will smell like onion," she grumbled before grabbing the salad prongs and putting some greens on my plate.

"Lisa, I happen to like my apples with an essence of onion," my father said with his mouth full of roast. His light teasing relaxed my mother's shoulders in the slightest, though it was clear she would still cling to small things and stress over stuff that didn't matter. One would think that upon losing her oldest daughter, her mother would be thinking about that rather than apples smelling like onions.

The mutter of my parent's unimportant conversation lulled me into a numbed state until Vita's bucket list poked out of my pocket, and I gently tucked it back in.

How could my parents have been thinking about anything besides their missing daughter? Was I the only one who loved her so fiercely that I now had a gaping hole in my heart where her laughter used to be?

"Alluna dear, stop playing with your food. Eat up," my mother said in passing while she spoke of the family car's need for an oil change.

Gripping my fork with white knuckles, I forced some food down my dry throat.

Vita could've been in danger somewhere. Who knew what dark alley she could be stuck in? Who knew what a vile monster could be doing to her in the middle of the night? Who knew how many times she tried to escape, only to find that her hometown police had given up on her? Too many nights had she been all by herself. Too long had she been abandoned by those who loved her most.

I never believed she was dead. Until I saw her rotting body myself, I knew she was out there somewhere. I knew she was waiting for me. And I knew I had to find her if no one else would.

With these thoughts circling my head like a swarm of vultures ready to swoop in on their prey, I found myself speaking for the first time and saying, "I'm moving to New York."

TWO

*I*mpulsive or not, I felt an unusual tug to do some soul-searching, if not for myself, then for my sister. The more I thought about it, the more it felt like the only thing that made sense in my miserable life. For once, I could take charge. Maybe even discover what happened to Vita along the way, especially with my newfound treasure map.

But my mother was less than supportive.

Her eyes narrowed. "You're going where now?"

"New York." My eyes remained on my uneaten plate.

"New York?" She repeated.

"City."

"You're going to New York City?"

"That's what I said." I finally locked eyes with my mother, silently standing my ground.

"Watch your tone, young lady," she scolded.

"I'm sorry," I said noncommittally, my mind a million miles away, mentally creating a list of things to pack. Though I couldn't form any rationale behind my decision, my mind was set in stone. There was no way I'd budge, not even if my mother decided to unleash herself on me.

"What in the world will you do for money? You've never worked a day in your life. You hardly know how to do your own dishes. Have you ever even done your own laundry? Maybe if you started taking responsibility around the house, I'd feel like you're ready. You're still a child."

She knew exactly what to say to make me feel incompetent. But she'd never understand the turmoil in my heart, and I couldn't expect her to.

"I'm twenty-two, Mom."

"You're behaving like a child with such ridiculous nonsense. Moving to New York City," she scoffed, "when you've never cooked for yourself or done your own taxes."

"Then I'll learn."

"It's because of Vita, isn't it?"

Well, that struck a nerve. I struggled with sticking to just "no" in a small voice.

"What's wrong with our town?" My mother continued. "What's wrong with our house? Am I just a bad mom, is that it?

Are you just trying to punish me for not being strict enough with Vita? I gave her all the freedom she wanted because she was so full of life and I couldn't stand in her way…"

What I wanted to say was, *But you could clearly stand in my way, Mom. Because I wasn't as strong as Vita. I wasn't as independent.*

What I actually said was nothing. There wasn't any room to speak. No room to stand up for myself, despite knowing I was dangerously close to my breaking point.

"…there is no way you are moving to New York. Vita wouldn't have wanted that." There it was. The straw that broke the camel's back. My mother returned to her plate as if she didn't just gut me.

"You have no idea what Vita would've wanted!" I yelled at my mother for the first time in twenty-two years. She looked just as shocked as I was with my outburst, but with that, I stormed away from the dinner table, grabbed the car keys off the counter and slammed the front door behind me.

The last time Vita and I went out together before she disappeared, we'd gone to our favorite Starbucks drive-through in Hershey, Pennsylvania. It was our tradition to go at least one night a week to visit the cute barista named Chex. Part of our tradition was gushing over his chocolate brown eyes for the remaining hour in the parking lot while laughing over our seasonal drinks. She always said she was rooting for us, claiming she'd be the best wingwoman.

All I had to do was get my driving license so that he would see me through the window.

Upset by the conversation earlier, I went to get the only thing I knew would cheer me up. A Peppermint Toasted White Chocolate Mocha. Vita's favorite signature winter drink. The only time she would hang up her pastels and enjoy the holiday season. It was half past nine and the parking lot of our Starbucks was empty, except for a few loose cars strewn around, sloppily parked. I watched Chex exit his Toyota and head to clock in for his night shift. Vita and I used to spy on him during our weekly check-ins. Not once was it creepy when we were doing it together, yet now, as I peeked timidly over the wheel, I felt like I was stalking him. It felt wrong to participate in this tradition without Vita.

She was always behind the wheel, proud and confident in her driving abilities. I was surprised I made it this far, considering the number of times I hit the curb pulling out of the driveway. This was entirely unlike me, storming out of the house like that.

But what choice did I have? When Vita was home, all the attention was on her and I was able to live my life as I pleased, perfectly content in her shadow. But the moment Vita disappeared, my mother started to suffocate me instead. I was the villain for wanting to cut my proverbial umbilical cord and actually make decisions for myself.

Chex ran a hand through his thick hair as he disappeared through the back door. I imagined him swiping his ID through the clock, vascular arms bulging with muscles beneath his green apron.

Eye candy was an understatement for him, even if he would forever remain just an innocent crush. Cars were starting to line up filled with the small-town residents and high schoolers who were looking to chill and light up a blunt in the parking lot or exchange some cheap liquor before the cops did their evening rounds.

It was my time to shine, as Vita used to say. I rolled down my window, allowing the crisp night air to tickle my face. Struggling to pull up to the drive-through station, I used every trick Vita taught me to avoid missing the blind spots. The last thing I needed was to total the car and prove my mother's point that I couldn't fend for myself in a big city. Did people even drive in New York City?

I was next in line. Nervously, I cleared my throat and remembered how Vita would put on a low voice to be seductive whenever she wanted to mess around with guys and get their attention.

"Welcome to Starbucks, what can I get you?" His dreamy voice sounded through the station. Normally, I'd be swooning in the passenger seat, but now, I had to make the order myself.

Low voice, I reminded myself. Calm and collected.

"Hi!" I exclaimed a little too enthusiastically, before slumping in my seat, ready to pinch myself for being too high-pitched. Clearing my throat again, I made another attempt, trying not to cringe.

"Do you have Peppermint Toasted White Chocolate Mochas?"

"Fresh out."

Damn. Change of plans. "Do you still have pumpkin?" My

attempt at a low voice sounded like I was recovering from a sore throat.

"It's the end of December," came the response.

"Is that a no?" Today must've been an off day for me to be talking back so much.

"I'll have to check for you." Chex did not sound amused. I supposed I was being an annoying customer who couldn't get with the times or change in seasons. But was it really my vice to want to drink pumpkin drinks all year round? If I couldn't have Vita's favorite drink, it certainly wouldn't be a crime to have mine.

"Yes, we have some pumpkin sauce left."

"Awesome. Can I get a grande pumpkin spice latte then, hold the whip?"

"Hot or iced?" He asked blandly as if reading from a script.

"It's the end of December." Throwing some sass back at him was the most empowered I'd felt in a long time, which was surprising considering this was the first time I'd ever spoken to him. Let him find me mysterious and ambiguous. Let the temperature of my caffeinated drink create an enigmatic character he'd like to know.

"Touché," he said and chuckled lightly. I could listen to him laugh all day.

"Hot, please."

"Your drink will be ready soon. Just pull up around the corner."

Just as I was about to lightly tap the pedal, he added, "And your name?"

My heart lurched. "Alluna." Maybe I was thinking far too deeply into it, but I'd made the man laugh. And we shared some banter. Vita would be so proud of me.

Vita and I were such frequent customers that Chex knew her by name. Every time we would pull up, he would stick his head out the window and try to get closer to her while handing her drink over. Vita used to say that a sure way to tell if a man was into a woman was by the slightest brush on the hands. I was so sure that once I pulled up, he would recognize me too, and perhaps try to get close to me in her absence. It was electrifying, driving on my own, talking to Chex on my own, independently getting my favorite drink. Seeing his face up close may make me faint.

By the time I pulled up to the window, I was practically bouncing in my seat. Making sure the car window was rolled all the way down, I contemplated hanging my arm out the window but decided to leave my appendages inside, still not fully trusting myself in a car alone. Was my clutch even parked? Yes, it was. It would hardly be long now before our eyes would meet and—

"Grande pumpkin spice latte for Alina, no whip."

My heart sank below the cement under Vita's car. Chex wasn't even looking at me. There wasn't the slightest mark of recognition on his face. How could there be? Vita was usually the one getting the drinks. I was hardly visible the other times. My name wasn't worth remembering.

But, maybe…

"Do you know Vita?" I blurted out. It was worth a try. I had to ask. Maybe this would jog his memory and he would remember me too.

Chex finally looked at me, his curiosity piqued. His chocolate eyes were like freshly melted hot cocoa. He handed me my drink without our hands brushing.

"Uh, yeah. She used to come a lot. Haven't seen her in a few months. Do you know her?"

"I'm her sister," I breathed. Chex was never aware of my existence. What was I thinking? How could I ever expect to stand a chance? I was nobody in this town.

"Oh, cool. Do you know if she's available?" He said, poking his head out the window and smiling at me for the first time. But I was no longer dazed by his presence and had no interest in entertaining something that would never happen.

Not bothering to look at him, I mumbled, "She's gone away," before driving away and going home, my pumpkin spiced latte not hitting the same spot it usually did.

"Welcome home, honey." My mother said once the sound of the car keys hitting the counter reached her hawk ears in the kitchen. She sounded so nonchalant one might never suspect there was a fight upon my departure. As if nothing ever happened. As if she didn't lash out at me. As if she didn't push my buttons to the point of provoking my ugly side. The table had been cleared and the dishes put away, the scene of the crime scrubbed clean. Shaking my head, I headed for the stairs as she came into the hallway and leaned against the wall, drying the last of the plates with her towel.

"Go wash up for bed, dear. I know you didn't mean anything you said earlier, my love." I was glad that at least my mother had the decency to understand that my words weren't out of anger but of pain. Nodding, I continued my way up the stairs.

"I know you don't actually want to move to New York." Halting on the next step, my hand tightened on the banister. Scratch that. My mother had no accountability. The way she casually treated my statement as a request before dismissing it was staggering.

"These are difficult times, my love. Vita's loss brings out negative emotions."

No, Mom. You did.

I gave her a long look before saying, "I leave tomorrow," and went straight into Vita's room to pack.

My suitcase was halfway full before I heard my father clear his throat by my door. Not wanting to meet his eyes, I continued to pack in silence, throwing in my entire fall-themed closet.

He sighed and took a seat beside me, gently resting his arm on my hand, a silent request that spoke higher volumes than it should've.

I reluctantly met his eyes and regretted it instantaneously. He searched my face for someone that wasn't there. He was searching for parts of Vita that were inevitably inside me, though our similarities ended with our dark blue eyes and dark blonde hair.

Vita's eyes always gleamed with excitement for what was to come. The will to live, the itch to love harder, deeper, unapologetically.

Vita was everything I ever hoped to be, and I was sure I'd be reminding her of that when I saw her again. When she decided this game of hide-and-seek had been playing far too long and all the players had given up. She won already. We didn't find her. Why didn't she come back already?

"What," I said softly, not wanting to lash out at him. My father never liked getting involved with family drama, particularly between Vita and our fiery mother. Vita was so much like our mother. It was astonishing. They shared the same vivacious ferocity and had a thing for making the most out of their valuable minutes.

They also clashed with the same stubborn, hardheaded personality traits. The way the house used to shake whenever they had arguments was truly a sight to behold.

My mother used to tell me that she felt too much power emanating from my sister the day she was born and felt in her heart that her name should be "Vita". A name to represent someone with a full life ahead of them.

I used to wonder if I was adopted until I took a hard look at my father and saw much of myself in him. The quiet, boring guy that no one paid attention to. The passive, mild-mannered symbol of peace who was a perceiver of life rather than a participant.

Sometimes I wondered if there was more to me than those parts of him. Judging by my outburst earlier, I was starting to think that

I hardly knew myself at all.

"Don't be so hard on her." My father squeezed my hand. As always, the voice of reason and logic cut straight through my emotions.

"She provoked me and then completely dismissed it," I tried.

"She's been through so much." It made no difference what I said to him. My father would keep defending my mother until I questioned my reality into existence and adopted his words instead.

Yes, my mother has been through so much. The laughingstock of our small community, as she kept telling me. The failure of a mother who couldn't keep her own daughter in check. The daughter that wanted to soar and soared too close to the sun.

I knew exactly what my father wanted from me. I watched him do the same thing for years to maintain his loving relationship with my mother. Absolve her of anything she said or did, no matter how severe. Forgive and forgive and forget. She's been through so much. She's sensitive. She's your mother.

An apology for making her upset was the last thing I wanted to do, but it wasn't about my feelings. He's taught me again and again that when you love someone unconditionally, you have to forgive unconditionally.

Vita should know I'd always forgive her unconditionally, even after disappearing like this. I would be sure to tell her that after I gave her one of our signature bear-hugs, the kind where we nearly squeeze the circulation out of each other. It's not done right unless we are blue in the face.

Vita was too big for our small town. She wanted much more out of life than completing courses at our community college and living the small-town life forever. She wanted grand. She wanted New York City.

I knew that by moving there, it wouldn't be an homage to her but more of a tribute until she was found again. I'd gladly return to welcome her with open arms the moment she came home.

I'd tell her all about my New York City adventures, especially those using her bucket list as a guide.

"Alluna." My father gave me a pained look. "Please. We can't lose you too."

"That's not fair, Dad." He was awfully good at making me feel like the worst daughter in the world. "I'll go crazy if I stay in this small town. I need to find myself."

"Grief makes people do crazy things…" He sounded just like my mother. Oblivious to my pain and what I needed to do for my own sake.

"It's crazy to want to move out at my age?"

"What about work or a place to live?"

"I'll find a job. I'll figure it out. That's the whole point. I can't depend on you and Mom to make all the decisions for me." He had to understand that.

"No, you depended on Vita for that."

I couldn't respond. He was saying something I was too prideful to ever admit.

The silence went on for what felt like an hour before he

conceded and sighed heavily. "I can't force you to stay. But please, at least give your mom a reason not to worry. Enroll in a class somewhere or something, will you? See if they can put you in a dorm."

"Fine."

"I'll talk to your mother."

"Thank you, Dad."

Of course, I'll pacify Mom. Of course, I'll do what it takes to uproot my life and finally feel like I was meant to do something in this life.

He kissed the top of my head with a sigh and left. Not bothering to listen to him groveling to my mother, I shut the door behind him. If all I had to do to appease her was act like my main reason for leaving was education, so be it. Hurling myself into research and deep-diving through Google, I was relieved to discover that I could shadow in a psychology class at a public college and get transfer credits should I ever decide to come back and attend the Hershey Community College. Out of all the available classes, psychology seemed the least stressful.

Besides, what was the worst that could happen? A newfound passion for psychology?

THREE

A week later, I was on the bus in New York City. It was a miracle that the college allowed me to shadow a psychology course before the start of the spring semester. They even accepted me as a part of rolling admissions and offered subsidized housing, which was their fancy word for a dorm. But this was no big college dorm like in Pennsylvania. The building was nowhere near the campus, which was only two connected buildings. I'd have to take the subway to and from class or walk thirty blocks. According to my research, walking thirty blocks was nothing to complain about.

But even after all the research I'd done on New York City, nothing could have prepared me for my first day there. No matter how many episodes of Gossip Girl I'd binge-watched. No matter how many times Netflix popped up to ask me if I was still watching Sex and the City, I knew I would be walking into a different universe from the one I'd known.

Pittsburgh was the closest thing to a city that I'd been to, but I knew that it was nothing to compare. I had to throw myself into the fire and hope I had the sense to walk the New York walk and talk the New York talk instead of burning to a crisp.

When I bid my parents adieu that morning, I made a mental vow to myself that no matter what happened, I wouldn't come crying home. No matter how many lonely nights I had, no matter how overwhelmed I got, I had to stay put. I had to learn to fend for myself, at least until Vita came back.

Speaking of Vita, I pulled out my phone and tapped onto the photo I took of her bucket list for safekeeping. The moment I dropped my things off in my apartment, I was headed to the first location on the list – Dumbo, by the Brooklyn Bridge. Apparently, Brooklyn was a part of New York City, too? Who would've thought?

After riding the bus for four hours, I had to transfer onto the train to get to my apartment building and walk a few blocks in Times Square, which looked nothing like the photos. I'd seen city lights and billboards, not this infestation of rats and piles of garbage. It was mind-boggling to me that the streets were packed with cars, yet masses of people marched onward at a pace I didn't think was humanly possible. If no one drove here, why were there so many cars?

I quickly got used to the stench of cigarette smoke and candied nuts by the time I entered the train station. Was I committing an UnNewYorker by opting for the train instead of just walking through the December chill to my building? Could a native smell the amateur on me all the way from downtown? The world may never know.

The train was moderately loaded with people glued to their phones, each of them with AirPods stuck inside their ears.

As the train started pulling out of the station, a homeless man entered my cart. Lowering my eyes, I was careful not to make eye contact and provoke him. He held out his raggedy baseball cap to each person, a silent gesture to ask for money. Sneaking a glance every now and then, I observed the pedestrians briskly shaking their heads without looking at him.

Preparing myself for my first official native act like a New Yorker, I held my phone in front of me, though I wasn't actually using it. By the time I tapped on the calendar app to look busy and scrolled back to the year I was born, he'd approached me.

Flexing my newly learned skill, I jerked my head and waited for him to move on, as he did.

When his back was turned to me, I risked a quick glance to see if he was getting off the train or moving to the next cart.

But he was speaking to the woman who was sitting across from me. His back was covering the woman's face, but I could make out her long blonde hair curled to perfection. I could also see her crossed legs and sparkly shoes.

He was directly asking her to help him. She shook her head and grasped her phone with her manicured hands. He called her beautiful. She didn't respond.

He asked her to go with him. The poor girl was visibly uncomfortable, and when we reached the next stop she bolted out right under his grasp and disappeared into the crowds. The homeless man moved onto the next cart without hesitation.

Quickly glancing at the above monitor, I counted a few more stops before my short walk to my apartment. I was eager to drop my things off and start my journey discovering the bucket list. Pulling out my headphones, I popped them in my ear but didn't play any music. Vita taught me that this was a handy trick native New Yorkers did to lessen the chance of interaction because no one wanted to be a friendly stranger, especially here.

Not that anyone would want to talk to me anyway. I was never the type to warrant a knight in shining armor, unlike Vita. She held men like putty in her hands. She knew exactly when to sway her hips and touch her hair to get any guy she wanted.

We used to discuss the importance of knowing how to act innocent while holding all the cards. Somehow, I was never able to pull it off the way she did. Every guy she dated truly thought she was naive until she decided she wasn't.

My love life, or lack thereof, was pitiful. I had one boyfriend when I was sixteen, but only because Vita was dating his older brother. Even though he put in some honest months with me, I always knew he just wanted to see Vita, too. Most of the time we hung out, he'd inquire if she'd be there.

But when I was sixteen, I really thought my feelings for him were real, as teenage emotions went. So when I lost my virginity to him, I never paid attention to how he never actually looked at me and preferred doggystyle because he "liked how my hair looked from the back". The realization that I was the closest thing to Vita hadn't dawned on me until well after he broke my naive heart. Coincidentally, it was soon after Vita dumped his brother.

At that age, my angsty teenage soul was far from wise, and I believed that was the best I'd ever get. Vita had a few more boyfriends until she realized she was going through them like tissues and had a sexual awakening.

She told me there was no point in pursuing a long-term connection when your mind wasn't ready for it. And she was absolutely right. If I couldn't imagine myself in a real relationship, why even bother?

When I was nineteen and she was twenty-one, Vita had a period of sexcapades that she never truly divulged to me, even though we agreed to never keep secrets. But she told me enough. Body counts were a "social construct", they weren't real. Society would prey on women regardless if they were prudes or whores, and it was difficult enough to survive among the double standards. We had to own our bodies and sexualities.

Her logic spawned my first and only one night stand when I was twenty. The man was older, I never knew his last name. All it took was one seductive profile picture, a swipe, and an address. He looked delicious in his photos, and the thought of him being interested in me made me giggle. We matched and met up the same evening at a hotel, and thankfully for me, he looked exactly like his photos, if not better. I'd entered that hotel with juvenile excitement laced with taboo delight.

But there was no romantic, candle-lit wining and dining. The moment I entered the room with him, the aggressive kissing began. Implied consent was enough for him. I don't think he said a single word. The kissing and love-making were nice, but there was something missing. I wondered if there was something wrong with me. I had a handsome man inside of me, someone who found me desirable enough to get a room, and yet I still wasn't satisfied. Even when I came twice.

The next morning, he was gone. He'd also unmatched me. No way of contacting him ever again. He ripped off the bandaid without any goodbye. Not that he really said hello to begin with.

Vita said I should've felt lucky. He made his intentions clear from the start and didn't string me along with false hope. We did the deed and dealt with our doing, and nothing more. What else could I have expected?

She was right again. She had this uncanny ability to go through men without a single emotional attachment. Maybe I needed more hookups to achieve that, but I couldn't do it again.

The whole encounter left me feeling lonelier than before. Britney was really onto something there.

So I swore off men. Even if I were crazy for feeling that way, I wasn't strong like Vita. I couldn't harness my feelings and use them as weapons no matter how many times she insisted this was our moment to have fun before having boring lives.

I'll tell her she was wrong when I see her again. I'll tell her about my adventures in New York without meaningless flings, and I'll tell her I had fun.

Once I reached my apartment, I practically threw my things on the ground without a second thought. I could unpack later, I had more important things to worry about. It was pointless to think about a pitiful past when I could create a memorable future that would begin with the first stop on the bucket list.

I shot a quick text to my parents detailing my safe arrival and headed back out. The fact that I was on my own didn't sink in yet, especially considering that I'd hardly explored my own apartment. As much as I didn't like the train, I was headed back there - determined to get to Dumbo.

This time, I made sure to play loud music through my headphones to drown out my thoughts. They had a tendency to bring me down, and it wasn't fair to the mental journey I'd embarked on. If I got lost in my own thoughts, I'd remember why I always lived in Vita's shadow; I wasn't meant to ever take the lead. She always knew what was best for me. My mother's voice would repeat in my mind like a broken record, a song I was tired of hearing. I'd be on my way back to Hershey. But I couldn't do that. For Vita's sake, I had to see my plan through.

The moment I got off the train on Clark street, I was stunned. The photos online didn't do this town justice. The cleanliness was the first thing I noticed, besides the high-end boutiques and expensive markets. I wondered how Dan Humphrey could've ever been considered poor living in Brooklyn. These apartment buildings were worth more than my name, and I just meant the studios. The lofts were probably worth a fortune. What real estate agents were the creators of Gossip Girl consulting with if they thought Dan was the poor one? Was I completely out of touch with reality? I'd half expected to step out into the trenches with rats scurrying around. Yet Dumbo was much cleaner than Times Square, the place that attracted millions of tourists every year.

I needed a grip on reality. Perhaps Sex and the City would be a more trustworthy reference point. There's rich, and then there's Chuck Bass rich. Maybe Carrie Bradshaw was more realistic. Then again, with her designer closet and writer's salary, I might have to scrap that show as a vantage point too.

The chilly breeze had relaxed some and allowed me to embrace the wintry air with warm arms as I donned my gloves and strolled to the park by the Brooklyn Bridge. The skyline didn't feel real. My mind couldn't believe that I was actually here, in New York City.

The nightfall sky was a starless void, but every window of every skyscraper twinkled like stars I could stare at for hours. The city was alive.

Taking a seat on the bench close to the river, I watched the reflection of the lights speckle across the water, turning tides shifting the perspective into a dreamy, trance-like blur.

I enjoyed the liveliness of the people around me and walking atop the bridge. Watching families stop to take photos and have picnics was nice. Some couples asked me to take their photo since I was occupying a prime spot.

Even though I was teaching myself not to be a friendly stranger, these moments were the opposite. I liked the idea of being part of someone else's forever. It made me feel less lonely.

A young group of friends stopped by my bench to snap some more photos, and I overheard them speaking.

"Dumbo is going to be full of YouTubers trying to make a buck," one of them said.

Her male companion lightly punched her in the arm. "Why?"

"Cause someone disappeared here. Shit's haunted now. And it's not like this is some secluded area someone went on a jog or something. People don't just disappear in a place that's this crowded," she responded while taking out a bag of chips.

"Another one disappeared? That makes four now."

The girl nodded. "Mhm. Just a few days ago."

"Then all of New York will be considered haunted at this point," another one said.

The disappearances I'd read about before. Could this be another one?

Something clicked in my head, but it couldn't be true. New York City was full of over eight million people. Four disappearances couldn't mean they were connected. And Vita definitely couldn't be part of it. She lived in a whole other state.

But this new nugget of knowledge remained curious to me, so I decided to investigate using the help of Inspector Google and Detective Search Button.

NYC disappearance

An article as recent as yesterday popped up, showing the trajectory of the disappearances. Cops were clueless beyond connecting the fact they were all women.

Scrolling down, I reached a list, detailing the last known whereabouts.

The latest one disappearance was in Dumbo just a few days ago, at the end of December.

The one before was seen in a coffee shop named Kaffeine in November.

And the one before that was in the Glitz nightclub in October.

And the very first one to disappear was last seen in Loeb Boathouse in September.

And Vita disappeared in August, where she was last seen at a bar. It couldn't be. My mind was playing tricks on me. I switched the screen from the article to the photo of the bucket list as my eyes bulged out.

The order of the disappearances all matched each of the locations on the bucket list.

Dumbo

Kaffeine

Glitz

Loeb Boathouse

I was about to lose my mind. This couldn't be. I was clearly going insane if I truly thought there was some connection to Vita. But what were the chances? She'd written this list way before she disappeared.

Was she leaving me clues? A trail of breadcrumbs? Was this bucket list a facade to truly understand what happened to her?

Vita may have been intuitive, but she was no psychic.

I could no longer stare at my phone. My brain refused to make sense of it all. The group of young teens was long gone, and I hadn't noticed their absence.

Standing abruptly from the bench, I headed over to the rail above the water and put my head in my hands. All I wanted was to follow Vita's dream and experience an adventure in New York, but these coincidences were becoming too intense for me.

I stared at the water, imagining my crazy connections forming a ball and urging it to dissolve within the light waves that settled below the surface.

My phone buzzed and I was glad to rid myself of my own insanity, even if it was my mother calling with the insanity of her own.

"Hello, dear." She sounded testy as if she were dipping a delicate toe into unstable waters.

"Hey, Mom."

"How was your trip? Did you get lost?" Only my mother could

find a way to demean me like it was her second nature. She wasn't like this when Vita was around. This new overly-protective mama-bear mode wasn't like her at all.

"Nope, I made it to my apartment alright."

"Sounds like you're outside. Where are you?"

"Exploring." I was finally free outside her grasp. The last thing I wanted was to climb back inside her womb, metaphorically speaking.

"Hm, alright." My mother didn't like that I was being vague but didn't push.

Alluna...

"What is it?" I asked my mom.

"What's what?"

"You just said my name."

"No, I didn't."

Confused, I continued my conversation with her. I must have imagined it. We started talking about groceries when it happened again.

Alluna...

I was sure I heard my name this time, and it didn't sound like my mother's voice. It was the gentlest whisper in the air as if my inside thinking voice took a life of its own.

Lowering my phone from my ear, I looked around, searching for a familiar face that might have called my name. Eventually, my eyes swept over the water. Only to find Vita staring at me intently as her head popped out of the water.

I was obviously hallucinating. It was just a trick of the light and wishful thinking to see her again, a cocktail my brain was churning to torment me further.

But I would recognize Vita anywhere, even miles away. Her crooked smile and always perfect hair were hard to miss. I stared at the hallucination and considered the side effects of extreme fatigue and dehydration. When did I last have water?

Absentmindedly, I hung up on my mother and approached the rail, my eyes glued to Vita in the far distance, but not too far to mistake her for anyone else.

The figment of my imagination winked at me and disappeared deep into the water, with a tail splashing the surface and disappearing behind her.

I burst out laughing. I was truly going crazy.

Not only did my brain find it ironic to show me Vita, but it also had to add something even harder to believe. A tail? At least I was being creative.

I stopped myself and headed home silently. I didn't believe in ghosts nor mermaids. What I did believe was there was something fishy going on. No pun intended.

All I could do was visit the other places on the bucket list and investigate any way they could've been related to Vita. There was definitely something unnatural happening. I just couldn't shake the feeling that I was about to get myself into something I'd regret.

FOUR

As much as I'd have loved dedicating my entire presence in New York City to investigating the bucket list, I still had to take my college course into account. Considering I arrived in the stark middle of winter, my only option to be accepted into the college was to shadow a psychology course before officially being enrolled in the spring semester. I figured it would work with my second job as a newly licensed detective since the class met three times a week on Mondays, Tuesdays, and Thursdays. Plenty of time to scope out suspicious crime scenes.

My first day shadowing the class was the following morning. Needless to say, when I arrived home, I went straight to bed without a single bite, mentally drained beyond belief, ready to sleep for ages.

Alas, my alarm clock sounded rather rudely at eight in the morning, and I groggily forced myself to look alive and attempt to have energy for the class. I was sent a copy of the syllabus so that I could keep up, even though I was shadowing in the middle of the curriculum. If I made a good impression on the professor in these few short weeks, she'd allow me to squeeze into her booked spring class.

Unfortunately, my departure from my apartment led to some rather unlucky events. With my bad fortune, the subway system was working atrociously today out of all days. Being stuck inside the train for an hour, unmoving, not having any cell reception, I truly wondered if it could've gotten any worse.

That is, until I ran out of the train station, officially late to class, and got shat on by a bird. Of course, at this point, screwing my tardiness, I ran to the nearest restroom inside the campus. Cussing like a sailor in front everyone, I furiously wiped at my jacket, now stained with greenish-brown droppings.

I swooped into the nearest Starbucks and peddled for some pumpkin spice as if my life depended on it. It wasn't like being even later to class would make a difference.

I arrived, pumpkin spiced latte at the ready, an hour later at ten o'clock. Out of all the classes I had to choose from, I was glad psychology was on the list as I found it fascinating. Perhaps I would learn something about myself and what happened the other day.

Holding my head high in indignation, I silently took an empty seat while the professor continued her lecture and took a moment to observe her.

Though her face was young and lively, her salt and peppered shoulder-length hair contrasted her youthful look. She had an extreme side part that emphasized her narrow face. Grey eyes sat in the sockets that emoted heavily. The theatrical neon blue eyeliner was a sign of her funky expression. Large, square-rimmed glasses sat low on her hooked nose. She had the look of a bird, cunning when needed and having lived many moons.

One thing I noted and appreciated was her relaxed nature. She'd hardly noticed when I walked in and didn't seem to care. That was good.

"Is that pumpkin spice?" Someone whispered next to me just as I settled in my seat. Looking up, I saw a lovely platinum-blonde woman that looked like she was straight out of a Barbie movie. Nodding in acknowledgment, I took a sip of my fueling coffee as a way to emphasize how much I needed it.

She whisper-chuckled and held out her hand. "Daisy Spiva."

Shaking her hand softly, I whispered back, "Alluna Day."

"Nice to meet you, Alina."

"Alluna," I corrected while cringing internally.

She shrugged and went back to listening to the lecture, and I followed suit.

Pulling out my notebook, I was prepared to copy anything that was on the board until I realized nothing was written besides the professor's name.

Dr. Sage Gusto.

Ah, this kind of professor. The type that lectured without writing notes.

Her class was a cocktail of wit and sarcasm, indicating she was proficient at her craft and wanted students to succeed. She used her hands expressively, which brought some of her inked skin into view. A dog paw on her left wrist and a dangly bracelet on her right.

As she waved her hands around to showcase her points, her necklace tossed around her neck, capturing my attention. An unusually large black feather set into a woven lanyard. Very unusual.

Her occasional jokes made the class laugh while she didn't even blink an eye, fully accepting her entertainment. I wondered if she used recycled jokes and knew which ones would induce the most laughter.

She mentioned there would be a teacher's assistant joining her team mid-semester, his first day being tomorrow. She might've mentioned his name. But I wasn't paying much attention, as my mind kept returning to the second spot on my list – the coffee shop Kaffeine.

I genuinely enjoyed listening to her speak and understood why she didn't provide any handwritten notes - they weren't needed. She was able to hold everyone's attention just fine without them.

When her lecture concluded, I made sure to be the last one out.

Hoping to apologize for my tardiness, I came up to her.

"Dr. Gusto—"

"Please, call me Sage. My Ph.D. is only meant to be rubbed in coworkers' faces, not students."

"Alright…Sage. My name is Alluna. I wanted to introduce myself and apologize—"

"Do I even know you?" she said, giving me a one-over.

"Oh, well-no. It's my first day shadowing your class—"

"Caramel macchiato with two Splendas, extra cream," she interrupted while shuffling her papers.

"Excuse me?"

"If you're going to stroll into my class an hour late because you needed your pumpkin spice latte, you should know my favorite coffee so that you can bring me one too." My words were knocked right out of me. This woman didn't miss a single beat.

I stuttered in response, unsure of what to say.

Her features softened. "I can see you're very academically oriented. If you want to talk about what you missed, you can discuss it with the TA tomorrow."

"Thank you," Turning on my heels, I left, completely fascinated and slightly intimidated by Dr. Gusto.

As I rounded the corner of the door, I almost walked right into Daisy.

"Hey!" I exclaimed in shock.

"Oh, hey! I was going to the library to study till you ran me over." Daisy nudged my shoulder playfully. She smelled like vanilla infused coffee, and it was intoxicating. Her brazenness reminded me of Vita, which hit a little too close to home.

I chuckled nervously, not accustomed to this much social interaction in one day. "Sorry."

"Are you new here? Haven't seen you before."

I fixed my bag over my shoulder. "Yeah, I'm shadowing."

"This late into the semester? That's brave. I can catch you up on everything you've missed. Want to get a coffee?"

Intrigued but cautious, I gave her the benefit of the doubt and raised an eyebrow. "Why?"

She twisted her pink lips in deep thought.

"I'd want someone to do the same for me." Her smile was infectious. It wouldn't be fair of me to assume the worst in everyone I met. Not everyone was my mother. If anything, having a friend in the big city wouldn't be such a bad idea either.

"Well, I do love coffee," I gave a small smile. She beamed and linked her arms with mine. We started walking down the corridor and discussed what sort of coffee we liked. It felt nice to share a commonality with someone, but I didn't want to commit another UnNewYorker by trusting a stranger. Maybe this girl just wanted to leverage someone to write psychology papers for her. Maybe she just wanted to vent about her pretty-girl problems.

"Never enough coffee," I agreed absentmindedly as we walked to the nearest Starbucks while simultaneously talking about how much we hated it and preferred lowkey coffee shop holes in the wall.

Before I knew it, we'd spent a whole hour agreeing on the too-burnt taste of the drinks but succumbing to the gravitational pull of the seasonal ones anyway. She'd also caught me up to speed with the curriculum and shared her notes with me from previous classes. I'd downed my second pumpkin spice latte of the day while she inquired as to what magical abilities I possessed to sniff out which locations still carried pumpkin sauce at the end of December. I told her I had a smell for it since I was a pumpkin in a previous life.

Talking to Daisy was refreshing, even though I didn't know much about her. It was nice to know that she knew nothing of me and Vita's name wasn't hanging over my head the way it did in Hershey.

I never had many friends outside of Vita, and I was curious to see if Daisy would want to hang out again.

"How long have you been in New York City?" Daisy had asked.

"A day. Is it that obvious?"

"A bit," she'd laughed. "From my born and bred eye, at least."

"What gave it away?" I mentally pulled out a pen and paper so I could start crossing out my UnNewYorkerisms.

"You can just tell, you know?"

"No."

"Exactly," she'd laughed. I mentally crossed out my entire self.

My social battery wasn't lasting too long, and after an hour, I knew it was time for me to go. I had extensive research to do. As nice as it was to talk to Daisy, I couldn't give her undivided attention much longer. My brain itched to discover more things that previously made me nervous.

I couldn't stop thinking about what I saw yesterday. Before long, a list of excuses longer than a CVS receipt took over my thoughts. I barely ate or drank yesterday, and New York City lights were akin to many illusions. What I thought I saw was utter nonsense and my body's way of saying I needed water.

And the coincidences weren't similar enough to scare me just yet. I wanted to look into the girls that vanished. Who were they? What did they have in common to attract larger forces to play?

"Alluna?" Daisy asked.

Realizing I'd zoned out on her again, I blinked a few times, reoriented myself to our conversation, and politely asked her to repeat herself.

"You mentioned another coffee spot you wanted to visit? I forgot the name, but it started with a 'K'?"

Kaffeine. The potentially dangerous second spot on the bucket list. A girl disappeared there last month. She could be dead.

But I was being silly. It was just a coffee shop.

"Oh, yes. Kaffeine with a capital K."

"Right! Let's go there and talk about how we are both the disappointments of the family. It'll feel classy with an authentic coffee." She winked.

I started standing up. "I do have to go now, but absolutely! Tomorrow after class." I promised while lifting my bag.

Realizing I was being abrupt and potentially rude, I halted and added, "It was nice to meet you, Daisy. I hope to roast more coffee places with you."

"All puns intended?" She smiled.

"Absolutely!" Waving, I headed out, questioning my social cues the entire way to the library.

I didn't want to be entirely alone in the apartment. My first night was hard enough as it were. My bags weren't even unpacked yet. I figured the library would be a better place to research.

Once I'd entered through the revolving doors, I realized I never exchanged phone numbers with Daisy. Whatever. I'd see her tomorrow anyway. I had more important things to focus on anyway.

If the library hadn't closed at ten, I'd have stayed there the whole night. The loudspeaker announcement to start packing up and return the checked-out laptops scared me.

Checking the time, I realized I'd been there for six hours, though it really felt like twenty minutes. All it took was one Google search, which led to fifty articles, Facebook posts, public Instagram accounts, even Twitter. I went as far as to locate the social media of the victims and lurk on their handles as well as their close friends and families. The last thing they posted. Their status. The missing person notices shared by dozens and the updates or lack thereof…everything, and anything that could lead me one step closer.

My stomach was rumbling. I couldn't remember the last time I ate. Coffee certainly wasn't a meal, though I was guilty of acting like it was.

The beauty of New York City was that it was easy to find an establishment that was open this late. Young professionals who weren't tied down by kids surely needed some grub to maintain their energy for their nonstop working.

The nearest place was a cute bagel shop. That would definitely hit the spot! I waltzed in with hunger on my mind, thinking I'd get a cheap and filling meal. Vita taught me this one too. I ordered a baconeggncheese under a single breath, feeling like the high and mighty New Yorker I now was.

Until the price came out to be ten dollars and my ego deflated. Ten dollars for a bagel?! I just committed another UnNewYorker. I could feel my mother's left eye twitching two states away and quickly shoved the bagel into my bag, hiding from her unwanted glare.

Now bitter and slightly resentful, I dragged my feet back to my apartment and ate angrily while continuing where I left off.

I'd come to realize that the only commonalities between these four women and Vita were that they were young, attractive women in their early twenties, and right before they all disappeared, their close ones described their behavior as "different" in the days leading up to their disappearance. That wouldn't have normally struck me as odd, but there was one thing in particular that stood out to me.

Each of them mentioned something about "dust". Detectives suspected this was a new street name for a certain drug that had yet to be identified, especially since none of the bodies were ever found and autopsies couldn't be performed. Beyond that, all four women shared symptoms of slurred speech, slow thought process, and slow responses in the few days leading up to their disappearance. Experts hypothesized that the commercial producer of the drug slipped it to all these women, waited for it to take full effect over the next few days, agreed to meet them somewhere, and the rest unknown.

As much as my heart was filled with pity for these women, I couldn't possibly connect them to Vita.

The last time I saw her, she was about to head to a bar. Straining hard, I struggled to recollect her exact words before she left.

She'd blown a kiss at me, saying she'd catch up with me later.

Well, before that.

Luca and Vaness are back together.

Not important. I have to dig further…

He's no match for me.

Wait. She spoke those words in passing while touching up her mascara. I almost missed them too. Why didn't I ask who she was talking about?

Could it be that she had a stalker? Was Vita being too full of herself and underestimating an obsessed fan?

But she mentioned nothing about dust. And she certainly hadn't been acting hazy or drugged up. I was the one who was in over my head. Let's be real. Vita was not connected to these other women.

She probably found a new boy toy and decided to move in with him for a few months and cleanse herself of social media. And our parents, I suppose. And me.

But she wouldn't do that either. And that didn't explain the connection between her pre-written bucket list to these disappearances. And my hallucination. Surely, my subconscious saw a pattern and indirectly was trying to tell me. Was Vita drowned and dumped into a lake?

Impossible. Vita would never let anyone drown her. She really had the capability to charm anyone she met.

Did she have a boyfriend I wasn't aware of? It was hard to keep track of the current men in her life with her tendency to go through them quickly.

And with that, I continued to research all her latest posts and statuses, photos she was tagged in, friends of friends who posted them, who liked them, as well as drugs and behavior and the victims and anything and everything - for the rest of the night and straight into the morning until I heard the birds chirping.

FIVE

*I*f I thought I was exhausted on my first day, this was torture. Blinking against the sunlight felt like weighted sandpaper slowly rubbing against my eyeballs.

Groaning slightly, I massaged my temples to counteract the sprouting blooming headache. I was so lost in my obsession that I spent the entire night glued to the screen, without making any real progress. If anything, I'd stunted myself further by having more questions and fewer answers.

Looking at the clock, I saw it was close to eight-thirty. Great. A second chance at a good impression, only to establish a tardy pattern. But Dr. Sage Gusto could kiss my pumpkin-spiced ass if she gave me hell for this. If she knew what I was going through, she might've understood. However, it was none of her business.

My movements dragged on as I tried to peel myself from my chair and get myself into an oversized sweater. A walking, moving blob that was hardly lasting two days without the cushion of my coddling parents who would've force-fed me nutritiously by now.

What if my mother was right? She must have known me well enough to say her piece. And now I was proving her right, every step of the way. I really had to pull myself together.

I had to own being late and make a point out of it. I was a New Yorker now, even if I wasn't doing a very good job.

So as I trudged through the city and waited thirty minutes for my pumpkin spiced latte because I didn't have the foresight to mobile order in the middle of the night in advance, I decided things could've been much worse.

I was about an hour late today. Again. Luckily enough, Dr. Sage Gusto gave short breaks at the beginning of each hour in the four-hour class, and I was able to slip in unnoticed while the students were socializing amongst themselves.

Sage spoke in hushed whispers on the phone, and she immediately saw me when I approached her. Looking unsurprised by my habitual tardiness, she finally raised an eyebrow when I set down a caramel macchiato with two Splendas and extra cream on her table and headed to my seat. I could feel her small smile behind me.

"I think she's warming up to you," Daisy said as I took my seat beside her.

I gave her a look as we said "all puns intended" at the same time and laughed together.

The break was winding down as the rowdiness of the class trailed into hushed whispers. Pulling out my notebook, I whispered to Daisy, "What topic are we on?"

She nudged my shoulder. "Did you ever actually look at the syllabus? We just finished talking about bipolar disorder. Now it's another one I can't pronounce, starts with an 'S'."

"Stress?" I guessed.

"You think I can't pronounce 'stress'?" Daisy whisper-yelled. "It was something like—"

"Schizophrenia," Dr. Sage said right next to us. Jumping a mile in my seat, I felt my heart leap from my chest.

"Yeah, that one," Daisy said.

"I wanted to thank you for the coffee, Alluna." I felt a gallon of appreciation for her remembering my name. Most people confused it with "Alina" or "Luna."

"Just don't make it a habit."

"The tardiness or the coffee giving?"

"Come on time with the coffee and I'll let you into my spring class."

"Noted."

Sage moved on to make her way to her podium and resume her lecture.

"Before I start the next topic, I'd like to introduce you all to my TA, who was working largely behind the scenes until today. For those of you who were wondering why your first paper had harsh grading, you're about to meet him."

A collective groan whooshed through the lecture hall. Good thing I started the class when I did. I supposed my first paper would've flunked me out immediately.

When he came out, my jaw dropped. I had to quickly close it so that I wouldn't look like a weirdo, but I would sincerely be surprised if my jaw was the only mandible that fell open.

I'd never seen anyone who looked like him before, with all his features being independently unique, and as a sum collection – a true piece of art. His fair skin and rosy cheeks gave him a boyish appearance, though he was anything but. Muscles were deceptively hidden by his slim frame, though his broad shoulders suggested otherwise. He could've been my age, if not younger. His youth gave him an aura of innocence that softened his features. He looked so open and free, like the breath of fresh air taken after being submerged in water a moment too long. His brown hair that was long enough to cover his ears had a reddish tint that I'd never seen naturally, and his green eyes had a sparkle to them.

He was beautiful.

His sharp canines flashed as he smiled at no one in particular.

"Good morning, everyone. My name is Reid. I'll be following Dr. Gusto closely for the remainder of the semester. You can find me during her office hours if you have any questions or need any assistance."

His voice was like silk. Smooth, delectable silk.

Chex couldn't even hold a candle to this man. I could feel my next little crush develop and flicker with butterflies.

He stepped down from the podium and took a seat at Sage's computer, sweeping his eyes over the class. Normally I wouldn't stare, but I couldn't stop. He was the most handsome man I'd ever seen in my life. Then again, I hadn't ever left the town of Hershey. There were no other real people to compare him with. He swept over me without a moment's hesitation.

Slumping into my seat, I was bitterly reminded of my encounter with Chex. Of course, Reid wouldn't look at me either. I was but one face among dozens of college students. I wouldn't stand out. Not like him.

"He's hot," I heard Daisy say next to me under her breath.

"Mhm," I agreed, not taking my eyes off him. The silver lining was that I didn't have to worry about looking like a creep. I could stare as long as I want.

Sage replaced him at the podium and began her lecture.

"Schizophrenia will be a large part of your exam so listen closely. It is characterized by thoughts and behaviors that seem out of touch with reality."

I heard about this disorder before but never knew the details. Finding it mildly fascinating, I tuned in.

"Symptoms include delusions and hallucinations…"

Reid sat at Sage's computer, typing. And I finally looked away. These symptoms sounded terrifyingly similar. Nausea racked me as the vivid memory of my hallucination picked at my brain. I'd heard Vita's voice so clearly, too.

"Hearing voices, paranoia, depression are big markers as well…"

I was about to lose my mind. Could this be the big reason why I experienced something so illogical? It would certainly explain the tail!

"Schizophrenia typically presents itself in young adults, though there are many theories that explain the reason for the onset. Could be hormonal changes, genetics, life-altering events that trigger the disorder…"

The more Sage spoke, the more she answered the questions that hung in my head like a noose. One by one, they wrapped up and resolved themselves while losing my sanity in the process.

Even Reid's inhumanly beautiful face couldn't sway my spiral. I had to speak to Sage after class. She may not have been a medical doctor who could diagnose me, but she might've had a referral to a psychiatrist or something.

If I nipped this disorder in the bud, I would go back to normal. I wouldn't be the kind of person who yelled at my mom or haphazardly uprooted my life. I wouldn't be seeing my lost sister with a tail. I wouldn't be turning into someone I couldn't recognize.

The remainder of the lecture was a blur. Even as I offhandedly agreed to go to Kaffeine with Daisy after class, I felt like my mind was a separate entity from my body. Once the lecture ended, my legs carried me straight to Dr. Gusto's office while my state of mind remained tangled and hazy. My sleepless night was getting to me.

I needed serious medication. The word Dr. Gusto used was "psychotropic." If "psycho" was in the name of the medications, clearly something was seriously wrong with me. I'd have to get monthly injections of clozapine. I might be shipped off to a state hospital. Oh, God, if my mother found out…

The sea of students carried me through the hallway in a loose wave until I quickened my pace and stepped away from the mass of students. Tremors rattled through me as I struggled to keep my eyes open when I reached Dr. Gusto's office.

I couldn't wait for my professor to answer her door. The state of my mental health was slipping away with each passing second. The moment my fist made contact with her door, I pushed it open with all my strength and stormed inside, knowing fully well that I was going overboard with my uneducated conclusions but unable to fight the intrusive thoughts.

Let her send me to the psych ward. Let them inject my veins with psychotropic medications. Let them take away all of my thoughts and hallucinations and voices and unraveling reality. Let them—

A hard slam knocked me straight to the floor. I didn't notice that I'd collided into something—someone rock solid while I was focused on my dismantling mental wellbeing. Feeling slightly dazed, I blinked a few times, internally making sure I wasn't critically injured, and looked up, ready to give the other person a piece of my mind.

But if my breath wasn't knocked out of me already, it surely was now.

It was the TA.

"Reid," I breathed.

"You can't watch where you're going?" He rubbed his head from the ground. It seemed I'd knocked him over too. He stood gracefully and didn't bother extending a hand to his assailant. I clumsily got to my feet and fixed my lopsided sweater.

"Um, no. I'm shadowing the class. Alluna is my name."

"Pardon?"

"Alluna."

"Okay, what do you want besides attacking me?" He asked rather demandingly.

"I need Dr. Gusto," I said nervously, peeking around him in search of the professor.

"What for?"

I spoke in a hushed tone, my eyes bulging out at him. "I think I have schizophrenia."

He paused, then burst out laughing. "Are you high?" He asked between wheezes.

"No. I had a hallucination and heard voices."

"No, seriously. Are you on drugs? Are they worth this bad trip?"

Immediately, my mind jumped to the victims I read about and the suspected drug they were on. He'd certainly hit a nerve.

"What? No! I'm not on drugs!" I was starting to get irritated.

He leaned in close enough that his earthy musk filled my nose and I forgot how to breathe.

"I can give you a referral to an addictions specialist. You're better than this." His condescending undertone made me want to scream.

 "Fuck you."

"Sorry, you're not my type." His casual demeanor was infuriating. It didn't help that the wicked smile was enough to melt me from the inside.

"Don't flatter yourself. Most girls don't go for this "asshole" vibe you've got going."

"I know exactly what most girls like." His eyes sparkled under the harsh lights, and I noticed how green they were for the first time. A vibrant emerald green that looked like contacts.

Realizing I was staring, I awkwardly straightened the straps of my bag, overly self-aware of my messy, underslept appearance. I was sure I looked like a junkie who hadn't slept or eaten in days.

"Go bother those girls then," I weakly responded, having no energy to retort with anything remotely clever.

"I will. And you can go home to Mommy and Daddy so they can help you get clean."

Stiffening over his words, I felt my eyes watering. Gritting my teeth and clenching my fists, I was ready to punch a wall - or Reid if he got too close. This intense anger was new to me, and it frightened me.

The door opened behind me and Sage's voice filled the room. "What's going on here?"

"Alina here wanted to speak with you." Reid leaned against the wall and crossed his arms, his eyes daring me to say something. He knew he was provoking me.

"Her name is Alluna." Sage corrected and looked at me. "Are you alright?" After giving her a small look of appreciation, I forced a smile on my face.

"It's not important." Turning on my heel, I tried to walk out with dignity, though I couldn't walk away fast enough. The last thing I wanted was to break down in front of the professor.

When the door closed behind me, I could faintly hear Sage scolding Reid. I might have imagined it, but I thought I heard her say *it won't work on her.*

I must have misheard. What couldn't work on me? Pressing my ear against the door, I tried to see if I could catch anything else.

A hand on my shoulder startled me and I jerked my head to see Daisy's concerned face.

"Are you okay?" She asked.

Shaking my head, I looked down so she wouldn't see my watery eyes. I was sure my picture of frizzy hair, unkempt appearance, and solemn countenance was worth a thousand words. I just needed to sleep.

"We can go to Kaffeine another time, hun."

Nodding, I took a deep breath and smiled. "It must be the jet lag. I mean— the metaphorical jet lag. Suburbs to city. Travel lag.

You know what I mean…" I was rambling. Daisy gave me an understanding smile and linked her arm into mine.

We walked to the subway station together and agreed to meet at Kaffeine the following day at noon. She didn't ask for any details and for that, I was thankful. It felt nice to make plans with a new friend, and I looked forward to feeling normal again.

Once we separated at the station, me going uptown and her going downtown, I kept thinking about my encounter with Reid.

What else could I have expected? He was just another asshole who held the power of his own attractiveness in his hand and welded it like a skeleton key, opening the hearts of anyone he wanted. He may have been the most attractive man I'd ever seen, but he was just another narcissist.

When I entered my apartment and crawled into my bed, I took pleasure imagining Reid as a balding middle-aged man going through his midlife crisis and struggling to tuck his beer gut into his trousers. The thought stayed with me as I slept for fifteen hours straight.

SIX

The moment I opened my eyes the next day, I knew that I was in over my head. But not in the same way I originally believed. I wasn't a schizophrenic; I didn't even have that in my family genetics. Both my mother's and father's bloodlines were relatively healthy and my grandparents died of old age, as did their parents before them. A speck of high blood pressure here and there couldn't possibly equate to my sudden schizophrenia.

Exhaustion was the only answer, along with the fierce longing I had to see Vita again. I hardly ate. I hardly slept. My first few days in New York were miserable, and I only had myself to blame. I'd spent all of Sunday traveling across states, visiting the first stop on Vita's bucket list, and losing sleep over a hallucination. Monday was spent stressing over my first day of class without a moments rest with my all-nighter. Tuesday was supposed to be better, until I let that narcissistic TA get to me. And today, bright and early on Wednesday morning, I had the whole day to recuperate and hopefully enjoy my third day in New York.

And Reid could kiss my suburban ass. There was no reason for me to let him get to me like that, and I vowed to myself he never would again.

Daisy and I'd agreed to meet at Kaffeine at noon, but I wanted to get there a little earlier to do some investigating on my own. Daisy didn't need to be looped into my delusional situation that Vita was connected to this second place on her bucket list.

I was ready to feel normal for once and not have that sleepless-chic look I had yesterday. Considering I still hadn't fully unpacked, I used the bathroom mirror to throw on some light makeup, inevitably brightening my face. I stared at my finished face, seeing the features I knew I shared with Vita. The same dark blue eye color and round shape. Bow-shaped lips, though hers were fuller. High cheekbones on a round face. Though I had dark honey-colored loose waves that reached my waist, she used to sport a champagne blonde cut just below her shoulders.

When the familiar twinge of longing started to wash over me, I turned away from the mirror, knowing I would undoubtedly avoid it for the rest of the day.

Once I'd made myself up to look decent, I headed straight there.

Something as simple as the weight of mascara on my lashes was enough to put an extra bounce in my step, which was exactly what I needed to walk the New York walk.

It'd snowed last night, a nice sheen of snow now coating the avenues of the busy city. I almost slipped a few times as the snow had hardened overnight, but I caught myself. If I could survive the New York City metro, then I could definitely handle some ice.

Online, Kaffeine was described as your "local, single-origin coffee shop that caters to each desire with their extensive menu options". The fact that this place had great reviews and was always buzzing with influencers had to mean that surely someone knew something about the disappearance of that poor girl.

I strolled outside in the light snow, appreciating the cold air compared to my stuffy apartment with the nonstop clanking heaters that sounded like someone was smashing their kitchen pans together all night.

Subtly walking to the beat of my song, I approached Kaffeine and was thrilled to see it wasn't too busy inside. A glass of peace and quiet was exactly what I prescribed to myself. I noticed a few people standing in line, but most of the seats were open. Checking my phone, I saw that it was half past eleven, more than enough time to investigate before Daisy came, but not enough time to sit there without shooting caffeine through my veins. Besides, I may as well take advantage of the off-peak time and more available baristas to help me.

I hoped Daisy would forgive me for trying a coffee before her, but the silver lining was that I'd have another excuse to order a second one if I didn't like the first.

Stepping inside, I stood in line behind a handful of people just as my song shifted to my ringtone. Clumsily pulling out my phone, I saw my mother was calling. It took a few tries to swipe on the answer button, as my gloves were thick and obscuring. Eventually, I succeeded and adjusted my headphones so that the microphone button was resting comfortably near my face.

"Hey, Mom, what's up?"

"Alluna, dear, I haven't heard from you in ages," my mother's worried voice sounded through the phone.

What I wanted to say was, *It's been two days.*

What I actually said was, "Sorry, Mom. I was really caught up with adjusting to the city and class." I had to be careful with every word, as I knew my mother's ability to cling onto each syllable was unparalleled.

"Oh, that's nice. You sound like you're outside. Are you wearing gloves and a scarf?" She babbled.

I stepped closer in line. "Yes, Mom. I'm dressed for the weather."

"Are those sirens I hear in the background? Who just honked? Are you looking both ways before crossing the road? Oh, dear, perhaps the city is a bit too suffocating. Are you sure you don't want to come home?"

As my mother continued to invalidate any progress I'd made as someone stepping into adulthood, I focused my energy on fumbling through my handbag in search of my wallet.

Muting myself from my mom to evade further humiliation, I quickly ordered the shop's seasonal special, a medium hot rose pistachio latte. Quickly maneuvering to the waiting counter, I unmuted myself before my mother realized my attempt at privacy during her speech and decided it was time to cut in and interrupt her.

"Mom." My tone was finite. "Please. I just need some time to unwind, okay?" I was ready to say something else until I bumped right into the last person I wanted to see and gasped reflexively.

He turned around, his soft features apologetic until his eyes fell to me and recognition darkened his face.

"What happened? Are you okay?" My mother asked through my headphones.

"Uh-yes. Sorry. I just ran into someone." I answered absentmindedly.

"Who? I didn't know you had friends there," my mother questioned, nosy as ever.

"I have to go, Mom. I'll call you later." I hung up before she had the chance to object and shoved my headphones in my pocket.

"At least you're being consistent with smashing into me."

I reminded myself of the mental vow I made.

"Hello to you too, Reid."

"Did the voices tell you to stalk me?" Reid wore a sneer that was inexplicably hateful.

There was no point in enabling him, even though his words

struck a deep nerve. He clearly wanted to get a rise out of me, and I wouldn't give him the satisfaction.

"No, I'm not." I rested my arm on the counter, completely unphased by him. He looked around the counter at the working baristas and sighed heavily as if the idea of standing next to me was torturous.

"Yeah? Then why else are you here?" He was poking and pinching and prodding and provoking.

I wouldn't allow him to push my buttons. He had no reason to hate me, I never did anything to him. I also had no reason to engage in any back-and-forth nonsense. Might as well just come out with the truth instead of explaining myself to him or look for excuses. To hell with it and him.

"I'm following my missing sisters' bucket list."

Reid shut his big, fat mouth for the first time and hesitated. Good. Now I put him on the spot and made him feel uncomfortable.

"Small double shot over ice with a splash of cream for Reid!"

He grabbed his latte and was about to leave before he turned back.

"I'd have preferred you saying you were stalking me." He looked me up and down and pursed his lips.

Was he for real? This man had no shame. He clearly lacked that subconscious voice that filtered tactless things to say.

He must've taken drugs of his own. How was it that he made it sound like he hated me but wanted me around at the same time? It was especially infuriating that his handsome face was enough to turn my knees wobbly.

"Rose pistachio latte for…Lena?" The barista called behind the counter.

I'd clearly said my name, even took the time to spell it. Was it UnNewYorker of me to expect that the wrong name was exclusive to Starbucks? Was I always going to be stuck with people not knowing who I was, unless Vita was around?

I hadn't noticed how fast I was breathing through my gritted teeth until Reid leaned in, his musky scent taking my breath away, and put the nail right in the coffin.

"Isn't that yours, Alana?" He knew exactly what he was doing.

I wanted to take his smirk, throw it to the ground, stomp all over it, and paste the trampled version back on his face.

"You know my name." My voice was low and deadly.

"Right, sorry." He threw his hands up apologetically, his eyes avoiding my glare. "Hey man," he called out to the barista, signaling for him to come back.

Could it be that Reid wasn't so bad? Softening my look, a little smile tugged at my lips. He gave me a little grin.

"You got her name wrong, man."

The gesture may have been small, but it was decent enough for me to reconsider my feelings toward him. Maybe even allow myself to admit how attractive he was. I couldn't stop staring at him.

"My bad," the barista said, though I was hardly paying any attention to him. "What's the right name?"

Reid turned to me, smirked, and said, "Her name is actually Lana."

With that, I found myself taking my medium rose pistachio latte and throwing it at him.

The lid popped off from the force of the impact and the hot coffee dripped off his brown jacket, his pants now covered in stains.

The look we shared in that initial moment was something I mentally documented forever. I wanted it painted and hung across museums internationally so that the world could forever enter this moment where I actually wiped the smirk off Reid's face. If looks could kill, I'd be dead already. He looked down at me like I was a cockroach that he wanted to squash, and his eyes were blazing. They might've even brightened at that moment, a green fire bursting at the seams.

And the look I returned was one of triumph. He could keep his words to himself now that he knew what would happen if he messed with me.

The moment lasted but a mere second until reality kicked in along with my humanity and I realized what I'd done.

"Oh, my God…" I couldn't believe myself. I had to look at my hands and remind myself that they were mine, the hands that actually threw the latte without an ounce of hesitation.

"What is *wrong* with you?" His voice was calm, and it was far more intimidating than if he'd screamed. But the fact that it was perfectly reasonable for him to ask is what killed me inside. What normal person just throws their coffee at someone?

"I-I…" I reached for the tissue dispenser and started pulling out one after another hastily. "I don't know what came over me." Passing him the tissues, I found it difficult to maintain eye contact thus longer.

"I don't care if you're on those drugs or if you're seriously mentally ill, you need professional help."

Stiffening, I sharply shook my head as if to delete what I just heard while trying to help him clean himself up. Noticing some bystanders looking in our direction, I realized the scene I'd caused. We were now the center of attention.

Feeling heat rush to my cheeks, I bit my lip to help ground myself and maintain my composure.

"Is there a problem here?" The barista that called me by the wrong name was leaning over the counter, inspecting the damage.

"No, um— we just— I just—" Words were becoming difficult. I wasn't one to be the center of attention and this was becoming more mortifying by the second. But my dignity was all I had left. Taking a deep breath, I relaxed my face, ready to explain away the situation and hopefully not be banned from my second spot on the bucket list before I had the chance to investigate.

As I raised my head to look at the barista for the first time, my breath caught in my throat and I forgot how to breathe.

The barista had wings. Iridescent, transparent wings that caught the light and created sparkling patterns with it. And they fluttered. The barista hadn't leaned over the counter to get closer. The barista was floating.

The barista lowered his head, exposing his pointy ears while examining the puddle of coffee on the ground.

I felt light-headed. Was I imagining things again? Was this another hallucination? I blinked a few times and wished away this vision, but the wings and ears remained.

I now had a second hallucination to add to my repertoire.

None of the other baristas were paying any attention to this one. They were going about their busy day preparing coffee as if nothing was about.

I was ready to rip my hair out of my scalp in individual chunks until I sneaked a glance at Reid to validate my own craziness.

But when I noticed that his mouth was agape and his eyes were bulging out, I finally understood that I wasn't crazy. He flung his eyes back to the barista, as if to confirm we were seeing the same picture.

He must've already seen the wings but played it cool, until he realized I could see them too, which was a whole different story. What could this possibly mean?

Reid quickly averted his eyes and resumed dabbing the tissues on himself as if nothing happened, but it was too obvious.

The barista with wings had disappeared into the back room, doing whatever baristas with wings do.

I grabbed Reid's arm and held onto it for dear life, my nails digging into his skin.

"You saw it, too." My statement was finite without any room

for questioning. Reid shook my arm off in and straightened his jacket.

"Saw what? You flinging your coffee at me?"

He was doing it again. One might even consider it a talent, the way he could get under my skin.

"Don't gaslight me, asshole. I know you saw it," I said under my breath, not wanting to attract any more attention.

"You should really lay off the drugs, Lana. Unless, of course, you want to see a doctor about that schizophrenia you were talking about." His eyes narrowed, but didn't meet mine fully. He clearly wasn't going to budge.

I wanted to press further, but Reid had grabbed his coffee from the counter and whooshed out of the shop so fast I hadn't finished processing my next sentence.

"We're out of tissues, ma'am." The winged barista's voice brought me back to the moment and I whipped my head towards him, particularly his pointy ears that didn't have any morsel of glue or plastic. My hand was just reaching inside the empty canister after I withdrew every tissue and I hadn't noticed.

Costume or not, I saw the man fly. Unless he was a master trapeze artist with hidden wires made to ensure top-notch barista quality service, I knew I wasn't imagining things.

I also knew exactly how I'd sound if I questioned the barista, especially with witnesses around. Instead, I asked, "Can you please help me with something?"

The barista took a quick look at his coworkers, most likely to make sure he wasn't missing anything and nodded his head back to me.

"A girl disappeared some time ago, and this was the last place she was seen. Do you know anything about that?"

He sighed. "I already spoke to the police about this. I was the barista at the counter that day, and some manic woman came in talking about dust being everywhere and asking us not to put dust in her coffee. She was pacing back and forth for hours, and stayed until the end of my shift. I have no idea what happened to her after that. As far as I know, she was never seen again."

SEVEN

*T*he class was about to start and I realized how awful I was the moment I walked in and saw Daisy's unhappy face. Even her thick blonde hair seemed to lose volume.

"You could've texted me that you wouldn't show, you know." Daisy was one card short of an understanding deck, but I couldn't blame her.

"I'm sorry for standing you up. Honestly, I was at Kaffeine pretty early but then I had to leave and I forgot to tell you."

The moment the barista told me the words that created nothing but more questions, I bolted out of there, feeling more unhinged than a broken doorknob. The duration of that Wednesday was spent mainly in bed, staring at walls and debating my decision to move to New York.

Until the stroke of midnight chimed from the clock and I was hit with another wave of inspiration to burn the battery straight out of my computer by researching anything I could, particularly relating to Reid. I'd stalked every social media platform known to existence, and couldn't find him anywhere. Not even under Professor Sage's LinkedIn connections. I realized I didn't even know his last name, which didn't leave me with much.

If anything, I knew nothing about Reid beside the fact that he was Sage's TA, liked a double shot over ice with a splash of cream, and was a level four sarcastic asshole.

No matter how much he wanted me to believe I was crazy or on drugs, I was starting to realize there was more to this story than both of us having the same hallucination. For any reason that he didn't want me to know, he saw the supernatural barista the same way I did, and it just so happened to be at the very location where someone disappeared, which just so happened to be on my missing sister's bucket list.

I knew I had to talk to him, and if I couldn't find him on social media, then I'd corner him after class. Dump latte after latte on him until he explained himself. I was at my wit's end, anyway. If Reid turned out to be a dead-end, I would be on the next bus home to my overprotective parents. There was only so much independence I could take, especially being the foolish UnNewYorker that I was, humiliated at every turn.

When I walked into class on time, for once, the next day,

Thursday morning, I realized how selfish I'd been. I didn't even have the decency to tell Daisy that I left Kaffeine and would make it up to her.

Was there even a point to tell Daisy the truth? I was so close to buying a ticket home that I hardly felt the need to salvage our blossoming friendship since I'd be leaving anyway.

But I didn't have to be a total jerk either. I apologized again and said there was a complicated situation, without going into detail. No point in adding that the barista with wings told me about the girl that disappeared in the same fashion as the others as per my sister's map of a bucket list, in addition to throwing my drink at Reid like a complete lunatic.

Daisy didn't really talk to me for the rest of the class, and as much as I wanted to make things better or make promises about the future, I had more pressing matters on my mind.

With each passing moment of the class, I waited for Reid to show up and hang out by Dr. Sage's computer, as he usually did.

But Reid was a total no-show today. And I was absolutely positive it was because of me.

There wasn't a single shred of doubt in my mind that he was avoiding me. But that wasn't enough to stop me.

When class ended, I wanted to tell Daisy I'd text her later, but she left before I had the chance. It seemed I really messed up with her. Yet another thing I was doing wrong and couldn't fix by myself. I never knew how to do the whole friend thing when Vita was around because she was everything I ever wanted in a best friend. If she could just come back from wherever she was, none of this would be happening.

Dr. Sage Gusto was gathering her papers at the podium when I approached her.

"Where is he."

"You were on time today, for once. No pumpkin spice holding you up?" She'd completely ignored me!

"Please, Sage. I really need to know where Reid is." I put my hand on her shoulder. She stiffened, her eyes darting between mine like she was playing ping pong.

She bit her cheek, failing to maintain her stoicism, and dipped her head, her voice hushed. "We can talk in my office."

A grateful exhale escaped me as I nodded and followed behind her prudently.

"How can I help you?" Sage closed her office door behind her and walked over to her desk, gesturing for me to take a seat beside her.

"Why does he hate me so much?" I slumped into my seat, sick and tired of not having any answers to my questions.

Sage sighed. "He doesn't hate you, Alluna." She hesitated as if she wanted to say something, but stopped herself. Another nonanswer.

I tried going in another direction, hoping it would get me some answers.

"Why wasn't he in class?"

"He was grading papers for me." Sage hadn't even missed a

beat. I must have looked like a hot air balloon since I filled my head with so much pride. Of course, the world didn't revolve around me. How big was I in the grand scheme of things to expect Reid to miss an entire class on my account? I really was full of it.

"Where is he now?"

"Poor thing hadn't eaten all day so he went to grab lunch."

I paused. Surely, I was missing something. All her answers were convenient and gave him a great alibi, though I couldn't shake the feeling that he was avoiding me. But I was sick of being the interrogator, it wasn't in my gene pool. It seemed I was drawing conclusions where there were none.

I thanked the professor for her time and gathered my things. There was no point in continuing. It wouldn't be difficult to go back to Hershey, all I had to do was grab my packed bags that I never bothered to unpack.

"Wait." Sage held her arm out to stop me before I left.

"Reid acts a certain way…because he lost someone."

I stared silently, willing Sage to give me any more crumbs, as informal as it was.

After a few beats of silence, I leaned in closer. "What happened?"

Sage hesitated. "It's his business. Just know that she was important to him and disappeared recently."

I felt as though I was about to melt into a puddle and go down the drain. I couldn't imagine Reid being loving and tender, especially with someone dear to him. Could it be that one of the girls that disappeared was Reid's girlfriend? I certainly didn't see that coming. What other reason could there be for him to have the same supernatural sight that I had in a place where one of the girls disappeared? As standoffish as Reid was, he was just healing his broken heart. I made a mental note to remember that the next time he made me want to punch him.

There must've been something connecting us. And this was definitely something far beyond normal.

"Who?" I asked, wondering which girl held the key to his heart. Sage shrugged.

"That's his business."

Even though my questions could fill an encyclopedia, Sage had just given me something far more valuable to work with, or someone, rather. Reid could help me. He had to know something or someone that was causing these disappearances. And if my theory was correct, there would be a clue at Glitz, the nightclub that was also the third place on the bucket list, where one of the girls was last seen.

I had to find Reid. If he really did get lunch, he would surely be coming back to Sage's office to finish grading papers. Gathering my belongings, I thanked Sage for her time and stood by her door, ready to pounce on Reid the moment he appeared.

"He's done grading papers for today, though." Sage's head disappeared behind her large desktop, the sound of her nails clicking on the keyboard.

Grumbling to myself, I left, right after Sage called out, "Try coming early for once and you might catch him in my office. Happy holidays and see you next year!"

Surprised by the weight of my frustration over not seeing Reid today, I worried over how much I'd wanted to see him. As difficult as his personality was, there was also something about him that was hard to resist. But it wasn't like I had feelings for him. I had a purpose behind my stalking; he had something I needed - information.

He could be as rude as he wished, I needed to don a thicker skin and pick his brain. And I couldn't take no for an answer, as much as he acted like my presence bothered him.

For once, I didn't feel crazy, schizophrenic, or on drugs. Something was certainly running amuck in this reality that I was starting to question, and Reid would help me figure out exactly what happened to Vita and the one he lost, unless he already knew.

And since I had to wait until the next class to see him again, I knew I had another problem to fix. Pulling out my phone, I started dialing quickly.

"What?" Daisy answered in the middle of a sigh.

"Let me make it up to you. Kaffeine part deux?"

"Oh, mon cherie. I thought you'd never ask."

We chuckled together. I was glad to hear that Daisy wasn't one to hold grudges. That was a big difference between her and Vita. Whenever Vita wasn't happy with me, she could go days without speaking to me.

But to Daisy, it was all water under the bridge.

I went straight to Kaffeine, excited to soothe my rumbling tummy with anything pumpkin flavored. I wasn't one to discriminate, the dessert could have pumpkin in addition to the coffee.

I realized that the year was coming to an end and tomorrow would be New Year's Eve, and perhaps I could spend it with my new friend to whom I've already managed to make a crappy first impression in the three days we've known each other.

She was surprisingly pleasant when I met her in Kaffeine, but I supposed I wasn't used to people letting things go so fast. I followed her to the corner and marveled at the layout since I missed it during my feud and possible breakdown the other day.

The whole wall was a window with a ledge big enough for two, which gave us the best view for people-watching indoors and outdoors. It was also secluded since the nearest table was more than a few feet away. A cozy throw blanket covered the ledge, giving it a homey and familiar feel.

"So did you get something last time you were here?" Daisy reserved the ledge for us by draping her tailored jacket gently over the blanket, and I followed suit with my own winter coat, though I couldn't replicate her graceful nature.

"Yes, the rose pistachio latte…though I didn't have a chance to sample it."

"How come?" She smoothed my jacket out for me, surely out

of habit.

I hesitated and played with my fingers. "Because I threw it at Reid."

Daisy gasped, her hand flying to her mouth as she burst out laughing.

"Reid? The TA?" She snorted through her laughter. "That's not how we pick up men in New York City, hun." Her laughter was contagious and I found myself laughing with her, the incident suddenly seeming less mortifying.

"I know! I mean, I couldn't help it. He really got under my skin."

"I'm sure you'd want him to get under something else, too." Daisy waggled her eyebrows suggestively and I lightly punched her shoulder.

"Why does everyone think I have a thing for him! I just met the guy, for Pete's sake."

"Oh? Who is everyone?"

"Enough!" I grabbed Daisy's arm and marched her over to the line. "No more Reid talk allowed."

She chuckled and gave me a look that said, *you're not fooling anybody, hun.*

Heat flaming my cheeks, I cleared my throat and glanced toward the baristas, the winged one nowhere in sight.

"If you say so." Daisy was not convinced, but changed the subject for my sake. "Would you like to hear about how I'm the disappointment of my family?"

"If you feel comfortable sharing."

Daisy let out a dramatic whoosh and stared at the menu, all signs of lighthearted humor gone from her face.

"My family is full of doctors. My father is a neurosurgeon and my mother is a cardiologist. My two brothers are in medical school and residency…and then there's me."

"No medical school for you?"

"You guessed it. My immigrant family isn't quick to brag about me and my fashion marketing degree. All I hear is how they came to this country without a single penny in their pocket to give my siblings and me a better life, and I'm wasting my potential with the privilege I was given."

I was pretty stunned. That was a lot heavier than I expected. Underneath Daisy's flawless curls and sophisticated clothing was just a sad girl whose family didn't accept her choices.

We ordered two rose pistachio latte's and resumed our conversation at the corner ledge.

Settling in, I pondered how much to let her in to my own family trauma.

"My sister was always the beloved golden child of the family until she disappeared in August. After that, my parents became so overbearing I had to move out."

My life in a nutshell. Without all the supernatural happenings, of course.

Daisy daintily sipped her coffee and nodded in approval. "Try the latte, it's good."

I allowed the warm flavors to circle my tongue, appreciating the taste. Though the latte was superb, my defining factor in a new coffee shop would always be pumpkin.

"A roast," I said. "I mean, a toast."

Daisy rolled her eyes.

"To new friendships and new blends of beans that don't give a flying fuck about each other's choices." Raising my whimsically decorated cup, I clinked with her. Daisy's smile was dazzling.

"Brewtiful words indeed."

We were about to resume our discussion and our venting about our families in particular when the sound of the news caught my attention. A person in line was watching the news on their phone without the headphones on, and the volume was turned all the way up.

Another NYC disappearance reported.

Oh, no.

This marks the fourth disappearance of a young woman in four months.

"Jeez, can someone give him headphones," Daisy muttered beside me.

"Another person disappeared." I gave her a sharp look.

The last place the woman was seen was…

"The Loeb Boathouse," I whispered. Daisy gave me a funny look.

The Loeb Boathouse in Central Park.

"How did you know?" Daisy set her coffee down.

Because it was the fourth place on Vita's bucket list. An iconic spot from Sex and the City. Vita and I'd rewatched the scenes that took places there a hundred times over.

But I couldn't tell Daisy how I knew. All I could offer was a small vague smile and a halfhearted, "already heard about it."

This disappearance happened faster than the others, typically there would be a month's gap, but now it was just a few weeks.

The poor girl was a college student at a nearby campus. She could've been someone in my class. She could've been me.

"Oh, okay. Do you have plans for New Year's?"

Shaking my head in the least pitiful way I could muster, I kept my eyes on my coffee. Me? Have plans? What a riot.

I winced internally as I realized this would be my first New Year's without Vita there to brighten the holiday spirit.

"You know, my family actually bought this Kate Spade dining set, but it came in a set of six! It would be so embarrassing for me, my two brothers, and my parents to only use five..."

I laughed at Daisy's inability to be discreet but decided to humor her.

"Well, I suppose I could do your family a favor and occupy the sixth dining set."

"Oh, you have no idea how much that would mean to them. Truly, you'd be doing us a huge favor."

Both our coffees were inexcusably empty. I was rudely reminded of this when we both went in for the last sip and were disappointed by the air in the cup.

I furrowed my brows in disgruntlement and crossed my arms.

"Pumpkin?" She smiled.

"Pumpkin."

Glee filled me at the thought of my addictive flavor, and by my new friend who was already starting to know me. Even if it was at an arm's length and I wasn't telling her the whole truth, she knew enough.

We both went back for our second coffee and stayed for a few more hours before Daisy took me shopping and truly made me realize the beauty of thrifting vintage clothes.

As much as I tried to be in the moment with her, I knew the moment I saw Reid again, my life would probably change. Thus far, I'd been running in circles with no anchor holding me down. I knew something dark was awaiting me, and I didn't care. I would do anything to find Vita again. I knew she'd do the same for me.

And so I enjoyed the last few days of my life before the descent into darkness truly began.

EIGHT

aisy's family was the picture of an eccentric family that wanted to feed every new mouth that came through the door. If I thought I knew boundaries with my own mother, everything flew straight out the window from the moment I met Daisy's mother, Katherine. At first glance, she didn't strike me as a cardiologist, until her sharp tongue really established her matriarchal tip of the totem pole, especially with Daisy's father, Michael.

The two of them were like two business associates always working together, which surprised me further. I always had this idea that doctors put work before their families, but based on what Daisy told me, her parents always tried to alternate their shifts so they could spend time with their kids. In fact, it was rare for the whole family to be together at once, except for holidays.

The moment I walked through the door, Daisy's mother wrapped me in a large hug.

"You must be Alluna! Come in quickly. It's freezing outside." She had a slight accent and rolled her r's. I realized I never asked Daisy where her parents were from but if I had to guess, I would say Slavic origins. Katherine ushered me in and looked me over, her blunt tongue working itself. Covering her hands in mine, she shook her head. "Your hands are like ice. We'll have to warm you up right away." She glanced behind me and clicked her teeth.

"Your jacket barely covers your butt." Not knowing what to say, I half-smiled and took my shoes off.

"I'll take that and that!" She scooped my shoes and my apparently deficient jacket and went to put them away.

She was gone in a moment. I felt both smothered and abandoned for a split second and wondered if this was how Daisy always felt. As if she heard my thoughts, Daisy put her hand on my shoulder and gave me a sympathetic look.

"Misha, make some tea for Alluna. She's freezing!" Katherine called.

"Misha?" I whispered to Daisy. She nodded.

"Misha is a nickname for Michael."

Not knowing if I was supposed to refer to him by the nickname, I remained silent.

Michael popped his head out of the kitchen for the first time and raised a bushy grey eyebrow.

"Early grey?" His accent was noticeable as well.

Confused as ever, I looked at Daisy for clarification. She shrugged. "He calls earl grey early grey. Does that tea suit your palate?"

"Yes, thank you." My voice was far too quiet to be heard, but Daisy was my saving grace.

"Yes, Papa, she'll take early grey. I'll have one too!" Daisy called back. Michael gave a thumbs up and disappeared back into the kitchen.

I heard some indistinguishable words in their language between Daisy's parents and whom I assumed to be her brothers.

One of them stepped out to the living room holding out some fluffy bunny slippers and threw them by my feet. I took the moment to observe his similarity with Daisy and noticed his bright blue eyes when ours met.

"Alex." He held his muscled arm out. Shaking his hand, I noticed his firm grip and had a brief invasive thought about his arm holding mine down.

"Pleasure. Alluna." Alex's dark brown hair swept over his face as he half-smiled.

"Nice to meet you, Alina."

Never mind. Gone, forgotten, not needed. No love story here.

"What are these for?" I gestured to the slippers, not bothering to correct him.

"For your feet. It's part of our culture." Daisy was in the middle of putting her slippers on and at that moment, I noticed no one was walking around barefoot.

Accepting them graciously, I was thankful Daisy and I shared similar shoe sizes and her warm slippers fit snugly against my toes and made them feel like friends at a campfire.

"Come meet my other brother, AKA the second nuisance of my life." Daisy pulled me into the kitchen while Alex trailed behind.

Daisy's other brother was sitting at the table, glued to his phone, when Daisy walked up behind him and messed up his tousled blonde hair.

"Yo, Leo."

He ducked beneath her grasp and fixed his hair, groaning in annoyance.

"What do you want? I'm busy."

"Save your porn for later, we have a guest."

Leo glanced at me for a moment and gave an approving smirk. "She legal?"

Feeling undressed and exposed, I reflexively covered myself and took a seat at the couch by the dining room, far from his leering eye.

Daisy punched his arm enough to induce a glare from him and she went to join me.

"Alex is in residency to be a neurosurgeon. He's alright, but he's usually got his head in the clouds. Leo is my twin, and he's pre-med, though I should've eaten him in the womb."

"Don't you wish," Leo called from the table.

Katherine said a few words in a scolding tone and flicked Leo upside his head. Giving me a warm smile, she motioned to the seats. "Dinner will be ready soon, come, come."

The conversation flowed between Daisy's family like a handball game, and they spoke without any filters or boundaries holding them back. When Katherine inquired if Leo was using protection, I felt secondhand embarrassment and blushed, though he didn't seem to care.

Katherine and Michael underwent a top-notch interrogation with me, asking me one question after another as if I was in an interview. My parents and I never shared this type of dynamic, and I struggled to keep up with their fast-paced nature. But in a weird way, it felt refreshing to be given front-row seats to the type of family that could talk about anything they liked.

Leo tried his underhanded version of flirting with me a few times. He said something about giving me a lesson on my own anatomy before Daisy flicked his head.

"What?" Leo rubbed his head in annoyance. "I'm just charming the girl."

"You call that charming?" Katherine said. "Did I ever tell the story of how your father charmed me?"

The entire table said, "one hundred times," in perfect synchronization.

"Well, it was the summer of 'eighty-five, I was in medical school..." Katherine began, while a collective groan ensued around me.

While I appreciated the hospitality of Daisy's family, I could see why she could only handle them in small doses. The way they doted on their sons for their career choices was fairly obvious. They hardly asked Daisy about how her education was going or gave her room to speak. I noticed she hardly bothered, especially standing in the shadows of her brothers.

Later on, in between dinner and the start of the New Year countdown, Daisy asked me to meet her in her room upstairs so she could show me her vintage collection.

I was on my way to her room when Leo cornered me, eyeing me up and down.

"I think we got off on the wrong foot." He blocked my path to Daisy's room.

"Pretty girls like you just make me nervous and then my tongue gets me in trouble."

"No worries." I tried to walk around him but he blocked me again with his arm.

"*You won't find her, and you'll die trying.*" Leo's voice was different, darker, menacing, unrecognizable. I stopped, wondering if I was hallucinating again because there was no way Leo would say words like that to me. But then again, I hardly knew what was real anymore.

"Come again?"

"I said, let me take you out on a date." Leo's voice was back to normal. I wanted to believe I misheard him, but the chances of his words landing straight on the bullseye couldn't have been an accident. Was it possible that the hallucinations I was having would lead me to Vita?

"Where is she?" I stupidly attempted, hoping his dark voice would come back and give me answers.

"Who, Daisy? I dunno, I think she's in her room. Anyway, what do you say? A night out on the town? Perhaps a Michelin star venue?"

My sister dated a guy like Leo once. I knew his type from her experience. He hounded her for a date until she agreed, and then he wouldn't let her out of his clutches far longer than she would've preferred. Guys like him think their perseverance should be rewarded with submission, but I knew better than that. He would never let this go while he thought I had the upper hand. All I had to do was let him think he was winning.

"I'll think about it," I said with a smile, and his arm dropped, granting me access to Daisy's room. Vita would be proud of me. She was always one to preach the power women truly held over men.

I made my way to Daisy's room, wondering if I'd ever get closer to any answers. The entirety of the night and holiday was spent with me avoiding Leo and thinking about how I'd approach Reid when I saw him again.

Three days later, when class resumed, I made sure to lurk by Sage's office far before the lecture started at sharply eight in the morning, a whole hour before the class started. I wanted to catch Reid the moment he came in and demand his help. No matter how much he got on my nerves, I knew he was my next step in my quest, whether I wanted him to be or not. I was willing to swallow my ego to work with him, but the question remained - could he? Or more importantly, would he?

The moment I saw his unmistakable auburn hair among the sea of heads heading down the hall sometime later, I shrunk behind a wall to make sure he wouldn't see me and waited for him to come to Sage's office.

I stepped right in between him and her door when he approached, and he paused, looking more irritated than ever.

His dark red eyebrows pressed together. "What a lovely start to my day." His sarcasm rang loudly. I crossed my arms.

He leaned in, his voice dripping with vitriol. "Is Dr. Sage's office on your dead sister's bucket list, too?" His malice would've made me tremble had it not been for my unfaltering will.

"Nope." I shook my head adamantly. "This time, I am stalking you." I made no attempt to speak inconspicuously.

"I know you lost someone, too. And I know you saw the barista with—"

His hand was over my mouth before I could finish, and my breathing stopped with how close his face was to mine.

"Shut up!" He hissed, looking around to make sure no one was around, though the scene didn't look very good in his favor.

"We can't talk here." He released my mouth and effortlessly

moved me to the side without flexing a muscle and quickly unlocked Sage's door. I was about to say something when he pulled me in roughly by my arm and locked the door behind him.

It was just me and him in the room. I could feel the heat emanating from his golden skin as he brushed past me and pulled me in closer, away from the door, away from the eyes and ears. Our close proximity was making breathing difficult, but I reminded myself of Reid's nasty nature and my goal in mind.

The word vomit ensued. "Okay, listen close. Enough with this gaslighting about me being on drugs or me being schizophrenic, I know you saw the wings. I know you saw the pointy ears. I also know you lost someone you loved dearly. I know there's something you're not telling me." I paused, and threw my reach at him, even if it was wrong. "I know you were avoiding me last week." His silence was confirmation enough. We were hardly a hair's length apart from each other, and his arm was still on mine.

Reid stared deep into my eyes with his blazing green fiery pit and realized our closeness when he put some distance between us, his eye contact never faltering.

"What do you want from me?"

"I want us to work together."

"*Me*? Work with *you*?" He scoffed. "What's in it for me?"

"We can help each other."

"Where I come from that's called prostitution."

I ignored him. "Don't you want know what happened to your…the person you lost?" I wasn't sure what else to call her. His girlfriend? Love of his life? His other half?

He stiffened. "You have no idea."

"Well, I want to find my sister. I have some good theories. I don't believe the victims are dead."

Reid laughed dryly. "You think your little "theories" are enough?" He held his hands up in quotation marks for emphasis.

"You don't know a single thing. You may not be schizophrenic, but there's something clearly wrong with you if you think you can find them."

I was starting to get better at seeing through his insults and seeing information between the lines.

"So you think they're alive, too."

He stopped.

"I see no benefit in working with you."

"Just give me a chance. A probationary period." I stepped closer to him and closed the distance between us. I wouldn't let him think he was the only deciding factor between us. "If you think I want to work with you, you're the delusional one. You've been nothing but cruel to me since the moment we met. You might not help me either. This probation is for both of us, not just me."

He was thinking. I could see it in his locked jaw and pursed lips. His unwavering eye contact. He was actually considering, which was a win for me.

"Think about it." Quickly checking my phone, I made sure to put as much distance as I could between us. "Class is about to start. Find me afterward if you're in." Turning on my heel, I brushed my hair back and walked away without waiting for his response. I'd already planted the seed in his brain, I needed to give it time to grow, hopefully in the right direction.

I could hardly pay attention during class, even with Daisy asking me to try a new coffee place sometime so we could roast it together.

Reid was sitting at Sage's computer as he usually did, except our eyes were locked the entire lecture. We were having a mental battle and seeing if either of us would back down.

"Woah, why is Reid glaring at you?" Daisy whispered halfway through the lecture.

"He's still mad about the latte I threw at him," was the best I could give. If this was my first time meeting him, his expression would've scared me. But I was stronger than that. If looks could kill, my returning glare would be no different from his. Two opposing forces that couldn't stand each other, but forced to play the same game. He knew it, too. And he hated it. For whatever reason that he hated my guts, he knew he needed me to find his girl again.

My confirmation was provided just shortly before the end of class when Sage handed Reid a stack of handouts to give out to the students, and just before he gave one to me, he growled under his breath, "Fine. Two weeks," low enough that only I could hear.

That was the first night I unpacked my bags.

NINE

The next day, I met Reid in Sage's office while she was teaching another class and we could have a private space to discuss our plans.

The moment I walked in with my pumpkin spiced latte, I handed over a double shot over ice, hoping to start new and make amends since we were about to get much closer. He hardly acknowledged my gesture, except to look at me to see if I was being serious.

"For me? I'm touched." Reid didn't bother to take the cup from me so I left it near him for good measure anyway, hoping he would follow my example and lay off the sarcasm.

"I have to head to Sage's lecture in about twenty minutes, so make it quick." He leaned back on his chair and rested his arms behind his head while I planted myself in a nearby chair, clearing my throat. Making sure to keep at least three feet between us, I hurled into my theories while avoiding eye contact. Reid had a way of making me forget my train of thought once he centered those eyes on me.

"This is going to sound crazy, but I have evidence that all victims are connected to my sister."

He laughed and rubbed his face with his hands. "You are way in over your head. These victims all disappeared in New York City. Aren't you from Bumblefuck, Arkansas?"

"Pennsylvania, actually." I wasn't going to let him undermine my theories before he even heard them.

"My sister was the first one to disappear, first of all. She—"

"Was she in New York City at the time of her disappearance?"

A frustrated exhale escaped my teeth. "No, but just listen—"

"Then she's an outlier and has nothing to do with the others, and my situation has nothing to do with yours."

I was losing him. Desperately, I shook my head and kept going. "Listen! Just before I moved here, I found this list, and every single location was—"

He crossed his arms. "Tell me something about you that would actually interest me, or I'm walking away."

"Stop interrupting me! If you would just give me a chance to talk for more than two seconds—"

"Do you masturbate?" There were now only two feet between

us as he leaned over his knee and became dangerously and uncomfortably close to me.

"Excuse me?" My eyes were on the ground, on his brown loafers, to be exact.

"You seem like you're on edge. So I ask again, do you masturbate?"

"I don't see how that's relevant."

Only one foot was now between us. Reid had leaned further over his knee and was now directly staring me straight in the face, and breathing had become a foreign concept, but I was starting to know better.

"If you're not going to listen, this isn't going to work." Meeting his eyes, I engaged in a silent battle between our eyes, a blue and green tango. To think I'd tried to be nice by bringing him a drink he would like and trying to be civil, and this was how he was responding.

For lack of better judgment, I went with my emotional gut instead of my rational gut. "Maybe you just don't care about the woman you lost."

I knew I'd struck a nerve when he venomously curled his lip and leaned away from me. Even though it felt like a victory in some ways, I somehow felt the brunt of my own lash at him and winced.

His eyes were blazing. "Don't you ever talk about her, or I'll kill you myself."

Swallowing nervously, I forced myself to meet his poisonous glare and continue our mission.

"Sore topic, got it." I shifted my legs awkwardly and tried to cling to the thoughts that were flying out of my head with every second I allowed his eyes to enter my soul and tear me to shreds. Clearing my throat, I tried not to imagine being on his bad side. After all, I needed his cooperation in order for this to work.

"Um. Anyway, I stumbled on a bucket list my sister made, I think I mentioned it earlier…" *Yeah, right before I tossed my latte at you.* "…when we ran into each other at Kaffeine." I was avoiding his eyes again. "Every single disappearance thus far has been linked to her list. The first spot was Dumbo, where the first girl vanished. The second spot was Kaffeine, where the second girl vanished, and so on and so forth."

I had Reid's attention. The poison had dripped from his countenance and melted into an unreadable expression, but I still had him.

"The last girl to disappear had been linked to the fourth place, the Loeb Boathouse."

"Interesting." Reid couldn't have sounded any more difficult to read. He could have been commenting on the weather with the control he had over his monotonous yet casual response.

"Then there's the other stuff. You know, the wings? Pointy ears?" Without waiting for him to intervene, I continued. "And that wasn't the first time either. In fact, I saw my sister at Dumbo."

His curiosity was piqued. His eyes shot straight to me, and I wondered if this was the only thing he didn't know already. "Oh? What did you see?"

"Well, I saw her in the water. With a tail." It sounded even more ridiculous out loud.

"Which is why you thought you were schizophrenic when we met." I nodded feverishly.

He pursed his lips and slumped into his seat, contemplating his next sentence. "Did she say anything?"

"Yes, she called my name. Two or three times, I think."

Could Reid actually help me? He was asking questions, after all. Maybe he knew which direction to point me in.

"Was that the only time you saw her?"

"No, well—yes. But someone else mentioned her to me."

"Who? In what circumstance?"

"I was spending the holiday with my friend, and her brother was, um." I shifted my weight again at the memory of Leo's unwanted advance and said, "Talking to me, when his voice suddenly changed and it sounded like he was possessed or something." I hoped Reid wouldn't catch onto my lack of explanation as to what we were talking about. The last thing Reid needed was to be involved in my personal matters, no matter how pitiful.

"What did he say?"

"Um, something along the lines of how I won't find her, and I'll die trying." Reid's interrogation was a bit of a shock to me. I hardly expected him to express such interest in the victims, though it seemed like he didn't have much to go off of. Or maybe he did. Maybe he had all the pieces and my few experiences were the missing ones that would pull the whole picture together.

He was silent. For the first time, he wasn't trying to penetrate my eyes with his own. His shoulders slumped as he pondered pensively, and I took the opportunity to really look at his handsome face and appreciate the solemn calmness that I hardly saw with him. Maybe he wasn't such a bad guy after all. He was just a lost soul with a broken heart, doomed to the unknown future of whether he would reunite with his lost love. Just like me with Vita. Every single day, I carried her absence with me and felt the merciless shards of loss lacerate my heart further and further into oblivion. I knew what it felt like to have a wounded heart that couldn't heal due to the wounds reopening before they could close.

"What about you? Do you know anything about the tails and wings and who knows what else is happening?" After everything I'd shared, I was curious to hear his side and ready to solve this together.

Much to my dismay, he was back to his old self.

"Oh, yes. You'll find all your answers when you follow the rainbow to the pot of gold in the end. A nice leprechaun will meet you and give you a lucky charm for it."

"Prick."

"Wouldn't you like to see?" He winked, and I sank into my chair, wholly perplexed by this man.

"Seriously. You have to tell me something now."

He shook his head. "Nah. I'd much rather entertain this 'probation' period," he said with air quotes, "and see the benefits that may come from this arrangement before I can trust you." His eyes roamed my body at the mention of "benefits." I found myself seeing through his perverted comments. He just wanted to be hated, it was easier. It was his defense mechanism to shield himself. I was no stranger to that - though I was the type to disappear in the shadows instead of lashing out at those around me. I was starting to know Reid better than he'd prefer, not that he'd ever admit it.

"So be it," I said against my lack of better judgment. "I was investigating every place on the list and using it as a map, if you will. I saw my sister in the first place, and I saw the barista with wings in the second, so I believe that anyone who was connected to the victims will see these things related to their disappearance."

Reid nodded in a slow drawl. Unclear if he was confirming my theory, I pursued myself, realizing that the more I articulated my tangled thoughts, the more I could shape them.

"I am going to the third place on the bucket list, the same place the third girl disappeared - the nightclub Glitz."

"And what do you plan to do there, dance the night away?" His tone was mocking, and if I had any pumpkin spiced latte left in my cup, it would be dripping off his shirt.

Giving him a slight glare, I exhaled. "You can put it that way. And you're coming with me."

"Me?" He scoffed. "I'm not much of a dancer."

"Neither am I. We are going to scope out the place and see if anyone knows anything about the third girl. Just like the winged barista knew about the second girl."

Reid's eyes shot to mine. "The Faerie," he corrected as he leaned closer again. "What did he know?"

"Quid pro quo." I smiled sweetly. "What is a Faerie?"

He leaned back, his interest lost. "Not today, Lana."

Gritting my teeth, I stood up. No matter how hard I tried to shake off his demeaning gag, it still got to me deep inside, in the place where I knew I was forgettable next to Vita. But he didn't have to know that.

"Meet me at Glitz tonight, eleven o'clock sharp," I said through my teeth.

Reid stood as well, his lanky height towering over me. He flashed his canines at me and spoke dryly. "It's a date."

Though I knew he was being sarcastic, a small part of me wished these were different circumstances and that I was actually about to go on a date with someone who cared enough about me to remember my name.

A quick glance at his watch and he was slinging his bag over his shoulder. "I have a class to catch. I'm sure you have enough time to think of more *theories* of yours. Maybe even hold my interest this time."

I wasn't going to let him walk all over me like that. "I'm sure you have enough time to make yourself less of an asshole. Maybe you'll hold my interest more as well."

He smiled and my knees were suddenly wobbly. "So I'm interesting in the first place, then?"

I clamped my mouth shut like a clam and cursed myself for not thinking my words through better.

"Enjoy class, and see you tonight," I said through a tight-lipped grimace. His ego was already so inflated he was a balloon about to burst.

Reid tipped his head, grabbed the double shot over ice, held it out to me like a toast, and bowed out of the room like the pompous ass he was.

I supposed that was his way of thanking me since he ended up accepting the drink. By the time I left, I realized my cheeks were burning, likely due to his comment. He was, in fact, very interesting to look at, and I seemed to completely embarrass myself while also being insulted by him.

He couldn't really hate me as much as he acted, though. Surely deep inside, he actually had a heart. If he even agreed to work with me in the first place and sit through this short meeting, considering my first impression involved a thrown latte and heated exchanges.

I had to believe Reid didn't hate me. And as much as I didn't want to admit it, I didn't hate him either. The entire way home, I pondered how I felt about him and realized he and his sarcasm was starting to grow on me, and I hated myself for every second of the way home.

After forcing Reid and his unfairly beautiful face out of my mind, I transformed myself into the goddess that lurked inside of me, shedding all modest layers of my usual self. I'd rummaged through my clothes and found a dress of Vita's that I brought with me, a skimpy black number that would surely draw some eyes.

I collectively decided with the angel and the devil on my shoulder that I would have a good time tonight, even if I was next to someone who could make me both out of breath and hyperventilate from exasperation. It was time for me to set my mind on something that would actually make me feel better. A night out on the town with myself. I could torture myself with thoughts of Reid later. Perhaps tomorrow while nursing my hangover.

Throwing on the dress in front of my vanity mirror, I was pleased to see that it fit me well, hugging all my curves and leaving little to the imagination. The long sleeves were adorned with intricate floral lace designs. My entire back was made of lace. The decolletage neckline left my shoulders, neck, and the better part of my cleavage exposed. The dress reached well above my knees, but the thigh slits came dangerously high. I would have to remember to pull my dress down every so often unless I wanted to give everyone at the club the full view of my panties. I will look good tonight, Reid be damned.

Hopping into the shower, I quickly washed my hair. Towel at the ready, I hastily dried my hair and started gathering my hair styling products.

Two hours later, my hair had been curled to perfection, and I was putting the finishing touches on my cosmetics. Opting for a dark smokey eye and defined cheekbones, I added some mauve lip stain to give me a sultry, seductive look. Puckering my lips at the mirror, I blew a kiss to myself, pretending I was Vita when she blew her last kiss to me before disappearing. A small gesture to remind me that I was in control, no matter how much Reid tried to remind me otherwise. It was his probation period, too.

I lightly ran my fingers through my hair, making sure the ringlets would loosen and look effortlessly perfect. Spritzing myself with my favorite fragrance, I reached for Vita's stilettos in the back of my closet, after slipping some pads on the back of the shoe to get a better grip. Vita had always been slightly taller than me, though we usually shared the same size. Her shoes were only slightly larger, but I still found myself shopping in her closet whenever I wanted to spruce up my style and venture out of my fall-themed closet. If anyone knew how to dress like a succubus, it was certainly Vita. Behind her spring-colored closet, she had quite a few leather pieces that would drop more than a few jaws.

Her rose-colored stilettos would surely shoot my height straight into the sky, but I wanted to feel tall and confident. My regular stature was average at best, though Vita used to joke that I needed to be watered to grow more, and I rarely wore heels. I hoped these shoes wouldn't tear my feet up for the lack of platforms, but I wasn't too worried. I hoped to ingest enough alcohol to no longer feel a single damn thing. Slipping my feet into them, I pretended I was Cinderella and this was my fairytale. Except in my version, I chose myself for my happily ever after.

Standing in front of the mirror fully, I examined myself. My body looked voluptuous in the way the dress clung, with my long hair almost reaching my waist in perfect loose waves. The dark smokey eye made my eyes look like an ocean at night, dark blue and intimidating. I was so tall in my shoes and I felt like a queen, about to grace the nightclub rooftop bar with her presence. They weren't ready for me. Reid wasn't ready for me. After all, I was a different person.

I was beyond ready to go unwind and have a fun night.

Just in time too, as it was time for me to head out. Donning my winter jacket and grabbing my small leather purse, I locked the door behind me.

The chilly air whipped at my naked legs, making me regret dressing so skimpily in this weather. The bar wasn't too far, perhaps a few minutes walking. I walked with as much confidence as I could muster, considering the fact that my toes had gone numb already.

Reid was already standing by the entrance, not a single hair out of place. He wore a long dark coat over a V-neck collared shirt. I tried not to stare too long at his pants, which were tight enough to cast a shadow in his nether regions.

His eyes fell on me and roamed all over.

"Aren't you a pretty little thing tonight."

TEN

O nly Reid could make a compliment sound underhanded, but I wouldn't have any of that. Even in my tall heels that could tip me over in a second, he still towered over me. But my boost still made its presence and I stood tall.

"Let's get inside, it's freezing out here." I swung my hips over to get ahead of him when he stopped me. Struggling to keep my balance, I almost keeled over but he steadied me rather roughly.

"Can't walk in Momma's shoes?" He crooned. I swatted his hand off me and clicked my teeth.

"Why did you stop me?"

"Considering the fact that you look like you wait street corners for a living, I'll have to keep my eye on you. Wouldn't want anyone to molest you and ruin our mission." He pulled me in closer by my waist and his musky scent took my breath away as I inhaled him in.

"I did say it would be a date earlier, but don't get any ideas. We will only act like a couple for the duration of this evening, and that's only so that I don't have to waste my time saving you from perverts at the bar." His grip on my waist tightened.

"Wouldn't want you to do me any favors," I breathed, intoxicated by him.

"Don't flatter yourself. It's just one less inconvenience to me."

"I knew you had a heart, after all," I said dryly.

I was standing way too close for comfort and was becoming increasingly hyper-aware of the heat emanating from his chest to mine.

"I'm glad you know elementary anatomy, now let's go." It was really difficult for me not to punch him. Though it wouldn't hurt him, I had to put him in his place.

"Don't forget, you're on probation too." Shaking myself off of him, I pulled out my ID. His hand never left my waist. Optics or not, it felt nice, even though the hand belonged to the biggest jackass I'd ever met.

Upon handing our IDs over for inspection, the bouncer jerked his thumb to the front door to signal his approval, as the two security guards beside him opened it and gestured for us to step inside. We headed toward the glass elevator that flew into the heart of the scraper that scratched New York clouds.

The moment we exited the elevator and stepped into the rooftop bar with the looming dancefloor, the pounding music hit my ears immediately, something techno with loud bass. It was so crowded that bodies were pressed up against each other on the dancefloor, moving together to the music. Clinking drinks and roaring voices were muted by the loud music. Bopping my head to the beat, I searched the bar for two open seats.

A young bartender with cropped hair came to us, wiping some glasses down and giving us water.

"Welcome to Glitz," he acknowledged us, "What's your poison?"

"Old Fashioned on the rocks," Reid shouted over the music. Nodding, the bartender turned to me.

"Margarita. Make it strong." Vita had always said that when in doubt, margaritas would always please the senoritas.

As the bartender disappeared, the song changed to a nostalgic pop song from a few years ago, heavily remixed by the DJ. Bopping my head to the beat, I watched him work his magic with his hands, skillfully preparing the drinks. Meeting my eyes, he smiled and rolled both drinks down the bar. Catching both, I nodded in thanks and took a sip.

My drink was definitely strong. The first sip went straight to my head. The music was roaring in my ears and all I wanted to do was mute my thoughts and dance. I downed my drink quickly as Reid left a twenty on the table. The song was getting louder, and I knew I was already gone.

Reid nudged my arm and I turned toward him.

"Aren't you going to force your boring old boyfriend to dance as any other girl would?"

I giggled. "Didn't you just give me the perfect opportunity to say I'm not like other girls?"

"Oh, I know your type. You act like you're not like other girls, but that makes you just like other girls."

"You don't know anything about me." Sober-me would be extremely embarrassed by the emphatic pout I gave.

He smirked. "Then give me something to know, Lena."

Throwing all discretion out the window, I giggled again and said, "Yes, I do masturbate."

Reid's eyes flashed and he grinned at me like I was the only person in the whole room. He extended his hand as a gesture to dance. Blushing deeply underneath my face full of makeup, I took his hand and allowed him to escort me to the ballroom of drunk college kids so we could share a waltz of grinding.

Reid was no dancer, but he understood the beat. He never let me go within more than a foot away from him, except to twirl me. We stepped to the catchy song without caring if we were good or not. I may have even spotted a genuine smile from Reid, but I couldn't be sure.

He surprised me with a strikingly low dip at the end of the song, and I allowed him to take control of my entire body as he swerved me over his leg and graced my cheek with the slight of his finger, and kept me there long enough to turn heads. Whistles and claps were cast upon us as everyone else gave us space and chanted for the lovely couple to kiss.

"Don't get ahead of yourself," I whispered to him.

He lifted me effortlessly back to my feet and swayed intimately, his entire body pressed against mine. He guided my head to his chest and I laid there without a care in the world. The crowd gave a collective *aww* and went back to their own drunken dancing.

When the song ended, he pulled away from me rather gracelessly, and for a moment, I missed the feeling of us swaying together. I must have really been going crazy. Supernatural hallucinations be damned, the most dangerous thing to do in this game would be to develop feelings for Reid. I was finally starting to understand what it meant to have a broken heart, even though we weren't together. None of this was real. He didn't care about me. He deeply loved someone else. I didn't matter. I was no one.

"I'll be in the ladies room to powder my nose." He batted his eyelashes at me and ducked out through the crowd. Thankful for a moment without his cunning smile clouding my judgment, I resumed my solo performance, my mind going blank with the music. I was supposed to do something important, something about an investigation, but it could wait until I could just finish dancing to this one song…

Allowing my body to become one with the music, my movements were fluid and rhythmic as I swayed my hips to the beat of the current salsa song that was playing, even if I didn't look good. I took a large sip of my drink and downed it, knowing I was playing with fire. As I got more intoxicated, the music started to blur. My dancing must've looked blurry too, but I didn't care. I was lost among all the bodies moving and jumping and spinning and swaying…

Time lost all meaning. The music was so loud I couldn't hear the thoughts in my head. I just wanted to dance the night away. My feet were crying in pain despite the alcohol, but I ignored them.

I tried to look for Reid but couldn't find him, though it was proving more difficult than usual since I was already seeing double. I was fine with dancing solo anyway.

I felt a hand on my laced back and stumbled over, thinking someone was trying to pass through. The hand remained, and I felt a chill from a fingernail that trailed.

Turning around, I saw who the hand belonged to. A tall, slender woman who was gliding to the music. The strobe lights in the club made it hard to decipher her facial features, but I noticed her pin-straight black hair and smooth skin. She was sensual in ways even Vita couldn't hold a candle to. Everything about her was inviting.

"Will your boyfriend mind?" She asked me in a deep, alluring voice.

I threw my head back and laughed harder than necessary. "He's not my boyfriend."

"Dance with me?"

To hell with it. I was so free tonight. Thoughts completely escaped me. Gladly, I started dancing with her. We looked hot.

She pressed herself close to me and I felt myself blushing, though the heat could've been from the alcohol mixed with my sweat. I could feel her long black fingernails tracing my skin, her cold fingers providing relief from the heat of the music. I was gliding with her, swimming through the other drunk fish in the sea of Glitz. She spun me to the beat of the song and I moved my hips sharply, feeling like I was on top of the world. The lights were so dark and my vision was so blurry I couldn't see her face anymore.

The music morphed into a blend of loud sounds that I couldn't discern anymore. A few more spins and I lost the woman in the crowd, but I didn't mind. It was nice to get down with a stranger without any commitments. I didn't know whose drink I was holding, and my subconscious reminded me that it wasn't polite to take someone else's drink. It certainly tasted much stronger than mine.

My hands and feet were tingling. I could no longer feel the pain in my feet. Worried that I danced my feet off, I stumbled in search of the bathroom to make sure they were still there. I was barely able to stand properly as I balanced myself against the wall. The music couldn't be heard from indoors, and I was able to hear my own thoughts again, but I found them to be jumbled and nonsensical.

Was I even in the bathroom? No one was around and I didn't see any toilets.

The room was spinning. My ears were ringing.

I gripped the wall tightly for balance, but my hand was tingling.

Who knew what was in that stranger's drink?

I found a door handle and opened it without any clue if I'd located the bathroom.

Darn. No toilets. I'd entered a fancy deck that was sectioned off for a private party that hadn't begun yet, hence the empty decorated seats.

I really needed to sober up. I'd let myself get too carried away. Carefully walking toward the deck, I allowed the cold night air to enter my nostrils and detox my inebriated self, washing away the drunkenness. The banister was a bit low for my comfort, but I also felt ten feet tall. I no longer trusted my senses.

I tried not to look down but curiosity got the best of me and I felt dizzy right away as I realized how high I was in the sky. I was above the city skyline, for reference. But the dizziness was certainly knocking reality back into me, and I took some time to level my breathing and sober up before continuing my quest to find Reid.

A hand fell on my shoulder and I jumped a mile, miraculously not flying overboard. Looking toward the hand, I recognized the slender fingers and long black fingernails. It was the woman I'd danced with. The slender goddess that intoxicated me with her sensual seduction.

She'd strayed far from the main dancefloor, as I had. Perhaps she needed the restroom as well.

"Hey! Were you looking for the bath—" My voice caught in my throat as I faced her.

She wasn't human. Whether I saw her true form under the harsh lights or not, I certainly saw them now.

Her skin was blue. Not like the hypothermic type of blue. More like someone dyed this woman's skin in a deep azure paint. Her pin-straight black hair reached well below her waist.

She cocked her head and stared deep into my eyes with her own. Only then did I notice her entire sclera was black.

But I couldn't be afraid of her. Why be afraid of a hallucination? There was no way this woman suddenly had blue skin, unless I'd accidentally sipped drugs from that stranger's drink. Might as well play it cool and see if she could entertain my notions.

She could have answers that I needed, since the investigation found me instead. I tried to keep my cool and match this creature's level-headedness.

"What's your name?" I asked calmly, forcing any ounce of fear to leave my body and dissipate into the cold air.

"Raine." Her voice felt like silk brushing against my skin and I shivered, but not from the cold. "And you're Alluna."

Nodding, I grasped her hand from my shoulder and held on tight. "Please, Raine. Do you know what happened to my sister?"

She dipped her head ever so slightly, her black eyes consuming me. My heart lurched with longing, a desperation for my sister roiling inside me like a plague.

"You're not asking the right questions." The monotone in her voice was alarmingly frightening, but I was far more interested to see what I could find out. Struggling to maintain my composure, I took a strained breath.

"What should I be asking, then?" I forced a monotonous tone to my voice as well, though my voice cracked on the last word.

Silence.

"Please help me, Raine. I need to find my sister." No matter how crazy I was talking to something that wasn't there, I couldn't leave a single stone unturned.

"Stop talking to it," Reid's voice interjected suddenly as he appeared by the door a few yards away, arms crossed, eyes darker than a black night.

If I had any water in my mouth, I would've done a spit take. Could it be that I wasn't crazy and speaking to a hallucination?

"You can see her, too?" My voice cracked with exasperation, a cocktail of relief that I may not have been crazy but certain trepidation that we both were seeing things. The barista wasn't any coincidence. This was real.

Raine unhanded my eyes from her own and slithered around as if she were moving underwater, lowering her head at Reid, not quite making eye contact. I held onto the banister for dear life as fear crept in and chilled my bones with the weight of the height looming beside me. Reid's face held no recognition for her while he completely ignored me and moved forward.

"She has nothing to do with this." If I didn't know any better, I'd think Reid was concerned for me. I could barely pinpoint the worry he tried so hard to hide in his voice, but the slight pinch of his eyebrows gave him away. In that moment, I considered how many seconds I had left before the blue woman hurt me…or worse.

Reid inched closer. "Let her go," he spoke plainly without a hint of fear in his voice. Time seemed to stand still at that moment. Raine released my hand and gave a small bow to Reid in a fluid motion.

"I can't do that." She slithered over me like a bodyguard, her movements almost in slow motion, as if she was swimming through the air.

"You think I care what happens to the girl? She's nothing. An insignificant little human." Each of Reid's words pierced through me like sharp blades. Not knowing what the truth was anymore, all I could do was watch their exchange unfold as I remained trapped against the banister, the chilly wind brushing against my back. But a small part of me couldn't help but wonder if I'd imagined Reid's worried voice earlier.

At this point, I had no idea who was more dangerous out of the two of them anymore. At least Raine had a soothing effect to her ambiance, even if she also wanted me dead.

Reid moved at a glacial pace while Raine floated around me, never quite standing still. Her blue skin almost glimmered from the reflection of the lights, like a sparkling sea touched by the moon's fingertips.

"Tell me what you want." He was only a few feet away, his hypnotizing voice deceptively calm.

Her voice was loud, yet still, a whisper echoed behind her

words. "I've come to deliver a message."

Reid was within hand reach, but he wasn't fast enough. Raine's cold hands iced my chest. I had half a second to meet Reid's eyes and see genuine fear there, a microexpression that I mentally saved forever. Less than a second later, I was flying. Or falling, rather. My grip on the banister had the sturdiness of a feather when she unleashed her inhuman strength and thrust me over the edge. Having no time to process, I had no chance to grab onto anything and suddenly, I was falling faster than ever.

The ground was a mere second away from being painted by my blood and guts before something caught me and whisked me back into the sky.

Knocked by the force of gravity being turned upside down, my head lolled backward like a bobblehead and I felt my cheeks flap like fish in the wind.

Is this what death felt like? Was I traveling up to heaven? Did God spare me the pain from shattering into a million pieces on the gravel?

Air was returning to me and the black of the wind was lightening. I could feel a hand tightly grasping my back, and another under my thighs. Was there an angel carrying me? Fighting the heavy air, I forced my head to snap upright and face whatever was next, in life or in death.

But there was no angel carrying me to heaven. There was only Reid, staring forward, an unmistakable glare on his face as we soared through the sky with nothing but the wind on his back and my body in his arms. I felt weightless, other than his fingers digging into my skin. I didn't even feel the winter's chill. Reid's fingers could've started a fire on my skin.

We were actually flying. The city skyline was at his fingertips.

It was beautiful. He was beautiful. His red hair whipped through the winds and exposed the smooth planes of his handsome face.

I must have been dreaming. Maybe I had died and this was all in my imagination.

That is, until reality sunk in, I wasn't waking up, and I was still thousands of feet in the air without a harness or parachute, in the arms of someone who already threatened to kill me once before, just a slip away from falling to my death.

Oh, and Reid could fucking fly.

Panic swept through my body as I let out a bloodcurdling scream.

ELEVEN

My scream was cut short as Reid buried my head in his chest. Now that I could no longer see the vast city underneath, it was oddly comforting that he blinded me. But that small sense of comfort was nowhere near enough to take away the rising panic, a fire within that was burning straight through any logical reason.

Mere moments later, I felt Reid touch the ground and scrambled out of his grasp without fully knowing where I was. Clumsily falling on my back, I made sure to put as much distance between us as I could, while assessing my surroundings and vantage point.

We were on top of a roof. A skyscraper, in fact. Somewhere Midtown. The Empire State Building wasn't far. The roof was also off-limits to pedestrians, as there was no way to go inside, other than a door with a large padlock hanging off of it. I was stuck here with Reid, and it was time to face the music. I reminded myself that he had ample opportunity to let me slip through his fingers, but he kept me alive for whatever reason.

Reid made no effort to come any closer. He was breathing heavily, clearly angered.

"Are you stupid or just unable to keep yourself safe?" He hissed, his voice venomous.

"Uh..." I rubbed my eyes, trying to manifest another hallucination as I stared at Reid, waiting for his wings to sprout like the barista at Kaffeine, or for his eyes to turn black and glossy like Raine, or for his skin to turn blue. Maybe even for him to grow a tail.

But Reid wasn't changing. He was the same unfairly handsome, condescending creature as before. With that, reality sunk in.

"You can fly?" I asked stupidly, clapping my eyes like an imbecile.

"That's your first question?" Reid quickly glanced around to make sure we were the only ones and slipped into the shadow cast by the overlying ledge, pulling me behind him. I supposed this way, no one would see me if I died, and my body would stay there to rot. But those thoughts couldn't stray past the back of my mind, as I grew increasingly overwhelmed with my new realization.

"Sarcastic fuck." I put my hands on my head. "Was that really a blue woman? Did you give me drugs or something?"

He loomed over me, evidently trying to establish a form of dominance or instill any fear in me, though by now it was clear that I was worth more to him alive than dead.

"What did the Syren tell you?"

"You know what she was?" I was getting angry. All this time, Reid was playing me for a fool. He allowed me to believe I was half-crazy and hallucinating with him when he could fly all along.

"What did it tell you?" He demanded again, ignoring my question. I could play this game too.

"How are you able to fly?" Struggling to remain calm, I bit my lip and tried not to think about how high this roof was.

"You haven't earned that information. If anything, you failed your probation." Reid's voice was rising. "I left you alone for half an hour and you went and became a magnet for trouble." His hands were squeezing my shoulders. "You had to go and provoke the Syren. You couldn't have just stayed on the dancefloor?" His fingers dug into my shoulders underneath his grasp. I didn't have the chance to answer once he started shaking my shoulders.

"Where did the Syren come from?" Useless as it was, I threw another question at him, knowing he wouldn't answer but desperate to try anyway. It was so cold on the roof that the wind drew tears from my face, and I had no idea if that was the only reason.

He was yelling now. "You can't even be trusted to keep yourself alive. And now I put myself in danger for showing you who I am."

"Well, maybe if you told me the truth from the beginning, I would've known not to leave the dancefloor!" Pushing his hands off my shoulders, I punched his chest with my fists, not holding back. Who did he think he was?

Reid stood far too close for comfort, curling back his lip. "My mistake for thinking you could handle yourself without my protection."

"You-you pompous asshole…what did you expect to happen? You gave me nothing to work with!" I still don't know if this is a result of drugs or a psychotic break, but I knew I was angry enough to punch Reid again. His earthy scent was confusing me. "You think you have the right to be mad at me? Do you even hear yourself?"

Reid was suddenly calm, and had the audacity to laugh at me. "You have no idea what you're getting yourself into."

I wanted to throw him off the roof. "I don't need you to find my sister. I can do it myself."

He cackled a little too loudly. "You're just a little girl who thought she was something just because she moved to New York fucking City."

To say he struck a nerve was an understatement. He knew nothing about me or what my truth was.

"Shut up shut up shut up!" My fists were like bullets, one after the other, aimed right at his stone chest. I hated myself for the tears I felt welling up in my eyes. He thought me weak, and maybe he was right. But he had no right to unravel my psyche like a ribbon.

"That's right. Go crying home to Mommy. Your sister is better off without you anyway."

I screamed and pushed him hard enough that he fell backward. Falling atop his chest, I pummeled him with as much strength I could muster, my cries filling the night air with their screeches. He laid there without any defense and took my beating, until I got tired and fell next to him, hugging my knees tightly and sobbing.

My bond with Vita wasn't unrequited, and I knew she loved me to death just as much as I her. And for him to have the gall to say that to me showed he didn't have a heart after all, just a rotting hole where his heart should've been. I wanted nothing to do with him anymore. I could find my sister myself. Her bucket list was all I needed at this rate, considering all my supernatural occurrences at every location I visited. Reid could go screw himself.

My low voice was hoarse, though I maintained a stern tone. "Forget our arrangement. Take me home. We can pretend like this never happened." I narrowed my eyes at him.

Reid stood up and shook the dust off his jacket like nothing had happened.

He sighed and chuckled darkly. "Can't do that. You know too much. I have to kill you now."

I felt a chill down my spine. "Are you serious?"

"Of course not, you gullible fool." Even under the dimly lit shadows, his eye roll was hard to miss. "Only goes to show why you wouldn't last a day in a real mission. You'd get scared of your own shadow."

"You've made your point. Now take me home."

Reid gave a devilish smile that was nothing short of mischievous and scooped me into his arms effortlessly. I tried not to strangle him with the arms I wrapped around his head, reminding myself that my dignity was all I had left.

"You won't find your sister without me, and vice versa. You have no choice but to work with me."

I tightened my arms around his neck. "You'll have to tell me what you know, then."

"Don't remind me."

My heart leaped as he whooshed into the air and flew me to the ground before I could blink. He managed to remain unseen by sliding down a dark shadow cast over a building by another. Setting me quickly on the ground, he disappeared into the night without a goodbye, just a quick, "Meet me at Sage's office tomorrow," then vanishing into the night before my eyes could process.

The moment I rounded the corner of the building, I was caught up in the millions of New Yorker's out on the town, none of which noticing a flying man.

Only then did I realize Reid had dropped me off on the opposite end of the city just to inconvenience me. I cursed his name along the two train transfers, one bus ride, eight blocks, and two avenues later to my apartment. My only condolence was that I knew I was getting closer than ever to Vita's disappearance, with or without Reid's help. I also knew that Reid was not to be trusted. I also knew he smelled really good and deserved to be cast into a barbecue. The moment my head hit the pillow, I was out like a light.

An abundant breeze rustled my clothes as I ran as fast as my feet could take me. The barren branches of the never-ending trees in my path whipped my limbs. A lump of fear surged in my throat. I didn't have much time. I was being followed. A steady stream of blood gushed down my arm, leaving a dripping trail as I raced through the forest. Another branch snapped into my cheek, undoubtedly leaving a mark. Ignoring the sting, I moved forward with trepidation.

The voice called my name again.

"Stop hiding from us," the familiar voice breathed into my ear, sounding so foreboding. No matter how fast I ran through the forest, whispers of the voice followed me. Not having a spare second to search for the source of the voice, I propelled myself forward, a bead of cold sweat on my forehead. My heart pounded louder than my thoughts, which were just yelling at me to run, run, run.

Flicking my eyes around, I searched for an escape route, but all I could see was the path ahead, hidden by trees. I knew I had to get there. My feet felt like they were welded to the floor as adrenaline shot through me. The voice tickled the back of my neck and I trembled in fear.

Tossing the last branch out of my way, I fell forward into the floor in a circular white room, with four seats and a throne in the center. Breathing heavily, I stared ahead, shaking uncontrollably. Again, I felt the tickle in the nape of my neck as the familiar voice whispered, "Naerin will find you, just like it found her."

An obsidian black feather laid there, covered in blood.

Blood that was dripping off Vita's lifeless body crumpled beside the feather.

A piercing scream resounded through the room.

My throat was burning from my screams as I jerked awake, covered in sweat, trembling heavily, crying hysterically. Spilled tears overflowed my face like a river escaping a dam. Wracked with heaving sobs, I gulped some air. Air felt thicker than water. I couldn't swallow. I was going to drown.

Sobbing uncontrollably, I tried to calm the tsunami in my brain that was drowning me, drowning each breath.

Desperately sucking in breaths between sobs, I flew further and further from reality. My nightmare continued chilling my bones even still, as I clutched my bedsheets with white knuckles.

Failing to make sense of anything, I continued my sobs until I ran out of tears. My heavy eyelids fell shut and I didn't fight my body's urge to knock itself unconscious. I was done being awake.

The next morning, before class, I felt like I was hit by a truck in my sleep. My eyelids were wearing me down, and the imaginary weights on my limbs made it difficult to move around. Rubbing my eyes, I tried to recollect the night terror that still shook me through the bone. The image of my poor sister lying lifeless in that room was enough to send me spiraling.

The dream couldn't have been my brain playing a cruel trick on me. That name, that word…I couldn't remember it, but it seemed important. Could it have been the name of the psychopath responsible for all the disappearances?

Vita was not dead. I didn't care how many people told me to give up. Even if I had a million more dreams about her lifeless body, I knew it wasn't true. There was a message hidden in that dream somewhere.

Raine wanted to send me a message too. She'd claimed that she came to deliver a message. Did that mean she was looking for me? Would she have claimed and slain me if she found me first? Even more importantly, who sent her? Was I doomed to become the next victim no matter where I went?

Racking my brain to remember the word from my dream, all I could recall was the first letter, N.

Perhaps Reid would know?

No—I had to get my mind off Reid. For a split second, I really thought we could help each other. Underneath his asshole mask, I knew there was a deeper side to him and I wanted to know it, wanted to know him. Even if he hated me. Texting Daisy, I asked her to meet for a coffee. She answered immediately that she thought I'd never ask.

After washing myself up, I found myself walking into Kaffeine. My body had taken me there before my mind could catch up. I hardly remembered getting dressed and leaving the house. I could have just as easily jumped off the Brooklyn Bridge and not realized.

"Welcome to Kaffeine, what can I get started for you today?"

"I'm actually looking for a barista that I spoke to a few days ago." I hoped the Faerie would give me something, anything.

"Oh, sure. What was his name?" The female barista adjusted her beanie.

I knew exactly how I would sound but still said, "I don't know."

She hesitated. I could see by her features she thought there was something wrong with me. And she couldn't have been more right. "Well, what did he look like?"

He had translucent wings and pointy ears, not that I would say that. Some things are better left unsaid unless I wanted to be checked into a psychiatric facility.

"He had dark hair." I tried to remember what he looked like but found it difficult, for some reason. It was only the wings and ears that I could easily picture. "His ears stuck out."

The female barista grimaced. "That's not a very nice way to describe someone."

Internally pinching myself for a lack of better description, I winced.

"Anything else you remember about him?"

"Yes. His eye color was…" I couldn't remember for the life of me and truly felt like I was losing my mind. "He had a deep voice."

Wow. You go, Alluna. Describe a dark-haired man with a deep voice in New York City and you'll really find who you're looking for.

Though I was far past saving, I shot my last shot. "He was making the drinks last Wednesday."

The barista shook her head. "Nah, our only male barista doesn't come in on Wednesdays. And he's bald. I think you might have mixed up this coffee shop with another one."

I stared at her while continuing to question my sanity.

She was getting annoyed. "So can I get you anything or not?"

"Yes, a small pumpkin spiced latte."

"Make that two!" Daisy ran up just as I finished speaking. I was thankful that she didn't hear the previous part of the conversation. As the barista rang us up and gave me one last weird look, I left some cash on the register without counting it and headed to the same counter where I distinctly remembered throwing my latte at Reid, unless that wasn't real either. The Faerie had asked if something was wrong, and Reid saw him too. I know he did. I think. Actually, what did I really know, besides the fact that Reid could fly?

"Hey, are you okay?" Daisy's hand on my shoulder didn't feel real. My out-of-body experience was becoming a little too candid, and I tried to force myself out of the clouds.

A strained smile took over my face. "Yeah…I just slept badly last night."

"Your coffee addiction is finally catching up with you." I could hear her concern behind her light-hearted joke, but I was glad she didn't press. Vita would've wanted to know everything, despite any boundaries. It was a nice change to see that Daisy could take a hint.

Vita, whose lifeless body dripped blood onto the black feather—

I wanted to throw myself off a cliff at that image.

But instead, I gave a small laugh, not meeting her eyes. "What better way to battle my addiction than to have more coffee?"

Daisy had loads to gossip about, and I allowed her to sway my unhinged mind and take me away from my troubles, but there was something I couldn't deny. Reid and I may have been seconds from ripping each other's throats out, but I had to know if he knew anything about my nightmare, especially that name that escaped my mind. Maybe he could still help me yet.

TWELVE

*T*hough I didn't want to admit it, I felt slightly better that Thursday, two days later, knowing I'd see Reid. The mission on my mind was far more important than our petty spat. As far as I knew, he wanted to find out what happened to the one he lost. Ultimately, we still had the same goal, and I had to utilize that commonality to its full potential. I had to find out what he knew and see if it would lead me any closer to Vita. Reid was not to be trusted, but he clearly knew more than I did. I had to do some digging and find out more about him. Including the fact that he wasn't even human!

With this knowledge, I decided to corner Dr. Sage Gusto by her office that day.

The moment I barged into her office holding an extra-large caramel macchiato with two Splenda's and extra cream, her first reaction was to say, "Oh, boy. What is it?"

Locking the door behind me, I invited myself to sit on a nearby chair and set the monstrously large coffee on her table.

"Is Reid here?"

Sage examined her drink. "Is there alcohol in this?"

I shook my head. "No."

She placed the straw between her lips. "Should there be alcohol in this?"

I nodded feverishly. "Yes, probably."

She took a few gulps and set it down, rubbing her temples. "Reid went to run some errands for me. This is about him, isn't it?"

My silence was confirmation enough.

"Go on, then. Grill me for the information you believe I possess."

I started with a vague question with purpose lined up against it. "Do you know where he's from?"

Sage gave me a questioning look. "Not really, but what does that matter?"

I gritted my teeth. "I just really need to know."

She sighed and took more gulps than I could count. "You're being awfully pushy for someone who should be on my good side. My spring semester is already booked, you know."

I exhaled slowly. "Please, Sage. I have my reasons for asking."

"His country is far away." She said as she sipped, giving me a weirdly understanding look.

Pausing, I let her words sink in. If I didn't know any better, I'd almost think she knew something. She certainly wasn't trying to hide it.

"Try me. I'm good with geography." I relaxed my elbows.

Sage downed the rest of her drink. "You wouldn't have heard of it. Besides, that's his business."

Narrowing my eyes, I took a jump, for lack of any rational reasoning. "Is there something you're not telling me, Sage?"

A small smile slighted her lips, as if she knew something I didn't. "Don't expect any answers from him. He is forbidden to speak on certain things. It's the law."

"Whose law?"

"The law where he comes from."

"Where does he come from?"

"The place that made the law."

I was ready to rip my hair out. "Is he human?" I exclaimed.

She shook her head, unsurprised by my question, confirming my suspicion.

"What is he?"

She shook her head again. No answer.

"If he is forbidden to speak on certain things, then how do you know what he is?"

"I was sworn to secrecy."

I had to ask, "Are you human?"

Her lips curled. Not quite a nonanswer. Somewhere in between.

Perhaps she was forbidden to speak of it too. She wanted to leave me guessing. My psychology professor might not have been a human either, who would've thought?

"Do you know what happened to my sister?"

Silence.

I huffed in exasperation. "Is there anything you can tell me? At all?"

Sage pondered and brushed a lock of her salt-and-peppered hair behind her ear. "Yes. You have only scratched the surface, and if you go on, you will die. Now would be a good time to cut your losses while you still can. Just go back home to Pennsylvania."

The thought of returning to my mother's smug face after less than a month of living in New York City was far more terrifying than the monsters I was beginning to face. And if that weren't enough, I would stop at nothing to see Vita again.

At that point, I knew I'd exercised Sage to the full extent, and she was a closed book under lock and key. The only confirmation I received was that Reid was not human.

"I'm not going anywhere. And if you can't help me, I'll find someone else who will."

Sage pursed her lips but didn't respond. Whether she thought me brave or unwise, I didn't care. I was willing to do whatever it took.

My eyes were glued to my phone when I left her office and headed down the hallway. I was desperate to find more clues. Willing for a sign to manifest itself, I pulled up Vita's bucket list once more.

At this pace, I'd only visited places after people disappeared there. Could I dare to lurk by the next place and see what happened to the victim?

I could've been the next victim that way. At least that way I'd know where Vita was taken.

Or perhaps I'd find more answers upon returning to Glitz in search of Raine, not that there was any guarantee she would be there. What message was she trying to deliver? Was it to me or Reid? I certainly got the point - never stand close to an edge where someone could toss me off. Was I to run in circles for the rest of my life?

"Hey, Alluna!"

Surprised to hear my name called, I tore my eyes from my phone and searched the busy hallways for a familiar face. When the person revealed himself, my heart sank.

"Hello, Leo." Great. The last person I wanted to see, next to Reid.

Hesitating, I glanced behind back at Sage's office, contemplating an escape back to her room. Feigning some interest to avoid his back-and-forth games, I sprinkled some life into my attitude.

I fixed my bag on my shoulder. "What are you doing here?"

He cornered me between a staircase and hallway. "Looking for you, silly."

A forced smile came across my face. Though I held Vita's

experiences in high regard, I never found out how she managed to shake off that persistent ex of hers. Either she didn't tell me or I didn't remember or I was too weak to understand the mechanism of her brain. If there was anything Vita taught me about men, it was that they loved the game, the chase, the thrill, the cat-and-mouse shebang. Keeping that in mind, I took an assertive stance.

"Well, here I am," I deadpanned.

"Did Daisy tell you to play hard-to-get? She wouldn't even give me your number."

Thank you, Daisy.

"Then how did you find me?"

"I take an elective on this campus and noticed you. You seem pretty on edge."

"I've just been really busy lately."

Leo shrugged. "Hey, I get it. Pre-med, remember? But I'll always make time for you. Remember that date you promised me?"

Giving him a sheepish grin, I snuck another glance at Sage's office, trying to think of a quick excuse to go back.

Sage's door opened and Reid came out. His eyes darted between Leo and I a few times, before he settled on my face, his expression unreadable. He was as still as a statue, his hawk eyes watching my interaction with Leo.

Wanting to get a rise out of him against my better judgment, I leaned in closer to Leo. If Reid wanted to act like I didn't exist, that was fine by me. But he was still a man, at the end of the day. Vita always said men wanted what they couldn't have.

I giggled, knowing Leo wouldn't even notice my change in tone. "Where did you have in mind?"

I could feel Reid's eyes burning through my back, and my smile deepened. Leo started talking and saying things that I wasn't listening to. I nodded and pretended to agree while turning back again.

Reid was giving me a look that said, *is that the best you got?* But as much as he tried to hide it, his lips were pinched ever so slightly. If I'd never met him before, I wouldn't have noticed. It was the most satisfying thing I've felt in a long time.

Reid broke our eye contact as he walked out of Sage's office, slamming the door loud enough to be heard down the hall and storming away. Even Leo glanced in that direction.

"It's a date, then?" He said.

"Mhm," I responded mindlessly, still thinking about Reid's reaction, but then I realized what I'd agreed to. "Wait, what?"

"Tomorrow, after class, I'll get you and surprise you."

"Oh, well, actually—" Any excuse I was about to give was pointless as Leo started talking about his elective and I gave up quickly. Smiling noncommittally, I tuned him out and realized the reality that was beginning to sink in.

Why was I toying with Reid? He'd almost killed me and could throw me off any building whenever he wished. He was an arrogant jerk who refused to help me out of spite. Most importantly, his heart belonged to someone else. What in the world was I doing?

Feelings were a liability. Even Leo would be a better match than Reid, not that I had any interest in him. Perhaps it would do me some good to give Leo a chance.

Leo was leaning increasingly close until his overpowering stench of a designer cologne filled my nostrils and traveled straight to my brain. The tendrils of an emerging migraine started to dance as I breathed through my nose, taming my thoughts.

My feelings didn't matter. I hated Reid yet I wanted to know everything about him at the same time. The novelty of his ability to fly was still fresh in my mind, especially the feel of the wind on my face as he soared me across New York City. The exhilarating feel of his fingers tightening on my back as he rose to heights only birds could dare to see. The way the breeze exposed the handsome planes of his face against the moonlight, his eyes practically sparkling. I hadn't forgotten that image of him, and I didn't think I ever would. He looked magnificent.

"I hope I'm not interrupting," Reid interjected as he appeared right by my side, completely cutting off Leo, who looked at him in astonishment.

I was drier than a slice of salami. "Aren't you light on your feet."

"Who are you?" Leo tried to stand closer to me, probably to establish dominance, but Reid didn't give him a chance.

"Reid." He flashed his pearly canines. "Just checking in on my student. We actually had a meeting to talk about her failing grade." He gave me a *tsk, tsk.*

My mouth dropped. Out of everything he could have said…

"I'm sure she can catch up with you later, Mr…?"

"Leo."

Reid nodded in acknowledgment, though I could sense the testosterone challenge between the two of them as they both tried to stand at their tallest. Reid won by a landslide as he looked down his nose at Leo with an air of arrogance. He knew he was about to steal me away and there was nothing Leo could do about it. Though I'd never been caught between two men like that, I couldn't deny the flattering heat that washed over my body.

"Good day, Leo." Reid sounded like he was close to laughter as he whisked me off in the opposite direction before I had the chance to say anything. But that was the least of my concern.

"I'm failing?" I hissed at him as Leo grew further and further into the background.

"Your last submission was so…uncolorful. Rudimentary at best."

"I'll show you colorful," I said as I flipped him off.

"Maybe if you included such personality in your paper, it would've gotten a higher grade."

"Fuck off."

"Was I interrupting plans with your boyfriend?"

"That shouldn't concern you."

"Are you taking him to the next stop on the list?"

I stopped in my tracks. "My life shouldn't concern you outside of our mission. Why do you care?"

He looked ahead. "I couldn't care less. Just wanted to know."

"I'm sure you have better things to do, like pour your feelings in a diary about your long-lost love." A low-hanging branch, and certainly a low blow, but I had no interest in preserving Reid's feelings. I wanted him as far away from me as possible. Or maybe I didn't. Those conflicting feelings were enough to make me tear my hair out.

Reid chuckled. "Is that the best you got?"

Reddening, I turned the corner and walked briskly, though he easily kept up with my pace. Realizing he wasn't leaving, I decided to use the nugget of information that my mind finally returned to memory and hurled it at him with all my might.

Looking him dead in the eye, I said, "Watch your tone, or else I'll make sure Naerin gets you too."

Reid froze, turning white as sleet of snow.

"What did you just say?"

"You heard me. Now stop playing these games and leave me be."

He grabbed my shoulder, stopping me right in my tracks. "Where did you hear that name?"

Smiling at him, I shook off his shoulder, ready to spit every ace up my sleeve just to shut him up. "Looks like this little girl knows more than you think."

Reid was a picture of hostility. I could tell he wanted to backhand me at that moment, and I couldn't have been any prouder of myself.

The halls had emptied, while the students disappeared into their lectures or left the premises. Reid grabbed me by the waist and hoisted me on his hip ever so slightly, whooshing us through the hall at the speed of light into a janitor's closet, my toes barely being off the floor, which he slammed closed the moment he threw me in against the wall.

Pressing himself against me with his hand on my throat, he lifted my chin all the way up so I could look him in the eye. "Don't threaten me ever again, Alluna."

Shocked by his use of my real name, I swallowed a huge lump, feeling the beat of my own carotid quickening against his long fingers. It felt like a hundred degrees in the tiny closet. I could especially feel the heat traveling to the core between my legs and had no idea why.

"Got it?" He squeezed the sides of my neck tighter. A bead of perspiration snuck down my forehead as I nodded, afraid to look away from the emerald fire in his eyes. This word that I said clearly had more power than I thought. I certainly didn't want to play around with this knowledge.

Releasing my neck slowly, Reid backed away from me and straightened his jacket.

"Good. I'll give you a moment to collect yourself."

Slumping over, I exhaled with my entire body and took a few deep breaths, processing what just happened. Reid made no mistake of showing me his strength, and who knew what else he was capable of? What else could he do, besides fly me to dangerous heights, only to throw me off? I didn't want to know.

Reid's eyes pierced right through my soul. "You can't keep these things from me."

Grabbing my throat, I breathed heavily, my voice raw, "That goes both ways. Quid pro quo."

It seemed he needed me now more than ever, and I had no choice, considering how close he could get me to my sister.

We left the janitor's closet completely covered in sweat and breathing heavily, just not for the reasons I would've preferred.

Jabbing myself for the dirty thought, I cleared my throat. "Do you know what happened to my sister?"

"Yes and no."

"Where is she?"

"The place where I'm from."

"Where is it?"

"In between."

"In between where?"

He glanced around, as he usually did, to make sure the coast was clear. "I can't talk about it here. Let's go to your apartment and I'll tell you what I know."

I burst out laughing despite the fact that Reid had just choked me, something I was still trying to comprehend. "Do you think I was born yesterday?"

"Are you doubting my intentions?"

"How stupid do you think I am?"

He glared at me. "Unfortunately, a lot stupider than I'd prefer, if you think I'd ever have any interest in you, especially like that."

Ouch. Well, that hurt.

Wait. Why did that hurt?

Reid just choked me.

And I kind of liked it.

I was ready to throw myself from a roof. What was wrong with me?

I never felt so alive. Especially seconds away from death, like when Reid saved me.

Exactly. Reid saved me. He needed me. No matter how much he wanted to act like he hated me, I was worth enough for him to keep me alive.

But he didn't have to save me from that awkward encounter with Leo. He couldn't hate me that much.

I just had to get the stupid notion that he was a good guy out of my head. Just because Reid was insanely hot didn't mean he could go around choking me and threatening to kill me, even if it sounded luscious coming from his lips.

Did I have selective memory?

That's right. Go crying home to Mommy. Your sister is better off without you anyway.

Those words had felt like they sliced me in half and left my innards in a pile to rot. And I doubted I would get an apology for them, either. All I could do was roll with the punches and hope I would finally get some answers, all while damning Reid and my traitorous lady parts in the process.

THIRTEEN

ou're kidding me, right?" I was surprised Reid's eye roll didn't get stuck in the back of his head.

"No way. Now is the perfect opportunity to visit the next stop on the bucket list, the Loeb Boathouse in Central Park." I shifted my weight and tried to avoid his condescending glare. "We can scope it out, see if anyone else tries to kill me to deliver a message, and then go to my apartment. You can explain yourself along the way."

"You really think this is the sort of conversation that will sound sane on the train?" He looked at me like I was nuts.

"Sane on the train is a myth. After the crazy people I've seen, I'm sure no one would take us seriously nor pay close attention."

Continuing my way through the door, I turned and waited for him to catch up so we could head to the subway station. Sensing his begrudging attitude, I kept going.

He was next to me a moment later, undoubtedly not touching the ground as he caught up with unbelievable speed. "Spoken like a true New Yorker," he muttered.

The joy that swept through my body was unmatched. I hadn't even realized what I said and how it came off, but if I was slowly starting to shed my UnNewYorker, then at least I was doing something right. Not that Reid had to know he'd complimented me, or else he would take it back. So I hid my small smile as we swiped through the turnstile and stepped out onto the tracks.

I wasn't bothered enough to lower my voice. "So, tell me. Who is Naerin and why are you so scared of her?"

Reid tensed like a rock and did his usual sweep of our surroundings. If the saying "the walls have ears" were real, he would be the picture perfect representation. Clearly uncomfortable, he responded with a low, stern voice.

"You want a microphone for your show?"

My mouth twitched as I cleared my throat, not taking his bait. As I waited for his answer, he watched a few people pass us by and walk at least ten feet away before he answered.

"Naerin is neither a woman nor a person." He hesitated. "Naerin is the name of the place I come from."

Nodding, I fixed my bag on my shoulder and lowered my voice a few notches. "So, the in-between place?"

"Yes."

"Are you actually forbidden to speak of it?"

"…yes…" He drew out the word nice and slow, as if it had every other meaning besides the definition. "How did you know that?"

Not wanting to give Sage away, I ignored his question. "Then how can you talk about it?"

"To hell with it. I've already broken enough laws by exposing myself and agreeing to help you." He gritted his teeth and I saw his jaw clench. "Still questioning if you're worth it."

I countered without a second thought. "I'm worth it enough that you didn't let me die on the roof."

He didn't answer. His silence was enough, and I took it as a token of a small victory against his incessant comebacks and insults.

"I have my reasons," was all he said. Another nonanswer.

Lowering my voice to a whisper, I continued my interrogation. "Why are you so scared of Naerin?"

He shushed me, I assumed out of instinct.

He'd lowered into a whisper so faint I had to concentrate against the sounds of the pedestrians, drunk and sober alike, chattering along like woodpeckers who survived on socializing. "You don't understand real cruelty or sadism until you've been there. The citizens survive by eating human souls."

Suddenly, I could feel my heartbeat through my chest and four layers of clothing. The image of Vita's lifeless body from my nightmare popped in my head and I pushed it away.

"Do the citizens of Nae—your place, live in New York?"

Reid laughed as if I asked a stupid question. "No. It is illegal to come and go as you please." His tone grew grim. "I ran away because I couldn't stand to eat human souls, and now they're after me."

"Who's they?" I'd only just realized my hands were shaking, and not from the cold. My body's attempt to shield me from my vivid nightmare only led to a physical representation of my inability to deal with the idea that my beloved sister was actually dead. Quickly hiding my hands in my pockets, I tried to conceal the anxious wave of shaking that swept over my body. My heart was going to jump out of my chest if I didn't collect myself soon.

The train popped into our vision, the squeal of the brakes so loud my thoughts were knocked right out of me, and for that, I was thankful. There were only a few people ahead of us, who boarded the train and sat on the opposite end of the cart. Noting this NewYorker move, I made a mental note to always sit as far away from strangers as I could.

We had a corner to ourselves. Reid sat one seat over, leaving some room between us. Though I was perfectly aware of the fact that he didn't like me, the distance stung. No matter how much I hated to admit it, his presence had an intoxicating effect on me. Even if his insults made my blood boil.

"The Keeper is now after me," he breathed as if he didn't want to say the word loud enough for the walls and seats and floor and ceiling to hear, looking around yet again to make sure no one was around. His eyes darted around the cart and through the window as if the pedestrians that were disappearing every second could hear us.

"The Keeper is the designated hunter, seeker, provider. Whatever you want to call it. The Keeper comes for the Marked soul and steals them, taking the soul all the way back to Naerin, where the Council decides which community will eat them and what others can nibble on the entrails."

Breathing was becoming difficult and my hands shook fiercely in my pockets as if each nerve and tendon was on fire.

"Who marks the souls? How does that work? And what is the Council?"

Silence. Too many questions at once, as it seemed. Or perhaps there was a limit to how much Reid would reveal on a public transportation system in one of the most densely populated metropolitan areas in the United States. Either way, I knew these questions had loaded answers and mentally pocketed them for later in one of the flaps of the folder within the binder of the encyclopedia of confusion and uncertainty going through my brain.

But, I was far from giving up, especially since Reid was talking at all. Hoping for better luck, I tried going down another route. "Are you saying that every single victim is definitely dead?" Vita's lifeless body flashed before my eyes again and I shut them tight, forcing the tears to stop welling up.

"Not exactly. It's complicated."

My eyes shot open. Reid was looking at me with a facial expression I'd never seen before. He was empathetic, an emotion I didn't know he possessed until this moment. His eyes even seemed to have warmed up with compassion. Only then did I remember he lost someone too and knew exactly how I felt. Maybe his hands were shaking in his pockets too. I was strangely comforted and felt like he understood me, even if all it took was an empathetic glance.

Besides, why would he even bother to embark on this journey with me if they were all dead?

"Tell me more."

"About which part?"

"Does the Keeper want to eat your soul, too? And what's complicated?"

The train pulled to a stop on 77th Street on the Upper East Side. We hobbled off together and made our way to the Loeb Boathouse, a mere ten-minute walk, though it felt like an hour. I'd already lost all feeling in my toes once we were outside, and I envied how Reid was completely comfortable in his light jacket. The weather didn't seem to affect him. I briefly wondered how cold it could be when he soared through the skies at night in the winter. And how warm he was when he held me close and pressed me against his chest—

"I'll be tried for fleeing illegally. And since I came to hide in New York, the Keeper has been looking for me here."

Nodding, I finally started to put the pieces together. Vita was the last one to be taken before Reid escaped and moved to New York, which explained why the recent disappearances all happened in the city. But that didn't explain how Vita made a preliminary bucket list with all the locations in which the victims disappeared.

"How do they know you ran away to New York?"

I knew I hit a sore spot when Reid's eyes looked like they would shoot flames at the next person who pushed through. "I trusted the wrong people."

"And the complicated part?"

Reid sighed. "They might not be dead if they were able to join certain communities, depending on the nature of the rotation and their ancestry."

"What are the chances?"

"Slim."

Right before we entered the path out of the concrete and into the jungle known as Central Park, I stopped and pursed my lips. There was something that wasn't adding up.

I eyed Reid suspiciously. "Why are you telling me everything now?" He stopped beside me and sighed. I could only imagine the battle going on in his brain, whether he should be honest with me for once. But to my surprise, he brushed a lock of hair behind my ear and my traitorous heart skipped a beat.

"I have nothing left to lose. I've already lost it," He whispered. I wondered if the thought of his lost love kept him awake at night. Did he have nightmares of her dead body too?

Less than a second later, his face returned to its normal, snarky self. "You don't see me bringing up that latte you threw at me. I can still press charges for that. Either you're in or not." His lip curled. "Stupid questions get stupid answers."

I wasn't even sure if Reid had let down his defenses or if he'd put up even more walls. Shutting my mouth, I nodded, my face reddening. I wasn't in the mood to play any games with Reid. All I wanted was to get more answers.

We walked past the barren trees and frozen benches until we reached the Boathouse, brimmed to the top with people waiting to get inside the restaurant.

"Well?" He was annoyed. "Do you intend to ask every waiter for clues to solve your little case?" His sarcasm was enough to warm my insides, but not in a good way. "Does it look like we have another mystery on our hands?"

After briefly pondering whether he deserved another hot latte singeing his skin, I decided to play his game. Smiling sweetly, I said, "Jeepers. They'd have gotten away with it too, if it weren't for us meddling kids."

For a moment, Reid seemed genuinely surprised I got his reference, though it should have been the other way around.

"It seems to me," I felt gleeful to catch him in such a small thing, "that in your time running away from the Keeper, all you've done to occupy your time was watch a children's cartoon about a mystery-solving dog. That's funny."

Reid cracked a smile as if he liked that I wasn't an easy target the way I normally was. "If you knew how I really occupied my time, you'd be scared to talk to me that way."

The roles must have really reversed since now it was my eyes that rolled in the back of my head. I knew a bluff when I saw one.

"I don't need to ask the waiters anything." I ventured around the restaurant into a small path that led to the lake. There were enough bushes to conceal us from most people sitting on the heated outside dining area, and the closest people to see us directly were all the way across the lake. All I could hope for was that no one else would wander into our corner.

Squatting by the water, I held a keen eye in every single corner of the visible lake. Every piece of moss, every stick floating in the water, even the water bottle in the distance that someone had littered. Though the water remained still, my eyes were wider than a hawks.

Reid squatted beside me. "What are you doing?"

"Any time I've been to one of the spots from the bucket list, I always encountered a magical creature, with or without you. When I don't look for them, they find me on their own. What better place to find a Syren than a lake?"

Turning to him, I saw him sweep over the lake as if the fish were listening to our conversation. Typical Reid. Always watching to see who might be listening. I supposed he picked up that habit when he fled his country and continued to be hunted in an enormously populated city.

"Why do we see them?" I asked, hoping this wouldn't be a question he'd avoid.

"You and I have a special connection to my country since we both lost someone. It has been known that people close to the victims often experience hallucinations and dreams since they may have encountered some of the magic that rubbed off the victims."

I pondered the last few days I spent with Vita. Was it possible that she was already touched, or Marked, and had unseen magic dripping off her? Was it possible that the last time I hugged her, it stained my skin or my vision?

"Does it mean—"

Before I had the chance to ask another question, something wet and cold grabbed my ankle and pulled me into the water with such force my breath was knocked out of me.

I didn't have the chance to take a full breath before something pulled me deep enough that the light from the sky faded into the murky darkness. The icy water felt like millions of needles piercing every inch of my skin, and I felt paralyzed by the cold.

Looking down, I forced my eyes open, only to meet glittering black eyes staring back at me.

Raine.

Her glowering blue hands yanked my ankle further and squeezed it with enough force I was surprised the bone didn't snap.

Her voice was as clear as day, as monotone as her blank face. "I can take you to your sister." She cocked her head, her smooth skin gliding with the water effortlessly. "If you trust him, he will kill you before you ever see her again." She walked on the bottom of the lake floor as graceful as a figure skater.

She knew where Vita was. Her face was so inviting, so comforting…

All I had to do was say yes. Just open my mouth and speak the word, the key, the portal to what my heart desired more than anything in the world. Maybe I was meant to be here all along. It was so easy to just say yes. As easy as it was to glide with her when the music poured into my ears. Her gaze was like a soak in hot water. I didn't need to be warmed. I didn't need to breathe. I just needed to say the word.

Mindless and hypnotized, I opened my mouth to answer her and gulped a large chunk of water. Freezing cold water. As it entered my lungs, I was reminded of my circumstances and broke out of my hypnosis in a state of panic. Kicking my feet, I frantically began a frenzy to release my ankle and make my way to the surface before I drowned or died from hypothermia. Her clench was like a vise under lock and key, and I knew I was seconds from death.

The moment I felt her grip release in the slightest, I whipped my head to look at her and didn't understand what I saw at first. It looked like a dark puddle of black water surrounding Raine's head. It was difficult to make out the scene since everything was dark underwater.

But when Reid swam around Raine's body and the momentum of his plight cleared the water, I finally understood.

Raine was swimming in her own blood. She was dead. A large gash marred her throat as she stared back at me lifelessly, the glimmer gone from her black eyes. Her hand had loosened around my ankle at that point, and before I could process what I was seeing, Reid was hoisting me under his arm and kicking off the ground to bring me to the surface.

Once we'd emerged, he roared for help as he laid me down on the cold ground. I was coughing up a lung at that point and choked at the water stuck in my throat. I barely noticed him slip a blade inside his winter boots, visibly clear of blood since the water washed it away. A few waiters from the restaurant scurried over with warm blankets and an offer for some hot tea on the house. I barely heard Reid explain that I tripped and fell into the water, and how he dove in to save me.

I hardly noticed them move me indoors and douse my hands and feet into hot water. I was shivering so hard that my fumbling hands slapped against my sides. Reid wrapped three warm blankets around me and rubbed my back. I was disoriented beyond belief, and wondered if I was dreaming again.

Eventually, when all sensation returned to my fingertips and the hot tea settled in my stomach, I noticed Reid's firm glare.

"Why?" My whisper was hoarse. "Why did you do that?"

He wasn't affected by the freezing waters at all, and he sat with his arms crossed, without any blankets. Reid cast his signature sweep around the restaurant, noting the servers that were giving us some space and privacy. Their kindness seemed genuine to a fault. If I were in their shoes, I wouldn't want to be held liable or sued by a clumsy consumer.

"She was going to take me to my sister." The tear that rolled down my cheek felt icy and burning hot at the same time.

Reid wrapped me in a consuming hug, allowing his heat to

wash over me, only to whisper in my ear, "Syren's are notorious for luring in their victims by using emotional manipulation. Can't you see she was trying to drown you?"

I tried to nod but was caught in a fit of shivers again. He hugged me tighter, but I knew it was only to prevent me from dying. I couldn't allow the gesture to mean anything more.

But no matter how hard I tried, after catching a glimpse of myself in some silverware nearby and catching sight of my blue lips and ashy face, I longed for some heat and, and—

And I waited for him to pull away so I could crash my frozen lips against his heated lips. For a single moment, I wasn't cold anymore. I even felt lighter in my seat, as if gravity no longer had a hold on me anymore. If I could keep that moment still, I would make it last much longer.

When he pulled away a single second longer than I expected, I felt heavier in my seat and the shivers had returned. The moment his face came into view again, he looked slightly different, though I could hardly place it. He seemed more ethereal. His lips were pinker, and his eyes had a sparkle in them.

I parted my mouth, filled with longing as I took in this new version of him. Reid quickly glanced around and I noticed his pointy ears. Was I imagining things? I knew I was baring it all within my widened eyes as I gaped at him and debated whether to steal another kiss before both of us would return to our back-and-forth game where we acted like feelings were a nuisance.

"Let's get you home," he said softly as he helped me to my feet.

The heat emanating from his body served as a crutch, as I wasn't sure I'd be able to return home in one piece without him. I could even feel when he lifted me on his hip ever so slightly and glided through the air at a speed most would have trouble discerning as super-fast-power-walker or inhuman. The entire way home, Reid walked, though I didn't feel his feet touch the ground. Some moments felt like he just floated with me home, but I couldn't really remember. I just floated with him.

There wasn't a single qualm that echoed through my head as we made our way to my apartment. All our prior talks about his intentions flew out the window. Maybe I was still disoriented. Maybe I had permanent brain damage. But all I wanted was a hot shower and a gallon of boiling tea.

His touch was comforting. I was ready to swallow my ego and drown my pride just to ask him to cuddle with me so I wouldn't freeze through the night.

My fingers rattled so much I couldn't open my own front door, but Reid silently helped, which I appreciated. He also kept all his comments to himself, and for that I was grateful. He knew now was not the time to insult me.

When he opened my front door and we stepped inside my apartment, I heard, "Alluna?" and my heart missed at least a few beats.

I wished I was hallucinating this time, but unfortunately, I wasn't.

My mother was standing there.

FOURTEEN

I had to blink a few times to make sure I wasn't imagining my mother standing there, in her usual narrow-eyed stance of judgment.

But she wasn't judging me today. Her icy blue eyes were centered on Reid as if he just crawled out of the sewer. Already knowing what she was thinking, I sensed an entire lecture about how my body was a temple and I was naive for allowing a man into my private apartment before establishing his true intentions - or in my mother's favor, locking a chastity belt in place and tossing the key out the window.

She was never overly conservative, but she made her views plainly known. If she knew what Vita was up to in her spare time, she would've had a heart attack long ago. The last thing she needed to know was what Reid was doing in my apartment.

I chose to break the silence, mostly because I couldn't stand being in the chilly doorway much longer and needed to warm up immediately.

"M-m-mom?" was all I could muster. I must've still been disoriented from my hypothermia. I could hardly think straight.

My mother broke her fixated stare and finally sized up my appearance, which was enough to tell a sad story. She gasped and her hand flew to her mouth.

"Alluna! You're soaking wet! And your lips - they're blue. Come inside right now." She lunged forward and pulled me inside with the gentleness of a quarterback. She thought she was being discreet by ignoring Reid, but I could see right through her.

Catching a quick glance of myself while I was passing the mirror, I saw I looked like quite a fright. The residue of my hideous episode was present in my swollen eyelids and the deathly pallor in my cheeks. My cracked lips were dry from dehydration. I looked like I'd aged a decade in the last hour.

For most of my life, I believed my mother to be a particular type of woman - someone who was righteous but came off the wrong way. I was finally beginning to understand that I was turning a blind eye to who she really was. A tyrannical force who couldn't bear to let her kids grow up. Perhaps that was why Vita was desperate to sneak out many nights and lead her own life. My mother surely made it difficult for Vita to steer her own reigns, and now she was imposing the same on me.

"Mom, what are you doing here?" I allowed her to sit me on my couch and nervously glanced at Reid, who silently maneuvered his way into my kitchen. He met my eyes briefly before finding my kettle and setting it to boil, investigating my cabinets for some hot tea.

My mother pushed her way into the kitchen, taking the kettle right out of Reid's hands before he had the chance to turn it on.

"I've been worried sick." Her voice shook with what I truly wanted to believe was concern. "You haven't been answering the phone. You always say you'll call back and you never do. And your poor father," she jerked her head towards me accusingly, "when was the last time you called him?"

My heart sank. I wanted to crawl into a hole and never come out. No matter how humiliating this was in front of Reid, my mother was right. I'd been so wrapped up in my obsession to find Vita that I essentially tore my parents right out of my life. But no matter how much my thoughts made perfect sense, I couldn't quite articulate them.

My mouth refused to work properly. My cheeks and jaw felt wired shut. My brain felt foggy from exhaustion, and my response was weak. Too weak.

"I've just been…preoccupied…"

"Preoccupied, huh?" She threw a glare at Reid. "Who are you? And would you care to explain why my daughter is about to freeze to death?"

She was blaming him, and she didn't even know what happened to me. And she was blaming me for being with him. My mother didn't even care to ask for any details, she just wanted to prove to everyone how incapable I was to fend for myself. And maybe she was right. But I would have rather frozen to death in that lake in Central Park than admit she was right. How could a bird learn to fly if its mother taped its wings shut?

Reid stepped aside and gave my mother complete space in the kitchen. After a hard look at him, I realized he was back to his human-looking self. His ears were no longer pointy, and he lost that sheen, the otherworldly glow he had right after I kissed him. Perhaps I'd imagined everything, after all. That seemed to be the pattern nowadays.

He'd threatened me for less, and I could only imagine what havoc he could wreak on my mother if he decided. My throat went completely dry at the thought of him threatening her. She could have him curled up and hugging his knees with a single glare before he had the chance to throw her off a roof.

"Reid," he said slowly, his velvety voice alarmingly calm. "Your daughter is my student. I'm the TA in her psychology class."

My mother's eyes bulged out of her head. "What business do you have seeing a student outside of a professional environment, Mr. Reid?"

"Just Reid," he corrected coolly. "We arranged a meeting to discuss her exemplary grade. Alluna is the best in the class and would make a perfect candidate to sit in the spring class semester that accepts few new students due to capacity."

"That doesn't answer my question. I don't see how my daughter's psychologically sound presence equates to her being soaking wet in the middle of the winter under your watch." My mother's sarcasm rivaled Reid's. If he thought he could undermine any shred of confidence that I had, he was now seeing what it truly meant to live without any self-worth.

Recalling how he lied effortlessly to Leo about my failing grade, I stared at him in contempt, knowing he may have met his match. Interesting that he was able to flip the script without the blink of an eye. Lying must come easily to him.

Reid chuckled. "We met in Professor Gusto's office originally, until she had to come in for an important meeting and couldn't share the room. By that time, we were both fairly hungry and decided to continue our meeting in the campus's outdoor corridor, where they were serving some free food for the students. A sprinkler fountain nearby was being repaired for leaks when, unfortunately, a spout burst, and Alluna was caught in the middle of a large stream of water. I had to make sure she came home safely so I escorted her myself."

My mother considered his words with the purse of her lips as she poured a steaming cup of tea. Whether she believed him or not, his words were so convincing I almost believed him myself.

"Mom," I croaked. She tensed and briskly gave me the cup of tea, urging me to drink it.

"Yes, honey?" She sat beside me on the couch and stroked my

hair, Reid forgotten.

"Why did you really come?"

She pressed a kiss to my forehead which felt like I was being branded. "To bring you home, of course."

I stiffened. "What?"

"You've lived here for what, a month? Haven't you had your taste of the bitter life in New York City? You know that without your father and I backing you, you'd never be able to afford living here. I knew something was wrong, and here I am, right as always. There's nothing here for you."

My eyes shot up to Reid instinctively, who didn't look happy. My mother couldn't have been any more wrong. The last thing I needed was to go home with her.

"I'm not going home."

"It's not an offer. I've made my decision. You're far too young and naive to live here. I'll give you a few days to pack your things, though it doesn't seem you even need that much time. Did you ever unpack your linens and dishware?" She shook her head. "No matter. I'm staying at a hotel nearby and will be back to take you home."

I felt like I was about to burst. I was so close to finding Vita, but my mother thought she could rip me away by dangling her financial advantage in my face? I was powerless to stop her, but I knew I had options.

"In the meantime, go take a hot shower. A bath might be better, but having a bathtub in that moldy mess of a bathroom would take up more square feet than your entire prehistoric pigsty you call an apartment." My mother sighed and stood, looping her bag around her shoulder, shooting another glare at Reid, and shutting the door behind her.

I could finally breathe in her absence. I might as well have been holding my breath for twenty minutes, or however long my mother decided to grace my presence.

I couldn't believe I ever thought she looked out for me like Vita did. The woman was a conniving snake who hid behind a mask of maternal tendencies. She couldn't spar with Vita anymore, so all she had left was the passive daughter who couldn't hold a candle to the way Vita talked back to our mother.

"No wonder you left home." Reid took her place on the couch with his own steaming mug of tea. I was too tired to do anything but nod. My head felt like it weighed a ton. Reid took my mug from my shivering hands and helped me stand and get to the shower.

"I may come from a dangerous place, but that was the most terrifying woman I've ever met. Seems you can handle a lot more than I thought." Surprised by his sincere statement, I waited for a sarcastic addition.

Lifting my head in appreciation, I gave him a small smile. He turned the water on and gave me a small smile back, before shutting the bathroom door. As the steam from the hot water clouded the bathroom mirrors, I slid down the wall and crumpled onto the shower floor, allowing the near-boiling water to seep into my skin and forgoing the thoughts that once seemed so important, but were now drifting away.

I thought I only closed my eyes for a moment, but when the water started to run cold, I was awakened by the uncomfortable sting of cold water on my steaming skin. Not knowing how much time passed, I cracked the bathroom door open, noting the darkness outside.

Wrapping my towel around, I tiptoed on the cold wooden floor in search of my slippers and pajamas before I stopped cold in my tracks like a deer caught in headlights.

Reid was on my couch. He never left.

He was caught in a deep sleep. I stared at his peaceful face that wasn't laced with a grimace or glare or sarcastic curl of the lip. Just his smooth skin, relaxed brow, and slightly parted lips. I considered waking him, but I couldn't bear the thought of disturbing his dreams.

For a second, I wondered if he was having a nightmare about the woman he lost, but his face was far too peaceful to indicate a dream gone sour. How could I disrupt a pleasant dream in such an unpleasant world?

I continued my light step into the kitchen, where I noticed a plate of peanut butter and jelly sandwiches neatly stacked. Next to the plate was a note that read *can't have you starving on my behalf* in Reid's signature sloping and bold writing.

Unable to hold back a smile, I inhaled the sandwiches in less than a second and pretended I was so light on the floor that I was flying so I wouldn't wake him. After finding my pajamas tossed under the bed, I quickly changed, tucked myself in, and entered dreamland.

Brisk raps on the door tore me from dreams I forgot momentarily. The knocking continued and I jerked awake. Rubbing my eyes, I ignored the knocking and tried to go back to sleep.

"Rise and shine, sleepyhead. It's me, Daisy!"

My eyes shot open and I practically heaved myself out of bed, lacking every bit of grace as I toppled to the floor, tangled in my own bedsheets. My heart raced as I clumsily rose to my feet, the perfect picture of embarrassment, hoping with every last fiber of my being that Reid didn't notice my fall of shame.

In addition, my mind flipped through about a dozen ways to navigate Daisy discovering Reid in my apartment. I fumbled through excuse after excuse, while considering if Reid would fit into my dresser. Ultimately, I decided I could shove him in the bathroom to avoid any unnecessarily awkward explanations as to why my TA spent the night at my place.

But to my utter shock, the couch was empty. Was he freshening up in the ladies room again?

Another brisk knock sent a wave of panic down my spine.

"One second!" I called out feebly before whirling around my small apartment in search of Reid.

He was nowhere to be found. A gust of wind blew at me and I faced my window, which was left wide open in his absence. He must've just flown away in the middle of the night.

Shaking my head at the lunacy of my own thought that was now my reality, I ran to the bathroom to quickly freshen up and greet Daisy, my anxiety having subsided immensely. My mother was already difficult enough as it were. The last thing I needed was to explain myself to Daisy.

Wrapping my cardigan against myself, I opened the door and her bright face greeted me.

"Don't tell me I just woke you up. Our lecture is in an hour." She waltzed in with a few paper bags under her arm while holding two hot coffees, which she placed on my kitchen counter.

"Coffee?"

"Not just coffee but pumpkin spiced coffee! I found a coffee shop that had pumpkin sauce all year round for you." Her smile was infectious, and I was ready to kiss her since I was doling out kisses anyway.

"That's so nice of you, what made you come over?" I started to get dressed for class, making sure to put on an extra layer as I still felt weak and cold from my time underwater.

"I never had a friend live so close to me that I could surprise them with coffee and morning bagels, and besides, we have so much to catch up on." She went into my kitchen and unloaded the bagels onto some plates while pulling out some small containers. "I didn't know what you liked on your bagels, so I got butter, cream cheese, and mayo."

After quickly putting on three fuzzy leggings and an oversized fleece jacket, I pulled my hair back into a ponytail and grabbed a butter knife my mother packed into my dishware.

"Cream cheese all the way." I smiled and started spreading. Daisy exhaled dramatically.

"Okay, good. I wasn't sure, but now I know you're thinking the right way." She held out her bagel pleadingly and I spread some cream cheese while laughing.

Vita never surprised me like this. She may have known what I liked, but most of the time, I would just go along with her mood or interest. I felt seen for the first time in a long time.

But that didn't change our bond. She was more than a sister to me, and it wasn't fair of me to cast her aside for one flaw that was so minuscule it didn't matter in the grand scheme of things. Vita was still my sister and no one would ever compare to the relationship we have. I wished she were here with us, enjoying the bagels and coffee. Though, I didn't think she'd like Daisy very much. She might view her as competition.

I was being ridiculous with my thought train.

After taking a few heavenly sips of my pumpkin-tinged coffee, I moaned slightly and held the warm cup against my cold cheek.

"Wow, Alluna, if that's how you sound after ingesting pumpkin coffee, I don't want to hear how you sound when you orgasm." Daisy licked the butter knife shamelessly.

I punched her arm softly. "Very funny." Taking another bite, I spoke with my mouth full. "To be honest, I can't remember the last time I was with a guy, let alone enjoyed it."

Daisy leaned against the counter. "Alright, I'm all for TMI, but I'm about to talk to you about something I'm not sure I want to hear about."

I knew exactly what she'd say.

"Is it about your brother?"

"Yep!" She gulped some coffee. "He told me you agreed to go out with him, and then the psych TA showed up."

Crap. Here I thought I could avoid talking about Reid since he disappeared through my window. I had to play it cool.

"Yeah, Reid? What about him?" I was suddenly avoiding eye contact even though we'd learned in class that eye contact avoidance was a textbook definition of someone who wasn't telling the truth.

"Leo said there was some tension between you and Reid," Daisy said between chews, giving me an incredulous look. "He thinks you two slept together."

"What? No!" I swallowed, hyper-aware of how defensive I sounded, even though I was being truthful. "I promise you. I haven't slept with Reid."

"I know you haven't. That's a completely ridiculous thought," Daisy said matter-of-factly. "He's your TA, and that would be an imbalance of power. Leo needs to get his head out of his butt."

I didn't bother responding and took another bite. I never thought about it that way. I'd been so focused on otherworldly matters that such human simpleties escaped my head. Not that Reid made any moves on me. He made it perfectly clear his heart belonged to someone else. The only reason he allowed that pathetic kiss was because I had almost died. I knew it meant nothing and so did he.

"What else did Leo say?" I asked, hoping to shift the topic away from Reid.

"He said you agreed to go out with him."

"Oh, yeah, well—"

"And I think it's a great idea! I promise you, he's a sweetheart underneath that player facade he has. Besides, if you get married, you'll be a doctor's wife." She winked at me. "You'll have super cute babies with blonde curls, and we'll be sisters." She smiled.

As if Vita's voice entered my head, I immediately felt her repulsion by the idea of me finding another sister. I could practically feel her distaste and had to remind myself that Vita wasn't here. Vita may not even be alive. I had to shed her overcasting voice.

Smiling weakly, I downed the rest of my coffee. "I think it's a little soon to think that far." Pausing, I decided to tell Daisy the truth.

"I kissed Reid."

Her jaw dropped. "Really?"

Nodding feverishly, I looked at my toes shamefully. "Yes. It didn't mean anything, but it's on my mind."

She shook her head. "Alluna, he took advantage of you. There's a clear imbalance of power there. He should've stopped you and set boundaries. I don't want him manipulating or blackmailing you now that he has leverage."

My mouth was speaking before I even processed my words. "Daisy, do you hear yourself? This is a twenty-something TA we're talking about. You're making him sound like a villain straight out of a Stephen King thriller or something. Don't you think he has better things to do?"

She pondered while I realized the intensity of my lies. I saw Reid murder someone. With his bare hands. My blood ran cold as I remembered the blade tucked inside his boots. He slept over my apartment with a murder weapon on his person, and I completely let that fact slide just because I was caught up in his handsome, sleeping face.

And he used to eat souls before he fled from Naerin. No matter how much he disagreed with the politics, he still ate souls at some point. A helpless victim that was plucked right out of their life and eaten by dangerous creatures with wings or tails or blue skin. I felt bile rise to my throat.

Reid never made excuses as to who he was. He never told me he was the good guy, and I couldn't romanticize him anymore. I had to push that kiss out of my head and focus on what was actually important - saving Vita.

"It was just the spur of the moment, and it definitely won't happen again." My tone was far more nonchalant after my revelation. "I think it's a good idea to go out with Leo, actually."

If my mother didn't pluck me from my life and eat me with her overprotective narcissism.

"I might be evicted," I said blandly. "Can't afford this apartment anymore." The lie came easily to me and I recalled the ease with which Reid lied to my mother. Could it be that he was rubbing off on me?

Daisy jumped up happily. "Come live with me for the time being!"

Smiling, I left with her to class, though my heart was lonely. We chattered and gossiped while heading to the campus like hummingbirds fluttering about first thing in the morning.

Once we entered the lecture, we took our usual seats in the back. I noticed Reid was already at the podium, and briefly wondered why he wasn't lurking by Sage's computer.

When the class settled down, Reid took the microphone. "Good morning, everyone. I'll be subbing for Sage today. She won't be coming in anymore."

Someone in the first row called out, "was she fired?"

Reid was as still as a statue. "She found another position."

A collective groan embodied the student masses, myself included. No one could engage a class as effortlessly as Dr. Sage.

Reid's eyes snapped to me and his brow creased. Unsure of what telepathic messages he was trying to send, I cocked my head in confusion. Not all of us had magic abilities to fly or heal quickly.

He clicked his teeth, swept over the class, which was now mostly socializing and gossiping about the professor, before bending his head and mouthing to me *the keeper got her.*

FIFTEEN

Reid resumed the lecture, though my mind drifted away into another galaxy. The sort of galaxy where people didn't have to walk around like sitting ducks, unknowingly snatched from their lives and unwillingly devoured by awful creatures.

I was brought back to reality by a buzz in my pocket. Pulling out my phone, I saw two texts, one from Leo, and the other from my mother.

I could picture my mother's taut face as she wrote, *I'll be over soon to help you pack.*

My fingers furiously tapped the keyboard without wasting a single precious second.

I'm in class for a few more hours, and then I have plans.

My mother's scrunched face flashed vividly behind my eyelids as if she were right in front of me. I knew she was staring at the phone with each passing second, deciphering my words. She knew something was up. I could feel dread sink into my skin like tar at the thought of my mother showing up and snatching me away before I finished my business with Reid. I was at my wit's end with the answers I yearned for swinging in front of my face while I blindly grasped for them. I knew I was so close, yet with my mother's overarching scorch, she was even closer to burning out the fire within my heart. I knew I couldn't give up, especially since all signs were pointing for me to go home.

Once my mother answered, *you can't dance around this forever*, I sighed with relief, knowing I'd kept her at bay, even if just for another day.

The second text was from Leo.

Looking forward to seeing you today!

I'd completely forgotten about our date amidst everything else going on. Considering the fact that my mother would be closely monitoring my behavior, especially after delaying her trip home, I was relieved to have an alibi by going out with Leo. Perhaps my mother would be gracious toward him, a guy, my age, studying to be a doctor.

Her distaste for Reid was more than obvious, and I never wanted the two of them in the same room again.

For reasons selfish and self-preserving, I responded, *likewise!*

Class dragged on at a glacial pace, and I was too preoccupied with my ever-so-tangled thoughts to concentrate. A few times, Daisy nudged me and asked if I were alright, but all I could give her were half-assed smiles and the pretense of paying attention to the lecture.

Once Reid concluded his lecture, I was on his tail, desperate to hear something, anything. He'd evaded the crowds with the agility only I knew the truth about. While the common passerby would assume he was a fast walker, I imagined his toes hardly touching the floor as he levitated just barely above human speed.

He'd reached Sage's office mere minutes before I caught up with him. Stepping inside the office, I was ready to pour my heart out, even if I didn't know what I'd say.

The words spilled out like a burst dam. "Reid, is Sage going to be okay? Where did she disappear? Was it at a spot from the bucket list? Where was she last seen? Did she say anything to you? Why was she Marked? And what about the Syren? Are there more of her? Are we going to the next bucket list stop together?"

I wanted to shoot myself for how desperate I sounded, but I was too busy hoping he would answer anything. I already felt like I was hanging off a rope with all the questions that were cutting off my circulation.

Reid ignored everything I said, as expected, and gave me a bored look. "Don't you have someone else to play with in the sandbox, Lisa?"

I was ready to scream and wished I had a latte to throw at him.

"I'm serious, Reid!" Crossing my arms, I tapped my foot impatiently.

He looked down at me, his annoyingly steel walls clearly back in place. "I couldn't tell you even if I wanted to." He sneered, curling his lip back in his signature fashion. "Must be difficult feeling powerless all the time."

I ignored him. "Reid, I'm not leaving here until you give me something."

His eyes washed over me. "I'll give you something, but I don't think you could take it."

I could see right through him. He was using this sarcastic facade of his to hide behind like a shield as if no one could see the truth, but I knew him better than that. But since he wanted to play games, I chose to play along.

"You have no idea what I could take." I made my way closer to him. He stiffened ever so slightly, his eyes darting to the open door where any student or faculty member could walk inside and catch him with a student.

"I already told you, you're not my type." He towered over me, his words sliding easily off his tongue, though his eyes hesitated as they loomed over my chest.

"It must be lonely without your girlfriend tending to your childish games."

Reid stilled at the mention of his lost love, his bare emotions giving him away. "As much as I'd love to give you a pity-fuck, I'm leaving."

Nodding, I trailed my fingers on his arm ever so slightly, just a whisper of a touch. He grabbed my arm and shoved it off him.

"I'm leaving New York. Forever."

I paused, my eyes widening. I hadn't expected that. I opened my mouth, ready to spew another fountain of questions.

Reid held up a hand to block my words. "Don't. Don't say anything."

I wasn't sure what to make of his words. I took a step closer. "Where are you going?"

He gave me a long look and started collecting some papers on Sage's desk. "I can't help you. The Keeper is already on my back, and if you stick around much longer, you'll get Marked too. It's too dangerous for us to spend time together." Reid's eyes were blazing as they enveloped me in the green fire that consumed me. All I wanted was to suspend disbelief for a single moment and press my lips against his. I couldn't stop staring at his full, supple lips that were begging for my own.

He must have noticed because he looked away. I was being too obvious. I was an idiot. I couldn't even hold true to my own mental vow. I was falling too hard and too fast. I was positive Reid thought I was a fool. I know I was. What was wrong with me?

"Reid, stop." I tried to block his passage through the door but he effortlessly walked right through my arm, though I didn't expect to have the physical strength. All I could hope for was for my words to have an impact. But why would they? I was no one to him. I didn't matter.

I was worthless.

He quickly surveyed the halls that were teeming with students, and he lowered his voice. "The chances are stacked against your sister. She's probably dead anyway. Just go live your life and forget you met me."

I took another step ahead of him. "Will you stop searching for your girlfriend?"

He stared back, utterly silent.

Narrowing my eyes at him, I said, "That's what I thought."

He gritted his teeth and clenched his stack of papers with white knuckles. The same knuckles that murdered the blue woman without the blink of an eye. The same knuckles that clung to me as he saved my life when she pushed me off the roof.

"It's different."

My voice came out weak but still holding onto its last straw. "You said you needed me. How else will you save her?"

He sighed. "I can't stay here, the Keeper is too close to finding me. I'll find someone else."

I was about to say something else, anything to convince him to stay or take me with him, but he interrupted me before I could open my mouth.

"I don't need you. No one needs you. You're just a piece of space that needs validation at every corner. Now that your sister is gone, you don't know how to make your own choices and just grow up. You'd be better off going home with your mother."

My body stilled and refused to process his words and allow

them to sink in. I knew I would suffer enough later. At that moment, I spat back, "Yeah, go on and insult me. Make me think you couldn't care less about me. Maybe you don't. I almost believe you. But you still saved me on numerous occasions. Don't you think that speaks louder than these words?" I was getting closer to him and I could feel his body heat wrapping around me, though I felt like I was on fire from anger. "You're just a coward who is afraid to admit he's heartbroken. Keep hiding behind this pretense, maybe you'll even fool the next girl. But I'm not done with you yet." My voice was starting to crack but I had to finish before breaking down. "I know Vita is still alive, and she needs me. I will *never* give up, do you hear me?"

Reid stared back at me, his features indiscernible, before sneaking one last glance at the crowds. "I'm leaving New York to go back to where I'm from. It's not an easy task."

I nodded feverishly. "I'm coming too. No matter what it takes."

He dipped his chin, his eyes searching mine, before softly touching my arm, an act of camaraderie, though it could have just as easily been a spider reaching the fly caught in its web. "You won't like the process." If I didn't know any better, I'd think he almost sounded concerned for me.

"Whatever it takes."

He nodded curtly and left.

The moment Reid was out of my sight, I burst into tears. There was only so much strength I could hold onto, especially when he threw daggers at my sorest spots.

Leaning against the doorframe, I quickly wiped my tears away, realizing I was in public, and having learned that the best place to cry in New York City was on the train. I had to keep it together.

My phone buzzed and I thankfully opened the text, ready to receive any form of distraction from Reid's words, that felt like they were still knifed right through me.

Daisy wrote to me that she was studying in the library if I needed her, and for a split second, I considered telling her everything. What was the worst that could happen? She'd call me crazy and ask if I were on drugs. Or, she could think I was having a mental breakdown. And maybe I was, especially if I thought that I meant anything to Reid.

I started walking to the library, hoping for some company to distract me when I felt a hand on my shoulder. Feeling startled and uneasy, I jumped in my shoes and nervously peeked behind me.

Leo stared back at me, a wide grin reaching ear to ear.

"You thought you could run off on me? It's time for our date." Though I'd normally cringe at the idea of going out with Leo, I was actually grateful that he was so persistent. These games I kept playing with Reid were wearing thin as they were, and I could barely handle much more. I was running out of petals to pluck in our does-he-hate-me-or-does-he-want-me game.

Smiling weakly, I fixed my bag on my shoulder. "Where are we going?"

Leo reached over and grabbed my bag right off my shoulder, slinging it over his own. "I did my research on you." He winked.

"I know you're a sucker for pumpkin coffee."

I couldn't help but chuckle, knowing Daisy gave me away, and appreciating his effort. "Can't argue with you there."

We started walking to a nearby cafe. Leo made sure to keep a respectful distance and maintained eye contact dutifully. A small part of me wanted to call him out on his intentions, but another part of me just wanted to be courted in peace without any mind games at play. I'd been conditioned by Reid to expect ulterior motives behind every sentence, and the last thing I needed was to ruin things with Leo because I couldn't stop jumping to the worst-case scenario conclusions.

We were seated at the cafe and he sat across from me, his eyes never leaving mine. The longer I stared at Leo, the more I could see he was truly smitten with me, for whatever reason.

"I actually have to study, so I don't have much time." Nervously tapping my fingers, I wished I were telling the truth. I wished my fate wasn't hanging by a thin thread caught between Reid's teeth. His perfectly placed, sharp teeth behind his full lips, that felt like a drug to be kissing…

"Alluna, I know I come off too strong sometimes." Leo looked apologetic for a moment, and ran his fingers through his hair. "I really like you, and I want to show you that." He smiled at me. "You're different."

I couldn't help but laugh. "Yeah, I'm not like other girls, right?"

He shook his head. "Nope. Most girls here are too shallow for me. Can't keep a conversation going at all. But I know there's a lot more to you than you let on, and I'd like to get to know you."

He ordered me some pumpkin coffee along with some finger food for us to share.

"What makes you say that?" I warmed my fingers with the hot coffee once it arrived.

"I'm good at reading people. Like I know you want your TA."

I almost choked on my coffee and dabbed at my face with a napkin. Leo settled into his seat.

"It's okay, you don't have to admit it. I can't blame you, he has the whole brooding corner guy thing going for him."

"What's your point, Leo?"

"He doesn't seem like a good person. Now back in the day, I'd offer to joust him for you, but I don't think you'd like that either. You don't like being the center of attention."

His insight was fairly interesting, and I didn't mind hearing his psychoanalysis.

"Are you practicing for psychiatry school or something?"

He chuckled. "Not at all. In fact, I'm gonna let you in on a little secret." He leaned across the table for dramatic effect and whispered, "I'm not actually in medical school. My parents don't know. They'd kill me."

He settled back in his chair, throwing some fries in his mouth. "I never wanted to be a doctor. Family pressure, you know? Daisy has been more than happy to take the fall as the family disappointment while I figure out how to tell my parents medical school is not for me."

There was more to Leo than he let on, too. Was this a thing all guys did? Hide behind a curtain face to avoid vulnerability?

He'd certainly piqued my curiosity. "What do you want to do, then?"

He shrugged. "Business. Finance. Who knows. Something that isn't medical school." He swallowed his food and looked at me. "I'd rather know about you. What's your family like?"

I tapped my coffee restlessly, unsure of how to answer his question. It wasn't a complicated question or anything, but how could I say that my sister was snatched by the Keeper of Naerin and was held hostage and potentially dead in a country where magical creatures survived off human souls?

"My mom and I don't see eye to eye." That should've been good enough, considering.

He nodded. "You and I both. Mine loves reminding me that she came to this country to give me a better life, and I will never know her struggles. As if I don't have struggles of my own. As if her overbearing pressure isn't a struggle already."

Leo shook his head and stared out the window. I couldn't believe how easily he was able to relate to me and make me feel less alone and certainly less crazy. Perhaps Leo was the type of guy I should be dating. Someone real. Someone tangible. Someone who couldn't fly and didn't come from a magical country that should've stayed in fairytales.

Sadly, Reid still held the keys to the mystery. I couldn't drop everything and leave my sister helpless and scared in the clutches of who knows what terrible monsters. No matter how much I wanted to be rid of Reid, I needed him.

After I'd finished my coffee, I shot Leo a grateful look. "I really like talking to you," I said sincerely. Talking to him was easy. From the bottom of my heart, I wished we met under different circumstances. I could only handle so much at one time. "Honestly, I'm kinda going through some things right now—

"Involving your TA, I bet."

I didn't confirm, but I also didn't deny. "–but maybe in the future we could hang out again." Finishing my coffee, I offered a small smile, hoping I wasn't giving him false hope. I had no idea where my feelings would take me in the future, but I still wanted him in my life, selfish as it was.

He raised an eyebrow and paid the bill. "I'm fine with just being friends, for now. Just be careful with that guy, alright? Anyway, there's no pressure if you ever want to just grab a coffee. Talk. Vent about your mom. Anytime."

I laughed and gently covered his hand with my own. "Maybe I'll take you up on that."

He smiled and handed me my bag before leaving the cafe.

I walked out feeling mentally hydrated, even though I didn't really tell Leo anything. I didn't have to, he could read the room, even if it was dimly lit. It was nice to just have a platonic date with no strings attached, though I knew Leo didn't want to be just friends. If I never met Reid, I could certainly imagine giving Leo a chance.

Perhaps, if I survived this whole thing with Reid, Leo could be my happily ever after unless I murdered Reid in the process and got arrested, of course. There were only so many unthrown lattes I could take before I lost it. Reid had a way of jerking on my heartstrings and making me want to smash his head in, while also making me want to kiss him until neither of us could breathe.

SIXTEEN

The breeze felt nice on my skin, a soft caress against my flesh. I shut my eyes and allowed my entire body to succumb to the licks of the wind, all the way down to my toes.

"You always liked the autumn breeze." I could hear Vita smiling through her voice. Opening my eyes, I smiled back, watching her soak in the sun.

"I hate the winters." I met her halfway and walked with her through the open, grassy field. The trees were starting to change color, the leaves splashed with yellow hues. We walked down the path and she bent to pick a flower off the ground and stuck it behind her ear.

All of the things that seemed so important in my life were flying away with each coming breeze. I was here, with my sister, and I was happy.

Vita twirled and picked more flowers, braiding them together and weaving a simple crown out of them.

I joined her activity and started braiding my own, though the stems I'd picked kept falling loose.

"Here, let me show you how." Vita plopped next to me and took my weak assembly of flowers, disarranging them and tossing them to the side.

"You have to make sure the root is long. Yours are too short to hold together."

She expertly reached into the dirt to pluck a few stems, wiping the dirt away and handing me a few well-plucked flowers.

"Try again," she instructed, before returning to her immaculately woven arrangement.

My second attempt proved more futile than the first for all reasons unknown. My fingers refused to hold the flowers in place.

A frustrated exhale escaped me as the flowers fell beside my feet, a gnarly mess that was too ugly to salvage.

"How are you so good at everything?" I dragged my fingers through the dirt, letting the soil escape in a slow drift.

Vita threw her head back and laughed. "You're just not trying hard enough." She placed her flower crown on her head and stood tall, a spring queen blossoming from her hibernation.

She extended her hand to me and pulled me off the soil, quickly dusting off some dirt from my behind and sides. Her eyes lit up with excitement.

"I know something you'll be really good at." She could hardly contain the glee in her voice as she tugged me forward.

"It's really easy, all you have to do is shut your eyes really tight and think happy thoughts. They'll lift you into the air and you'll fly." She yanked my arm forward as we started sprinting through the field.

Once we reached the hill at the end, I looked over in fear but realized the slope wasn't steep and if I failed, I'd just roll right into the soft grass just a few feet below.

"Oh, I don't know..." Hesitation took up the forefront of my mind. Vita was always so good at everything; I would always pale in comparison.

"Come on, I know you can do it. It's going to be so much fun." She released my hand and walked on her tippy toes to the edge.

"I'll go first to make you feel more comfortable."

Vita faced me, held out her arms as wide as she could, and shut her eyes, a peaceful smile enveloping her face. The gentle wind brushed her shining hair behind her shoulders and rustled the crown on her head as she fell backward, allowing gravity to take full control.

Instinctively, I reached for her to halt her fall. But before I knew it, she was flying!

Vita's laughter sounded like cherry blossoms taking root and turning a simple meadow into a masterpiece. Her happiness was so infectious I found myself grinning widely as I watched her float on the air as if she were lighter than air itself. What I wouldn't give to join her. To soar in the air as freely as she could. To achieve her level of happiness. To fly next to her.

She gestured her hands frantically and floated right by the edge.

"Come on, Alluna! This feels amazing!" She called to me before doing a wide loop through the air and laughing like a child on a snow day.

My toes were hanging right off the edge. All I had to do was listen and I'd be free too. I'd be with Vita. We'd fly away together. It was everything I ever wanted.

My eyes were welded shut from nerves. I doubted pliers could pry them open anymore. My brain was a nexus of electricity, with each jolt being a happy moment between Vita and I. The nights we spent giggling in her bedroom. The times she did my makeup against our mothers permission. The time she let me sneak out with her and go for a drive with the most popular guys in school. The days we binge-watched Gossip Girl and discussed which of us was the Blair or Serena.

I couldn't have been more elated. My mind was free and flying, and I knew my body was about to be free and flying, too.

"Hurry, Alluna!"

I held my arms out the way Vita did, allowing the breeze to inch me forward.

"It has to happen. Remember that all of it has to happen!"

Her wording confused me, but maybe I misheard her. The wind

was picking up and the temperature was rapidly decreasing. But it didn't matter.

My mind was free.

I was ready.

"You have to jump *now.*"

I wanted to see the look on Vita's face when I finally did something right. I wanted to see her face light up even more at the sight of me flying next to her. I wanted to tell her how excited I was.

I opened my eyes.

And my excitement dropped like rocks tumbling down a mountain.

Vita was nowhere to be found.

There was no meadow. No grass. No hill. No gentle breeze. No flowers to pick by my toes.

Just me, standing at the ledge of my open window in my apartment, seconds from tumbling to my doom.

My breath hitched in my throat as fear seized my entire body and paralyzed my limbs.

Don't look down.

I looked down.

Oh, god.

I was so close to the edge. Seconds from death, even. I would've been splattered on the pavement if I didn't wake up and open my eyes.

Using unparalleled forces that didn't feel like they belonged to me, I propelled myself away from the window and landed on my floor, breathing heavily and feeling my heart violently thump against my chest like it was trying to escape a cage.

I could feel each breath catch in my throat as I edged farther and farther away from the window, terrified of what I'd almost done.

Was I sleepwalking? Was I possessed?

My nightmare from a few nights ago flashed in my mind. Vita's lifeless body with her blood going *drip, drip, drip—*

Had I taken that last step, my body would've also been lying lifeless on the ground, specks of my blood going *drip—*

Could this have been a sign? Was this my mind's sick way of telling me I was going to die if I went after Vita? As if I hadn't heard it enough already. At every twist and turn, all I've heard was how I would fail and how my weakness would lead to my death.

But I wasn't ready to rationally process just yet. I was too busy hugging my knees and shaking horrendously, a mixture of the freezing winds blazing into my apartment and my own fear coursing down each vein.

I was too afraid to approach the window, even just to close it. I feared myself. What if I was still asleep?

I pinched myself.

Ouch.

Wincing, I stood carefully, making sure my eyes were wide open so I could clearly envision each step. My legs cooperated and I started to calm down, though it took everything inside of me to just close the window and hook the latch as quickly as I could before I was overtaken by another narcoleptic episode and hurling myself to my death.

If I could restrain myself to the bed, I would've.

Instead, I surrendered to the couch, feeling slightly comforted by the extra distance.

As I pulled my comforter over my head and fell back into darkness, I settled into the only condolence that made me feel better - I saw Vita again, even if it was just a dream.

"What don't you get? Pumpkin pie is gross, but pumpkin coffee is superb." Daisy took a sip of her sweetened coffee for emphasis.

Leo looked at her as if she had five heads, each sprouting with varying degrees of lunacy.

When he finally turned to me, I knew he wanted to see if I would join Daisy in her absurd ideology. If this would've been any other day, I would've enthusiastically educated him on the principles and fundamentals of pumpkin flavoring.

But after my terrifying night, I felt like a shell of myself, even more than usual. I'd spend most of the day holed up in my apartment staring at the godforsaken window.

Until Daisy invited me to get cookies at midnight, of course. With her and Leo. I couldn't have been happier at the opportunity to escape from myself and my thoughts.

We splurged at Insomnia cookies and went hunting for coffee.

I wouldn't sleep that night anyway, might as well enjoy it.

With all that being said, I couldn't allow Leo too much fantastical thinking, even in my battered state.

I nodded to Daisy. "She's absolutely right."

Leo gawked at me. "You women are crazy. Pumpkin is a flavor."

"Pumpkin is not a flavor, dear brother. It's a concept."

"A philosophical way of thinking, even," I added, a small smile tugging at my mouth.

Daisy and I shared a laugh before I glanced out the window. The cookie shop was open until three in the morning, a perfect place to start a sleepless night.

If this were my hometown, I knew the streets would be bare. No one went out unless it was in a car. Yet this big city was buzzing as usual, teeming with a cocktail of socialites chirping through the proverbial social op forest and friends gathering to drink and smoke the night away into oblivion. It never failed to amaze me how any second could turn into an adventure in New York City.

Maybe these were the type of adventures I was meant for. Not hunting down mystical creatures from a magical country that ate human souls, or embarking on a journey to said magical country with someone who was hardly the good guy of my story.

Daisy and Leo were perfectly…human. Leading their human lives with human problems. As much as I wished I could relate to them, I felt myself drifting farther and farther from the natural human realm.

I thought back to my impromptu kiss with Reid, how I felt myself lift ever so slightly. Could that have been a result of his magic, or just my imagination?

Something flashed before my eyes. Blinking, I jerked my head, trying to catch the object that moved at an inhuman speed. Through the dirty window, I saw it again.

Was that a little boy?

Internally shaking my head, I scolded myself. Not everything in my peripheral vision was going to be a supernatural hallucination.

The boy walked alone, and the longer I stared, the longer something felt off about him. He was all dressed in leather material, almost like a leather jumpsuit. The boy was all alone in the middle of winter, and he was barefoot. Even the back of his head seemed dirtied with leaves and sticks.

The boy turned to me, and my heart stopped. His teeth were all fangs that slid past his lips, the irregular contour misshaping his mouth. Dried blood coated his chin in red-black scabs.

He ran up to the window, staring right at me, and snarled loud enough for the whole avenue to hear.

Jumping in my seat, I pulled back, falling right into Leo.

"Are you okay?" Feeling his hand on my shoulder, he helped me sit upright.

"Who is he?" Daisy asked, glancing toward the window.

I looked at her with bulging eyes, feeling like all the blood was sucked out of my body. She could see him?

Leo didn't release my shoulder as concern flooded his eyes. A quick glance at the window and his eyes widened.

"Y-you can see him?" I whispered shakily.

"Of course, we're not blind." Daisy huffed and grabbed her bag. "Let's move away from the window."

I couldn't believe it. Maybe I wasn't crazy after all. Maybe these weren't hallucinations. I had to look back. I had to tell Reid about this terrifying little boy. I had to—

The little boy was gone.

Instead, there was a homeless man smiling at us through the window. Facial wounds tainted his face, cuts all over his chin. He made a gesture with his hands indicating he wanted money, smiling at us expectantly.

"Come on, Alluna. Let's go." Leo tugged my arm and I allowed him, feeling like a complete idiot. Who was I kidding? Was I really stupid enough to believe the world would work in my favor for once?

I wasn't safe anywhere. These hallucinations were following me everywhere, even in my sleep. I wasn't safe. At this rate, I should've been afraid to leave my apartment.

But instead, I felt a surge of tenacity settle in my bones. The feral little boy didn't harm me. He was just another clue. Reid would tell me what he was.

Leo, Daisy, and I grabbed another table away from the windows. My mind was racing with new ideas and theories as Leo and Daisy started arguing about something unrelated.

While pretending to listen and giving noncommittal nods, I quickly sent an urgent text to Reid to meet me. Without a moment's waste, he answered, saying he would be in my apartment within the hour. Locking my phone and discreetly putting it in my pocket, I returned to Daisy and Leo's not-so-civil war.

"You're Mom's favorite. It won't matter when you tell her the truth and break her heart. She already has one doctor son in the family, anyway." Daisy finished off her chocolate chunk cookie, washing it down with her coffee.

Leo briskly shook his head in defiance. "Mom will kill me for not telling her sooner. Do you know how many of our international cousins think I'm about to go to an Ivy medical school?"

Daisy rolled her eyes. "Half our international cousins still think I'm pre-med. Big whoop."

I interjected lightly, eager for a moment's distraction from the problems that seemed much more important than Daisy and Leo's sibling quarrel. A small part of me wished my problems were human-sized again. The best I could do was pretend.

"If it makes you feel better, at least your mother talks about you to international cousins. I was never anybody in my family. Not like my sister was."

Daisy gave me a pained look full of pity. I never went into detail about Vita's disappearance, but it wouldn't take a genius to know how much it hurts to lose a sibling. I also gave her permission to fill Leo in on the details to spare me from repeating the tragic story.

Leo's look was identical to Daisy's, and for a moment, I saw their resemblance for the first time. The way both of their brows crinkled in the same place, the way both their eyes looked wet in that sad, puppy-dog type of way. How both their ears reddened slightly. They even sighed at the same time. As much as they acted like they couldn't stand each other, I knew their bond was deeper than words. It made me miss my sister more than ever.

Daisy grabbed one of my hands and squeezed it. "Let's make a pact." She gave a silent look for Leo to take my other hand and he did, after a quick check that I was alright with it, which I appreciated.

"We'll be there for each other. No matter how weird things get." Her eyes traveled between Leo and me as if her words weren't obvious enough. "This is a big, lonely city. Friends come and go. People get too caught up with work to remember what really matters. We choose our family in New York."

She looked at me directly. "I choose you, Alluna."

Her words were touching, but I couldn't help but wonder. I wasn't used to having friends, and I certainly haven't been a great one.

"Why me?"

Leo answered for Daisy, and I was sure he took the thoughts right from her mind by the way she nodded in agreement. "Because you've been through it. You're not surface-level. You know what real pain is. You get it."

I took the last cookie from the box and split it into three pieces - more than a toast, but also to seal our words with one last yummy bite. We held our cookie pieces up in the air and touched them before gobbling them down. With a full mouth and in the middle of a laugh, I said, "I choose you guys, too."

SEVENTEEN

My happiness was short-lived the moment I parted ways with Daisy and Leo and headed home. All I could think about was my never-ending nightmare, awake or asleep. I'd only been in New York City for less than three weeks, and everything I'd ever known was already turned upside down. I'd only known Reid for two weeks and he was already taking up more space in my mind than anyone else outside of Vita. I'd already been stupid enough to kiss him.

I could hardly tell if he wanted to be around me, but I couldn't let that stop me.

I figured he was already inside my apartment before I even walked in. I'd unlatched my window before meeting Daisy and

Leo. To think I'd come to this place in my life where I had to start leaving my window open on purpose in case my psych TA wanted to fly in for a visit. Could that thought get any more preposterous?

The moment I opened my front door, I knew he was waiting for me. It was eerily silent, and I felt he was there.

Nevertheless, when I saw him sitting cross-legged in midair, I knew he meant business. He almost looked like he was meditating, with his eyes shut tight and his face pensive. He didn't acknowledge me until I shut my door, took off my jacket, and took a seat on my couch. Not knowing what mystical forces he was trying to channel, I dared not interrupt him.

Only when I settled into my couch and stared at him for a few full minutes did he open his eyes and look right at me.

"Were you meditating?" My question hung in the air like dead space, and I briefly wondered how long he pondered whether to give me a sarcastic answer.

But to my surprise, he was more mellow than usual. "Not exactly. I was trying to see."

"See what?"

"Anything, really. I'm sort of locked out, and my magic blinds me from the path to Naerin."

I crossed my legs. "So how will we get there?"

He cocked his head, his body slightly turning toward me, still suspended in midair as if the weight of gravity no longer existed. *"We?"* There it was again, the snarky, condescending Reid I knew very well by now.

I nodded. "Yes, *we*. You know I'm coming with you." Whatever sarcastic retort I'm sure he had up his sleeve stayed dormant for now, though by now I knew it would come out spontaneously, at his whim. But there were more important things at hand than Reid's sass. "I saw something else today, and I wasn't even at a bucket list location."

He perked his head toward me. "Do tell."

Swallowing the lump in my throat, I went through about a million versions in my head before settling on the one that sounded the least insane. "Well, it was a little boy, I think. He had this leather…skinsuit? He was barefoot and had scary teeth."

Reid nodded along with my words. "Yeah, it's getting more dangerous. Those boys are not to be messed with. It means the Keeper is getting closer."

"What are they?" I asked.

"Dangerous. Unpredictable," Reid said as if that was all I needed to know.

I recalled how the previous victims had mentions of dust. Did they also have hallucinations right before the Keeper stole them? Was I just a blinking light waiting to be taken?

"What do we do?"

Silence. Reid's eyes were shut again.

Trying to sync with his mellow attitude, I gave him some time, hoping he would give me more than that. But when he closed his eyes again and creased his eyebrows, I ventured forward.

"Why does your magic blind you from the path?"

He hesitated, his eyes remaining closed. "It's complicated. In layman's terms, no one can leave or enter without the Keeper's permission. The magical folk can't see the path in Naerin either. I had to starve myself for months to dull my magic and escape. Barely survived the journey. I had to become more human and weaken myself."

"So you'll have to become more human to return there as well?"

"Bingo."

"But how? You're already not eating souls here." I narrowed my eyes at him. "…right?"

He opened his eyes and chuckled. "I have not. That sort of practice only exists on Naerin. There's a ritual and procedure that involves magic that doesn't exist in this realm."

Exhaling in relief, I thought about his words more. "Then how can you dull your magic on this realm?"

"The human realm and Naerin wax and wane together. Yin and yang. Push and pull. I'd have to ingest human matter here to weaken my magic."

I let my mind wander and grimaced. "Human matter, meaning…?"

His canines flashed. "I could eat a human." He landed on the floor and stalked toward me slowly. I knew he was just trying to scare me and wouldn't give him the satisfaction of falling for it.

"You won't eat me." My statement was just as definitive as it was a warning to him.

Reid stopped and leaned against my kitchen counter. "I can eat your boyfriend."

"Leo is not my boyfriend!" I exclaimed, jumping off the couch and pointing my finger at him. "Leave my friends out of this!"

Reid chuckled, and I felt like a fool for falling for his bait. He lived to push my buttons and bring out the worst in me. Taking a deep breath, I willed myself to calm down.

"Is there any other way?"

Reid genuinely considered my question. I could tell his mind was working through every nook and cranny.

After a long while, he answered with the last thing I expected him to say. "Do you remember when we kissed?"

Of course, I do, Reid. It's not like it's been on my mind for the last three days or anything, but sure, let's pretend it was no big deal.

"Oh, yeah. Vaguely."

"When you kissed me, did you feel lighter?"

Remembering the moment our lips met, I recalled the feeling of slightly lifting off my seat, and how I wondered if I had imagined it.

Nodding slowly, I said, "Yes. I also saw your pointy ears."

Reid's eyes widened slightly. "Very interesting. Just as I thought."

I was about to jump off the couch. I wasn't crazy. I didn't imagine his ears.

"Tell me."

"Push and pull, remember? My magic conceals my true self while I am in this realm so I can blend in with humans. As my magic dulled, yours intensified and you saw my true self. I know my magic dulled because I felt heavier, more tied to the ground than usual."

"So if we kissed again, you would see the path to Naerin?"

Shaking his head, he fell backward, following gravity. Stopping himself halfway before he fell to the ground, he remained horizontally afloat, as if he was lying in bed. Crossing his arms behind his head, he stared up at my ceiling. "Wouldn't be enough."

I regretted my next sentence before I even said it. "What if you kiss other girls?"

Reid genuinely laughed as he rose a few inches higher in the air and held his stomach with his hands. "Still won't be enough." He looked at me for a few moments, before flying onto the couch next to me.

I shifted my weight as my leg started tapping restlessly. "Then how?"

He held up three fingers. "There are three steps, and you probably won't like them."

"I'm listening."

"This process will take some time, but we can help speed it up by having me ingest some matter every day, to slowly build up the weakness."

My mind was traveling in about a million directions, but I wanted to make sure I knew what he was getting at. "So, you want to kiss every night?"

"That would be the first step, yes."

"Oh."

"There's worse things you could do." He narrowed his eyes at me, and I looked away, feeling my cheeks reddening. With his hand on my chin, he turned my face back to him, and I was ready to melt at his touch. "You have to really be into it. Otherwise it won't work."

"Why not?"

Reid smirked and brushed my hair out of my face. "How effective is ingesting your matter if you're lazy about it? The more hormones you produce, the stronger the matter is. I need you to be a hundred percent in."

I knew this would be a mistake. I knew I was already falling head over heels, far too fast, but I couldn't stop. Reid wasn't even the good guy. I've watched him murder someone. Yet the thought of his hands wrapped around my throat made my insides tingle, and out of sheer impulsivity, or pure longing, I breathed, "I'm all in."

His smirk widened into a grin. "I'll be the judge of that."

He gave me a lingering glance as his burning hand traced my thigh. I thought it would catch fire. My lungs expanded with a huge intake of air as I felt what was coming next but wasn't sure if my body could handle it. The smile that played on his face was dangerous. His grazing fingers left an electrifying tingle wherever they landed. He was toying with me, and I wanted him to keep playing.

Reid couldn't know how much power he possessed over me, how I would crumble under his touch. Feeling my heartbeat hard enough that my chest could hardly hold it in, I took care to remain still, not leaning in, not giving him the satisfaction.

His hand grazed my collarbone and moved to gently caress my neck. Feeling exposed, I was ready to explode. He leaned in, placing a kiss on my neck, sending shivers down my entire body. Unwillingly, my body leaned into him, almost fully closing the distance between us. I wanted him, no matter how wrong it was. It felt right in my mind, in my body, in my throbbing core.

His mouth reached my ear and ever so slightly grazed past it with his lips. "I'll show you what it looks like to be all in," he whispered into my ear. I had to remind myself that this was all pretend, all part of the grand scheme, though he was awfully convincing. The first step. Weakening his magic.

I didn't care about those details. How could I, when my body squirmed under his touch, under his hypnosis? I wanted his lips to take mine already and could hardly stand each passing second that they didn't.

He cupped my face with both hands and slowly went in. I could hardly bear to wait any longer. Taking his time to tease me, his lips pressed against mine so sweetly, so warmly. It was perfect. My head was swimming with lust, and I allowed my body to relay the message by pressing against him.

Pulling apart emphatically, I bit my lip. His eyes flashed with lust as he pulled me back in by the nape of my neck. This time, our slow dance was over. It had transitioned into a tango as our mouths found a rhythm together. His lips devoured mine, and I sighed into him, wanting to feel every part of him on me. The moment his tongue met mine, I could feel myself lifting slightly, barely off the couch, but enough to feel less of my body weight sitting upon it. Our passions continued to dance as he pulled me onto his lap with more ease than usual, considering I probably weighed less at that moment, running his hand down my waist and lower back. My body fit into all his nooks and crannies perfectly, and it felt sublime. Knowing this moment was meant to happen, I allowed his hands to explore my body while gravity departed further.

Tangling my fingers through his shining auburn strands, I kissed him harder. My fingers traced his sharp jawline as I held his chin softly, keeping his lips on mine and tasting every part of it. Just as my hand was about to betray my impulses and slip inside the drawstring of his sweatpants, he took hold of my wrist again, not allowing me access.

"No," he whispered into my mouth, giving me one last kiss before pulling away.

Panting heavily, I considered pouncing on him. My mouth was throbbing from our intense kiss. My chest was rising and falling quickly, my heartbeat racing. I felt lighter than air, and I feared I would fly away if I stood up.

He looked magical again. His pointed ears were back, and I could see the glimmer in his eyes, even under the dim lighting. He had a slight aura that was iridescent, and I wondered if that was his magic. He was living, breathing magic. I was in awe.

Reid stared at me, his features indiscernible, before clearing his throat. Realizing I was still sitting atop his lap, I awkwardly shuffled over to the couch, trying to calm my breathing and not stare at him longer than necessary.

"Was that okay?" I asked, reminding myself that he only did it for the cause and nothing more. I couldn't allow myself to believe any of that was real, though he could've fooled me. I briefly pictured him kissing his girlfriend like that, and felt like a masochist.

He nodded, out of breath himself. "Yes. It's harder for me to fly."

I couldn't look at him, but still had to ask, "How do you know, if I was on top of you?"

"You being on top of me wouldn't stop me from flying."

Recalling how he saved me from Raine's push from the rooftop nightclub and how effortlessly he soared while carrying me, I blushed.

Anxious to shift the topic and not give my true emotions away, I asked, "How long until the first step is complete?"

Reid jumped up off my couch and I could see him trying to lift himself into the air, but it took more effort than usual. "No idea. I have to see how long it will take for my full magic to return. For now, we can settle on nightly appointments. How does that sound?"

Nightly appointments to kiss a magical creature to dull his magic and open the magical path to an in-between realm where my sister was taken captive so I could potentially rescue her and, most likely, perish in the process. Nothing like a typical week in New York City.

Reid pulled on his jacket and drifted off the floor to get his shoes. My mouth was still throbbing from our kiss, and I hated myself for wanting more.

"Well?" He looked back at me. "I'm not one to beg. I'll find someone else if you're not in. It's not like there's a shortage of desperate girls who are touch-starved in this city."

Ouch. Wincing, I answered, "I'm in."

Reid unlatched my window and threw it open all the way.

"Wait," I said.

As he stepped on the ledge, he turned back, the sheen of his magic creating a shadowy glow on his skin.

"What are you?"

"A special breed of Faerie," he said as he fall back through the window and disappeared into the night.

EIGHTEEN

rust me on this one, Mom." I shuffled into the lecture hall as my mother's voice grilled me through the phone. Her stern voice was the type of quiet that was scarier than being yelled at. "Alluna, it's been four days since I saw you. I won't be telling you again."

"There's nothing to tell, I heard you the first time."

"Watch your tone. When we return to Hershey, you'll be grounded for a lifetime. I'm not sure what degenerates you've been spending your time with, but I don't even recognize you anymore—"

"Mom, I am twenty-two years old. You can't ground—"

"Don't interrupt me. As I was saying, you have become a

complete—"

"Mom!"

"*What!*"

The lies poured out of me smoother than maple syrup and I didn't miss a single beat. "I will come home. I have to tie up a few loose ends first, and I need a few days." Lying was a necessary evil at this point. "If I finish this final, I'll be able to get credit for this course and transfer it to the Hershey community college when I come back. You don't want me to retake the course for no reason, do you?"

I could feel my mother's pursed lips and flared nostrils through the phone. "Fine. The moment your final is over, you will be on the next bus to Pennsylvania. Have I made myself clear?"

"Crystal. Gotta go. Class is starting." Hanging up as fast as I could, I slumped into my seat, rubbing my temples. My mother's uncanny ability to infantilize and demoralize me was more than I could handle. I'd much rather take my chances with the murderous feral boy or a vengeful Syren.

If only I could tell my mother the truth. There was no guarantee I would be in the human realm at all, let alone sitting in a psychology final. Chances are, I might be dead long before I even reached my sister, especially considering how I've been faring with the Naerin creatures in my native realm.

The moment Reid left my apartment last night, I knew our investigation would get more complicated with the addition of these "kissing appointments" that we agreed to do each night. We also agreed to report to each other if we noticed any changes in each other's magical auras.

By the time I woke up this morning, the magic had worn off me. My stance on the ground had returned to normal, and when I saw him in the lecture hall by the podium, I could no longer see the iridescent sheen that was previously rolling off his body.

We agreed to continue our investigation by revisiting Kaffeine after class in search of the Faerie, though Reid doubted we would see him again. He mentioned something along the lines of them "not being seen unless they wanted to be," to which I countered something along the lines of "the same should go for us."

"Wanna get lunch after class?" Daisy took her seat next to me and looked at me expectantly.

Giving her a sheepish shrug, I avoided her eyes, feeling like she could see right through me. "Sorry, I have to discuss my grade with Reid after class." Guilt washed over me for not being truthful, yet the protective barrier trumped all other emotions. The less Daisy knew, the better.

"Your grade, huh." Daisy definitely didn't believe me, not for a single second. And I couldn't blame her either. I barely believed my own lie.

"I know you're not telling me stuff but like…be careful with him," Daisy paused. "And please keep Leo in mind. He really likes you, so if you aren't interested, then don't waste his time."

Nodding without giving any information away, I pulled out my notebook and tuned into the lecture, or at least pretended to, feeling like the worst person in the world.

"You never told me who marks the souls and what the Council is." I sped up my pace to keep up with Reid's inhuman one.

As usual, a quick glance around to make sure no one was listening before he lowered his head toward me. "Could you be any less discreet?" He hissed at me through his teeth before whispering, "The council of the Five was created at the origin of the realm, thousands of years ago. They hold monthly trials in which a human soul is marked for the Keeper to deliver. Once the Keeper bewitches the human and transports them to Naerin, the human has the option of being devoured and lost to the world, or joining them, their soul bound to Naerin for eternity."

We quickly made our way into the crowded coffee shop and took our place in line. I nudged his arm, urging him to continue.

"Most humans choose to die," was all he added, before looking around to make sure no one was eavesdropping.

"Why?" I asked.

"There are things worse than death," he said through gritted teeth as if he knew from personal experience.

Immediately, my mind jumped to my sister. She wouldn't— couldn't. Knowing her and how much she loved life, I knew in my heart that if she had any opportunity to stay alive, she would take it and make it work. That is, if she fell into the slim chance of joining them. Recalling how Reid mentioned ancestry, I pondered our own. Do we come from a long line of Faeries or Syrens? How could someone even know that? Wouldn't that mean we had magic too? My questions were only piling up worse than before, and I tried thinking about something else just to calm my buzzing brain that was itching for answers. It was beyond exhausting to gain one answer but end up with ten more questions in its place.

The baristas were buzzing about as usual, with no wings in sight. I didn't know what I was hoping for, but considering all the occurrences that continued happening whether I sought them out or not, surely paying a visit with Reid would spark something magical, especially since both of us were tied to victims of the Keeper.

Lingering behind the other customers, we waited for the large group to order before taking their place at the front of the register.

"Welcome to Kaffeine. What can I get started for you?" The barista asked with a pleasant smile.

Returning his smile, I said, "A large pumpkin spice latte and a double shot over ice with a splash of cream."

"You remembered," Reid breathed down my neck, and I could feel the goosebumps rise.

"It's a talent," I responded casually as if we were just two plain humans going about their day, not in search of a barista with wings.

We stood by the counter, and for the first time, I noticed sadness on Reid's face.

"What is it?" I asked.

"She loved coffee, too." His shoulders slumped forward and he pinched the bridge of his nose. My heart broke for him. I could only imagine how difficult it was to maintain his composure in public. He never brought her up. I imagine it was too painful for him, especially considering his circumstances.

I told him, "I'm so sorry for your loss."

I had to tell him that. Unsure of how many others bothered to say that, it was important to me that at least one person told him. Maybe no one else knew. Maybe he was all alone in his grief. Breaking all boundaries, I reached over and grasped his hand, sharing in his pain. I knew what it was like to be alone after losing a loved one. The pain was indescribable and only grew like a tumor. No one deserved that.

At that moment, I realized that I might've been the only one who knew the truth of what happened to his girlfriend, even with the missing bits and pieces about his native realm. What could I say? She's in a better place? She's no longer suffering?

So I did the only thing I could do as a human in the normal human world - provide emotional support and be his crutch, if only for a moment. If I could shoulder his burden, I would. I would take on the pain that I knew so well by now and give this person that I barely knew a moment to breathe...the way I wished someone would do that for me and the gaping hole in my heart.

I knew what it was like to break all composure and have all walls come crashing down. It was more important than ever for me to be there for him, despite the double-edged sword I felt oozing into my back. As much as I shared in his grief and felt us bond over our shared distress, I was also bearing witness to the true love he held in his heart for someone I could never replace.

He repeatedly told me I wasn't his type. He's said cruel things to me again and again, and he's flat out using me to get back to the love of his life.

Yet the way we kissed last night was the most exhilarating I've felt in my entire life. I felt like I wasn't alive until that moment until he claimed my lips for his own and showed me what it felt like to belong to someone.

And to think I volunteered to go through that every single night…just for him to return to someone else…either I was a total masochist or I hated myself.

The corners of his mouth turned upward, and he gave me a genuine smile tinged with slight surprise. "No one's ever said that to me and meant it."

"Yeah."

He squeezed my hand. "I'm actually sorry for your loss too."

I couldn't help but return his genuine smile and squeeze his hand back.

Our coffees were served quickly through the window and I turned to look around the shop again in search of the Faerie.

Instead, my eyes fell on Daisy, who'd just walked through the door. With Leo by her side.

Both their eyes fell on me, my hand on Reid's, the way he was smiling at me, and our close proximity. I was ready to die at that moment. Truly. I wished I could peel my face off and throw it out the window.

Leo couldn't have looked more despondent if he tried. And Daisy just shook her head as if she wasn't surprised. I knew she didn't believe me in class and she was right not to trust me.

Reid noticed my hand tense and followed my gaze to Daisy and Leo. Clearing his throat, he separated his hand from mine and grabbed our coffees from the window, acting like he didn't even know me. But it was too late, and we both knew it. After quickly sharing a look, I felt like my body jerked awake.

"I-um." I nervously looked back and forth between my fake life and my real one. "Uhh…bathroom," I said to no one and sprinted as fast as my feet could carry me through the crowds of customers. I wanted to escape both lives. I no longer wanted to pretend that I wasn't falling for Reid and doubting myself every step of the way in our investigation. I no longer wanted to lie to Daisy, a true friend that was showing me there was more to life than my lost sister, and Leo, someone who didn't deserve what I was putting him through.

I was tired of lying to everyone. I was tired of lying to myself. I wanted to bury myself in a hole. I wanted to hide behind my sister.

Running into the bathroom, I splashed some cold water on my face to settle my nerves, though I felt like I was about to burst.

Not long after, the bathroom door flung open and slammed the wall as Reid flew inside, hardly bothering to mask the invisible space between his feet and the floor. He hovered a few extra centimeters higher than usual as he locked the door and approached me.

"Calm down. The more you overreact, the worse this looks. We just came here to discuss your grade." He was by my side, taking deep breaths with me. "Remember why we came here. Remember what truly matters."

Nodding, I wiped my face with a paper towel and matched his breathing rhythm. He was right. Worse crimes have been committed than going to a coffee shop with a TA. We came here for a reason. We had a mission to complete.

As I looked up at him to inform him I was ready to go back out, I noticed movement in the mirror. One of the stalls right beside us was cracking open too slowly to be normal, and I saw glimmering eyes staring right at us.

Right at Reid. As I saw the eyes bulge, I acted before I could even think.

"Look out!" I exclaimed while pushing Reid with as much force as I could muster, while the stall door flung open, and the Faerie barista with wings flew out while aiming at him with a boiling cup of coffee.

Reid, completely taken by surprise, fell backward, but caught himself before he planted his ass to the ground and picked himself back up.

The boiling hot coffee spilled all over my top in the process, the hot coffee seeping through my shirt and burning my skin. Screaming out in pain, I clung to my arm as the Faerie kept his blazing eyes on Reid, his true target, and lunged again.

Reid was more prepared this time and using reflexes I never

knew existed, pulling a blade out of his boots and stabbed the barista right through the eye. The barista gurgled as if he were choking before falling backward, his unseeing eyes staring at the ceiling. Reid hardly looked at the Faerie before getting some cold water on my burning skin. My flesh was searing to the touch, and everything hurt. Furious tears spilled down my face.

"Make it stop," I sobbed, not knowing what I meant by that. Reid stilled, his eyes widening.

Without any hesitation, his lips crashed on mine as both his hands grasped my cheeks and held my head tenderly. This kiss was nothing like last night. Last night was full of lust, or pretend lust, or unrequited lust, or whatever it was.

This kiss had a purpose, and I sensed it with each passing second as the pain began to fade and I was able to move my arm again without it feeling like it was being torched. He was healing me.

A few moments later, he pulled away and quickly assessed me. My shirt was completely stained with the hot coffee, but my skin was back to its normal color. My face lost its splotchy redness and puffiness from the tears.

"Better?" He asked me, determination lacing his features.

"Yes. Thank you." I looked over at the dead barista and almost did a double-take. He no longer looked human, and I was sure that Reid's kiss gave me true vision. The barista looked like a shriveled-up old man with scars all over his face, his pointy ears sticking out of his hair.

Blood seeped down his cheek as the blade protruded from his face, a grisly sight to see.

Reid was completely unfazed as he placed his leg on the man's chest to level himself and pull the blade out of the eye. I had to look away as the sight of the man's head was starting to resemble ground meat, and I could feel my breakfast making its way back up.

Reid quickly rinsed the blade and tucked it securely back in his boot. The same blade that slashed Raine's throat underwater in Central Park. Who knew how many other things Reid killed with that blade?

"We can't just leave him here." I was starting to get panicky. Jail time would certainly impinge on my mission. Our mission.

Reid hesitated. "I'll have to eat him."

My jaw dropped. "Are you serious?"

"No, I'm choosing now as a time to fuck with you. Yes, I'm serious," he snapped at me.

Shutting my mouth, I crossed my arms. We had no choice. We couldn't risk being seen like this and charged with murder.

Watching Reid fall to his knees a few inches off the ground beside the body, I felt like I was about to heave again.

"Will it take long?" I dared to ask.

"I'm not eating with my mouth. Like I told you before, it requires magic. Just don't interrupt me and make sure no one comes in." He turned back to the body and took a deep breath.

A part of me wanted to watch, while another part wanted to run away and hide. Curiosity got the better of me as I saw the most unusual thing in my life.

The entire process must have taken five minutes or less. I watched as Reid's body glowed more than ever, his magical sheen expanding to coat the corpse. The corpse started to look like it was glitching and twitching, before becoming intangible and soaking into the sheen, before disappearing completely, every drop of blood along with it.

As if it never existed.

When Reid stood up in his tall frame, he looked anything but human. His cheeks were fuller, his shoulders broader, his eyes smarter. A true predator. An overcasting shadow trailed behind him, shimmering ever so slightly in his wake. He was full of magic, and we both knew it. As he looked at me, I knew we were thinking the same exact thing - all our progress since last night, wiped away. He'd not only restored his magic but enhanced it by consuming this creature.

We were back at square one.

But at least we knew the limits of him ingesting my matter, as he liked to put it. And we knew we had to keep dulling his magic before we could reach the second step.

"You saved me," he said.

"Huh?" He was the one who healed me and got rid of this nasty thing.

"You pushed me out of the way."

Oh.

Well, yes. I did.

"Of course, I know you'd have done the same."

His hesitation not only disappointed me but confirmed how little I meant to him.

I was ready to throw in the towel and just give up on the entire mission just to spare my weak heart until he gave me a long look and said, "You're everything she wasn't."

Unsure of what he meant by that, I unlocked the door and gestured for him to follow me. A line of people waiting by the door groaned and glared at us, obviously assuming the worst, as we awkwardly walked past them.

Right before we got to the door, I noticed Daisy and Leo staring at me from a table not too far away. They'd seen us exit the bathroom. There was no hiding it.

But this time, I didn't want to cower and run away. I had to own it, especially since they didn't know the truth. Let them assume the worst as long as they were alive and safe. Reid and I left Kaffeine and I wondered if they'd ever forgive me. If I could ever tell them the truth.

But before I could dwell much on the topic, Reid said, "I was wrong about step one. The only way we can get to Naerin is to skip to step two."

NINETEEN

After our series of unfortunate events at Kaffeine, I was the first to suggest we revisit Dumbo at the same spot I saw my sister in the water my first day in New York. I'd come to realize that Reid had already eliminated the beings connected to three places on the bucket list already. Raine, who'd pushed me off the roof at Glitz, then tried to drown me by Loeb Boathouse. The Faerie, who aimed to maim Reid in Kaffeine.

"Just don't get any ideas about killing my sister if she pops up again in Dumbo," I'd said, recalling my hallucination from my first night in New York. A large part of me hoped she'd come since I'd be able to find out what happened to her.

"And if she tries to kill you?" He'd responded.

"She won't."

"But what if she does?"

"She *won't.*"

If we saw my sister again, I'd have some inclination about her safety and any information about Naerin. If we didn't, then perhaps we'd discover something else together.

And so the following day, we set out to walk across the Brooklyn Bridge and scout the area where I had my first hallucination before even meeting Reid.

It was an unusually warm day, especially considering it was nearing the end of January. I was careful not to dress in too many layers in case something else tried to drown me today, though I had no intention of going close to the water.

While we walked together, I occasionally glanced down the bridge, thinking I might spot movement in the water.

"Why do you think the barista targeted you while Raine targeted me?" I said to get the ball rolling and hopefully fill in the missing bits and pieces in my swarming nest of questions.

Reid was dressed even lighter than me, a short-sleeved green shirt hugging against his torso, contrasting his signature boots that undoubtedly concealed the blade he always carried with him. At this rate, I rathered he had it than not.

He quickly glanced around before responding, "It's possible you were Marked already and Raine was trying to scare you and make you paranoid before the Keeper came for you, like the others."

Reid looked behind us, his jaw clenched. "Not that I'm any safer. I know I'm being followed." His head turned to me and his urgent tone was imperative. "We don't have much time before we are captured. We have to get to my country first if we want to live through this."

"Will you tell me the second step then?"

Reid stopped and walked over to the fence. We were halfway across the Brooklyn Bridge by now. The warm weather and sinking sun made for a perfect walk. If the circumstances were any different, I'd imagine us on our first date. Getting to know each other's likes and dislikes. Does he like olives? The pulp in his orange juice?

My wandering thoughts brought sadness to my face before I could conceal it. Looking over the fence, I watched the city hum and the skyscraper lights turn on. The sun was close to disappearing behind the buildings, and the sky was straight out of a painting - red, orange, and pink tones washed across the canvas, reflecting off the windows.

Reid didn't want to tell me the second step. I could tell. But we didn't have time to play games anymore, not with the bullseye on both our backs. Yet he still had a knack for keeping his information to himself, despite the urgency. By now, I'd learned the best way to gain his knowledge was to be as stubborn as him.

"Reid, look at me."

His unfairly handsome face met mine. His hair looked like the sun's rays specifically reached down and painted it as a personal masterpiece. His striking green eyes were bright enough to pierce right through me, but I wasn't scared of them. Of him.

His thick eyebrows were drawn together as he observed every inch of my face.

"I'm not sure if you're aware, but if you don't tell me the second step, we won't be able to do it."

He scoffed. "Look at you, explaining something to me." But he was smiling. He liked when I played his game. Spoke his language. To my surprise, I liked it too. I liked when he brought out passions within me I didn't know existed. Before I met him, I wasn't one to have outbursts. But when I was with him, I felt alive. I felt like my soul came to the surface and wasn't hiding behind anyone. Behind *her*.

"You're right," he sighed before his eyes darted to mine and he raised an eyebrow. "For once." Even his sarcasm was starting to dull down. I had to keep pushing.

"Will you tell me or not?"

Reid's eyebrows scrunched together more, tainting his flawless face, creating lines that shouldn't have been there. "You have to understand something first."

"I'm listening."

He leaned in close and lowered his voice. "Eating the Faerie was a major setback and we won't have time to slowly dull my magic again. I didn't expect my magic to bounce back tenfold like that. Only goes to show I'll need one huge overdose to decrease it fast."

Nodding, I responded, "I've gathered all that. I assume that's where step two comes in."

"You should be able to guess what it is already."

My thoughts went into overdrive. If it were that obvious, I shouldn't even be asking.

I went through everything in my head again.

Reid's magic was dulled by ingesting human matter. The way he put it, it waxed and waned opposite from Naerin. When he ingested the Faerie, his magic came back. Us kissing only gave a minuscule dose of dulled magic, as we could tell by him feeling heavier and me seeing his true self while being slightly lighter.

He needed an overdose of matter. And he didn't seem to want to eat a human the way he ate the Faerie. If he did, he wouldn't have left Naerin in the first place.

If a kiss was a small dose, what would be an overdose?

I stared between his eyes, searching for answers, even though it felt like it was staring me right in the face. Either my mind didn't want to accept it and I was being willfully ignorant, or it was dangling right within reach and I had to just open my eyes and grab it.

You have to really be into it. Otherwise it won't work.

How much more would I have to be really into it to give him an overdose-level blast of magic dulling power if a kiss wasn't enough? What other way could we be connected without him eating me and long enough to follow the path back to Naerin?

Unless—

Oh.

Oh.

"You mean…I have to…we have to…" I couldn't even finish the sentence.

Reid gave me a pained look before nodding slowly as if the idea tormented him, and I knew exactly why. Not only did he hardly tolerate me, but he also loved another.

"We don't *just* have to 'do it,'" he said while using his hands for quotation marks. "We both have to finish. Together."

I was about to ask him why and opened my mouth, but I quickly closed it. I wouldn't be able to handle a sarcastic answer, and the more I thought about it, the more I understood. If he finished inside me, we would be connected for days, which would secure our passage without the path flickering out halfway. That part made perfect sense. But what I didn't get…

"Why do I have to finish for it to work?" Societal double standards be damned, I had to ask.

Reid's lips twitched. "Because our souls have to connect, and we both have to give a hundred percent. There won't be enough juice to fuel the blast, otherwise." He gave a small chuckle. "Out of everything you could have said, that was your question?"

My cheeks reddened and I started walking ahead of him, remembering when he'd said that the more hormones I produced, the stronger the matter would be.

"The sun is setting. Hurry up. Put some pep in your step," I responded hastily, hiding my face and getting a few steps ahead.

I felt him behind me, though his steps were lighter than a feather. He didn't bother catching up to me, and for that, I was thankful. He was giving me some time. Letting the second step sit with me until it no longer held any power over me. I was glad he had that much decency, at least. I mean, along with killing other people for me, and stuff.

He let me get to the end of the bridge and step into Brooklyn before matching my step.

"Where exactly did you see your sister?" He asked as we rounded the road and walked along the cobblestone streets.

"This way, by the park." I led him toward the picture-perfect scenic lawn beside the bridge that displayed New York like a gem.

I could finally understand why he waited so long for me to know the second step. I could only imagine how much he detested the idea himself and how he was still letting it sit with him.

Before long, we reached the same bench I was occupying when I'd heard the group of teenagers talking about the disappearance, my mother called, and I heard Vita calling my name.

A small part of me was nervous to see her again. What if it wasn't actually her, and the creature was violent and murderous? I didn't know if I could withstand that. We sat on the bench, overlooking the sparkling lights ahead. My eyes were trained on the waters in the same spot I'd seen my sister before.

"What was she like?" My question felt like a blade I was dragging along my skin, not quite hard enough to cut but sharp enough to hurt.

Reid's eyes were sad and far away. "I thought she and I could rule the world together until she was stolen from me."

Despite my conflicting feelings, I was sad for him. I knew what it felt like to have someone stolen from me.

"I'm sorry."

Reid gave me a long look, and I couldn't tell if he wanted to lash out with a sarcastic remark or just open up, for once in his life. Who better to vent to than someone going through something similar?

"I'd light the world on fire for her."

"I know." I'd light the world on fire for Vita, even if I wasn't strong enough to light the match.

"We're so alike, but have the worst things in common." He was looking at the water too, his eyes distant as if he were caught in a memory. A positive or negative one, I wasn't sure.

This mysterious, faceless girl who held Reid's heart in her palm had her own flaws. The same flaws as him. Was she unfairly beautiful? Sarcastic? Have a thirst for danger? Would slay someone without a second thought?

I could never imagine the kind of girl that would be good enough for him, but that one statement alone told me enough. Reid didn't like to be bored. He loved adventure. A girl by his side who could not only keep up with him but challenge him past his limits. This girl checked all the boxes to a fault. Perhaps she had no limits. Perhaps they could never just sit down and have a normal conversation.

Were they like Chuck and Blair? Toxic but hopelessly passionate to the point where they created flames from their love? Or were they like Carrie and Big? Always trying to run away from each other, only to end up together, against their best judgment?

My next question was deep enough to cut this time. "Do you still love her?"

"Always," his response was faster than the crack of a whip. "But you know what that's like. With your sister."

"Yes, of course. She's the most important person in my life," I said without hesitation.

"Why?"

Taken aback, I repeated, "*Why?*"

"Yeah. Is it just because she's your sister?" He tore his eyes from the water and observed me.

"No." My tone was fiercer than I expected. "She's not like other people. She's not just a face in the crowds. This is her world and we are all living in it."

"You sound like a side character in her story."

"It's not like that." Reid didn't get it. It was different comparing a romantic love to a deeper-than-family one. "She looks out for me in a way no one else can. She knows me better than I know myself. I'd do anything for her. I just want her back." My voice cracked on the last sentence and I angrily looked away, not in the mood to be mocked.

To my surprise, Reid pulled my face back by the chin and gave me a long look. "You have a good heart. She's lucky to have you as a sister."

Hearing these words from him made them feel loud and true, considering he wasn't the type to dish out warm words.

"Careful there, I almost didn't catch the sarcasm." I couldn't believe his words were genuine. Reid was too good at acting like he didn't have any real feelings.

But this time, his face wasn't changing. He had a pained look on his face. Maybe he was thinking about his girlfriend. Maybe he was experiencing empathy for the first time in his life. Maybe he just pitied me. I never really knew with him.

If anything, he seemed a little surprised. "I wasn't being sarcastic."

I couldn't get too used to this tender side of Reid, it was dangerous. Especially considering the flutter I felt from his touch. I never would've thought I'd end up sitting here and bonding with Reid over our shared losses. Out of everything we experienced together, this had to be the most intimate moment we ever shared.

I was about to say something else until I noticed something moving in my peripheral vision. At first, I thought it was a crow or raven and didn't pay much mind. But then I realized crows and ravens weren't common in New York City.

My eyes whipped to the bird, and I realized it was something completely different.

"Reid, look." I pointed in the direction and his eyes followed my gaze.

The object was certainly flying, and I saw black wings, but it was definitely not a bird. It was a small Faerie, about the size of my hand. I could barely make out her pointy ears and long hair until she zipped away quickly and was too far out of sight.

"Faerie?" I asked him.

"Yes."

"Why was this one small? Why were her wings black?" This Faerie looked nothing like the one from Kaffeine, who was a human-sized male with iridescent and see-through wings. This one had a shimmery aura surrounding her, though it was tinted black, like her black see-through wings.

I was especially surprised that she didn't try to attack or kill us. On the contrary, she seemed like she was in a hurry to get somewhere and flew right past us without a second glance. She was already long gone, somewhere in the direction of lower Manhattan.

Reid was deep in thought. "Because the one from Kaffeine was a threat and sent to harm us. This one came straight from Naerin."

"I thought only the Keeper could come and go."

"I thought so, too." Reid did not sound happy. "I think it means the Keeper is getting closer and sending spies."

"Then why was she flying away from us?"

"She probably already saw us and is on her way to tell the Keeper about our location." Reid quickly stood up and pulled me up too. "We should go. It's not good to stay in one location too long."

Longingly glancing toward the water, I yearned to see my sister again. "But what about—"

"No," he interjected briskly. "If we haven't seen her by now, she's not coming. Come on." He tugged my arm and we headed back to the city. Sadness washed over me. I'd gotten my hopes up. I really thought I'd see her again. Even if she tried to kill me, I hoped I'd see her. I wondered if I ever saw her to begin with. Maybe that was a real hallucination. I hadn't met Reid yet, hence I probably wasn't Marked by proxy yet. Maybe I was actually crazy.

"Did the black wings mean she was dangerous?" I asked while we sped up our pace to the train.

"No. Faeries are harmless unless provoked. I think she was just sent as a spy."

We barely caught the train and slipped inside seconds before the doors closed and it started moving.

Hoping I would continue the momentum, I kept going. "Why are some Faeries small and others large?"

"Are you calling me fat?" There it was. The famous sarcasm. Here we go.

Giving up, I changed tactics. "What about the first step? Are we discarding it completely?"

"If you wanted to kiss me so badly, you should've just said so."

Clamming up, I pursed my lips. I liked Reid better when he was being real with me. But beggars couldn't be choosers. "You know what I mean."

After considering it for a moment, he said, "Might be better to keep it up. Hopefully build my tolerance for that big blast when it happens, and get used to the idea."

He had a point. It would all be for nothing if the overdose knocked him out and left him unable to make the trip to Naerin. In addition, we had to make sure we could take it all the way for it to work. I wouldn't know what to do with myself if we took that step now, and the more we kissed, the more comfortable I'd get. At least, I hoped so.

We found ourselves in my apartment soon after.

I found myself on his lips not long after that.

TWENTY

The next morning, I woke up knowing Reid was gone. Last night, after we concluded our "appointment", I noticed I was able to sense where he went, almost as if I felt an invisible tug. I supposed that meant we were connected temporarily by way of him dulling his magic by giving me some of it. I wondered if he felt a pull to me too.

My window was wide open, another clear indicator. He must've slipped away at some point in the night or morning, or whenever he felt like it.

Closing my window and throwing on a warm sweatshirt, I rubbed my eyes and tried not to think about last night. My lips were still swollen from our session.

For a moment, I wondered what the distinction was between exchanging saliva or blood. Perhaps blood would be stronger, but it would also be painful and unpleasant to me. And I'd have to drink his blood too, and I wasn't aware I was part of a vampire adventure. Just a Faerie one, for now.

Putting some chapstick over my lip, I realized how much I still didn't know about him and Naerin. I hoped he was warming up to me enough to trust me with more information. I couldn't imagine going to Naerin with him and not knowing what I was walking into. He owed me that much. Especially because of that massive second step that he dropped on me like a bomb. Well, I dropped it on myself like a bomb, after I'd pieced it together. But still.

What would Vita say if she knew about all this?

Closing my eyes, I imagined she was sitting next to me. She'd have woken up looking flawless as always, a mug of hot lemon tea in her hands to start off the day. She'd be wearing her favorite pastel silk pajamas and fuzzy pink slippers. The corners of her mouth would be slightly upturned, and she'd twiddle her fingers the way she usually did when her hands felt restless.

"What do you care, he's insanely hot. Plus, there's no strings attached since you know he has someone else," she'd say.

"But my feelings are the problem. I don't want to complicate things," I thought back to her in my head.

I imagined her throwing her hair behind her shoulder and shaking her head. "Then you know you're the problem. Let go of your feelings, live in the moment, and know that this is just physical."

I'd have rested my neck on her shoulder and sighed deeply. "Vita, you know I can't do that the way you can. I wish I could."

"Then repurpose your mindset. Remind yourself why you have to do this," she'd have said in a matter-of-fact tone. By now, she'd probably be getting frustrated with me since the answer was so obvious in her head.

"To save you," I'd say, before sitting back up again and grabbing her hand. "I'd do it to save you."

She'd fix my hair or pluck some lint off my shirt. "So you'll be my hero, my savior, and also get a good fuck out of it. Remind me what's the bad part again?"

I'd laugh and shake my head. "Only you can take a bad situation and make it sound like a good one."

She'd light up, smiling widely. "Anytime, sis." She'd lean in close and give me a wink. "Don't tell me you're not curious about the size of his package."

"Okay, okay," I'd say and look away shyly.

After opening my eyes and returning to reality, a small smile stayed on my lips. I made some lemon tea in her honor and spent the morning thinking about how great it would be to see her again.

When I sat down to drink the tea, my phone buzzed in my hand. Unlocking it, I saw a text from Reid.

Grading papers today. Do me a favor and try not to die. See you tonight for our appointment.

I sent back a thumbs up emoji before throwing my phone beside me, not wanting to think about our appointment. We were still going to be sticking to the first step for now, but I knew I wouldn't have much time to prepare for step two.

Each passing day was another opportunity to be scouted by a Syren, Faerie or feral little boy, and who knew what other creatures were next? Each passing second was another moment for the Keeper to find us and bring us both back to Naerin to be executed. From the way Reid made it sound, the soul-eating process was far from pleasant, and I'd be better off slitting my throat rather than endure it.

Maybe I should just suck it up, listen to my imaginary sister, and take the second step. Be done with it. Go forth onto the path, march into Naerin, save my sister and his girlfriend.

Yet here I was, stalling and stalling.

I'd only known Reid for three weeks, but it felt like we were thrown into something where every second where you don't know if you'll live or die feels like an eternity. We've survived countless things together. We entered hellfire together. We're both risking death. Would it really be so bad to take the plunge while we still could?

I could only imagine how horrible it would be if the Keeper beat us to it and we were too late when all we had to do was just jump into bed together.

But one more day couldn't hurt. The Keeper was already biding their time by sending spies and threats left and right, making sure we were cornered at every turn. Two of the Keeper's spies were killed in the process.

I had to believe I had more time.

When I finished my lemon tea, I decided to reach out to Daisy and Leo and make sure things were good between us. I wanted to honor our pact and make sure they did too. They didn't have to know the extra details to cast aside the judgment of seeing me with my TA.

Hey guys, I typed and pressed send. Immediately after, I sent a follow up text. *Lunch at 1?*

A few minutes passed before Leo sent a *sure* and Daisy *ok.*

I knew they weren't happy with me. I was hardly happy with me. But I couldn't go to Naerin before making sure I still had my friends. If I ended up turning dead, I'd want someone to miss me, as selfish as that was.

After quickly getting ready, throwing on some light makeup, and pulling my hair back into a messy bun, I wore a pink tank top with a long black cardigan over it. Pink wasn't my preferred color, but I always felt like Vita was with me whenever I wore it. Though after the stern talk she had with me in my head, I wasn't sure I wanted Vita with me right now. I was already putting her words to shame by not heeding them.

If she were in my place, I know she'd have seduced Reid and have him wrapped around her finger, before discarding him once she was done with him.

I walked out the door knowing I had a lot of explaining to do. Unfortunately, I had no idea how I would twist the truth to make it make sense, especially since my reality hardly made sense anymore.

I saw the two of them walking near the campus entrance where we'd agreed to meet. Initially, I was ready to call out excitedly and run up to them, until I saw the looks on their faces when they spotted me.

Disappointment. Betrayal. Unhappiness.

A massive cocktail of emotions splayed over both their faces. Just like at Insomnia cookies, I noticed how similar they looked when they were both feeling extremely similar things.

Cowering back slightly, I swallowed the lump in my throat and tried my best to play it cool. There was only so much worse it could get from this point on.

Also, from the standpoint of future me, yes, I jinxed it.

"Hey," I said as we reached each other. "I was going to go study in the library for a bit, but I'm pretty hungry now."

They shared a not-so-discreet look.

"Yeah," Daisy said at the same time as Leo said, "Sounds good."

I never liked when tension hung in the air. Whenever Vita was mad at me and didn't speak to me for a few days, those days were the worst. I wasn't one to handle them well.

"Guys, please. I know you're mad at me, and I know I messed up. Can we talk about it?" I didn't care how desperate or pathetic I sounded. I just wanted things to be normal with us.

Leo gave a strained smile and said, "I just thought you were different."

Ouch. I deserved that.

Daisy added, "If you were just honest with us…" and trailed off, shaking her head.

"I know. I'm sorry. It wasn't fair to you guys." Lowering my face to the ground, I thought about how I could make things better.

"How about lunch on me and we can talk about it?" I offered halfheartedly, knowing my lies were far from over.

They were both sullen as they trudged behind me to the campus library. There was a coffee shop inside that was pretty subpar, and on any normal day, I'm sure Daisy and I would've come up with a dozen bad coffee puns already. But now was not the time. Now, I just had to reach into my pathetic need to be needed and have my friends forgive me. Have someone care when I died trying to save my sister.

I hoped I could smooth things over with them and make sure that when I departed to Naerin, they'd care.

The coffee shop barista, a petite girl with long black hair, informed me they didn't offer pumpkin, and I begrudgingly ordered a chai latte instead, grumbling under my breath. After ordering Daisy's favorite, a caramel macchiato, and Leo's favorite, a flat white, I picked up a few sandwiches as well as a bag of chips and pretzels. Once I collected all our drinks and peace treaty snacks, I joined Daisy and Leo in a nearby booth.

As hard as Daisy tried to hide it, I sensed a small appreciative nod toward her favorite drink, which she accepted graciously. Sending her a warm smile, I hoped I could get my intentions across.

Daisy sighed. "Alright, fine. You have the stage. Go on and explain yourself."

I pretended my latte was alcoholic and took a shot for good measure and good fortune, before jumping into the version of the truth that made the most sense - the one where I wasn't lying, just omitting details.

"The truth is…Reid and I aren't in a relationship. Honestly, he has a long distance girlfriend that he adores, and they're on and off. We bonded over some stuff and kissed in the heat of the moment, but we have no interest in getting together."

Was it the heat of the moment, or was it the magic surrounding him that made him taste like ecstasy and light my skin on fire?

"Then why did you make it sound like you would give me a chance?" Leo sounded awfully accusatory, and I wondered if honesty was something both him and Daisy valued dearly. Noticing Daisy protectively lean over her twin brother, I swallowed the lump in my throat.

"I thought I understood my feelings." I looked him directly in the eye. "But I was lying to myself. I played with fire, thinking we were just connecting over a loss, and then one thing led to another and…" Trailing off, I sighed.

"Then what were you doing in the Kaffeine bathroom together?" Daisy asked, her arms crossed.

The one question I hoped we could avoid, because there was no way I could answer it honestly, though I tried to take bits and pieces of the truth.

"When I saw you guys, I felt really guilty and ran away like a coward. He followed me to see if I was alright." Yeah, and then we were attacked by a barista Faerie and I was burned and Reid stabbed him and consumed him like a slab of meat. But yeah, we talked about our feelings too.

Leo munched on some chips. "Are you still going to see him?"

"Yeah," was all I could say. Not much else to offer. "But I won't lie about it."

Daisy frowned. "He's taking advantage of you."

Nervously gulping down some more chai, I said, "The winter semester will be over soon. Our relationship has no relation to my grade. Either way, we aren't together. I have no interest in being with him." Why did that part sound like a lie?

"Please forgive me for not being honest. I'm figuring everything out along the way, and I messed up in the process. I don't want to hurt you guys. You're my friends. I haven't forgotten about the pact." I pushed the bag of pretzels into the center. "Please accept my peace treaty. I'm waving the white flag here."

Leo sighed. "I did say I'd be patient, but it seems like there's nothing to wait for. Right?"

Shrinking into my seat, I twiddled my fingers. "Probably not. But I would still like to remain friends if you're willing."

Daisy was waiting for Leo to give the final call. They shared a look before Leo turned back to me and reached for his flat white. "Thank you for being honest. I forgive you."

Daisy uncrossed her arms. "I forgive you too."

A wave of relief washed over me. I really appreciated how Daisy and Leo were accepting and forgiving. I was used to the way Vita wouldn't speak to me for days over less.

"Now that we got that out of the way, tell me, what's new with you guys?" I threw some chips in my mouth.

Daisy sat upright and looked at Leo quickly for silent permission, before saying, "Actually, we have big news. You'll never guess what Leo—"

"Hi! Sorry to interrupt, but did you want anything else before we close the cafe before dinner?" Recognizing the petite barista's voice, I was ready to tell her we were fine and pleasantly plump from our helping of chips and caffeinated cups.

I still had the straw in my mouth when I turned to her and almost choked on the chai in my mouth.

It was happening again.

She was no plain barista. Her skin was blue and her eyes were black. She gave me a knowing smile, as if she were calculatedly watching my every move. Coughing and feeling the drink go down the wrong throat, I knew I had to be careful and not give anything away in front of the others. It was hard enough with the feral little boy that turned out to be a homeless man at Insomnia Cookies. The best I could do was pretend I accidentally choked.

"Hey, Alluna, are you okay?" Leo sounded concerned as he

reached around and firmly rapped my back. Nodding and feeling my face go red from all the attention on me, I calmed down. Collected myself. Poker face plastered.

"Yeah, I'm alright. We're good here, right guys?" Smiling casually, I acted like I wasn't terrified for my life since Reid and his hidden blade weren't here to protect me should this Syren decide to kill me.

Leo and Daisy nodded simultaneously, hardly paying attention, and pulled out their phones.

Smiling sweetly at the Syren, I pushed the empty bag of chips toward her. "We are done with these, actually."

The Syren's obsidian eyes were black and cold as she scooped up the bag and crinkled it under her long, black fingernails.

"I was looking for your TA, actually. Have you seen him?" Her monotone voice lacked any hint of defeat.

I was more than ready to play.

Daisy looked up from her phone. "Alluna, didn't you mention he was—"

"No," I interrupted, feeling the Syren's eyes burning into my head. "It wasn't Reid I was talking about." Daisy gave me a weird look but didn't question it, returning to her phone.

Laughing politely, I answered, "He *is* impossible to track, isn't he?" Knowing my double entendre was equally as satisfying to me as it was infuriating to the Syren, my grin only widened when she squeezed the bag of chips harder.

Her voice was razor sharp. "It is very important that I find him.

Are you sure you don't know where he is?"

She was no match for me. I would never give him up, and I made that very clear. "I'm not sure why you think I'd know, but even if I did, I wouldn't tell you."

"Alluna!" Daisy exclaimed, before whispering, "Don't be rude!"

A smile flickered on the Syren's perfect face. "I'm sure I can find him myself. Sorry for bothering you." She slipped away as Daisy smacked my shoulder.

"What has gotten into you? She was just asking a simple question."

I slumped into my seat, twiddling my fingers the way Vita did. "Just got bad vibes from her, is all," I mumbled.

Leo turned over and watched the Syren walk away. "I think I'll ask her out."

Daisy planted a smack on his shoulder. "Stop embarrassing me! You don't have to ask out every single female that gives you attention."

He rubbed his shoulder and grumbled, "She has a nice ass."

I could feel my nerves start to rack up, knowing the Syren was hunting Reid now. Why didn't I point her in the wrong direction to save her time? I could've said he went to Connecticut and gotten rid of her. Instead, I made a fool of myself. Put on a show in front of my friends for something they didn't even understand.

"So, as we were saying, you'll never guess what Leo did!" Daisy said.

Leo smiled sheepishly. "I finally told my mom I wasn't in medical school."

"Oh, my gosh!" I clapped and hugged him tightly. "That's amazing! I know that wasn't easy for you. How'd she take it?"

Daisy and Leo exchanged a glance. "She's not speaking to either of us. She thinks I convinced him to drop out and that I'm a bad influence." Daisy's delicate shoulders slumped.

I grabbed her hand and squeezed it. "Your mom will understand someday that he made his own choice. She just needs time."

"You don't know our mom. She's like the devil when it comes to this sort of thing," Leo said.

Smirking, I responded, "I know the type."

We finished off our drinks and parted ways at the library desktops nearby, where we spent the next few hours studying.

When I came home, I was ready to meet Reid for our "appointment" and tell him about the Syren.

But he was already inside my apartment when I came in.

And he was definitely livid.

"There you are," he snarled, before sliding up to me, throwing me against the wall, his hand pressing against my throat. "I'm going to kill you."

TWENTY-ONE

Struggling to gasp some air into my lungs, I choked out, "What?" Feeling his thumbs press into the sides of my neck, I felt myself growing weaker while I tried hitting his chest.

"Do you realize what you did?" He asked softly, towering over me, using his advantage of strength against me.

"N-no…" my voice came out strangled. Would this really be the end?

Reid finally released me and I fell to my knees, grasping my throat, and coughing up a lung.

He kneeled next to me and lifted my chin up at him. "You're nothing but a weakness. A liability. This was a mistake."

Keeping my hands around my throat protectively, I muttered,

"What on earth are you talking about?"

His scoff was enough to break the illusion I had about us. The one where we could actually get along, he didn't hate me, and having feelings for him wasn't a mistake.

Reid pulled me up, giving me a pathetic look that made me want to crawl inside my own skin. "I was followed because of you."

"By the small Syren?" My voice was raw, hoarse. He gave a small nod, looking at me down his nose as if he couldn't stand the sight of me. "I-I don't understand. I was loyal. I didn't give anything away about you."

Reid suddenly pressed against me, backing me straight into the wall, his forearm pressing against my throat, his eyes blazing. "And that's exactly why you're weak. You admitted you knew me. You taunted the Syren. Don't you think that gives away more than my location?"

"I-I…"

"I-I," he mockingly whined. "Yes, you." His arm pressed harder.

The moment I started seeing black spots in my vision, I knew it was time to fight back. There was no mercy from Reid. Only tough love and leveling the playing field. He didn't get to just walk all over me like this. I didn't know the customs in Naerin, but I would not tolerate this physical abuse.

My knee went exactly where it was meant to go - right into his groin, hard and fast. Reid winced, his eyes widening, before releasing me and backing away. He knew his game was over.

But I wasn't done playing.

Balling my fists, I could feel my anger rising. "You have no right to come into my apartment and choke me." Pointing my finger at him, I made no effort to lower my voice. "You have no one else but me. I don't have to help you. I have no obligation. I'm over here trying to make this work and be civil with you, but you've been nothing but an arrogant ass."

Reid crossed his arms, but didn't respond. Maybe he wanted to see how far he pushed me.

I was far from done. "I stayed *loyal* to you and didn't give your location away. I did what I thought was best at that moment. Besides, we were already spotted together by the black winged Faerie, among other spies. It's no secret we hang out together. So I don't see what I did that was so terrible to deserve this!"

Reid lifted a few extra centimeters off the ground as if he already wasn't tall enough.

"Clearly, I have to spell it out for you since you still don't get it." He gravitated closer to me. "Wouldn't it be in your best interest to act like you're my hostage and helping me unwillingly? When the Syren found me, she knew there was something going on between us. I don't know what you told her, but you definitely got that message across. If the Keeper finds out about our plan and the three steps, we are done for."

I was speechless. Was he really saying…

"Are you saying you care about me?"

He clammed up for once. He didn't want to admit it, even though his words were confirmation enough.

I couldn't believe him. "You didn't want the Syren to know you cared about me and your solution is to come here and choke me?"

He brushed a lock of hair behind my ear, sending wildfire down my back at his touch.

"What happened to the Syren?" I looked up at him.

Reaching into his boot, he pulled out his blade, covered in dried black-red blood. His eyes were trained on mine as he pressed the blade against my throat gently. The blade covered in the Syren's blood.

"Don't ever forget who you're dealing with," he whispered. My breath caught in my throat and I shut my eyes tightly, afraid of Reid. Afraid of how excited I was feeling. Afraid of the adventure he pumped through my veins. Afraid of how turned on I was.

"Duly noted."

The tip of the blade disappeared from my neck. He tucked it back into his boot and stepped away from me, facing my window.

"You have to be smarter about what you say. You can't just act all proud that you know where I am. The Syren read between the lines."

Against the moonlight, Reid looked like a shadow. His silhouette was as still as a painting, illuminated by the faint shimmers I could barely make out against the air. It had been a day since we last kissed. The magic had just about worn off by now, his aura barely discernible. But I wondered if something stayed with him every time we kissed. Something more than just magic.

"Did you eat her too?"

He shook his head, a few strands of his auburn hair shimmering in the moonlight. "I don't have time to eat everyone that stands in our way - we'd never get to Naerin that way."

"Touché."

He turned back to me. "I think there's another thing we need to do."

Clutching my throat, I managed, "Oh? Step four?"

"No. Not in that way." Reid's eyes roamed over me before settling on my face. "There might be situations where you won't have time to think - only act."

"What are you getting at?"

He straightened his shoulders. "If we are ever surrounded or need to flee, you have to trust me and jump."

I cocked my head. "Jump where?"

Reid's wicked smile was capturing my heart and holding it hostage. There was something about his canines that made me want him to bite my lip. "I can show you better than I can tell you."

Subconsciously backing away from him out of fear I'd launch my mouth into his, I reminded myself that this man - this Faerie just held me in a chokehold. I should have been angry. But against all reason, I was incredibly aroused.

"It's dark outside." His face was one of mischief as he started leading me by the hand to the window.

I didn't understand the punchline. "Yeah?" I prodded, wanting to be in on the joke.

"Like I said, trust me." We stopped by my window as he unlatched it, opening it all the way. With one foot on the fire escape outside, he held his hand out to me.

"Take my hand." Obeying instantly, my hand was on his. He effortlessly lifted me out to the fire escape that was dangerously high above the street on my eighth floor. Suppressing a shiver, my heart hammered in my chest. Don't look down, don't look down…

I looked down.

Fear tormented me as intrusive thoughts invaded my mind. How long would it take me to slip? A second, really. And the fall? Maybe another second. In total? Just two seconds for me to break all my bones and be dead and gone.

Reid steadied me, holding my hand tightly.

"Why are we—"

"Trust me." Pacified by his tranquilizing voice, I stopped shaking. Reid had a plan.

But the moment he stalked toward me like a predator, I felt all my trust in him disappear and drain down the sewer. The smirk on his face was a telltale giveaway on what he was about to do to me.

His face lit up as he braced himself.

He wouldn't dare—

Absolutely not—

He pushed me harder and faster than I could comprehend and I knew I was done for. Sheer terror wrapped itself around me like a cloak that was digging in and spreading, the tendrils of panic reaching every fiber of my being. I had no time to think. I had no time to process. I had no time to scream.

I was ready to meet my doom.

Until Reid swooped in and caught me as I was a hairs length away from spilling my entrails onto the pavement.

He landed on the ground gracefully, one arm under my knees and the other gripping my waist tightly, pressing my chest against his.

Smirking at me, his voice was filled with delight. "See? Good practice."

I was ready to rip his head off and toss it into the next borough. "Good practice? Good *practice?*"

Hauling myself out of his arms, I did the thing I've been desperate to do from the day we met.

I punched him in the fucking face.

Let his perfect face be tarnished. Let me put him in his place for once in his self-serving life. I was surprised I didn't shatter my wrist in the process, and my hand definitely hurt. But it was beyond worth it to see the look on his face.

Any damage that I'd inflicted on Reid was wiped away in seconds. His red face returned to its normal rosy color before I could blink. His shock was quickly replaced with an unimpressed look.

"Are you done playing?" He sounded bored.

Panting heavily and still recovering, I gritted my teeth. "Don't *ever* do that again."

He smiled. "Don't act like you didn't like it. There's nothing like feeling alive when you're so close to death."

"I'm not like you where I can heal in two seconds. Pain hurts. Death hurts."

"What a human thing to say."

"I'll take that as a compliment because at least I appreciate life and don't take it for granted."

His smile disappeared. "I certainly don't take life for granted. Pushing limits and breaking boundaries is my way of enjoying it." He looked around at the empty street.

"Put your arms around my neck," he instructed.

"Absolutely not. If you think I'd ever—"

"Oh, shut up and just do it. I'll show you how much life can be enjoyed in a way you've never seen before."

Silently, I did as he asked. Scooping me back up, his gaze was one of adventure when he looked down at me and whispered, "are you ready?"

Before I had the chance to answer, Reid bent his knees and soared into the night sky at a speed no human would catch with their naked eye.

I was dropped back into my body, knocked into reality and my stomach dropped. Gripping his neck to the point where I was surprised I didn't choke him to death, I thought I was going to pass out.

Reid beamed, his dazzling smile shining in the moonlight. "Look around," he told me.

I opened my eyes to the world around me when it suddenly hit me.

We were flying! I was flying! And this time, it wasn't because I was close to death. My memory from the night at Glitz felt like a fever dream, similar to when he'd just pushed me. But this was different. This was what it meant to be alive.

Laughing with joy, I observed the city in wonder. Dozens of city lights twinkled like stars below me. We were so high in the air that no one would see us. We became one with the clouds that the skyscrapers were touching. The hum of the nightlife had decreased to a whisper as we flew above the beeps and ambulances and drunk college students and everything *human*.

He maneuvered his arms and shifted me around him so that he was now carrying me on his back. I hardly realized it until I saw the city with new eyes. He flew with his arms spread wide, his laughter carried by the wind. The air was colder, but Reid's unnatural warmth felt like a furnace and I was provided with enough heat that the cold air felt refreshing against his scorching skin.

Reid ascended at a frightening speed. He was gliding past skyscrapers and even ran sideways on one, before pushing off with his feet and gaining momentum.

I was a bird, flying with the wind. Reid was fluid with the air, allowing the breeze to control which direction we went. Breathing felt easier after he skyrocketed above the smoke and pollution.

I trusted him with my life during our flight and couldn't explain why. Our connection was cemented the moment he lifted us into the air. It was one thing for him to expose himself and his secret to me, emotions in the raw. It was another thing for him to have full control over my fragile thread of life. Even when we soared thousands of feet above the ground, I never felt safer.

Even when he landed on the antenna of the Freedom Tower, hanging onto the spire mast with nothing but his fingertips, I felt safer than I would be crossing the street. Even when he let go of the mast and allowed himself to freefall backward, tumbling against thousands of feet of air working against us, and I could have flown off his back at any moment, I felt safer than on a kiddie roller coaster.

It was perfect. I was elated. It was one of the best moments of my whole life.

The moment he landed us gracefully back on my fire escape, I decided I would throw all my doubts out the window. The way we had just taken control of the sky completely shifted my perspective. I was finally able to understand Vita's mantra to live in the moment. The way I felt right now certainly wasn't finite, but it was exhilarating. The way I wanted us to kiss right now was a feeling I never wanted to give up. I was tired of holding myself back, denying my true feelings. I could deal with the consequences tomorrow. But right now, I was free. Flying.

I could hardly wait until we stepped over the window ledge back into my apartment. I was hungry for him. And I made sure he knew it.

Leading him to my bed, I pushed him on his back and straddled him, locking my feet under his to secure my grip. Caressing his beautiful face under my fingers, I brushed his hair out of his face. Taking my time to devour each second before our lips met, each second that we salivated for each other, I dragged it out - knowing the edging was torturing us both. I knew he wanted to kiss me. His lips inched closer to my lips and parted in longing, and I loved the feeling of making him wait.

But I couldn't hold out much longer.

His lips were warm and soft and inviting and seductive.

I could feel his magic seeping into my system when our tongues slid over each other. I had to lock in my feet to keep from lifting slightly off him. I wanted our bodies to touch. I wanted to feel his skin against mine. His warmth enveloped me and brought me closer as he kissed me as I'd never been kissed before.

Even though I wanted to continue kissing him forever, I forced myself to pull away and get a good look at his true self. His pointy ears were perking up, and the glow was back. He looked like a dream.

Judging by his crooked smile and the way his arms wrapped around my sides, I knew he was no longer interested in being underneath me, though he was far from done playing with me. He squeezed my ass before hoisting himself up, wrapping my legs around him, and making sure I was sitting right on top of his nether regions. Feeling it poke against our clothes, I bit my lip, imagining it springing out.

Reid tangled his hand on the back of my head and pulled my hair, not enough to yank it out, but enough to maneuver me in any direction he wanted. His other hand wrapped around my throat, forcing my mouth open all the way.

Not too long ago, I was afraid and angry of him choking me, but now, I loved it. Sensing his true dominance that he had yet to unleash, he expertly laid me down on my back, while keeping his hands in all the right places. Pressing down hard against me, I knew he wasn't using his flying ability at all. Every second of kissing was just bringing him down closer to me. Interestingly enough, I was slightly lifted, as if an eighth of my pull to gravity was just shaved off. We were pressed against each other like magnets. I was enveloped in his aura. I could feel it.

His kiss had left the realm of passionate and sensuous and entered a new territory - a predator taking its prey. He kissed me harder and stronger, sweeping his tongue over mine and grabbing onto my bottom lip, sucking it and biting it. I could feel the tinge of my own blood swimming between our mouths and was startled at how aroused it made me. More than ever, I wanted him to take me and plunge himself deep inside.

Catching him by surprise by forcing my tongue in his mouth, I caught his bottom lip between my teeth and decided to level the playing field. Biting down hard, I sucked on his broken skin, knowing I was ingesting even more magic in the process. His blood tasted different from mine. It tasted lighter. Like the salted wind of the sea. I never thought I would be into this, and with anyone else,

I'd never even want to try, but with him, it excited me to have a part of his magic inside me. It made me feel stronger than ever. Knowing I had broken skin and drawn blood just the same as he did to me, it felt invigorating. Thrilling. Intoxicating.

He didn't let me suck for long before he pulled away and grinned, his mouth painted red. Licking his lips, he closed his eyes and savored the taste. Following suit, I swept my tongue over my lips, expecting to taste a mangled mess. To my surprise, my skin wasn't broken at all. It was sealed as if he hadn't broken it. His lips were healed too. He must've healed me while kissing me, which explained why it didn't hurt at all. Relishing in the taste, I liked knowing we already had a part of each other inside us; a symbol of our unity.

I also knew I was incredibly wet, yet I couldn't go all the way tonight. My mind wasn't letting me, despite the way my body hungered for his. But the moment was still, without a doubt, one of the best moments in my life, secondary to the flight he took me on, with or without my consent. I loved how he pushed my boundaries. I loved how he knew what my limits were and showed me what I was missing.

I wanted to fly with him forever.

TWENTY-TWO

The rays from my window warmed my skin as I stirred awake. My eyes fluttered open and closed quickly, the light blinding me. As my tongue ran over my perfectly healed mouth, I thought back to last night and felt a different kind of warmth deep inside.

Just as I was going to roll out of bed, I met resistance. Did someone restrain me? Looking down in bewilderment, I saw an arm draped over my waist, total dead weight. I'd recognize those fingers anywhere. They were wrapped around my neck less than twelve hours ago.

Reid had fallen asleep with me. And we cuddled all night.

I really must've been dreaming. Reid had never stayed overnight, ever. I always assumed he had better things to do; he certainly acted like it.

I'd never had a guy stay the night. Definitely never had a guy big spoon me through the night. It felt nice. Felt like home. A cozy, warm, inviting home, where someone was always waiting for me.

As amazing as it felt, I still couldn't believe Reid had done that on purpose. I hardly remembered going to bed. All I recalled was being exhausted and especially worn out after our appointment. It was very possible that he just passed out and his mind led him to think he was with his girlfriend again and the cuddling provided some comfort.

Sensing some movement behind me, I knew he was coming to. Holding my breath, I pretended I was still asleep, unsure of how to act around him. This could've gone one of two ways; either in my best interest or my worst. And knowing my luck—everything always goes wrong.

Reid slithered his arm off me fluidly and almost imperceptibly. If I were truly asleep, I wouldn't have noticed the change. He slowly lifted off the bed, making sure to be as quiet as a mouse. Knowing he was floating nearby, I considered saying something. But the cowardice within me kept me paralyzed until I heard him unlatch my window, an action he couldn't mute no matter how careful he was.

Just as the lock snapped, I sat up. Rubbing my eyes for dramatic effect, I looked at him sleepily.

"Do you always sneak out after a night of cuddles?" I willed my face to play the part of a just-woke-up, innocent Alluna.

He clicked his teeth. "I knew you were awake. People don't hold their breath while asleep."

Crap. Well, no use in playing that role anymore.

Using my normal voice, I inquired, "You got me there. Still doesn't explain the cuddles."

"It's all preparation for step two, baby. " With that, he saluted me sarcastically with one eyebrow raised, and fell out of my window. I could barely make out the shape of his body as he zipped through the sky.

Sadness overwhelmed me that the old Reid was back. The Reid I detested with a passion. I couldn't understand why he was so hot and cold with me like night and day. One moment he acted like couldn't care less about me and the next moment he was furiously making out with me before soundly cuddling up behind me.

How many times did he have to remind me that we were just two individuals working together toward a common interest? Just because he was thinking with his other head during our appointments didn't mean a single darn thing.

Vita used to tell me time and time again - you know a guy isn't actually into you if all he wants is sex.

I wanted to beat myself up. I'd set myself up for failure, thinking I had a chance with Reid. If only I could just disconnect my brain during our appointments and reconnect it as needed.

My emotions were taking up too much space in my head. If I could just delete them, life would be swell. But unfortunately for me, I was alone with my thoughts and I didn't like it.

Getting out of bed, I tried to keep my hands and mind occupied but my thoughts raged on like fire, burning everything in their path. Once my thoughts turned dark, I knew I had to get out of my apartment.

Shooting a quick text to Daisy, I asked if she wanted to grab some coffee. Almost instantly, she responded when and where. Thankful for her availability, I chose the nearest coffee shop as far away from Kaffeine as possible. That place was traumatizing enough, even though their coffee had bean amazing.

We settled into a nearby, hole-in-the-wall coffee shop not too long later.

"You look like you have a lot to spill, so go on," Daisy said instead of greeting me as she set her jacket and bag beside me on the couch.

"I need a shot for this." I shook my head. "Maybe a few shots…of espresso," I winked. Daisy rolled her eyes and we ordered together.

Once we sat down with our piping hot concoctions of perfection, I braced myself. "So before you say anything, I'd like to remind you of the clause in our pact where we wouldn't judge each other."

Daisy's mouth dropped. "You had sex with Reid."

"No!"

Her eyes narrowed. "You said you'd be honest."

"I am!" I insisted. "We made out last night and then he passed out and cuddled me."

Daisy's eyebrows raised even higher. "Okay, and?"

"And I'm definitely falling for him. I feel so stupid getting involved with him." I took a sip for comfort.

Daisy put her hand on my shoulder as she leaned back against the couch. "Alluna, you know you can walk away at any time, right?"

"I can't."

"You can. It's not like you're handcuffed to him."

In a sense, I was. If I walked away from him, I would also be walking away from any hope of seeing my sister again, if she was still alive. That last shred of hope was the only reason I was still sticking around.

"He doesn't care about you. He's only using you for his own benefit."

"You're right." Couldn't argue with her there. Daisy didn't have to know all the details to make that conclusion. It was obvious to everyone - even me, though I couldn't stop turning a blind eye and making excuses for it.

Setting my drink down, I put my face in my hands. "I just can't escape my feelings for him."

Daisy hugged me and I slumped into her. "He's super hot - I'll give you that. But he's not the last hot guy you'll ever meet."

"I know…"

She stroked my hair. "Put yourself first and walk away. Find someone who makes you happy and isn't a toxic mess."

"I will. But now isn't the right time."

Her hand stilled. "Do you hear yourself? When is there ever a right time to walk away from someone who isn't right for you?" She sighed, evidently disappointed in me. Couldn't blame her. I was disappointed in myself, too.

"Daisy, just trust me when I say that when the moment comes, I'll be running away as fast as I can. But—"

"There is no but. You have full control over your life and your actions, not him. You make the moment, not him. You choose when you want to make yourself happy. Not him." Daisy's brows were furrowed, and I could tell her sincerity was genuine. "If you're not ready to make the right choice yet, that's on you."

Staring deep into her eyes, I knew she was right in everything. Maybe if she had all the details, she'd understand. Maybe I could give her a little more…

"It's just…he's helping me. Deal with the loss of my sister, I mean."

Daisy gave me a pained look. "Alluna. I know he's not a completely terrible person, and that's what makes him toxic for you. He gives you a few redeeming moments and you start to think that maybe, it's not such a bad idea. But he's still your TA, at the end of the day. He met you when you were his student, and it doesn't sound like he makes you that happy. When you talk about him, you look sullen."

"I do?"

She nodded. "You're always hiding something with him. I get it, he's your dirty little secret. But this isn't high school anymore.

It's just someone in a place of higher power manipulating you."

Crazy to think I never thought about that aspect. It seemed too unimportant, too human. Under normal circumstances, maybe it would've gotten to me. I was falling far too deep within his magical life to notice nor care.

There was no point trying to get Daisy to understand a situation I could never truly confess. No matter how hard I tried to humanize him and our relationship, the fact in the matter was that we were anything but - and I had to take these secrets to my grave. I knew Reid would personally slice my throat if I told anyone about him.

Why wouldn't he? It wouldn't be hard for him to find someone else to sleep with to go to Naerin. Maybe that was why he was so hot and cold with me. Maybe he finally realized that my feelings made things too complicated. We could've easily already slept together. We could've already been in Naerin. He could've already been reunited with his girlfriend.

But where were we instead? Playing games with each other to pass the time while the Keeper hunted us like animals?

I was going to be sick. I never hated myself more than I did at that moment. I was the problem.

"Alluna, are you okay? You look pale." Daisy rubbed my back, concern laced all over her pretty face.

"Yeah, um. Just dehydrated, I guess." Hiding my face, I took a few chugs of my now lukewarm coffee. "Let me get us some snacks to go with the coffee."

"Alluna…"

"Croissant? Pastry?" I stood up, avoiding her face.

"Alluna, please…"

"Understood. I'll surprise you." Reaching out of her grasp, I walked away to the cashier like a coward, too afraid to face Daisy, too afraid to face myself.

And the worst part? I had no idea how to get out of this situation. Maybe I was going about it all wrong. The faster we had sex, the faster I'd get to my sister. This delay was exactly what was killing me…

What was I so afraid of? Getting attached? I was already fucking attached.

Grabbing two croissants and a big baguette filled with protein, I came back to Daisy, ready to change my pace.

"Let's go for a walk and get some fresh air. Maybe sit in a park somewhere and eat?"

I knew she wanted to persist with her earlier point, but I was glad that she chose to drop the topic for now. "I've been so selfish anyway, only talking about myself. The stage is yours. Regale me of the tales of you and your brother against your mother," I joked lightly, trying to lighten the mood.

We strolled down East Village, a completely different setting from our usual Midtown meetups. The streets were buzzing with college kids mingling and eager to use their ding-a-lings. It was nice to be among crowds I was supposed to be a part of - a life I should've been living.

"Oh, dear. My mother has declared war on me personally. She

really thinks I'm a terrible influence and told me that if I didn't convince him to go back to pre-med, she'd disown me."

I couldn't help but chuckle, knowing Daisy wasn't being completely serious.

"We should introduce our moms. I think they would have a hoot together."

Daisy laughed. "I think they'd either get along fabulously or blow each other up - there's no in-between with people like that."

We walked all the way to Washington Square Park and settled on some benches, finishing our coffees and helping ourselves to the food I brought.

The weather wasn't too harsh, but we knew we wouldn't be staying out for long. Less than five minutes of sitting down and we were already walking towards the direction of a subway.

Exhaling deeply, I twisted my hands in my pockets. "Sometimes I wish I stayed home. Didn't come here, didn't meet Reid, didn't strain my relationship with my parents."

"Don't be such a negative Nancy. Think of the positives that came from you coming here, now there's an exercise. Go ahead." Daisy looped her arm around me and stared at me expectantly.

Pursing my lips in deep thought, I finally answered, "Of course, I met you. I'm learning what it's like to be independent and self-sufficient. I chose a pretty great city to come to, I mean let's be real. Name one place that beats New York City."

"Have you ever been to Los Angeles?"

"Okay Daisy, you're missing the point here. Anyway, New

York City is a paradox within itself. So many people here…yet it gets so lonely. I'm really lucky I met you, and I'm really sorry for all the times I upset you. Daisy, you're a really great and supportive friend."

"Aww, see? The benefits of this exercise. I get some compliments out of it, too. I think you made the right choice by coming here. How else can you make mistakes, learn from life, fall for the wrong guy, meet lifelong friends, and so on and so forth?"

Though the mention of falling for the wrong guy stirred some sadness in me, I knew she was right, yet again.

I was ready to applaud her wisdom until I saw something that took up my attention. I knew I wasn't imagining things.

A quick flit and something flew across my vision. Something tinted black. Whipping my head to the other side, my eyes scoured the environment.

Before long, the small black-winged Faerie zipped to the other side. Almost knocking heads with Daisy, I peered around her to see the small thing and get a better look.

The Faerie had already made its presence known - why hide at this point?

It was good at staying in my peripheral sights, never getting close enough for me to distinguish any personal features.

I was sure that the Faerie was female, that was my only indicator. She was wearing what looked like a dress made from dark leaves that radiated dark dust.

The moment the thought entered my head, my blood ran cold.

Dust? Had it really come to this? Was this Faerie the final omen before I was taken just like the others?

Recalling how the Faerie from Kaffeine mentioned one of the victims speaking about dust, I was ready to pass out. I had to tell Reid. This wasn't about our feelings anymore. This was much bigger than that. Our lives were at stake.

For all I knew, I wouldn't survive past the night.

Daisy felt the sudden change in tone, intuitive as she was. "You're thinking about Reid, aren't you?"

Smiling weakly, I hid my face with my hair. "Yeah. I'll be okay, though. Thank you for listening and everything." Her grip on my arm tightened protectively.

By then, we'd already reached the nearest subway. In this up-and-down weather, I couldn't care less about how many subway transfers I'd have to make just to avoid being in the cold.

As we descended down the stairs, the black-winged Faerie zipped across my view again, finally perching atop a corner just out of my sight, watching us, watching me. I didn't bother trying to get another glimpse at her - the message was already received, loud and clear. I bitterly considered saluting her for her hard work.

The underground subway station proved to be even colder than the outside chill. Internally cursing myself for pulling yet another UnNewYorker, I pressed closer to Daisy, hoping we could stay warm through body heat.

"I don't understand. How can it be even colder here?" I muttered, almost to myself.

Daisy chuckled through her chattering teeth. "Welcome to New York City, baby."

I gave an unamused *hmph* in response, my eyes subconsciously darting through the station. I felt like Reid. No wonder he was always sweeping his surroundings. I could've never known there would be so many creatures around us.

The train came soon and we departed quickly. Holding my phone just out of Daisy's view, I quickly texted Reid.

Saw the black-winged Faerie again.

Staring at my own message, I remembered how particular he was and deleted it, retyping *saw the black-winged butterfly again.*

He'd appreciate that. I think. I actually didn't know. But it seemed like he would.

Pressing send, I put my phone back in my pocket and rejoined my conversation with Daisy about our mothers. It seemed we had more in common than I thought. Different ships, same sails.

Daisy and I parted ways at the next transfer and I hurried home, too cold to check my phone, anticipation flurrying through me like a snowstorm. Desperately, I had to know what Reid responded. With all my might, I traveled home as fast as I could.

When I finally entered my apartment an hour later, I pulled my phone out in an unparalleled frenzy.

But there was nothing from Reid. Typically, he would answer instantaneously. I knew he saw the message.

He chose not to answer. He was ignoring me for reasons beyond me. Perhaps he didn't deem the message important enough.

Perhaps he fled to find another to take to Naerin. It finally hit him that I wasn't worth it.

Flinging my phone away from me and hoping to take my train of thought along with it, I buried my face in my hands. I wanted to scream. Punch something. Punch him.

Even when he wasn't with me, he brought out the worst in me. The double edged sword part of it was even worse. If he were here, I knew I'd forget all these current thoughts and be overtaken with desire to devour him, his mouth, his everything.

What if I was taken tonight and he never bothered to answer? What if the Keeper found me before he did and I was dead and gone in Naerin?

I couldn't live my last day like this.

Heading to my couch, I pulled out my laptop, turning on some mindless reality show to distract me.

A breeze from the window caught my attention. Didn't I close it?

Putting my laptop aside, I walked over to latch it shut. There was something laying on the ledge.

A black feather.

At first, I thought a bird had flown in and shed its feather.

But this was no ordinary feather. It was massive, and seemed familiar. Picking it up and carefully examining it, I noticed it was bound to a woven lanyard. A necklace.

Sage's necklace. She wore it to every class.

It was also the same feather from my nightmare. Laying next to

Vita's body.

Speechless, I carefully set it down and backed away. Could Sage have been the Keeper all along? Was my dream just a direct vision of what happened? Nervously, I turned the feather over, examining every crevice for dried blood. It was completely clean, dry, and intact. In perfect condition. This feather had never been ruffled. What if my dream was a future vision instead?

I had no idea. But this feather didn't end up on my window ledge accidentally. It was a sign. For what? I couldn't know. There was only one person who might.

Ignoring the double texting boundary, I quickly sent another text to Reid.

Discovered something important.

Staring at the two messages stacked neatly, sent a few hours apart, I frowned, wondering if he was purposefully choosing not to respond.

It was also eight o'clock already. What of our nightly appointments?

I considered reminding him, but he knew. I knew he knew. What was the point, other than to rub the salt in my wound? He was actively ignoring me, and I had bigger things to worry about.

If he chose to show, I'd tell him about the feather and the Faerie. If he didn't, I would pursue my investigation alone.

Placing the feather carefully on my kitchen counter, I tried testing its magic. While keeping a finger on it, I jumped, trying to see if it lightened gravity's grasp on me.

Landing normally, I frowned.

The thought of licking it crossed my mind, but I didn't know where this feather had been.

I clasped it around my neck and walked over to the mirror, expecting something to happen.

I looked the same. Nothing changed.

Exasperated, I carefully took it off, put it inside my cabinet and resumed my reality show. Tomorrow, I'd wash it and try ingesting a strand. But I was done for today. Too many things at once.

The reality show provided a temporary comfort, until I fell asleep on the couch, waking a few times throughout the night to see if Reid came.

But he never showed.

TWENTY-THREE

hen I awoke the next morning, I decided to throw all double standards and social boundaries out the window. I didn't have time to mope around until Reid decided to show me the light of day again. I was better than that. I had bigger fish to fry.

After washing up and overthinking my next move about a thousand times, I finally dialed him for the first time. I didn't want to walk into class and awkwardly avoid him, we didn't have time for that. We'd never spoken on the phone before, only curt texts every now and then.

Putting my phone on speaker, I nervously twiddled my fingers as the dials began.

He picked up on the sixth ring, about two seconds before I

passed out.

Hearing him exhale slowly through the phone, I felt a certain comfort hearing him breathe. He was still alive and safe. A wave of relief splashed over me.

"Yes?" His smooth voice was too seductive to be fair to me and my poor, weak, human heart to bear.

I cleared my throat. "Ahem." Don't mess this up, he's already temperamental by nature, I reminded myself.

"There's a few important things I need to discuss with you."

I readily pictured his snide face and sarcastic response at the ready. He'd either mock me or make me sound like a total idiot.

To my surprise, he was neutral - a trait I knew was infrequent in his nature. "Go on."

He wasn't hot nor cold. He was a middle ground I wasn't used to. Not quite approachable, there was still a certain coldness about his tone. But he wasn't so far detached either. Just a not here nor there middle. An in-between.

Sighing, I tried my best to sound like I wasn't freaking out on the inside. "You'll have to come over so I can show you before class. You kinda owe me one for giving me the cold shoulder yesterday out of nowhere." Pausing, I contemplated my next statement before throwing all reason out the window. "I'll consider forgiving you if you bring me coffee."

Hanging up the phone, I felt a mixture of satisfaction, fear, triumph, and anxiety. At least I was smart enough to hang up before he went snarky again.

Considering whether I should wait for Reid to come knocking on my door, I smiled and shook my head. That wasn't his style.

Leaving my window totally unlatched and wide open, I covered myself in maybe four layers to balance the strong winds.

Not more than thirty minutes later, Reid swooped in through my window, holding a perfectly balanced tray with two plastic cups diagonally facing each other.

His feet didn't touch the ground until the tray was sitting neatly on my kitchen counter. Even then, he took my drink out and offered it to me, completely horizontal with the air, as if he were lying down.

"I hope this meets your standards." Handing me my drink, he stayed in the midair position until I took a sip. Giving him a long, hard look, I carefully sipped the coffee. The moment the pumpkin sauce hit my tastebuds, a huge grin overtook my face. It was perfect.

Reid was trying not to smile, but he couldn't fully conceal a small grin.

"This is amazing. Thank you."

His toes barely grazed the ground. "Will you tell me now?"

"Yes. But only under one condition."

"What is it?"

Knowing I would probably rile myself up and explode on him, I made no attempt to hold myself back. I had way too many pent up emotions by now.

"You have to tell me what was up with you yesterday." I had

no intention of giving him a single second to make me doubt myself. "What did I do to deserve that? Why would you leave me hanging all day and ignore my texts?"

My hand gripped the plastic cup tighter and I forced myself to loosen, not wanting to waste any of the precious drink, though it was difficult to remain calm and my voice was rising. "You said so yourself that we are running out of time. How in the world am I supposed to feel comfortable sleeping with you if I can't even trust you to keep your end of the bargain? Huh? What's your excuse? What's your magical, sarcastic reason?"

My hands were shaking and my eyes were wet. Angry tears were threatening to spill over, but I didn't care. I'd riled myself up by now, knowing Reid would drive me over the edge and bring the worst out in me anyway.

But again, he did the last thing I expected him to.

"You're right." His feet were planted on the ground and he faced me like a human, unable to just fly away at a moment's notice. His shoulders slumped over and he stared at the ground.

My lip quivered. "I just want my sister back. Not all these mind games you're playing with me." My voice cracked, but I was past the point of caring.

"You're right. You didn't deserve the way I've been treating you." His neutrality was making me nervous. I wasn't used to it.

"Why do you hate me so much?" My voice was nothing but a whisper now.

Reid placed his hand on my cheek and wiped a tear away with

his thumb. "I don't hate you, Alluna." His use of my real name somehow made him seem more real, more honest. But I was still so confused.

"Then why do you act like you do? Why are you so cruel to me?"

He grimaced, wincing his face, before finally meeting my eyes. "Because I'm scared to fall for you, and I think I am."

"You're…what?"

His second hand caressed my other cheek as he gazed into my eyes, before tearing his away. "I…listen, I can't always explain my feelings, but what I'm feeling for you is far different from what I ever felt for her."

There was no way he could ever—

For me—

"How?"

"You feel like home."

I was in a daze, unsure of how to handle what he said. "So you ran away from me."

"To be honest, I wanted to call you today right before you did. I couldn't stop replaying the look on your face yesterday when I left…I felt terrible. I was relieved when you called." He caressed my cheek, before turning away from me and facing the window again. Pacing with his feet a few inches above the ground, he said, "I feel guilty for caring about you. I would still give the world to her, and I don't know what to do."

He stilled, and his next words shattered me. "It might be better for us to stop now before it's too late."

As much as his words felt like a dagger slicing against my heart, and as much as I wished he dragged his hidden blade across my throat instead of saying that since it would've hurt less, I saw his point. Which made it hurt even more. How can I argue with him when he's right? We were both hurting each other by being together in whatever mess this was.

"Reid, I..." I wasn't even sure which side to argue. "I can't imagine the guilt you're feeling right now, of course I'm in a completely different situation than you. I care about you too, as much as you drive me crazy." Walking up to him, I placed my hand on his shoulder, pushing down so he could land on the ground and I could reach better. "We're in too deep to stop now. We know what we have to do. Let's just take things one step at a time."

Pausing, I considered my own words. "Actually, you never told me what the third step was. You know, after we...yeah."

Reid looked down at me and frowned. "Once we are connected and I can see the path to Naerin, I have to tap into your soul to access it. Like a road. I'll use your soul to fly there with you."

And here I thought having sex with him would lead to attachment issues. That was nothing compared to him tapping into my soul. I couldn't even imagine what that would entail, and what side effects would linger. The things I was willing to put myself through for Vita...

"Do you have to tap into my soul right after we finish?" Would I have any time to recover from the second step and prepare for the third? That was my actual question.

He hesitated. "It doesn't have to be immediately after, but remember - the path will only be there while we are connected. Once I…finish, the path will only remain open while my seed is in you. You're probably more educated in human anatomy than I am. You tell me, how long does it stay in the female body afterward?"

Knowing my cheeks were flaming, I avoided eye contact. "I dunno, a few days?"

"There's your answer. And I'm assuming on the last day, it wouldn't be as potent. My best guess would be to make the journey within the first twenty-four hours."

"How long does it take to get to Naerin?"

"Time moves differently there. It's hard to say, but in human realm hours, I would guess overnight."

"So we would have to take that into account as well, and make sure the path stays open for at least twelve hours ahead?"

"Yep." Reid's stare was burning into my head.

I needed a second to think. This was a lot to process, but I was glad I asked. In a way, it made sex seem less of a powerful thing compared to him tapping into my soul. I shouldn't be afraid to have sex with him. If anything, it sounded like he wanted it too, which turned me on more than anything else.

Grabbing my coffee, I took a few sips. Reid flew onto my couch, staring out the window, his handsome features of his face smoothing out as he settled into a plain-faced stare.

I wondered if he was thinking about the same thing I was. What would happen if we made it to Naerin? If I was reunited with my sister and him with his girlfriend? What would happen next? Would we keep in touch and become pen pals? Would he forget about me?

I couldn't think about that right now. As I'd said before, one step at a time. Those problems sounded like tomorrow's problems anyway, which was exactly when I'd face them.

Reid was looking at me again. I couldn't stop staring into his green eyes, wanting to climb into them and see what he was thinking for once.

"What?"

He was neutral. "Nothing. Just thinking."

Staring at him, I responded, "You really know how to diffuse the tension." Before long, my face grew grave when I remembered. "I didn't just call you over to yell at you."

"Then why?"

"Well, I was with Daisy yesterday and I saw the black-winged Faerie again." Watching his reaction, I was sad to see him frown again and distort his handsome face.

"Did the Faerie approach you?" He asked.

I shook my head. "No, she was just watching me."

"Hm." I didn't like the sound of his hm. It didn't sound good.

"And there's one other thing." Walking over to my cabinet, I carefully took out Sage's feather necklace. "When I came home, this was on my ledge." Walking over to the couch and sitting next to him, I presented the feather.

He examined it carefully. "So?"

"It was Sage's necklace. She wore it every day. How could that have ended up on my ledge?"

He grasped the necklace carefully and shook his head. "I have no idea what this means."

"Oh." I leaned against the couch, crossing my arms. "Another dead-end, I guess."

"Not quite. I'm sure this means something, we just have to figure out what." He placed the feather on the coffee table pensively. "We never investigated Sage's disappearance. Maybe we can find some clues in her office."

I sat up brightly. "Yeah! Good idea."

Reid flew off the couch and gestured for me to follow him to the window.

"Reid, it's the middle of the day. Someone will see us."

He threw his head back and chortled. "Silly little Alluna. My magic conceals me from humans when I'm flying."

"And me?"

He shrugged. "You better hold on tight."

Nervously walking toward him, I bit my lip. "Just don't drop me," I said as he leaned down for me to clasp my arms around his neck and lock my legs around his waist. Turning back, he smirked. "Maybe I will. But then I'll catch you."

"Reid…"

Laughing, he hurled himself out the window and I tried not to scream as he freely fell toward the ground, allowing gravity to pull him down. Just before we smashed into the ground, he swooped upward and let go of gravity's pull, creating his own wind and force with the air.

As usual, I was amazed at the sights around us, especially knowing we were invisible to the average human eye. Just when I thought I had enough of Manhattan, Reid showed me the skyline from a new angle, halfway high of the skyscrapers. We were close enough to the ground that I could make out individual faces of people rushing to work, but still high enough to see the tops of lower buildings. Reid was also flying at a leisurely pace and the wind wasn't knocking my hair all over my face.

He was completely horizontal, and I was laying atop him.

"Sit up," he instructed me.

Eyes widening, I slowly sat up, making sure my legs were secure underneath him. My hands were clutching his shirt with a death grip, but I was able to sit upright with him as my chair, or magic carpet ride. Hoping he wouldn't whoosh forward and knock me off my balance, I relaxed my grip and stared around me in wonder.

"Let your arms go!" He called out to me.

Feeling a rush of adrenaline pumping through my veins, I opened my arms as if I were greeting the air with a warm hug and laughed with exhilaration.

We weren't too far from campus by now. Eventually, I laid back down on Reid's back and rested my head on the nook of his neck, hugging him from behind.

I was having the time of my life until the black-winged Faerie shot past me again.

"Reid, look!" Pointing in her direction, I saw her nested atop a streetlight, watching us soar by. "It's her again!"

Reid looked down at her too but didn't change his speed. "Don't provoke her. Let's just get to Sage's office."

Frowning, I looked ahead with him as we approached the campus and he landed us in a corner quietly and walked out as if we weren't just flying. Reid was awfully good at acting human.

Following him, we made our way into Sage's office, which was left wide open. Her stacks and folders were left untouched, and I felt a pang for her, hoping she was safe and alive.

Only after Reid closed and locked her door did he say, "We are really running out of time."

TWENTY-FOUR

Okay, I'm ready. Do you have access to all her passwords?" Cracking my knuckles, I made myself at home in Sage's leather chair and scooted closer to her desktop, pushing the stacks of papers aside. Reid lingered behind me, closed the shutters, and made sure no one could peek inside and see us.

The last thing we needed was an accusation of tampering with the professor's belongings, and for Reid to lose his job by enlisting the help of his student.

"Yes," he murmured and reached around me to type in her password. His chin was resting on top of my head as his arms brushed against mine and I sighed, wanting to lean into him and feel his entire chest on my back.

"We only have half an hour before the lecture starts, so do your thing."

A swift moment later, we were in. Reid's warmth disappeared behind me as he went toward the shutters to glance around and keep a lookout. Quickly rummaging through Sage's files, I found nothing but the syllabus, submitted assignments, and lecture notes.

I had to dig deeper. She wouldn't have left any clues out in the open for anyone to find. I had to think smarter like her. Just as I was about to enter her hard drive and search every document created within the last two weeks, my phone started to buzz.

Pulling it out of my pocket, I saw it was my mother. Quickly glancing at Reid, I took the call while he stared right at me.

"Hey, Mom," I said in a low voice.

"Am I interrupting something, dear?" I knew what my mother really meant - what was I doing that she was unaware of?

"I'm just studying. The final is coming up," I lied.

"That's exactly why I called. I want to know when I should be expecting you home." My mother made it clear she wasn't here to play any games. Knowing how she was, I knew the best way to get her off my back was with a straightforward answer. She was never one to be emotionally understanding.

Smiling so I could sound casual, I relied on the truth to sound honest. "Actually, my final is in exactly a week - January twenty-fourth. Grades will be in within the following week. I think two weekends is realistic."

"And when were you planning on informing me? Must I pull

teeth every time to know what's happening with you?" She was doing it again. That thing where she had to play the victim in every situation while remaining the narcissist who was blind to her own effect.

"Mom, please. I don't want to fight."

"I get it. I'm the bad guy. I'm a terrible mother because I care about your safety." Only my mother could find a way to twist the situation like that.

Resorting to old habits, I did exactly as I'd trained myself for most of my life. Appeasing her and begging for forgiveness was the only option.

"No, no, Mom. I know you're just worried about me. I'm sorry for making you upset. Everything is okay. I want to ace this exam so I can get full credit for this course, and then I'll be on the next bus home, I promise." The lies spilled out of my mouth with such ease I almost believed them myself. In a way, this was supposed to be the truth. I wasn't really lying. I was merely telling the truth in a different reality where everything happened the way it was supposed to if my life didn't turn upside down.

"Make sure you spend some extra time with that TA of yours, if he likes you enough, he might give you some information about the final," she said suggestively. Interesting that she was coaching me to be an opportunist after the rude way she spoke to him when they met. I almost laughed at the irony. She was the only person who was telling me to spend time with Reid, and if she knew the truth…

I didn't even know if I would make it to the final, let alone next weekend. Reid and I could embark on our path to Naerin any second now by how things were going. There was no guarantee I would ever come back. My mother would lose both her kids.

Glancing up, I saw Reid staring right at me, his brows furrowed and lips pursed. I wondered if he also had the magical ability of superhearing and would attest to me being probably the worst offspring in the world.

"Alright honey…your father wants to have a word." Hearing the phone get shuffled and a muffled "David, it's Alluna. Have a talk with her," the phone was finally placed against another ear.

"Hey, kiddo." My father sounded nervous, and I knew my mother put him up to this, as usual. It was never enough for her to guilt me, she always needed him to back her up. Classic for them.

"Hey Dad, it's been a while." I never called him in my entire time here. I never called either of them. I really thought I would've, but it never seemed important.

"Yes, you've been in New York City for four weeks, but I guess you didn't have time to call."

Wincing, I looked at the ground. Why was I punishing my father for the grievances I had with my mother? Would it really have been so hard to just pick up the phone and dial him?

After some silence, he said, "It's alright, I understand. You're experiencing life on your own and meeting new people. I was in your shoes once. Just…" He sighed heavily. "Remember that your mother has a talent for overthinking herself sick. Especially after what happened to your sister. She just wants to make sure you're safe."

"I know, Dad…"

"We love you very much. Don't forget us."

I wanted to cry, but I smiled through it, and a single tear rolled down my face as I said, "I'd never forget you. I'll be home soon."

The moment I hung up, I burst into tears. No matter which way this would realistically go, I would break their hearts, and probably end up dead. I was about to walk into a minefield to save someone that might not even be alive, with no ticket back home.

I could already imagine my parents receiving the call about me disappearing. How my mother's eyes would widen, how she would shriek my father's name, how she would collapse in his arms and hyperventilate until she finally took a Xanax and passed out for the next two days. How they would lie in bed together, staring at the wall, the empty house, knowing they were helpless to stop their second daughter from disappearing, knowing their attempts to get me home weren't enough. How my mother would wish she dragged me home when she came to visit because that way, even if I hated her, I would still be alive. How my father would rub her back all night and comfort her, only to turn away and hide his face so she wouldn't see the tears rolling down his cheeks.

My mother may have been a narcissist, but she wasn't evil. She still loved my sister and I, in her own way. I could never hate her. She had her own wisdom about life that she wanted to share with her two daughters, and soon enough, she would have none.

I didn't realize how hard I was shaking until Reid wrapped his arms around me and I completely lost control. Sobbing into his chest, I buried my face in his shirt and cried and cried and cried.

He held me close and didn't let me go until I was able to take a single breath without choking on it.

"Shh…it's okay," he whispered to the top of my head.

"It's not. I'm a terrible daughter and a terrible person."

"You're not a bad person." Reid stroked my head. "If they knew the full story, they'd understand."

Struggling to catch my breath, I fell back down on Sage's leather chair and tried to reorient my mind. We only had fifteen minutes until the lecture, and I certainly didn't want to walk out of the room looking like he just killed my puppy.

"I-I have to focus," I said while my hands went on autopilot, searching every document Sage created before she disappeared. Reid backed off and let me do my thing while hovering in the back, flipping through the stack of papers on her desk, and searching through her cabinets and closets.

After finding nothing but lecture-related documents on her hard drive, I was ready to give up and slam my head against the keyboard. Groaning audibly, I ran my fingers through my hair, tearing my eyes off the screen.

"Anything?" I asked Reid as he was bending over and rummaging through her things. "Nope. You?"

"Nothing here either."

"Wait, I think there's something here." Jumping up, I sped

toward Reid and practically knocked him over.

"Watch it, woman!"

"Where?" I demanded, getting in his way and stuffing my head in the cabinet.

"Here." He moved the stack of psychology books off the bottom cabinet and revealed a string underneath. A hidden compartment, by the looks of it. Tugging on the string, the small pocket creaked loudly as he lifted the top.

Inside the small compartment was a photo. A small, pencil-drawn photo, covered in dust.

Reid carefully took it out and smoothed out the dust so we could get a better look at it under the lighting.

"Is that…are those Faeries?" I asked in wonder. Reid nodded in astonishment. The drawing was very old and made on parchment I'd never seen or heard of. It was a dulled green and had faint green lines crisscrossing through it. Almost like…a leaf?

"Did this come from Naerin?" I asked. The fine detailing was so small there was no way a human drew this, especially on material as delicate as the leaf.

"I think so…the dried leaf paper is common over there." He was just as shocked as me.

There were three Faeries sitting on a tree branch, looking at each other and laughing, the moment captured forever. Their wings were tucked low, facing downward. I could hardly make out the details on their faces since the paper was so old, but I could tell they were all happy. The forest beneath them was evergreen and full of trees and lights. There was something in the corner, but the details were too fine to make it out. A dark shape with…wings? Perhaps a close up of a bird?

"Is this what Naerin looks like?"

"Not anymore," Reid said sadly, before putting the photo back in its place and carefully closing the compartment.

"What do you mean?"

"Naerin used to be a safe place full of life until there was a change in power thousands of years ago that forced the citizens to eat souls, and life was drained from the ecosystem. Most of Naerin looks barren now, and the people are starving." His face was grim as he closed the cabinet.

"Class is about to start, you should go. I need to prepare some things for the lecture."

Nodding, I stood up. "Let's meet back here after class and continue our search?"

"Deal."

"Were you crying because of Reid?" Daisy asked as she settled into her seat.

"What?" Remembering my episode after my phone call with my parents, I realized my eyes were probably blotchy and puffy. "No, I wasn't."

Pulling out my notebook and clicking my pen, I copied the notes from the board. "I've been going through some family stuff."

Daisy gave me a pained look. "I'm sorry, I didn't mean to assume."

"I know you're just looking out for me." Smiling at her, I hoped she'd believe me. Reid may have been a huge part of it, but my main issue was within myself and my feelings.

"So Leo has moved on from you and has his eyes set on someone else."

"Oh, who?"

"The girl from the library, remember? The one you were rude to for no reason?"

The blood drained from my face. The petite Syren spy was still alive? How did she survive?

We were definitely done for.

"Oh, good for him…have they gone out yet?"

Daisy nudged my arm. "Why, you jealous? Realized what you're missing out on?"

Laughing nervously, I shook my head. "No, I'm just surprised. She didn't seem like his type."

"Girl, have you met Leo? Everyone is his type. Anyway – you are off the table, right?" Daisy smoothed out her sleeves.

Of course, I was off the table. There was no guarantee I'd be alive for him to make a move. But what I actually said was, "Yeah. I just want to focus on myself."

"And Reid."

"Well, it's—"

"Complicated. I know."

Slumping into my seat, I was more anxious than ever. Reid and I were doomed. Either the Keeper would catch us and have us executed, or we would go on a suicide mission to Naerin and get executed. I had to talk to him about the plan after we made it to Naerin.

The entire duration of the lecture was spent with me twiddling my fingers while twiddling my thoughts into every possible outcome until my brain spiraled into a black hole.

"You weren't paying attention to the lecture, were you?" Reid closed the door behind him as we resumed our search in Sage's office.

"How can I?" I turned to him, balling my fists. "No matter which direction I start thinking, I end up in the same place - dead."

"Of course you'll end up dead with that attitude. If you want to be like that then don't even bother coming with me." Reid walked around me and started knocking on the floorboards and testing their dullness.

"Reid, please. We never even touched on what will happen after we get to Naerin. The least you could do is tell me that." Kneeling next to him, I helped him go through every corner of every floorboard.

"Assuming everyone is alive and well? Willing to go back?" He asked, and I nodded briskly, eager to hear the next part.

He paused, frowning. "If they are alive, which remains a slim chance, we would still have two obstacles." He held two fingers up.

"One, they would be bound to Naerin forever because they would have rejoined as citizens." Bending one finger, he wiggled his other one. "And two, we would need the path again and they wouldn't be human anymore." His other finger went down.

"So what does that entail?"

"Assuming we don't get captured in the process of trying to save them?"

"Of course Reid, of course!" My knocking became frantic.

"If you are still human by then, we have our path to come back here, as long as your body is safe when we leave. But the other part would be difficult…"

"Reid, just tell me!"

"We would have to go to war and overthrow the Keepers!" His eyes were blazing and I felt like he was about to set me on fire with just his gaze.

"There, you got your answer. Happy now?" He muttered.

I was starting to see why he kept things from me. The more he revealed, the worse it got.

We silently continued our knocking until we finished the entire office, including moving the cabinets and desktop to the side and checking those floorboards too. Nothing. Nada. Zilch. All we had was that hand drawn photo, with no indication where it came from and who it belonged to. Sage might not have even known it was there to begin with, considering all the dust that was collected. It looked like it hadn't been touched in decades.

"By the way, you did a pretty terrible job with the Syren that followed you. She's still alive." Knowing I dropped a bomb on him, I reveled in the fact that for once, I was the one surprising him with information, no matter how dark.

He sat up. "What? Impossible. I killed her."

Shaking my head, I sat up too. "You must've thought her dead until she healed herself, cause she's dating Leo now."

"That's not good."

"No shit, Sherlock," I threw back at him, using the full force of the sarcasm I got straight out of his handbook.

"Alluna…" He hesitated.

"Yes?"

"The second step…" He trailed off, knowing I was fully aware.

"No, I…not yet. I need more time." Standing up, I crossed my arms. With all the new information that was constantly being dumped on me, I had no time to process something as human as sleeping with someone, no matter how arbitrary it seemed now.

Reid was getting angry. He was breathing heavily. "I don't want to push you…you have to want it yourself. But every day, we get closer to getting captured. There are spies everywhere. Do you or do you not want to save your sister?"

Now I was angry. "Don't you dare mention my sister. Of course I want to save her."

He bared his teeth at me. "Just don't waste my time. If you don't want it, I'll find someone else who does."

Slamming my fist against the cabinet, I shrieked, "Wasting *your* time? You're the one who always keeps me at arm's length and never tells me the full picture!"

Reid laughed darkly. "Still not sure if you can handle it..."

"Caring about people's feelings doesn't make me weak. It makes me self-aware, unlike you, you self-serving, selfish asshole."

Folding his arms, Reid's face was plain. He lost interest in our spat. Too boring for him. "While you sit there and think about your precious *feelings,*" he mocked, "I have more important things to worry about." He walked toward the door.

I knew he was resorting to his cruel sarcasm as a coping mechanism. Still, I couldn't pretend his words didn't sting.

Feeling my eyes water, I jerked my head away from him. "I know you have feelings too. You just don't want to face them."

Noticing his presence tense beside me, I knew I was right. He was careful not to scream to the point where people in the hallway could hear, but he definitely raised his voice as he whirled back toward me. "You want feelings? Fine. I know you want me, and I want you too!"

With that, he walked out of Sage's office and slammed the door, leaving me alone with my worst enemy - my thoughts.

TWENTY-FIVE

I wasn't able to spend much more time in Sage's office, especially considering the fact that nowhere was safe, and eyes were always on me. I also wasn't in the mood to see anyone or anything. All I could do was get myself home in one piece, reprimand myself for caring too much, and muster up the strength to just let my feelings go and do what needed to be done.

The moment I entered my apartment, the solitude shook my bones and I left before my keys could fall on the counter. I wanted to clear my mind and walk.

Fresh air would do me some good.

Heading down the nearest block, I walked into a coffee shop to grab some iced coffee to keep me company.

As my mind drifted to my parents and the guilt I felt for what I was about to do, I shoved all thoughts of them into the box of forbidden thoughts and shoved it to the back of my mind.

Instead, I focused on my surroundings. My reality. It was January seventeenth. I was walking along Park Avenue and forty-eighth street. My favorite boots were on my feet, warming my toes. My hand was freezing against the plastic cup dripping with water, but every sip of the coffee was like a breath of fresh air. The weather was on the colder side, and there was a breeze every so often that blew my hair behind me. The streets weren't very crowded, except for the restaurants and bars beaming with socialites.

There. I tethered myself back to the ground and out of the storm clouds that were holding me hostage.

I just had to keep going.

My mind lost all sense of time when I popped my headphones into my ears. Before I knew it, I was on ninetieth street.

Turning toward Central Park, I finished my coffee and tossed it in a nearby trash can. A large lake spanned across dozens of blocks with benches lining the perimeter.

The sun was setting as the short day was coming to an end, and the park was dispersing. People were going home to their families, back to their human problems that may have been important to them.

Occupying a small bench overlooking the water, I allowed myself to immerse in the scenic view before me. The water reflected the giant buildings as if they were painted on upside to mirror the image above. The water was still, and the image wasn't moving.

Feeling someone sit next to me, I tensed slightly, already on edge, considering previous experiences. Sneaking a glance to my left, I was right to be wary.

The petite Syren was smoothing out her long azure dress while crossing her legs on the bench. She had to be here to talk, or else she'd have struck already.

"You found me," I said wanly.

"It's not that hard. You're always glowing," she responded in that monotone voice I'd come to recognize. Raine had it too.

"If you wanted to kill me then just do it already." Surprised at my own candor, I wondered how far I'd come since the first time I saw a creature from Naerin.

Smoothing the lines on her face, she resembled the water ahead. Ever so still with slight movements that didn't shake the scenic image. Syren's were hypnotic, and I couldn't stare at her for too long before falling under.

"Who are you?" I demanded, hoping she would give me some answers.

"Zura." She sat so still that I wondered if she would pounce if I blinked. My eyes remained open as if that was my telltale sign of her impending attack.

I had to stall while I thought of an escape plan. "What do you want from me?" My eyes darted from side to side inconspicuously, analyzing every direction around us.

She ran her fingers along the seams of her dress. "I'm not here to kill you, if that's what you mean."

Gritting my teeth, I made sure my voice was clear and strong. "Then why are you here?"

She ignored my question. "You're really missing out on Leo. He's a great kisser."

My mouth parted in surprise, but I wouldn't take the bait. I could tell she was stalling. She didn't just come here for some chit-chat. Something was definitely up her sleeve. She may have been monotonous, but her micro-expressions gave her away. The slight twitch of her brow, the barely there upturned lips. If I looked close enough, she was smug. I just had to avoid those black eyes. They'd put me in a stupor. I had to be careful and not give in to her taunt.

"You came here to talk about Leo?" I made my voice as monotonous as hers to match her level.

"Humans are fascinating. They have so much…emotion." She ended her sentence in a whisper that sounded like we were in a cave and almost submerged in water, and the hiss echoed throughout.

"Just answer the question or stop harassing me, and leave." I've learned that cowering was never the answer with these creatures, even Reid. Better to act tough and see whose bark was louder. Though as I've learned with Syrens, whose bark was more monotonous. Whose bark was more unbothered, more level-headed like an untouched body of water.

"Harm won't come to you if you do as I say. Come with me to Naerin."

"I'm not going anywhere with you. I like my human realm, thank you very much."

Zura sighed, looking bored. "Let me put this into terms you'll understand better. Come with me, or I'll fill Leo's lungs with water tonight and watch him slowly choke to death while you and his sister watch, and then take you to Naerin anyway."

Stiffening at the vivid image she painted, I responded calmly, "I'll kill you with my bare hands before you could ever hurt him."

"Was that a no I heard?"

"Go drown yourself and leave me and my friends alone."

Shrugging, she sighed. "Fine. Have it your way. Don't say I didn't warn you."

Her arm shot out and grabbed mine with force I didn't think possible from such a small creature. Her black claws grew longer and dug into my skin, ripping through my jacket. Yelping, I yanked my arm back out of pain, only for her claws to sink into my skin and leave a bleeding tiger swipe.

Not holding anything back, I kicked her away from me, and smashed my heel on her arm enough to crack the bone. Her lack of reaction startled me, but I couldn't waste a single second. Without waiting for her to heal, I was on my feet and running for my life toward the nearest exit.

Before I could take more than a few sprints, I felt something wet wrap around my leg and heave me back, throwing me off my own momentum and catapulting me right onto my stomach. Looking behind, I saw a wave of water wrapped around my leg like an unbreakable vice, a tendril of icy steel that was moved at the Syren's will. She stalked toward me at her leisure, not bothering to rush. I must've been an easy target for her.

Struggling and squirming against the grip on my leg, I desperately whipped my head around in search of something to throw at her or incapacitate her. Nothing but dirt and small pebbles were scattered around me, besides the lake that she was utilizing her power with. My fruitless attempts to kick away the water only made it wrap tighter around my leg, cutting off the circulation. Gasping in pain, I frantically waited for an epiphany to light up in my head and save myself.

"Are you ready to go now?" Zura was standing by my feet.

I was too late. All this was happening because I didn't take step two with Reid. If I could strangle myself, I would. All the chances we had…all the time we wasted…

I just had to stall and hope for Reid to realize something was wrong. I wasn't sure how, but I was out of ideas.

"I'm not going anywhere with you." Spitting at her, I angrily continued my useless fight.

"Your choice," she reminded me as another wave of icy steel knocked my head into the pavement, the sharp ground tearing into my skin and throwing my brain against my skull. Moaning, I cradled my head and tried to gather my surroundings, though my vision had gone blurry. Was I concussed?

Kneeling next to me, she swiped her finger at my bleeding arm and sucked on it, an orgasmic look on her face. "All that time you're spending with Reid has gotten to your head. You're not invincible like us. You're just a weak, pathetic human."

I couldn't answer, I was too busy moaning and focusing on staying conscious. The moment I gave in and blacked out, I was gone. I had to keep kicking while I still could.

As more tendrils of her icy steel wrapped around my appendages and tightened around my waist, I started seeing black spots in my vision.

She lifted me off the ground using her water and walked with me carried besides her, unable to move at all.

Just as I was to succumb to the comforting darkness, something flashed before my eyes and knocked into Zura's face.

Stumbling back, she uttered a sound that was a mix between a snarl and an echo and clawed at her face. Her grip on the water loosened and I fell back to the ground, regaining full control of my limbs. Adrenaline kicked in and I jumped to my feet, fighting the pounding in my head. I could rest later.

Zura's face was covered in a ball of shimmering dark dust. She was blinded by the dust as she ferociously dragged her claws against it, trying to rip it off her face, though it clung with a life of its own.

Swaying unsteadily, I knew I had to get moving before I collapsed. Another flash before my eyes and I saw my savior.

The black-winged Faerie.

Could it be that she wanted to deliver me to the Keeper herself? Was there a contest between the Keeper's spies? I didn't care anymore.

For the first time, she was close enough that I could make out her long, dark hair. Her face was clouded in the dust and I couldn't decipher her features, but I recognized her leafy dress.

Nodding thankfully to her, I started limping away as fast as I could. When I'd fallen, I must've sprained my ankle in addition to my injuries as I couldn't move as fast as usual.

The small Faerie extended her arm, and a bolt of dust shot through her and toward me like an anchor. It hit me like an icy hot flurry of air. She was pushing me forward and giving me speed. Like a strong wind, I was able to escape faster while she held Zura at bay with her dust.

Allowing her wind to become my crutch, I half-limped, half-carried myself away from the scene, jumping into the first subway station I saw. It was a miracle no one saw this exchange, but I suspected the magic she used on me was also concealing me from other humans. I walked like I was invisible and no one batted an eye. But this was also New York City, so maybe everyone did see me but didn't deem me worthy of attention anyway. I certainly picked the right city to fight off magical creatures.

My blood was dripping to the ground when I finally hurled myself down the escalator at the train station on eighty-sixth and Lex. Thankfully, I ended up in a station that would deliver me at a close range to my apartment. I knew my mind was made up before

I set foot on the train. There weren't any more chances I was willing to take; this encounter had been my last straw.

The moment I entered my apartment, I dialed Reid and put the call on speaker as I sank onto my couch, peeling my torn jacket off me and assessing my wounds. As I lifted my top over my head, the pounding headache returned and a stream of blood was running down my face by my left ear, where Zura knocked my head into the pavement. My arm had a gash of her claws running alongside my left deltoid, all the way down to my forearm. The cut was superficial, but enough that my skin was ripped in jagged lines.

He picked up on the third ring. "Yes?"

Breathing heavily, I slumped over, ignoring the pain all over my left side. "I was attacked."

"What happened?" He sounded alarmed, his worry sounding through the phone. "Are you hurt?"

"Yes…just come over…and…I'll tell you…" Trailing off, I laid on my right side, unable to continue. The dust from the Faerie had worn off, along with the adrenaline. I wasn't able to stay awake much longer.

"I'll be there in two minutes." Reid hung up and I closed my eyes, knowing what was to come and finally making peace with it.

Reid was kneeling at my side by the time I opened my eyes again, whether two minutes had passed or two hours, I wasn't sure.

He sucked in a breath. "Who did this to you?" He growled as he delicately turned me over. Words failed me as I whimpered in pain. "Stay awake, Alluna. Look at me."

My eyes fluttered open to see his concerned face. "Let me heal you," he said as he put a hand on my cheek and caressed it gently. Nodding, I moaned in pain.

His lips pressed to mine hard and fast, parting mine and shoving his tongue inside. This was not a passionate nor loving kiss, this was fuel. He was pumping his own magic into me so I would heal from my wounds. I could hardly return his kiss, but at that point, neither of us cared. He was healing me, not kissing me. It stopped feeling like a kiss when his tongue swept my mouth in a rhythmic motion, making sure I would ingest as much of him as fast as I could.

Feeling the slices on my arm seal up painlessly, I was able to sit up and accept his kiss. He continued consistently and expertly as my headache faded and the gash by my ear closed up, and my ankle returned to normal.

Less than five minutes later, it was as if nothing happened. I was perfectly restored.

Pulling away, I exhaled, shaking my head. "Thank you, Reid." Grabbing his hand, I pressed it back against my cheek because it felt nice and I was sick of fighting against what I really wanted.

"What happened?" He asked, cupping my cheek and stroking his thumb along my face.

"The Syren. Zura. She found me and tried to blackmail me into going to Naerin with her. I refused, and she attacked me. She almost got me, but the black-winged Faerie saved me. I have no idea how I made it home." Putting the weight of my head against his hand, I looked up at his concerned face, watching him process what I said.

"Is the Syren still alive?"

Looking away, I felt ashamed. "I don't know. I escaped before I saw how it ended. The last thing I saw was the Faerie blinding her with her dust." Tears welled up in my eyes. "I'm sorry, Reid. I'm sorry I couldn't defeat her. She's probably on her way to the Keeper. I failed, I—"

"Shh, it's okay." He pressed my head into his shoulder and hugged me tightly. "I shouldn't have left you. I should've known she'd be back."

A muffled cry escaped me as I clung to his shirt, staining him with my tears. "This is all my fault."

"Snap out of it, Alluna." He stroked my head. "I can't leave you by yourself anymore," he whispered as he pressed his forehead to mine. "I have to be by your side to protect you, always."

I knew what he really meant. He would be by my side until I was ready for step two, unless the Keeper struck first.

My voice cracked. "I just—I can't keep fighting against my feelings for you. I want it, and I want you…"

"Then stop fighting it," he said as his mouth claimed mine in the completely opposite fashion from before. "I want you, Alluna," he said into my mouth. "Not just because we need to get to Naerin. Every day, I question whether I fell for the wrong girl." He stared deep into my eyes as he grasped my other cheek. "She would never consider my feelings the way you do. You're the most selfless person I've ever met." His lips crashed to mine again hungrily and I let him, knowing I could no longer fight it.

"I know I'm selfish for wanting you, and wanting this. It really turns me on knowing you want me too." Reid's warm lips were causing the butterflies in my stomach to rumble as I ached down below, yearning for him. All of him.

Putting my hands on his chest and pushing him away, I observed his lust-filled face as his eyes devoured mine.

"I think—no, I know I'm ready. We must hurry before Zura gets to the Keeper."

He cupped the back of my head, his eyes blazing. "Are you sure?" He leaned in and kissed my neck, before leaning against my ear and whispering, "I will ravage you. I will make you come again and again on my fingers, on my tongue, and on my cock, and I will absorb every second of it." His hot breath on my ear gave me goosebumps and I shivered as his words ran a chill down my spine. "Are you sure, Alluna?"

Nodding feverishly, I pulled his face back into mine and finally answered, "Yes."

He smiled darkly before rolling up his sleeves. "Tell me when to stop."

TWENTY-SIX

He threw me against the wall, pinning my arms above my head, locking his hand to my wrists. Lost in his sudden dominance, I tried to unlatch my hands. He tightened his grip. A sharp breath from the pain traveled down to my core, aching for more. His other hand went around my throat, gently squeezing it while still allowing me enough air supply. His eyes raked my entire body, stuck in this compromising position, already belonging to him before he even went inside. Trying to angle my head for our lips to touch, he moved his head so that I couldn't reach him.

"Tell me you want it," He said softly, his eyes piercing into mine.

"I want it," I begged, admitting defeat and succumbing to him.

"All in due time, sweetheart." He enjoyed teasing me.

My entire being trembled for his touch, yearning for his mouth on mine. His trailing fingers on my waist sent me into a frenzy as I cocked my hips up with longing. I couldn't handle it much longer. My shallow breaths hitched as his fingers came dangerously close to my core. He pulled them away and lightly chuckled.

"Sadist," I hissed. He lowered his head and nudged the tip of my ear, sending goosebumps down my arms and legs.

"I'm just getting you ready for me, baby." He whispered in my ear, nibbling on it softly. I was about to burst.

His fingers resumed their journey and lightly traced my hips, going lower and lower until he reached my center. While he barely touched me, I was already gasping at the sensitive feeling as he traced circles excruciatingly slowly, teasing me to my wit's end. He claimed my mouth with his own, biting my bottom lip as he moved his finger lower and plunged it in. I gasped into his mouth and he breathed it in, not letting my lip go. Shuddering and giving into his touch, I let go of any inhibitions. He methodically moved his finger deep inside, hooking it against my membrane each time he dug it in, sending me into outer space.

A second finger was promptly added just as his tongue entered my mouth, tangling mine in a twist of fiery passion. My moans could not be concealed as he was sending my body into pure bliss. Keeping his two fingers steady and consistent, his thumb circled, driving me over the edge. I couldn't hang on much longer. His fingers expertly stroked the inside and outside of my wetness, bringing me closer to explosion.

His touch was so sensitive my hips were thrashing involuntarily but he unforgivingly stroked me until I detonated on his fingers. His tongue never left my mouth as I twitched under his touch, his fingers continuing their pattern.

"Keep going, baby." He said into my mouth, as I continued pulsating under him. Relentlessly, his fingers never stopped their crusade inside me, making sure to hit the right spot with each thrust. He waited until I stopped twitching and slowly removed his fingers, torturing me with a few extra circles before bringing his hand before his face, examining it. His fingers were soaking wet with my juices, and he licked them one by one.

"You taste ready for me," Reid said. Through my panting, I sucked in a deep breath. "But not yet." His mouth returned to mine as I tasted myself on his lips. I quivered under his touch, lost in the spell he put me under.

Lust surged through me as I cursed my body, betraying my mind. Reid's hand gripped my throat like a vice, and he gently squeezed it, eliciting a moan from my mouth to his. He pulled away for just a moment to hungrily look me over before his lips came crashing down again.

Feeling meek in his strong grasp, I trusted him with my body and soul. I wanted him to ravage me on his terms, for him to finally take me as his own. My body belonged to him, and he knew it. I could feel my own pulse bounding through my carotid artery as his burning hot hands pressed against my neck.

Reaching down to unbuckle his jeans, he moved his body out of my reach, suspending himself in the air.

"I'll take care of that myself." Releasing my neck, he undid his belt and undressed swiftly. Struggling to handle my nerves, I observed his perfect body as my heart kept racing. He put his scalding hand down between my legs, and I gasped from his touch.

"You're dripping wet," he said as blood rushed to my face and I looked away, feeling shy. His thumb on my chin, he turned my face towards his, hunger seeping from his glowing green eyes.

"Keep looking at me, baby," he instructed. I struggled to keep eye contact, but he had me in the palm of his hand. Obeying submissively, I lost myself in his darkening eyes. Unwavering, he reached behind me and undid my bra in one fell swoop. Reid came in for a long, passionate kiss. His tongue grazed mine ever so slightly, and I shuddered.

"Let's get you out of those soaked panties, shall we?" If I thought I couldn't get any redder, I was mistaken. I would probably bleed out if I nicked myself on my cheek at this point. Lifting my hips for him, he slid my panties out under me.

Reid lowered himself onto the bed and climbed over me. His hardness was pressing against my thighs. Pinning my wrists above my head, he slowly dragged it over me. My moans were getting increasingly louder. I couldn't take much more of this teasing, and I was *thisclose* to plunging my hips into him immediately.

"You're trembling," Reid whispered as he kissed my neck, giving me goosebumps everywhere. His length continued to trace the insides of my thigh, getting soaked in my wetness.

"Keep looking at me." Reid's eyes burned into mine. Words failed to reach me as I just nodded, looking up at him, wanting to take all of him already. His muscled chest and arms held me tighter.

"Look at me," he growled, and I immediately brought my eyes back to his.

Before I could blink, the fingers were replaced with something much thicker. Lifting my hips to meet his, I moaned as he thrust into me, deep and fast.

"You're mine now," he whispered into my ear, thrusting harder, his hand around my throat, his breath on my skin. I had no strength to hide my moans and squirms and released myself. He put his arm under me around my waist and held me so close that almost every part of our bodies were touching. Our sweat intermixed as he drove himself inside. I pressed against him, our bodies becoming one as he continued to enter me with his unforgiving strength.

My moans were silenced by his hand around my mouth. I couldn't hold anything back as he took me at his own mercy. He moved his mouth closer to my ear and nibbled on it, making me shudder and squirm against him. He unlatched his arm from my throat and moved it down… touching me in the right place while thrusting harder, deeper. Ecstasy poured through me as he kept touching me with a constant speed, making sure to match up with the rhythm of his length. He heard me moan as he kept touching me, shuddering as he knew he moved my body closer and closer to my explosion.

He kept going, whispering in my ear "Submit to me." I knew exactly what that meant. I tried so hard to keep it in, but I knew I already lost. He kept thrusting and touching me as he got closer and closer with me.

"Come with me, baby." He growled in my mouth as he bit my lower lip and blood was exchanged in our dance of tongues. I barely felt a pinch before the wound closed up and held his lip between my teeth, moaning loudly. Biting down, I felt him smile as our blood mixed once more just as we both erupted. Right as I felt myself finish, he was throbbing and pulsing inside of me. I could feel my body stick to his like a magnet as his magic dulled and spilled into me. My soul felt lifted, and my connection to him was secured. My body didn't feel human anymore. I felt ethereal. I was glowing too.

I shook against him as he continued to torturously rub his finger on me while his thick length ravaged me, feeling like I belonged to him and him only. My blood dripped down the side of his mouth and he licked it, slowly slowing down and keeping his full length inside until every last drop was deposited.

Just as I was about to roll over, he held his arm on my chest, locking me in the position, and said, "Uh uh uh. I'm not done yet."

Reid gave me a mischievous look and flew to my desk, returning less than a moment later.

Holding some duct tape I'd used to pack my things, he tore off a strip with his teeth and taped me shut below. My eyes widened as I felt my cheeks heat up.

"Now my seed will stay put without spilling out. You'll keep this on all night. Understood?"

I nodded shyly as he pressed a kiss to my forehead. "Good girl."

Reid collapsed beside me, our limbs entangled, holding me tightly, his sweat glistening under the moonlight, his pointy ears visible more than ever.

I was out of breath as if I'd just run a marathon, my chest heaving as I was hyperaware of the tape sealing me shut below. "Do you want to…"

"Not now." He was out of breath as well. "We wouldn't make the journey, we need rest. First thing in the morning, we go."

I was out like a light before his head hit the pillow beside me.

The next morning, I woke up next to Reid, who remained sound asleep as I loudly exited the squeaky bed. Not all of us could fly and gracefully move around. I went to wash up while carefully removing the strip of tape, blushing madly.

Staring at myself in the mirror, I was still in a daze. I was also coated in a sheen similar to Reid's. Quickly checking my ears, I noted they were still my good, ole' human non-pointy ones. But I could lift a few inches off the ground, much more than usual. My reflexes were sharper. I could probably heal quickly. I was ready to make the journey. I was ready to save my sister.

And the most important part - I didn't regret last night a single bit. I hadn't expected the dominance from him, but it was so erotic that I was salivating for more.

Hearing my bed squeak, I knew he was coming to.

Excitedly jumping back onto the bed beside him, I ran my fingers through his tousled bedhead, noticing how his hair shined in the stream of the sun coming through the window. His eyes remained closed as he smiled.

"Hey," he said, still half-asleep. Wrapping my legs around his torso, I straddled him, fully putting my weight on him as he continued to lay there. Putting my hands on his warm chest, I explored his body greedily, drinking in the sculpted perfection that was this man.

Reid opened his eyes and I was struck by the green pigments in his irises, encapsulated in glittery specs that seemed other-worldly. I suppose they were, considering he wasn't born human.

Lost in his green ocean, I failed to catch the smirk that crossed his face, until he cleared his throat dramatically. Not following, I gave him a questioning look. He moved his eyes around, gesturing for me to look around as well.

We were both floating a few feet above the bed.

Startled, I clung to him desperately, nervous to slide off my saddle. I didn't even realize he'd lifted off the bed. We were floating together, me laying on top of him, while he was gliding on the air effortlessly. How extraordinary!

"Hey!" I exclaimed in wonder, an exhilarated laugh escaping. I felt as free as a bird, allowing nothing but the air on my back to carry me forward.

"Wrap your arms around me," Reid instructed, and I followed through. He flew upright, his arms around me, and took me on a ride, circling around my apartment in a slow dance. I felt weightless in his grasp. I could only imagine how it would feel to fly in an open sky, how effortless it was for him. This felt amazing - I was beyond ecstatic.

Reid maneuvered his arms so that he held me bridal style. Wrapping my arms around his neck, I was awestruck by him.

Reid dipped me suddenly and I gasped, laughing with him. He was careful to make sure I was safe and secure and wouldn't bump into anything. My body fit into his arms perfectly, and I never wanted this moment to end.

Reid gently laid me down on my bed while still not touching the ground. He hovered over me, his legs levitating upwards towards the ceiling. Pressing a soft kiss to my forehead, he nudged my cheek with his nose gently.

"I'm going to get some things that we need for the trip. I'll be back in less than twenty minutes. Will you be ready to go then?" He was already at my window, waiting for my confirmation before taking off.

"Yes." Getting off the bed, I started getting dressed. "Go."

Reid was gone in the blink of an eye and I closed the window and latched it shut, knowing Reid would come knocking when he returned.

Donning a pink top so that Vita would have a piece of home

when I saw her again, I slipped into my black high-waisted jeans, debating whether to wear my comfy sneakers or fashionable boots. Considering that I would probably be running for my life, I opted for the sensible former. If there was anything that living in New York City had taught me, it was that comfortable shoes were a must.

As I reached for some chapstick, a gust of wind caught my attention. Turning towards my window, I saw that it was wide open. Supposing that I forgot to latch it all the way, I quickly used the last of my strength to push it down, sealing the cold morning air outside.

Returning to my dresser, I applied a coat of chapstick, my lips feeling moisturized as I rubbed them together. Touching my lips, I remembered the feel of Reid's on them and blushed, smiling to myself.

Another gust of wind blew in my direction. Slowly looking up at my window, I saw it was wide open. Did I not close it? I must have thought to have shut it all the way, whereas the strength of the wind reopened it.

Leaving the chapstick on the dresser, I went to inspect. The whistle of the wind met my approach as I braced myself against the pane, sticking my head out carefully.

Was Reid back already?

My eyes searched the skies for the familiar auburn hair or glint of the emerald eyes. Disappointment lurched through me when I was met with nothing but the empty air.

Something wasn't right. Feeling uneasy, I retracted my head and started to push the window back down, intending to lock it shut this time. But it wouldn't budge. It was stuck all the way open. Surprised, I pushed harder, to no avail. I looked closer at the joints and tendons of the window frame. Maybe a bug flew in there and got stuck. Perhaps bird poop acted as adhesive and sealed it shut.

It was completely free of any outside disruptions.

My knuckles turned white from the force I applied to try to push the window down. The sighs of the chilly air surrounded me, causing me to waste energy by shivering.

Sucking in a deep breath in the hope of filling my lungs, I pushed with all my might, putting most of my weight on the window.

I stopped when I realized the issue might be within the operating handle on the sill. Leaving the window alone, I bent by the ledge, scrutinizing the arm.

Wiggling the handle to and fro, I found that it was working just fine, only furthering my frustration. Huffing, I stood straight, still looking at the window ledge.

The ghost of a shadow dimmed my peripheral vision and my gaze darted outside immediately. Peering out, I tried to look for Reid again. When I saw there was nothing outside, I exhaled in dismay and tried to close the window again weakly. This time, it obeyed without question. I barely had to put any pressure on it. How odd.

Assuming I wasn't pushing at the right angle, I shrugged off the weird experience and turned to select a suitable perfume that would make me smell nice while I begged for my life.

But the moment I turned, I was met with a flurry of air that was blown into my face that felt both icy and hot. Inhaling, I felt it travel up my nostrils and enter my veins, as well as travel to my head. My vision blurred quickly and I could hardly make out shapes in front of me as darkness consumed me quickly and everything faded to black.

TWENTY-SEVEN

*S*tars brightened the sky in the pitch of the night. The glow of the fireflies twinkled around me, as though the stars traveled down to earth and chose to sparkle all around me.

Stars were all around me.

The smell of the freshly mowed grass reminded me of hay and summertime compounded into a manicured pillow for me to rest upon. Coarse leaves tickled my bare feet as I completely flattened myself against the ground, enjoying the view of the starry night.

I was lost in a sea of stars.

Vita's hand found mine, putting a smile on my face. We laid side by side in contentment.

Time was standing still.

"Mom will kill us if we come home with dirt all over our clothes," I mused aloud.

I was sinking in the pool of darkness.

"Mom needs to chill," Vita retorted.

My head was barely afloat.

I laughed. "I love you, Vita."

I didn't know if I was still awake.

She turned her head toward me and grinned from ear to ear, squeezing my hand gently. Her hand was softer than the cotton pillows I slept on every night.

I didn't know if I was still alive.

"I'll visit every weekend," She promised. Vita always kept her word. I held her integrity in high regard and took her very seriously.

I had no eyes to see, no mouth to speak, no ears to hear.

"Can I come to visit you at college?" I asked earnestly.

I was just…there.

"Of course!" She exclaimed. "But don't think I'll be dragging your fifteen-year-old ass to frat parties - not gonna happen on my watch."

The stars were swirling in a whirlpool of lights.

Our laughter filled the air like chiming bells attached to the billions of stars that sparkled ahead.

I succumbed to the void, my thread of life unknown.

Part 2

TWENTY-EIGHT

*A*re'yew daft, Hill?"

"Aye?"

"Tie up this wench before she comes to."

The gruff voices were muffled. I felt some shuffling before the stinging of some rope rubbing against my wrists fully brought me back. Hearing some grunts near me, the intense smell of rum wafted through my nose. Willing my face to remain slack and eyes closed, I didn't move.

"Dell, come get a whiff of this one. It smells delicious."

The other voice came closer. "Looks delicious too." The closer one smacked his lips as the two voices cackled.

"Love me a young one."

"I'd pillage that."

More cackling. Completely disgusted, it took everything inside me to remain still and not give away my consciousness. I tried to make sense of my surroundings while keeping my eyes shut tight. My hands were bound behind my back, and they were touching something solid. I was laying on my side. Ever so slightly, I pressed my fingers against the flooring. It felt wooden.

I knew I was outside by the soft breeze. Apart from the smell of wood and rum, I couldn't gain much from my sense of smell. The two voices had disappeared somewhere, but I didn't open my eyes. There might be more of them.

Waiting until I couldn't hear their boots anymore, I dared to crack open one of my eyes, trying not to move my face. I was at the corner of the floor, facing the edge. Seawater was visible to the eye. The ship was not sailing, as the water appeared to remain still with soft waves lapping against the ship. I must have been midship, by the look of it.

I couldn't move my hands to get out of the rope, even though I could sense it was tied sloppily and my thin wrists could easily slip out. If any of them saw me move, they could take me somewhere much worse. I had to think of a plan to escape.

What did I know about pirate ships, besides badly written movies and cartoons? They tend to have a plank used to force someone to sink to their watery death. Keeping my head on the ground, my eyes traveled up, searching for a plank.

No such beam was in sight, nor were there any openings to roll off of. Considering my vantage point, I could estimate that the height of the deck wall was not very tall. I could easily just jump off of it. Whether there were rocks in the water that would shatter me into a million pieces, I didn't know. But I would much rather do that than be a prisoner to these pirates.

Alas, I couldn't gauge my chances since I couldn't see behind me. For all I knew, someone was keeping watch on me. Perhaps other men were stationed at their post and I was within clear vision. Listening extra hard, I could hear boots in the distance, but none right next to me.

I didn't have much time. The two voices I heard. Dell and Hill. They could be back at any moment. I didn't have time to be afraid. I didn't have time to question myself. And with that thought steering the mast of my mind, I surged to my feet, took a deep breath, and heaved myself over the edge, plummeting straight into the water.

I hit the cold water headfirst with a loud splash, immediately sinking. My hands wriggled through the rope and I was able to free myself. Forcing my eyes open, the salt water stung my eyes as I assessed the murky waters. I couldn't return to the surface within plain sight of where I jumped from. I had to emerge elsewhere. But I couldn't see anything around me besides the sternpost holding the rudder, keeping the ship afloat.

I kicked my feet and swam around the post, hoping to emerge at a different point and assess my surroundings.

My eyes and nose popped out quietly as I tried to remain hidden, concealing most of myself underwater. Taking precious breaths of air, I scanned the area. The boat was docked in a peninsula within a beach of the island. A crescent moon of water surrounded by mountainous terrain and an overgrown forest with canopies shooting straight into the sky. A small cove connected the beach to the forest. The cove was my only chance to escape into the jungle and hide.

"All hands on deck!" I heard someone yell from the ship. "The soul's escaped!"

My breath caught in my throat and I held my breath as if they would hear me from all the way down in the water. This was not good. I did not have much time. They would most likely see me emerge from the water and be completely visible on the beach before I reached the cove. I only had extra seconds before they would spot me and chase me. I had to move fast.

Moving my arms swiftly, I paddled towards the shore, trying not to attract much noise from the water. The ship was not docked far from the bay and the water became shallow within minutes. I was able to stand and run for my life. The water was already knee-deep.

Not helping the splashes my feet were making as I sprinted ahead, I kept my breath steady as I pushed myself ahead. My lungs cried for rest, but I could not stop. They might have already seen me.

I barreled past the sand, the heavy saltwater weighing down my soaking wet clothes. The sky was cloudy with no sun in sight.

What a strange dream I'm having. I never thought I could feel such vivid fatigue.

"It's headed for the cove!"

At my speed, I thought my legs would explode. Adrenaline coursed through my veins. A thin layer of sweat coated my forehead as I pushed myself to go faster. The cove was right up ahead and I would disappear in the trees.

My calves were burning. My shoes pounded into the shore, sand flying all over me. The wind whipped my hair back from my face.

I had no time to turn back to see if they were following me. I could only go forward.

The moment I reached the cove, I threw myself into the crowded trees, not aiming for any particular spot.

But I wasn't safe lying there on the ground. Picking myself up with great effort, I bounded deeper into the forest, searching for a sheltered area to rest.

My legs were crying and I thought I would collapse. I had to stop.

A large weeping willow came into view, its graceful drooping branches offering shelter. The slender, oval-shaped leaves were large enough to conceal multiple people. I dove straight to the heart of the tree, protected by the layers upon layers of thick leaves.

I collapsed onto my back, giving myself a moment to breathe. My heart was pounding so hard against my chest I thought it would pop out. Gasping in short breaths, I allowed my body some time to rest. I was not a very active person. Running like that left me completely winded.

Is this what dreams felt like in the moment? Hyperrealistic until I woke up and couldn't remember such intense feelings? Even in my nightmare a few weeks ago, I remember how I was running, but I don't remember the weakness, tiredness, and lack of energy. Maybe my body forgot that part the moment I woke up. Maybe when I woke up after this dream, I'll only remember escaping from pirates that I didn't even see and running into a forest.

Bells sounded nearby. Immediately sitting up on full alert, I swept my shaded surroundings.

The bells were coming closer. I whirled around only to find a small figure flying towards me. Its wings fluttered so fast they almost disappeared to the eye. It was barely over half a foot tall and resembled a small person.

A faerie. Female, by the look of it.

Her short hair was bone-white and awkwardly cut at differing lengths, and she was muscular for her small frame. Her dark eyebrows and wide eyes were expressive as she approached me curiously, her pointed ears perking. She didn't seem dangerous and I relaxed my tense shoulders.

Holding my hand out for her, she landed on my palm and observed me as I observed her.

Her now-still glassy wings were transparent with translucent detailing in the irregular design. Her skin was so pale I could make out the veins crisscrossing down her arm. She looked like a fighter with her muscles. She also looked weak at the same time, with her hollowed cheeks and sunken eyes. Wrapped in a leaf tied at the waist with a piece of twine, she stood tall.

"Who are you?" I asked her. She lowered her wings with a low bell.

"Moone." Her voice was not high-pitched the way I assumed it would be. It rang clear to the ear despite how small she was.

"Are you a Faerie?" I asked stupidly, even though it was pretty obvious.

"I am." Moone was cautious with her words. I could sense she was wary of me, and I took that as a good sign.

"What are you?" She asked, looking me over, searching for something. Confused by her question, I answered to the best of my understanding, thinking she misspoke.

"I'm Alluna."

Moone shook her head furiously. "No. *What* are you?"

She meant her initial question exactly as it sounded.

Hesitating, I responded, "Human."

Moone backed away on my palm, muttering, "My Avis," her wings raising, becoming increasingly nervous.

"What are you doing here, human?"

"I don't know. I woke up on a ship by the cove and escaped here."

She was shaking her head. "It can't be," She gently fluttered off my palm and flew right up to my face.

"You have to follow me," Moone insisted, the veins in her neck bulging out.

Standing up, I nodded. She disappeared through the branches and I followed the sound of the ringing of her wings.

"Where are we going? Where am I?" I asked, barely keeping up with her quick flight.

"Naerin."

I halted midstep and tripped over a rock. This dream was going on far too long. I pinched myself a few times, ignoring the pain and the realization overcame me.

It couldn't be, but—

I wasn't dreaming.

I was actually in Naerin.

Shock coursed through me, more biting than my pinches. There was no way I was in Naerin. Those pirate-sounding beings were just a figment of my imagination, along with Moone. My subconscious was playing a cruel joke on me by taking Reid's description of Naerin and creating a metaphysical plane within my brain.

But if that were true, why wasn't I waking up? Why did I still feel the scratch from the rock I tripped over? Why did I still feel the dried sand stuck to my jeans and on the soles of my feet? Why was my hair stiff from the dried saltwater? Why was the smell of grass and dirt still wafting in my nose?

Denial or not, I had to keep moving. I could battle with my internal self later, once I was in a safe environment. For now, I can treat this as my new reality.

That is, unless Moone was a threat.

Though thus far, she hadn't exhibited any threatening signs. She might have even known Reid before he ran away to my world - and became my world. Maybe she could tell me what happened to my sister and his girlfriend.

My gait swayed and the blood drained from my face when I realized.

You're always glowing. What Zura had said. It wasn't hard to find me after my nightly kissing appointments with Reid. By sleeping with him, I basically put a neon sign with a finger pointing to myself. I thought I'd feel relief that I finally made it to Naerin, but considering the odds stacked against me - I couldn't have been more afraid for my life.

Opening my mouth to allow my fountain of questions to spill out, I realized Moone's glow was missing. I was so wrapped up in my thoughts that I lost her in this swelling forest that seemed to enlarge the deeper I went.

The labyrinth of trees paid me no favors as I was completely lost. The weeping willow from which I ran was nowhere in sight. Too frightened to call out Moone's name, I hid behind the nearest trunk. I couldn't attract any attention to myself - the pirates could very well be nearby. The last thing I wanted was to be in their smelly, greasy clutches.

A rustle nearby sent my heart straight to my esophagus as I clamped my hand over my mouth, my breathing accelerating like an engine. My instinct was to run, but I couldn't risk being seen. Pressing my back against the thick trunk, I carefully peered around.

A naked figure was digging through the ground up ahead with their ass in the air. Their skin was completely wrinkled and leathery-looking, and I wondered if they were part-reptilian. As I peered out more, I accidentally stepped on a branch. The crack was deafening, and I careened behind the trunk, holding my breath.

The rustling stopped. Maybe I scared the small half-reptile away. Carefully glancing around again, the figure was gone. Exhaling in relief, I returned to the trunk.

The figure was right in front of me.

It was not a part-reptile creature.

It was a little boy dressed in a suit of a dried, leathered fabric of sorts. Just like the little boy I'd seen outside Insomnia Cookies with Daisy and Leo. Maybe this one was nicer.

"Hello." I kneeled down to the boy's height to be at eye level and establish rapport. The child stared at my shoes, showing no signs of understanding. Maybe he spoke a different language. I tried again.

"What is your name?" I hoped he would sense my friendliness.

The boy bared his teeth and growled. His teeth did not look human. Uneven, chipped fangs surrounded his two front buck teeth, along with more sharp canines jutting from his gums. He was even scarier than the boy I saw before.

His dirtied long fingernails swiped at my face and scratched my cheek. The wild child stared at the blood on his fingertips and brought it to his mouth. After licking the blood, his pupils dilated to the point of his entire iris being a black hole. He howled and started jumping up and down, swiping at me again.

Abruptly moving my head, I fell to the side and quickly picked myself up. The boy hissed and swung his hand out, his leathery hood coming into view as it bounced around his shoulder.

It was a drooping sack of the dried texture. I could have sworn I saw some hair coming out of it but didn't have time to focus on that.

Ducking from another swerve, I jumped behind a tree. The boy roared, the ear-splitting sound drowning out my thoughts. I was operating purely out of instinct on autopilot at this point. The boy charged toward me and I darted a few trees away.

He caught up to me quickly and pulled the hood over his head. My jaw dropped.

The hood was a human head with nothing deeper than the skin, with holes for eyes. A mustache was visible toward the mouth. The edge of the hood was a mouth permanently cut open. My eyes traveled to the rest of the boy's suit when it dawned on me.

The boy was wearing someone else's skin.

I was about to heave when the boy bolted, his claws open and ready to inflict more damage.

I ran for dear life.

My tired legs carried me through the dark forest, the sounds of the little boy guiding every step. Hoping to gain some traction, I took a few lefts and rights to get the boy off my trail. Hiding behind a tall stump, I gave myself a single moment to catch my breath.

Something warm slid down my cheek and pooled at my chin. Thick and red, it dripped to the ground. I was bleeding. That savage little boy cut my cheek open. Pressing my hand against my cheek, I tried to stop the bleeding, unsure of how deep the cut was.

The rustling started again. The boy was getting closer. Gripping the trunk for balance, I briskly scanned the area. My hand left a bloody handprint on the trunk, barely discernible against the dark bark, but still visible upon closer look.

Snarling filled my eardrums as the boy came into view, a few yards away. Saliva dripped from his cracked lips as he dropped to his hands and knees, preparing to charge.

I backed away while shielding my cheek, the blood seeping through my fingers and dripping down my arm. A stray branch caught my ankle and my knees buckled, sending me toppling. My arms flew out to soften my landing, but I still managed to end up with a face full of dirt.

The boy stampeded like a wild ox, his fingers clawing through the ground as he gained momentum, his fangs lengthening, irises turning black. Instead of crawling back, I completely froze. My limbs were completely paralyzed as I accepted my fate. Inundated by my exhaustion, I closed my eyes, ready for the pain.

"Alluna!"

My head snapped up as I saw Moone zooming toward me. She was running her hands up her body as though she was collecting the immediate air and threw the gust of reflective wind at me. She turned backward and furiously flapped her wings at the iridescent ball of air to channel it in my direction.

The opaline air was both icy and hot, the same way it felt before I was home. But instead of fainting, I was growing weightless by the second.

I was lifted slightly into the air.

"Push off the ground!"

Flexing my calves, I launched myself into the air with the boy being a hair's length away.

He howled and jumped to catch me, but I was spinning upward with no control over myself.

"Fly, Alluna, fly!"

My mind was drawing a blank. Holding back a spat that the average human can't just fly, I held my tongue and did the only thing I could think of.

I strained like I was constipated.

Nothing changed.

Flapping my arms around like an imbecile, I snagged a tree branch and hung upside down, having no control of direction or speed. Grasping the branch tightly, I pulled my body towards the tree limb and wrapped myself around it, afraid to let go and fly up to space.

Moone's laughter rang through my ears. She flew up to my face and held herself up by my nose for support. I was not amused by her jovial throaty guffaw as I felt wholly inane, stuck to the tree, leaves sticking out of my hair, dirt everywhere. I was positive I looked like something a cat would drag in from the street.

The boy barked a few times, scratching the tree, before giving up and scuttling away in defeat.

Wrinkling my nose in contempt, I waited for her laughter to subside so she could kindly get me off the branch.

"What was that thing?"

Moone's laughter was cut short as she gazed at me sadly, flying away from my face.

"That, my dear, was a Pheraboy. We tend to avoid them."

No wonder Reid ran away from this ghastly place. That demon boy was something straight out of a nightmare.

"What was he wearing?"

"Scraps," was all she said. I didn't bother asking for details and clutched the branch tighter.

Moone held out her hand. I stared at it, unsure of what she expected me to do next.

"Take my hand."

I raised an eyebrow.

Moone tugged at my white knuckles. "Take it," she repeated.

Shakily lifting a hand, I extended it. She grabbed my pointer finger and tugged, signaling me to let go of the branch. Warily, I loosened my grasp, trying to see what Moone was trying to do. My entire body started flying into the air, but her hand grasped around my pointer finger kept me in the same sphere as her as she flew forward, guiding me behind her.

Gaining momentum with her speed, my legs leveled with the

rest of my body as we zipped through the forest.

"Where are we going?"

She looked back and shrugged. "Can't tell you."

TWENTY-NINE

The location was hardly a secret as I had no recognition of the winding forest. We flew for what felt like a lifetime until Moone told me to close my eyes. Trusting her with no rational justification, I went along with her order. I just hoped she wouldn't let go of me and leave me awkwardly stuck in the air.

I felt her guide my body past more trees while some leaves lightly grazed my skin. My scraped cheek stung as the dirt clung to my skin mixed with my dried blood.

My mind was stuck on my encounter with the Pheraboy. I was not built for this kind of lifestyle, to fend for myself in the woods. To describe me as skittish would be an understatement. Even seeing a rat in the subway was enough to send me a mile into the air. I'd hardly mastered becoming a New Yorker, and now I had to start from scratch as an UnNaeriner. I was so quick to give up and allow myself to become the feast. I couldn't last a single day on my own here. This meant I needed to form alliances fast. They might know how to contact Reid in some otherworldly way that didn't involve cell phones.

"Don't panic." Moone's grip on my finger disappeared.

How could the small Faerie think that telling me not to panic would result in me not panicking? I, of course, did what any person would do upon hearing that. I panicked.

Flailing my arms and legs around, I turned upside down again, my ass in the air. Opening my eyes, the upside-down world taunted me as I continued my unequipped process. Spotting Moone nearby, she flitted swiftly all around my body, collecting the air that surrounded me.

Oh no, she wouldn't…

She turned upside down at the same level as my face and smiled.

"This might hurt."

She swiped her small arms, gathering the air that kept me afloat. And then I fell.

The sudden rush dragged me down like a chain of weights was attached to my leg. I fell headfirst straight into a dark hole jutting out from an enormous tree. Having no time to assess my surroundings, I shielded my head as I bounced between the hollowed hole, screaming all the way down. Gravity pulled me down faster as the steep slide narrowed.

Popping out of the threshold, I somersaulted onto my back and laid there in a daze, seeing stars. Every muscle in my body hurt. I didn't know how much more of this I could take. Not bothering to get up and make sure I was safe, I remained on my back, imagining that I was back home in New York, in my apartment. What I wouldn't give to be on my comfortable couch and blasting my air conditioning. Not in this humid dark cave with unknown perils in every corner.

I finally understood why Reid didn't want to tell me about Naerin. This god-forsaken island was just a large tumor that metastasized to human earth, preying on souls alike. I could not imagine Reid wanting to partake in such horrors and sick perverted savagery such as this.

He is beyond admirable for deserting this land of predators and running away to create a better life for himself. I longed for his touch more than anything else, even more than my air-conditioned apartment and fuzzy slippers.

Time lost all meaning as I laid there. Moone made her way down and flew right past me, zipping around the corner. Hushed voices were heard, but the words were unintelligible. When was the last time I drank water or ate something?

Ah. The night before Reid and I…oh, God. How would Reid know I was taken? I just disappeared without a trace.

Tears welled up and I bit my cheek. I couldn't cry now. I had to be strong. I had to shed my pampered city-girl skin and be tougher than this. There were much worse things than a chipped manicure.

Sitting up, I groaned as my ribs protested. Looking over my dirtied clothes, I noticed rips and tears all over my top, as well as dirt and sand all over my legs. Lifting my shirt, I examined the abrasions on my stomach and sides. I looked like I was beaten up with bruises everywhere. Lowering my shirt, I rose to my feet, ignoring the pain that shot up my sore legs from all the running. Even flying was tiring.

I followed the voices around a few corners until I emerged into the first extraordinary thing I've seen in Naerin.

A bright blue lake with crystal clear waters was overhead, somehow not spilling downward. Vibrant fish swam through, minding their own business. The entire room was illuminated by blue hues, as though someone took a paintbrush and stroked blue filters everywhere. Even the air felt different. Amazed by the magic that kept the lake as the ceiling, I tried to see what was above it. Some trees were seen, and bits of the sky.

So the hole took me through the large tree and underground. An entire maze was constructed here, with multiple pathways. The perfect hiding place. Unless this maze was known to every creature on the island, that is. But if it were, then why would Moone tell me to close my eyes before dropping me through the hole?

Giving her the benefit of the doubt, I continued toward the voices. Walking past the lake room to a forked path, the voices sounded from the left side. I followed them into another room that had a small pool coming out.

Noticing Moone first, I walked up to her. She was standing on a tall rock off the edge of the pool and speaking with another Faerie with dark purple hair that reached below her waist and pale ivory-colored skin.

"Our wings will be clipped for this." The dark-haired Faerie snapped at Moone.

"I know the risk, but I have a plan." Moone was calmer than still waters.

Just as I came closer, the vigilant Faerie sensed my presence. Her wings lifted in awareness as she gave me an icy lavender glare, her eyes striking deep into mine.

"So this is the pathetic human you saved." She turned back to Moone. "By the unsolvable Avis, Moone, you should've left her to the Phera for dinner." She lifted into the air and disappeared faster than lightning.

Moone shook her head and motioned for me to come closer and dip my tired feet into the pool. Unlacing my sneakers, I tossed them to the side and took a seat next to the large rock, leaning on it while dipping my weary legs. The cool water soothed my aching legs.

"So…that was Nova," she said sheepishly.

"I thought Faeries were charming," I sighed as I felt some life return to my body.

"You have much to learn here."

"If I survive long enough."

Moone winced. She didn't like that. I couldn't blame her; I

didn't like it either. But optimism was hard to find in this mess I found myself in.

My exhaustion was taking over. As much as I welcomed Moone's help in bringing me to this safe space and wanted to hear more, I could feel my eyes closing against my will. Pulling my legs out of the water, I pushed my back against the rock and leaned my head backward on the stony surface.

"I'll just close my eyes for a moment," I said to nobody, not caring if my eyes would remain sealed forever.

Voices beckoned me to return to the land of the living. My limbs tensed as I guarded myself. Looking around prudently, I jumped to my feet.

All the pain was gone. I was completely well-rested, though my mouth was still paper dry. Touching my cheek, I was clean and washed, free of any blood-infused dirt. My stomach and ribs were free of bruises too. My wrist was completely healed even though black spots were present before I passed out.

A male voice startled me and I jerked toward the pool, completely mystified by what I saw. He was different from Raine and Zura…somehow, just more.

At the other side of the pool, a male head gaped at me. I couldn't be sure, because his entire sclera was pitch-black with no pupils in sight. His skin had a blue tint and was as smooth as silk. He revealed more of his face as he swam closer to me. His full lips had a blue hue. He was breathtaking. I came closer to him and lowered myself closer to the water. His sculptured face was well-defined, though his age could not be determined by the lack of wrinkles and creases.

My mind was completely blank as I submerged my hand in the water, lost in the vast onyx pool of his eyes.

His mouth turned downward.

"You're the human." His voice was pure velvet with a gentle lilt. He raised a webbed hand out of the water and touched my arm, sending an electric pulse through it.

Snapping out of my trance, I snatched my hand back, completely terrified. I knew exactly what he was and what he could do to me.

He was going to drown me. And I was more than happy to let him, after letting myself get entranced by his eyes.

I jolted backward, and he raised his webbed hands in an act of harmlessness.

"I won't hurt you." His lilting voice was impossible to resist, but I believed him.

He pointed to himself. "My name is Echo."

"Where is Moone?" I asked cautiously, still unnerved by how effortlessly I fell under his spell.

"She will be back shortly. She is gathering the others for you to meet." Echo lifted himself out of the pool and sat by the edge. My eyes trailed down to his scaled tail that started from his hips. It was a deep cerulean, darker than his skin tone. His physique was impeccable, completely chiseled.

Similar to Moone, he was very muscular, but also thin. His hip bones were jutting out under his tail. They all looked hungry like they hadn't had a full meal in months. I suppose that was exactly what happened. They were all being slowly starved.

Echo ran his hands through his long black hair, removing the wet strands from his smooth face. He seemed perplexed but mild-mannered, and for that, I was thankful. I didn't know how many Nova's I could handle at once.

Several voices were chattering on top of each other as they neared the small room I was occupying. I was beyond relieved when I recognized Moone's among them. Nova was chiming in too, still the hothead she pertained to be. And another voice that sounded strangely familiar…

It couldn't be…my mind was about to explode.

The three Faeries flew into the room as my suspicions were confirmed.

Moone and Nova were the first ones I saw, and flying right behind them was the same black-winged faerie who had become my savior. Except this time, I could finally see her face.

Dr. Sage Gusto.

"Sage!" I exclaimed, ecstatic to see her again. In her smaller form, that is. She was now just over half a foot tall with darkened wings attached to her back. She still wore the same wide-rimmed glasses, her salt and peppered hair falling loosely below her shoulders. She was the same zany professor I'd come to admire, just in a miniature version. And with a few pounds lost as well. Her cheeks were jutting out and her jawline was much sharper than before, her leaf dress hanging loosely on her thin frame.

"Alluna!" Her excitement matched mine as she flew up to me and hugged my finger tightly.

"I can finally communicate with you!" She twirled for me, showing off her wings.

"I can't believe this," I said in awe.

"What? Like you've never seen a Faerie with a psych Ph.D.?"

I chuckled with her.

How peculiar, indeed.

"Sage, what happened to you?" Since Sage was part of this clan then my concerns were instantly alleviated. She would explain everything to me. She fluttered pensively.

"It's a long story with me and I'm sure you're already overwhelmed…"

Shaking my head furiously, I wasn't going to be left with more questions.

"Tell me everything, including the feather."

She pressed her lips in a hard line.

"For generations, I've heard from my family about a strange land with strange creatures, and that I was a descendant. My grandmother gave me that feather, which was said to have come from this island many moons ago and provided magical protection." She smoothed out her dress. "The feather was giving me the heebie-jeebies that day, and I felt that you had to have it. I knew you believed me, deep down."

She looked between everyone's faces and I wondered if this was the first time she was sharing her tale to someone with a tail in the room.

"Can you believe that the same day I gave my feather away, I was taken? That night, I was about to go to bed when I was suddenly hit with an icy hot blast of air and woke up here."

Just like what happened to me.

"So the pirates got you too," I deduced.

"Huh?"

"The pirates brought me here," I explained.

"You mean the Phantos, the pirate specters. And no—" She hesitated. "They weren't supposed to do that. They broke the law."

"They broke…the law?"

"Only the Keeper is allowed to bring back the soul. The Phantos don't have the full power to transfer a human. Your body is still in the human realm."

I paused. "Then how can I feel pain and hunger if I'm not physically here?"

"Your soul still has all senses intact."

"But why did they bring me?"

"You were Marked, my dear," Sage admitted sadly.

"Then why didn't the Keeper—"

"You ask too many questions, *human*," Nova's irritated voice cut through. "Do you realize the danger you've put us all in?"

Nova looked down at me with disgust, her nose wrinkling.

"We'll be executed for breaking the law by hiding you."

Moone put her hand on Nova's shoulder and rubbed it gently. "It's for the cause and you know it."

Nova crossed her arms and huffed, lifting her chin up. "The cause," she scoffed, "is dead. Just like Raine and Pine."

"You knew Raine?" I interjected. Everyone ignored me.

"She can help us win." Echo trailed his long fingers on the water, sounding bored.

"*It* won't help us do anything except die," Nova stated venomously, looking at me like a cockroach that needed to be squashed.

Sage turned on her. "Get your frontal lobe in check, Nova. *She* is the answer to our prayers, you single-celled fool."

Nova fisted her hands as the flare from her opaline wings reddened from anger. She pointed a menacing finger at Sage. "You don't know who to pray to anymore, half-Nae. Keep talking like this and I'll clip your shit-stained wings myself." On that note, Nova flitted away, leaving us stunned. I'd noticed that Sage's wings differed from that of Moone and Nova, and was starting to put the puzzle pieces together as to why.

"Half-Nae?" I ventured.

Moone answered, "It's a derogatory term used to describe someone who was originally human and chose to live their miserable remainder of life bound to Naerin instead of dying with integrity. Her wings are darker because they were formed from her soul's ashes."

Sage stiffened as if she was just struck across the face. Even the Faerie on her side held some disdain for someone who chose to remain in Naerin. Everyone judged her for choosing to stay. The tension hung heavily in the air.

Sage's face drooped with wavering hope. "It doesn't have to be miserable forever." Her eyes met mine. "Alluna can save us all." With that, she flitted in the opposite direction, disappearing behind the corner.

Hoping I wouldn't ruffle anyone's feathers, I attempted to lighten the mood. "Must be nice to have wings to help you fly out of the room dramatically for emphasis."

Echo released an unrestrained belt of laughter, a stark change from his usually monotonous nature. "I like this one."

Giving a half-smile, I looked at Moone. She was hardly hiding her ill-concealed smile, definitely humored. I could tell humor ran sparse around here. In my short time here, the disposition struck me as gravitating around every-man-for-himself nihilism, stemming from self-hatred and misanthropes alike. It was quite the paradox; they didn't know who they hated more, themselves or anyone around them.

Feeling way too springy on my toes, I geared up to Moone, "You healed me." I was ready to run a marathon, though that would be the last thing I would do.

She curved up her eyebrows. "I did, how did you know?"

"Faeries have healing abilities," I thought back to every time Reid healed me.

"Where did you get this knowledge?" Echo sounded.

I hadn't the slightest idea how to classify Reid. "This guy I'm with told me. He ran away from here to live in my world. Maybe you knew him?"

Moone's face paled as she and Echo exchanged looks.

"Haven't heard of anyone running away from here in a very long time." Moone was paper-white.

"His name is Reid—" I realized I didn't know his last name nor if he had one. "Just Reid."

The creatures shrugged. "We do not know anyone by that name."

A wicked smile crossed my face. "He must have done a very good job, in that case."

They nodded, remaining apprehensive.

My eyes were downcast. Reid might not have any idea that I was taken. He told me himself, time passed differently here. What if it had only been seconds since we said goodbye on my realm? All I could do was hope that once he returned to my apartment and found me missing, he would realize what happened and come running straight to Naerin before my soul was stolen from me.

"You should rest, it's getting late. We have a big day ahead of us tomorrow." Moone's voice impaled my inner monologue right through the core.

Skeptical, I tilted my head quizzically, peering intently at her. When she did not elaborate, I asked, "Why?"

"I'm to teach you to fly."

THIRTY

aving no indication of how much time passed since I passed out on a rock covered in soft moss in a nearby room, I trusted Moone to wake me in time for my lesson. I slipped into a coma the moment I laid down, completely lost to the world.

Awakening from the sound of arguing voices, it took me a moment to recollect where I was and come to terms with my new reality. After a few failed self pep-talks, I switched into autopilot mode, focused on the action directive at hand. My flight yesterday was beyond pitiful and I knew I had to improve on that skill above all others. I couldn't even dream of facing another creature headfirst and daresay, fighting. I hardly maintained the skill to swat a fly in my air-conditioned apartment, I'd be too nervous.

I had to have the element of escape up my sleeve, at least until I toughened up and earned some mental calluses, so to speak. Based on how fast I gave up yesterday, I knew I had a long journey ahead of me.

It was imperative that I held out until I was reunited with Reid so he could guide me to my sister. All I needed to do was to stay just barely out of the Council's reach. Survive with the protection of some Faeries and a Syren who hardly knew if I was worth fighting for. I had to show them they could trust me.

Sitting up and rubbing the last of the sleep from my eyes, I noticed there was a small pile of fruits near me, neatly stacked. An apple, a banana, and something that could have been a mango, or papaya or guava - I didn't know nor care. I gobbled up the nearest fruit that I assumed would be sugary - but I found it had no taste at all. I could have just as easily been eating the air, considering it had the same flavor but with added texture. Could this be the reason every single creature I've met looked starved? Was the food even real?

It certainly felt real. I juggled the apple, noting the color and weight. It was crunchy like an apple. But the taste?

I bit into it, chewing slowly. No taste at all. Just pure, crunchy nothingness.

Not wanting to finish the tasteless fruit, I tossed it to the side. Hunger continued to rumble in my stomach, but this meal was so bland and flavorless that I would just as rather continue to my lesson on an empty stomach. Might be better for my nerves anyway - not having anything to regurgitate and vomit.

And so I followed the voices, hoping Moone's magic dust would be kinder to me today than yesterday's disaster.

They led me to a nearby hatch that exited in a secluded part of the forest, assuring me it was safe to practice there. I couldn't tell the difference between any part of the forest so I accepted their word without much thought. For the next hour, the flying lesson commenced.

It was a disaster. If I thought I was subpar yesterday, today was miserable by comparison. I spent most of the time hanging upside-down, gracing the sky with my butt. For the life of me, I could not figure out what I was doing wrong, and neither could the rest of the brigade, though I suspected Nova wanted me to fall and break my neck. Her scorn was present the entire lesson. Echo was lurking mutely in a nearby pond. He was not a merman of many words.

Every time Moone coated me with dust, I would immediately lift up, roll right over and remain stuck while upside-down. She'd have to gently maneuver me back in place and take away the dust so I would fall back to my feet.

The number of times I almost heaved from all the blood rushing to my face was insurmountable. It was a miracle I didn't faint as the short lesson concluded.

All my energy was drained with nothing left to salvage. I couldn't even eat my hunger's worth as all they had to offer were tasteless fruits.

I was leaning against a tree, forcing myself to keep focus. The pond that Echo was occupying was beside the tree, and I caught a glance of my haggard self. My matted hair coated in sweat was not a good look. All this after a mere hour's work.

Nova mirrored my thoughts. "It isn't capable. Why couldn't they have Marked someone stronger?" She hadn't moved from her spot on a low branch. The entire lesson, she'd scoffed every time Moone gave me encouraging words and frowned whenever I failed.

Moone somehow remained patient. "We just have to keep trying."

"Nova is right." There was no point in pretending anymore. I was a walking target, dragging all of them along. "I am not capable of saving you, and I wish I could." Getting to my feet, I knew what needed to be done.

"You have to take me to my sister…if she's still alive."

Moone asked, "Who is your sister?"

"She was taken by the Keeper a few months ago, and I need to save her."

Moone flew up to my face, her expression sorrow. "We have no idea what happens to the souls after the rotation if they don't come to us. Even if your sister was taken here, none of us would know."

I was ready to drown myself, but I couldn't completely give up hope. Reid had to have more information; he wouldn't have embarked on this journey with me otherwise. If everything I did was in vain, I wouldn't have the strength to go on. I had to trust that Reid would help me.

Sage, who had been fluttering pensively, settled on a nook nearby.

"You can't give up on us that fast." Her expression was rigid as she wrapped her thin arms around herself.

"Figures," Nova scoffed. "Least it has the sense to agree with me."

Moone contemplated. "Lest you forget, there's not been a single soul besides her who evaded the Council, even if by sheer, dumb luck."

"That luck is bound to run out. And I don't intend to be on the losing side when it does."

"I don't want anyone to get hurt. Just please, my purpose here is not to wage this war. All I want is to find my sister." My mind was set. Even though the others didn't want to admit it, Nova was right. She understood the implications of helping me and the odds against my favor.

Moone shook her head sadly. "You poor thing, there's so much you don't know."

"Then tell me."

"Do you even know what our purpose is beneath the Weeping Willow?"

The tree Moone had sent me tumbling into.

"Obviously, it doesn't know anything," Nova interjected from above.

Ignoring her, Moone continued, "These words are forbidden, so I'll only say them once. We are Anti-Keepers."

Fear crossed from Nova's face to Sage's to Echo's, as they rapidly looked around nervously as if the trees had ears.

"There used to be more of us, but they were picked off and executed one by one."

"Most of the Nae are comfortably numb in this predatory lifestyle, but we want to return to the land of peace we once were. The only way to do that is with the help of a soul. And now you're here." Moone's eyes flashed with hope.

"You have the wrong person…" I trailed off, astounded by how much hope Moone had in me. "I-I can't even fly with your magic air."

"Faerie dust," Moone corrected. "And it's alright. We can keep you hidden beneath the Willow. No one knows of it but us, because we built it and concealed the tree and surrounding area with magic."

Explains how I was able to practice flying out here without fear of being seen. In any case, I could not be the one to lead them away from their servitude and into a land of harmony.

I shrunk back, not meeting anyone's eyes. "Please take me home." My voice cracked. If I could return to the human realm and find Reid, we could return to Naerin together. It was the only hope I had left.

I never asked to be dumped into this mess. I just wanted to find Vita, bring her home, return to my normal life, and pretend this never happened. Just like Reid, I wanted to escape Naerin. I felt so constricted that I could hardly breathe from the claustrophobia of all this information being thrown at me.

"Shame," Echo spoke for the first time all morning. The pain in his voice stung like a lash, that singular word slicing right through me. He wanted to believe in me too. I could never tell when he was looking right at me since his obsidian sclera left a vague impression. But I felt his dark eyes burning into me, filled with disappointment.

"I'll take her home myself," Sage's voice interrupted the silence. "She never volunteered to be a part of our war." I welcomed Sage's defense, knowing she was the only one who would understand my turmoil. She was a lowly human just like myself not too long ago.

"Thank you." Gratitude replaced the ache in my heart. Soon enough, I would be home, safe and sound, reunited with Reid—

"You don't call the shots around here," Nova snarled.

"I don't need your permission, Nova." Sage struggled to remain calm. "Besides, you don't want her here anyway." She was smug as she pointed out Nova's flaw in her argument.

Turning back to me, Sage said, "I will take you, but you'll have to know how to fly." Sage perused me.

"I'll do anything it takes."

"Pity." Any semblance of friendship that was slowly forming between Moone and I was getting more distant by the second. Her face lost any inkling of hope that was previously there. "Farewell."

Wincing, I couldn't look at her anymore. But Sage had a point. Even if I was the first and only person thus far to have fallen into the wrong place at the right time, in their case, it didn't mean that I was obligated to do anything. As selfish as that was, I just wanted to take my sister and return to my New York City life with New York City problems. I wasn't built to handle anything beyond superficial life problems. I could still hardly handle Vita's disappearance, even though it has been four months. I was emotionally weak. Physically, too. If I stayed, I would lead them all to their deaths, including mine.

I didn't have to answer to Nova's snark anymore either, so I paid her huffs no attention as I focused on Sage.

"I'm listening."

Her face was grim. "Flight is the only way to travel to your realm."

"How did the pirates get there then?"

She grimaced. "The Phants took a fairy and crushed her until she was nothing but Faerie dust and used her as fuel."

Flinching, my fear of the Phantos only worsened. The things they were capable of…were beyond despicable.

Sage started collecting some of her surrounding air, collecting her dust. I could tell she needed a vast amount for the long journey ahead.

"A batch of dust is enough for a few hours in the air," Sage explained as the barely visible ball of air grew in size. The longer I stared at it, the more I could see some reflective particles, similar to that of the Faerie's wings.

"You won't have enough, half-Nae." Nova flew over and effortlessly doubled the batch as it went from the size of a chestnut to the size of a beach ball. Though it took Sage great effort to collect dust, it flowed from Nova like a shower. It seemed that even though Sage was now a Faerie, she didn't have the full capabilities of a full-blooded Faerie. Or full-dusted Faerie, by the way they made it sound. I wondered if Faeries bled. What coursed through their veins? Dust?

Peculiar, indeed.

Selfishly, I wondered if Sage had what it took to bring me home. Scolding myself for such an ungrateful thought, I focused on how lucky I was that she volunteered in the first place. I was already being selfish enough for abandoning them.

I thought of the mighty heroines I read about in my epic novels. How courageous they were, how they excelled at being leaders, how triumphant they were. What would any of them do in my place? Certainly not run away like a frightened mouse. They would start their battle plan and lead the citizens of Naerin out of this grisly war, out of their starvation, into a better life.

I was no hero. I was just a city girl. All they needed was another soul to help them. Really any other soul was a better choice than me. I was a coward.

These thoughts circled my brain as Nova and Sage created a ball large enough to coat my entire body and threw it over my head. Feeling the familiar icy hot blast, I felt myself lifting into the air and sent up a silent prayer.

As usual, my center of gravity shifted and I found myself falling upside-down yet again, powerless to stop. I'd fly home upside-down if that's what it took.

"Here's a lesson for you," Nova said spitefully as she sent a whoosh of air in my direction, shooting me into the sky with full force.

"No!" Sage and Moone cried out, but they were too late.

I screamed as I somersaulted vertically at a speed that made me dizzy. Branches and leaves cut right through my arms and legs, as I managed to hug my knees and protect my head and chest. A few deep slices caused me to cry out.

After I passed the tips of the trees, I felt a small vibration as I entered the open sky. I must have broken straight through the magical barrier. Anyone would see me now.

Crying from fear, I was powerless to stop my trajectory.

But my flight was cut short rather quickly as I smashed right into another flying object, hitting me with so much force that the dust was knocked right off me, and I fell back down headfirst.

Right before I hit the ground, the smasher-in-question swooped in and grabbed my legs and waist before I crashed.

And when I lifted my eyes to see whose muscular arms had saved me, I was beyond relieved to see that it was Reid.

"Reid!" His familiar strength gripped me closer, the shock on his face paralleling mine.

"Alluna! I've been searching for you for days." He gently landed on the ground and set me down. Days? How long had I been here?

"I was taken right after you left my apartment. I—wait, how did you—"

"You're hurt!" Concern flashed over his eyes as he assessed the fresh scratches marking my arms and legs. "Who did this to you?" He demanded.

"The biggest villain of all," I said gravely. "That tree." Pointing to the nefarious tree, I resorted to my default setting in times of stress - making jokes when no one wanted to hear them.

Reid followed my gaze and rolled his eyes, before wrapping me in a tight hug.

"Tell me what happened," He demanded.

"The Phantos brought me here. I escaped into the cove on the beach and met the Ant—well, you'll meet them." Just barely catching myself on saying the forbidden words, I hoped my correction wasn't obvious. Reid has clearly been gone from Naerin for a long time, he might not have any idea about this secret organization. It wasn't my secret to tell either.

Licking my dry lips, I continued, "They were actually about to take me home by teaching me to fly, though, for the life of me, I could not get the hang of it," I rambled, still in shock that my precious Reid was here, "until I smashed right into you…you, who aren't telling me how you're here."

"Happy thoughts," Reid said softly. "Happy thoughts lift you into the air."

Just as I was about to press on my unanswered question, the others stormed in.

"Who is this?" Moone asked just as Nova asked, "How are you on the ground?" Just as Sage said, "Good heavens."

Echo appeared on two long blue legs, astounding me further. He crossed his arms and leaned against the nearest tree in the background, observing us mutely.

"Who are you?" Moone insisted.

Reid's hand around my waist slightly tightened, keeping me close to him for protection.

"This is my…this is Reid," I explained, gesturing to him, "Who was about to tell me how he came here."

Reid eyed each of the three fairies, especially making long hard eye contact with Sage, and the shadowed Syren lurking behind before his eyes finally fell on me. He blinked a few times, clearly not used to being the center of attention after all that evasion.

"The Keeper, along with the Council, have been hunting me ever since I fled. They finally found me, but I escaped and was fleeing into the forest in search of a place to hide."

My hand flew to my mouth in horror. Could it be that we were on the same ship?

"Come with me, Reid." I took his hands and clasped them in mine. "Let's find them."

His eyes were full of sadness. "We can't."

Sage stepped—flew in. "Why?" She demanded.

"They can track us wherever we go since we were both Marked."

I gasped, not wanting to believe it. I was so close—so close to her, only to find out it was a useless plan.

"What do you propose then?" Moone chimed in, her pale skin turning sallow.

"Even if we find the ones we lost, we can't leave safely unless we win the war." Reid's hoarse voice cracked. I vaguely remembered him telling me this before, but my brain just so happened to delete that knowledge since I was dealing with other obstacles, but I could see he really meant it.

"Unless we win the *what?*"

"We have to fight."

No, no, no. My mind had been set. I was prepared to return to my average *human* life with *human* problems. What coffee should I order today? Am I taking the train or walking? Am I cutting class?

Not this otherworldly war that I knew nothing about in this fantasy land with fantasy made-up creatures that I preferred to remain in storybooks and fairytales.

I had to get out of here.

My legs were carrying me somewhere without any inclination to where I was going. I could feel Reid's strong arms wrap around me, prohibiting me from running.

I couldn't breathe. I was going to be sick.

A great tremor overtook me as I shook with tears racing down my cheeks. I didn't want to be here.

I hardly wanted to be alive.

No longer able to hold myself up, I crumpled in a disheveled heap as Reid went down with me, cradling me as I sobbed into his arms. He stroked my hair in the same way he comforted me the other times, but I couldn't shake the hysterics. Gut-wrenching sobs tore through my chest as I realized that I would most likely die here. Not knowing what to do, I punched Reid's chest in exasperation, in frustration over my life being torn away from me. He did not react and held me closer, rocking me side to side like a baby. Every few seconds, he wiped my wet cheeks.

The sounds of my wailing and suffering and shaking echoed through the ground and grass and trees and leaves and branches and sky.

Reid chewed on his lower lip as his eyes grew wet. He felt my pain. He understood me and really felt my pain. I never felt closer to him than I did at that moment, knowing he was thinking of another. But he never let a single tear fall. He wanted to be strong for me. For us.

My sobs were slowly calming down. My chin trembled as tears of pain continued to fall down my cheeks. I settled into a catatonic state in his arms, unable to move or speak or breathe.

Reid signaled the Faeries, exchanging some incoherent words that I could not understand. Everything was blurry. My mind, my thoughts, my emotions, my body, my soul.

Not too long after, I felt the icy hot blast of air shot right into my face. But instead of lifting into the air, I sank down, down, down into the place I wished I could remain forever... unconsciousness.

THIRTY-ONE

I woke up lying down on Reid's lap in the lake room, calming blue hues tinting every corner. He was grazing my shoulders, lightly running his cool fingers up and down my arms.

Cool fingers?

I sat up, the stark difference striking me. His skin was always scorching hot before, but now it felt cool to the touch. I wondered what other differences he had in Naerin.

"Awake?" Reid asked carefully.

"Yeah…did you knock me out with Faerie dust?"

"Yep." He didn't even bother trying to deny it. I wasn't even upset. If anything, I felt much more level-headed after my episode.

"Do you see why I am the worst person to fight?" It wouldn't take much convincing. Anyone would see that. "I just cried like a baby because I can't handle any of this."

"You don't give yourself enough credit, Alluna." Reid leaned in closer. "You escaped from the Phantos all by yourself. You made friends on your very first day here and were protected."

"I'd hardly call Nova a friend."

He sighed. "I spoke to her while you were out." My interest was piqued. "You have to understand, they have been through hell. They are in hell. Every day is a battle. They've been through so much, it's only natural for them to be rough around the edges."

He made sense. But still, I couldn't shake Nova's blatant disregard for me and wondered if there was a deeper reason.

He leaned in closer and pressed his blue-tinted lips to mine, surprising me further.

Pulling away from his lips, I said, "Don't tell me we need to maintain our appointments here, too."

Reid chuckled. "No, I did that because I wanted to."

A rumble through my stomach interrupted our conversation. The hunger was taking over. Pulling away and pressing a hand to my stomach, I peered at Reid, groaning softly.

He frowned. "I know."

"Fruit tasted like nothing." I accused bitterly, though it wasn't his fault.

"I know," he repeated, his face in deep thought. "The hunger will go away eventually."

His words did not make me happy.

"Won't I starve to death?"

"No one dies in Naerin."

No wonder Nova was so mean. She just needed to eat. All of them needed to eat. I imagine I'd be cranky too after an eternity of no food.

"How long was I out for?"

"The rest of the day and night."

"What do we do now?" My questions felt robotic.

"Now we must plan."

"No, we have to find them first. What's the point of planning something involving other people that aren't aware of it?"

Reid sighed. "There's a lot you don't know about the way things work here."

There it was again. A plea for ignorance. I had to really put my faith and trust into him.

"Then tell me," I said blandly, knowing I'd still be left with questions.

Reid stood and gave me a hand.

I opened my mouth, about to say something until he gave me a crooked smile and shushed me.

"We have all the time for talking, but not for this," He whispered as he kissed my neck. I shivered, goosebumps appearing on my arms. He ran a trail of kisses up my jawline before his mouth claimed mine. I didn't care if he was distracting me. My need for his touch was stronger.

He pushed me back against the hard rock wall, his hand on my throat and his tongue dancing with mine. My lust started taking over my hunger and I allowed it to take over my entire body as my hand gripped his hardness through his pants.

Someone cleared their throat loudly and we pulled apart like two teenagers caught in the act by their parents.

Nova looked at us like she wanted to smite us.

"If you wouldn't mind, we have things to discuss," she said angrily as she flew out of the room, her wings red.

Reid shrugged sheepishly and held out his hand to lead me into the other room, but not before whispering in my ear, "I like to play with my food anyway."

In a new corner of the underground maze, the Faeries were situated on a flat rock. Moone and Nova kept some distance from Sage, which I marked internally. I found this to be surprising, but then again, I knew nothing of the relationship between Moone and Nova. At first glance, I thought Moone and Nova didn't get along, yet they still stood near each other, an air of camaraderie present regardless of their perpetual bickering. Sage hadn't yet made it into their inner circle, and I wondered if she ever would.

In the absence of any bodies of water, Echo was sitting with his blue, shiny, hairless legs crossed. He struck me as European with his features, but I could not be sure. I imagined him as a human I'd pass on the street and the image of him sitting daintily at a quaint Parisian cafe with a croissant in hand came to mind. Above all, I wondered what happened to his tail. I hoped Echo had no intention of hurting us. Who knew what he was capable of in his starved state of mind?

I was a walking meal for any of them. It was imperative for me to remember that. But now that Reid was by my side, I knew he would protect me. We still had our common goal, even if we were dancing around our true feelings and purposefully ignoring what would happen after we found the ones we lost.

Moone was right before when she said I had much to learn.

Reid and I plopped down next to Echo and formed a small triangle with the flat rock in the center. A makeshift control room, where we the generals can discuss war tactics and strategies. All that was missing was the war table with pawns guided by sticks as we figured out where to strike.

"Where did your legs come from?" I didn't bother waiting for the others to start, I had to know. Echo's expression remained colorless, though he raised an eyebrow.

"My hips," he answered, a smile tugging at his lips. His humor was remarkably dry for someone who survived in a wet environment.

I laughed nervously, hyper-aware of Reid's presence, even though we weren't technically together.

Deciding to try again, I rephrased my question, "What happened to your tail?"

Sage spoke for him. "Syren's get temporary legs when they are out of the water, but they have to return to the water within a day."

Catching her drift, I gawked at Echo. "Does it hurt to walk?"

"Like walking on glass." His demeanor was perfectly flat. I would've never guessed that he was in pain. But I suppose most creatures in Naerin were so used to hunger and pain that they hardly felt it anymore.

It was finally starting to dawn on me that the creatures were not the problem. They did not choose to live like this. There was an overlying issue that stemmed from the Keeper based on what Reid previously implied.

For the first time, I considered what it was like to live on this land and empathized with them. It seemed I would have no choice but to stay and fight for them, and I was starting to see what I was fighting for.

"What is this war?" I asked nobody, hoping someone would finally tell me.

A collective sigh, even from Reid, was my answer. Until Moone spoke.

"There is no war currently."

I couldn't be more confused if I tried.

She continued. "There would be a war if we continued to break the law and fight against the Keepers."

"So you want a war?" I surmised.

"None of us want a war. But it might be the only option."

"I don't understand."

Moone and Nova exchanged a glance and for the first time, I saw genuine fear on Nova's face. I briefly considered that her tough act was a facade used as a coping mechanism. Though that didn't excuse her belittling comments to Sage or me.

"The reason why we live the way we do is because of the Keepers laws—"

"Keepers, as in plural?" I thought there was only one Keeper.

"Yes. There is an entire society of Keepers, and they live like royalty. Whenever a Keeper finishes their sentence and retires - so to speak, they live in a community and command everyone around."

"What if you just didn't follow their laws?" My question felt half-witted but I had to ask.

"We have no choice. They are the only ones who can bring us sustenance. If we don't follow their rules, we'll all die."

"I thought no one dies in Naerin."

"No one can die organically, but we can be slaughtered."

Not me, but my soul. I wasn't even considered a person here - nothing but food. I could tell by those who'd referred to me as "it."

Sage added, "A soul was the beginning to their magic and can be the end."

"But then what would everyone eat?"

"Long ago, Naerin did not survive off souls. No one remembers the old way as most new citizens were not alive during that time. We do not know how Naerin lived before, but breaking the rule of the Keeper is the first step."

"And how do we do that?"

"You have to—"

Moone was interrupted by a resounding quake from the walls above us. Bits of rock crumbled as the sound of stampeding roared in our ears. Even though I knew the spot was magically concealed, I still closed my mouth shut, scared to make any noise.

"They're hunting you," Nova said in a sing-song voice as if waiting for me to get caught, her lavender eyes stuck to the rumbling ceiling.

Reid's head snapped up to the ceiling as if he were trying to see through it. Dread roiled in my stomach and I felt my bounding pulse through my chest as anxiety overcame me.

But I couldn't break down in tears every time something inconvenient happened. I had to be better than that.

Trying my best to allow Reid's cool temperature to chill my blazing emotions, I took a deep breath. No gushing tears came rushing to the surface. Astonished and slightly amazed by my own durability, I was able to calm myself down for the first time without having to depend on Reid or Faerie dust.

Maybe I could actually do this.

We waited to resume our conversation until the stomping subsided, but my thoughts digressed to an unrelated topic.

"Wait..." I said before Moone continued what she was previously saying.

"If I can't physically go back to my world, can I contact someone?"

Reid narrowed his eyes as he glanced sideways at me, suspicious of whom I would contact. I couldn't blame him -

obviously, he wouldn't want me to go rambling about his world. And as much as I understood that, I had a different idea.

Sage answered vaguely, "There are ways."

I immediately straightened up. "How?"

"Dreams."

My nightmare flashed before my eyes. The nightmare with my sister, and Sage's feather.

"You sent me that dream?" My voice was hoarse. "Was that a vision?"

"No. It was a clue."

Relief poured through me.

"Can you put me in someone else's dream?" I inquired.

She was sparse with her words. "Yes," was all she said, and all I needed to hear to confirm my suspicions.

"Whose dream?" Reid demanded, making it clear he would have to approve.

I took a deep breath, knowing exactly how he would react.

"Daisy."

"Absolutely not," Reid said as his nostrils flared in anger, his jaw clenching. "You can't tell another human about any of this."

"Reid, she's the only other human I can trust."

"She's just a human," he snarled.

"So am I. Have you forgotten?" He was doing it again, bringing out the worst side of me as my volume increased. "Sorry that I'm *just* a human here, but I'm going to do this with or without your support!"

"Contact her, and she'll die too." He was venomous.

"At whose hand, yours or the Keeper's?"

"Keep testing me and you'll find out." He was notorious for assuming the worst, especially with the scant amount that he trusted. Reid walked out of the room, his footsteps unheard as he flew somewhere unknown.

The others stared incredulously before Nova decided to say, "Well, he sounds really secure in your relationship."

Shooting her an unfiltered glare, I tried my best to ignore her. There was no point in engaging with someone like Nova. Her pleasure in upsetting others said more about her than me. I had to give Reid some space, knowing him. He would return ready to have a logical conversation on his terms.

But I had no time to waste. So I focused back on Sage, not caring if Reid would forgive me.

"I need you to send me into Daisy's dream," I pressed, not willing to take 'no' for an answer.

"It won't be easy," Sage hesitated, but I shook my head to silence her.

"Whatever it takes."

Sage gave me a contemplating stare and flew onto my shoulder, holding onto my ear for support.

"Daisy is not asleep right now but I can put her in a micro sleep-like state. She may think she is simply zoning out. I need to tap into your soul to find her and then channel you. I won't be able to hold it for long, so try to make it fast."

Nodding, I closed my eyes, trying to relax my nerves.

"Will it hurt?"

"No, dear. Just don't resist."

And with that, I allowed Sage to stroll right into my soul.

I felt like I was being put under anesthesia. Darkness surrounded me. Before I knew it, the world around me dissipated and turned black. Nothing was visible to me besides my hands and feet. I blinked a few times, trying to make sense of my surroundings, but the blackness did not change with my eyes closed.

I was able to take a step forward, so I must have been standing on something. But distance had no meaning anymore. Neither did any of my senses besides my limited vision.

A firm hand on my shoulder startled me. Whirling around, I was face to face with Sage, who was now her lanky human size.

"Sage!" I threw myself around her, appreciating her old form. She hugged me back tightly.

"How?" Incredulous, I observed her missing wings and non-pointy ears.

"We are in your head," she smiled, "This is how your subconscious wanted me to look."

I missed the human Sage. Even though her loud personality stayed intact in her Faerie form, there was something about her wingless form that made me feel less alone in this world of magical creatures.

Sage put both her hands on my shoulder as her face grew serious. "Listen very carefully. I will open a door that leads right into Daisy's mind and dream. You will only have a few minutes. Once the door starts shrinking, you *must* return."

Nodding, I said, "Okay."

"Alluna, I mean it. If you do not return through that door in time, you will be stuck in Daisy's mind forever, and will only have consciousness when she dreams."

Feeling faint under her grasp, I nodded again. The severity of Sage's words was clicking in my brain and I realized how perilous a task this would be. Lowering her hands from my shoulders, she gestured her head to the side, signaling me to go.

The door was about a hundred feet away. The light inside was so blaring that I had to shield my eyes while I bolted toward the door. Without any specific words in mind, I knew I had to get my message to Daisy before it was too late.

As the door got closer, I was able to see what was inside. Rows of chairs leading up to a podium. Our psych lecture hall. Jumping headfirst into the door, I fell forward and landed on my face. I could have just as easily stepped through the door calmly. Looking around, I saw a handful of students taking their seats. They all ignored me as if they didn't see me, and their faces were blurred out, like in a dream. Noticing Daisy on her way to take her seat, I charged forth, sitting in my usual seat next to her.

"Oh, hey, Alluna." She took out her laptop and pulled up her lecture notes.

As much as I wished I could allow her regular dream to continue, I was about to turn it into a nightmare. Hoping that her conscious brain was still in there, I shut her laptop, gaining her full attention.

"Daisy, it's me."

She rolled her eyes. "I know it's you. You're Alluna."

I shook my head. "No, Daisy. You're dreaming right now. I came into your dream."

Daisy was not comprehending my words. She looked around the lecture hall, and then back at me. I was wasting time and started to shake her shoulders. The moment my fingers touched her body, she gasped, her eyes bulging.

"Oh, wow," Daisy said. "Guess I'm having a lucid dream."

"No, I came here to give you a message."

"What are you talking about?"

"Daisy, I don't have much time. You have to listen to me." I creased my brows, my anxiety creeping up on me. "My body is in my apartment. You have to make sure no one buries me. I will be back."

Her mouth gaped. "Your *what*? I don't—"

"Yes. My body. I can't explain everything right now, but my soul was stolen. You have to protect my body," I insisted.

"What a horrible nightmare…" She trembled nervously and braced herself to run away from me and my scary words.

I grabbed her arm before she could leave. "If you don't believe me, go look when you wake up. You'll find my unconscious body.

But I am *not* dead."

Daisy was speechless.

"Daisy, I am so sorry for everything. Please do this for me. I will return to my body and give you the explanation you deserve." I vowed, glancing over to the door, which was still standing.

"I...wow, my mind is clearly being cruel to me." She didn't believe me.

"You don't have to believe me right now, but you will. Just please, don't let anyone bury me."

The door was starting to shrink. It was time for me to go.

"Daisy, I have to go. I'm not sure if I can contact you again, but just trust me. Everything will be okay." I turned to the door, but she grabbed my arm.

"I don't understand," she pleaded. "You have to tell me more."

I jerked my arm back, but her grip was too tight. The door was getting smaller and smaller. Panic was rising in my chest.

"Daisy, please let me go. I will explain everything later." I had no idea if that was even true, but my priority was to get out of there.

Yanking my arm out of her grasp, she looked at me with hurt in her eyes. I was leaving her again. Even in her dreams, I was abandoning her. Guilt wrenched through me as I sped to the door, which was already too small for my adult size. Luckily for me, I barely managed to squeeze through before the door sealed itself shut forever.

I was back in the black space. Sage, who was covered in sweat, eyed me nervously.

"Close call there," she commented, panting heavily. The amount of inertia it must have taken for her to keep that door open - I could see she was wiped out.

Nodding, I grabbed her arm.

"Let's go back."

She put her hand on my arm and strained, her veins bulging out of her forehead.

Giving me a look of panic, she whispered, "We're stuck."

Blood drained from my face as I stared at her in shock.

"What?"

"Just kidding." Her chuckle traveled through the black dimension. Punching her arm, I willed myself to relax. Sage was quite the trickster.

A blink of an eye later, I was back in the cave. Like waking up from anesthesia, there was no grogginess or confusion. Just an alert and oriented Alluna who delivered her message.

There was no guarantee Daisy would heed my warning. She might even forget her dream when she awoke. But I knew that I planted the seed in her head, and hoped she would at least march over to my apartment purely out of a sneaking suspicion that something was wrong. Once she found my body, she would know I was really in her dream.

Uncrossing my legs, I stretched them out and considered how I would do damage control with Reid. Moone, Nova, and Echo were still there, observing me.

"Very interesting," Moone commented.

"Hm?"

"You're fine," She added wondrously. Sage was lying down on the rock back in her Faerie form, breathing heavily, her hand on her forehead, completely red from exhaustion. Kneeling beside the rock, I lightly stroked her back with my finger, blaming myself for her state.

Even Nova looked surprised that I was fine upon my return. Was I not supposed to be?

"What?" I asked.

"You should be worn out too," Moone explained. I shrugged, feeling as right as rain.

Nova clicked her teeth. "It might be useful to us after all."

Turning on her, I did not hesitate for a single moment when I retorted, "Have you always had such a sunny disposition?"

She ignored me and flew away, but I was certain I didn't imagine the corners of her slightly upturned mouth. She could handle the bark she dished out and liked it.

Echo sauntered away as well, presumably back underwater.

It dawned on me that there was an entire island out there with communities that I knew nothing about. Echo was probably returning to the other Syrens who wouldn't dare put themselves at risk.

Or the Faeries. Did they fly home every day acting like nothing was amiss? Like they hadn't been discussing war plans that would involve every citizen of Naerin?

Moone wrapped a coating of her Faerie dust around a feverish

Sage and took her aflight by the hand. "I'll bring her back to the Tesek Glen, where the Faeries live. You can have some privacy with Reid." Moone gave me a knowing look. Clearly she thought of some interesting ways I could get him to forgive me.

Nodding, I watched Moone guide Sage through the corridors. Sighing heavily, I was nervous to face Reid now and have even more to explain to him. As I turned to head down to the lake room and start searching for him, I was startled to see Reid leaning against the wall with his hands crossed.

"What are you—"

"I never left." When I went into my own soul with Sage, he'd stayed put right there, despite our argument. Typical Reid. Saying terrible things, but still sticking around in case of trouble. He may have driven me crazy, but I knew he was dependable in that regard. His fight-or-flight response was impeccable.

"I have nothing to apologize for, I did the right thing." I jutted my chin out at him.

He shrugged. "Her funeral."

THIRTY-TWO

We settled into a private room filled with soft moss to lay on. His fingers were circling around my shoulder blade, tracing an invisible design. Fitting my head in the hollow of his neck, I held his hand, trying to warm it with mine.

The day was both draining and exhilarating. I hoped Reid would fight alongside me, not against me. As the night fell, we retreated to a private corner, all other members of the Anti-Keeper society gone. Our argument was forgotten. Connecting with our bodies seemed like the next best thing. I didn't want to question it. I was living in the moment, no matter how short.

Leaning against my elbow, I lifted myself above him and put my hand on his cheek, getting excited.

"The Faeries placed a barrier spell around this area," I hinted, ignoring all the sirens in my subconscious telling me to stop playing with fire. But it was too late, I was already living in my moment.

He put his hand over mine and breathed in my scent deeply.

"Can we go outside?" I breathed, yearning for the elated feeling that swept through me the night we soared through New York City. When he didn't answer, I nudged him slightly, adding, "You can teach me to fly."

Reid sat up and gave me a crooked smile. "Sounds like you're in need of a good lesson."

He lifted me bridal style and flew us out of the nearest exit.

It was the first time I was experiencing Naerin in the nighttime. And for the first time, I saw the beauty that was once there. During the day, the trees looked barren and shriveled. But at night, the warm light of the moon illuminated the peace that once was. It was the stillness of the sparkling waters, the slight breeze in the tree branches, the soft hum of cicadas orchestrating the night.

It must have been beautiful once. A land of peace. No corruption, no feasting on souls. Just beautiful peace. The sky was dotted with billions of shining stars, which was something I never saw in my polluted city. The starry night stretched until it met the sea, which was visible in the far distance.

I was at peace for the first time. The view was spectacular, and I longed to see more of Naerin but held myself back.

Bracing myself and locking my knees, I jumped, landing back

on the ground with a loud thud.

"I suck at this," I berated myself in disgruntlement.

Reid put his hand on my shoulder and held back a laugh.

"You're probably running low on dust." Patting my back, he circled around me and back-flipped onto a low branch on which he perched with one leg, the other leg dangling and swinging back and forth. I realized he never had to worry about keeping his balance. He never failed to amaze me.

"You could've mentioned that earlier, show off," I muttered, and tried again unsuccessfully.

"Happy thoughts are the key," Reid reminded me from his branch.

Wracking my brain for happy thoughts, I was surprised to find they were all involving him. The first that came to mind was the night we made love. Every touch, every smell, every taste was divine. And when we flew together. I had never felt more alive.

My feet were no longer on the ground. Bewildered, I looked down and saw I had lifted about a foot off the ground. And I wasn't upside down either!

Clapping excitedly, I shouted, "I did it!"

Reid's grin was wider than I'd ever seen. "I knew it wasn't the dust," he laughed.

Thinking harder about my happy memories with him, I focused my energy on that. Waking up next to him in the morning, the sunlight elucidating his flawless features. The feel of his lips on mine, his hand in my pants. Any time he carried me in his arms, my favorite, and held me so close our hearts were touching.

I was lifting higher and higher, completely in control of my center of gravity. It was amazing - I was amazing.

And for just a moment - my thoughts couldn't be happier as Reid and I circled each other like two leaves twirling in the wind.

Reid's lips found mine and he kissed me hungrily and passionately, his cool hands holding me close by my neck. I matched his energy and tangled my fingers in his hair, allowing the night breeze to control the direction we swayed into.

Wrapping my legs around him, I straddled him mid-air, pressing my hips against his and gyrating them against his hardness. He cupped my ass, squeezing hard enough to elicit a squeak from me.

Chuckling softly, Reid tugged my shirt over my head and tossed it to the ground, leaving me in my bra. I swiftly removed his shirt and pressed my bare skin to his muscular chest as he unhooked my bra, letting it topple.

Losing myself in the moment, I didn't notice his pants went missing until Reid laid on his back, ending up with me sitting on top of him with my legs dangling. His fingers found my center and rubbed my sensitivity as I struggled to keep myself upright with the intense pleasure I felt.

Taking hold of his length, I stroked him until he stood erect, hard as a rock. Reid waggled his eyebrows at me, signaling for me to take a seat on him.

"Time to take you for a spin?" I giggled as his hands caressed my breasts.

"I think you're tall enough for this ride," He said, putting his hands behind his head.

Moving my hair to the side, I placed my hands on his chest, using him as a surface to keep my balance as I lifted my hips and guided him inside. Just as I positioned him at my entrance, he thrust deep and fast. Losing my balance, I gasped and fell forward onto him. He wrapped his arms around my waist and held me steady against him as he continued pumping inside.

My lips returned to his as I moaned into his mouth, his enormous shaft entering my core. He groaned with me, running his hands all over my body as if he couldn't get enough of me.

Breaking apart from his tongue massaging mine, I left a trail of kisses down his jaw and onto his neck, sucking his skin softly and licking the sweat. He tasted good.

The entire time I was riding him, Reid's floating body hardly moved from the spot, though he occasionally lifted a bit higher.

Once we reached the barrier and felt the small vibration of the hooded magic, he hesitated before lowering himself.

"You want all of Naerin to see?" I purred as he reached down to touch me.

A spark flashed through his eyes as his pointy ears reddened. We were flirting with danger, and it was surreptitiously provocative. Where it would normally make my skin crawl, I was dangerously turned on.

He pulled me in for another kiss and lowered himself back into the safety zone. He sucked on my bottom lip as his touch brought me closer to erupting.

I could feel him throbbing inside me just as he said, "Come for me, baby," and we exploded like fireworks together in the air as one.

Awakening in Reid's arms the next morning, I was already wishing the day would end. Only during the night of Naerin could I truly feel peace. Even the monsters under my bed have a bedtime. But now that the island was waking up, I was on edge, always looking behind my back.

I knew Reid felt it too. From the moment I laid my eyes on him, his face was grim, last night's adventurous and carefree spirit - dead and gone. The fire we'd played with – long since burned out, leaving the charred coals of reality.

Hand in hand, we entered the war room, where the Faeries were dipping their feet into the water, carefully avoiding their wings.

"Where's Echo?" I asked carefully, remaining wary of everyone.

"He couldn't make it," Moone answered, rubbing her arms with the water.

"Why not?"

Moone shrugged. "Syrens have always been vague." Flitting into the air and shaking the excess water off her limbs, she added, "Besides, if a Faerie in our community suspected anything about our group, we would have to lay low, too."

That made sense. I nodded to Sage. "You're looking much better today."

She smiled weakly, her wings sagging. I winced at the dark circles swelling under her bloodshot eyes. She must've had a rough night with no nutrition to pull her through.

My own stomach grumbled in protest. Perhaps I'd snack on the fruits full of air later and use my imagination to add flavor.

Nova glowered at me more than ever. Not bothering to humor her sass today, I completely ignored her.

Moone tended to Sage's weary body by wrapping a warm leaf around her while speaking, "We don't have much time to stand here and do nothing. We must strike first."

"And how do we do that?" I asked.

Moone rubbed Sage's shoulders over the leaf, creating some heat through the friction.

"We use you as bait," Nova said. Reid's hand squeezed mine.

Knowing I had to be brave, I blindly answered, "Tell me what to do."

Nova's cruel smile deepened.

"No," Reid interjected. "We can't just put her in danger like that."

"Save the caring boyfriend theatrics for the bedroom," Nova snapped, flying over to his face and wagging her finger straight at him.

"He's not my boyfriend!" I exclaimed while blushing at the

memory of last night and hiding my face. Reid gave her a look and waved her away, not bothering to answer her.

Nova gazed at Reid lingeringly and did not say more. She retreated to Moone's side and kicked her feet on the ground, pacing thoughtfully. Noting her behavior, I realized she was very quick to back down from Reid. If anything, she never glared at him or directly regarded him with disrespect.

My attention was brought back to Moone when she said, "We will surround the enemy when Alluna walks. We have the element of surprise."

Reid shook his head. "Not an option. We hide Alluna here until they get the next soul and we can take advantage of the Council meeting to sneak into their headquarters and face the Keepers. If they surrender, which I doubt they will, we can bring everyone home."

Moone softened her voice. "You may be able to save Alluna, but what of the rest of us?"

My heart broke for Moone. She never wanted any conflict, let alone a war. She was the most peaceful being I'd ever met. I trusted that if she felt this was the best way, this was not a decision made on a whim. It must have been premeditated.

Reid hesitated, unsure what to say. I couldn't blame him either.

"Let's slow down here," I said, my thoughts racing. "Moone, what exactly is your plan?"

"By the unsolvable Avis," she muttered under her breath. "Alluna, you must get into the Keeper Society down below and see if the rumors are true."

"What rumors?"

"Those in the name of the Avis."

Reid stiffened. He must have known what this Avis thing was. They all did.

Moone continued, "You must cross the Pit of Poison Tears to reach the entrance to the Keeper Gate, which will take you below the island into the Keeper Society, where you'll then be a fly on the wall."

"How does this involve me being bait?"

"They must see you so they could alert the Keeper and have the Gate unsupervised so you can get in."

"Say 'hello' to Echo on your way through the Pit," Nova said sarcastically from the corner.

Reid stepped in front of me.

"I can't allow this," he spoke for me, sensing my tongue was tied in a knot.

Sage tried to say something but was overcome by a fit of coughs. Slightly unwrapping her leaf blanket, she sat up and cleared her throat.

"Reid," she managed to say. "Alluna will be under our watch the whole time - she will be protected. The Pit will be harmless."

Reid shook his head. "She can't get near the Pit. I don't trust them."

My heart was split in two. As much as I wanted to help everyone, I just wanted to go home.

"Isn't the most important thing to find my sister first? I still don't even know if she's alive!"

"We have to have our plan secured before we leave the protective barrier and expose ourselves," Reid said dismissively.

Reid's voice started to overlap with Moone's as they both continued making choices on my behalf. Funny, since no one cared about my opinion on the matter.

Not that I had an inkling of what to do myself.

But still.

Would have been nice to include me in this topic of life or death - or based on the way they made it sound - death or death. Death by waltzing into my own death trap or death by being hunted to death?

Death, death, death.

The word was starting to lose meaning to me after being repeated so many times.

Discreetly excusing myself and feigning the need to pee, my heart pounded through my ears as I calmly walked away, picking up each step with added swiftness. Reid could easily hear my steps, and fully knowing this, I had to be out of his ear range before I could pick up my pace.

Echo had briefly mentioned the location of the Pit earlier, and I didn't care how reckless I was being. Each step was driven by my need to find Vita.

False hope or not - I couldn't think of anything else.

The dark paths were starting to wind together as it dawned on me that most of this labyrinth was a mystery to me. I really only knew a handful of rooms, and I was on the verge of losing myself to this wooded insanity.

Mentally backtracking my steps after making a few circles, I eventually found a wall of leaves with light coming through it.

Hurling myself toward the leaves, I emerged into a sunny wooded area surrounded by barren trees taller than my Upper East Side Building. The leaves were all brown without a single hint of life on them. Like the remainder of Naerin, this wood was in a state of decay as it was left untouched to rot.

I raced through the trunks, trying to put less weight on each step.

Perhaps I could fly.

Summoning a happy thought, I remembered my last birthday with Vita, when she hugged me so tight I thought my ribs would crack.

The soles of my sneakers hardly lifted off the ground and I strained with all my might, rallying the last of the Faerie dust that clung to my skin. I just had to keep going.

How my sister decorated the entire house with balloons and made a scavenger hunt with gifts. How I'd never felt more loved than then.

Struggling to keep the memory alive, my feet weighed me down by the second before my full weight was stuck to the ground. Exhaling in frustration, I gave up since I'd used up all that was left from the last time I was dumped with dust.

No matter, I was starting to see a clearing through the trees and raced to it.

A shallow river was coming up ahead and I leaped over it, noticing the barren trees lessening around me.

Alluna

Unsure if I imagined my name, I somewhat slowed. I wouldn't be surprised if my mind was deceiving me in my state of hunger and dehydration. I waited to hear my name again as I continued down my path.

When nothing came, I sped up.

"Alluna?"

This time, I knew I didn't imagine it. The voice was far closer and far clearer.

Muddled by nerves, I followed the sound of the voice, gearing to the left, where a small batch of trees stood.

I could barely make out a shape moving through the trees, but it was surely there.

"Hello?" I called out softly.

"Alluna!" The shape stepped out of the trees.

It was my mother.

"Mom?" I stared in shock.

"What's happening? Where are we?" She was scared. Her breath caught in her throat as she tried to contain herself.

I didn't want to believe it. Did the Keeper go after her? Was she meant to be used as leverage? To bring me out of the shadows?

I hugged her tightly and collected her hand. "Mom, don't worry. I'll explain everything."

The idea of finding Vita could wait. This was real. This was now.

My mother was a walking target just like me. I had to bring her back to the caves and make sure she was safe. Tugging her hand, I started to head back to where I'd come from. Her hand was shaking in mine.

I would make them pay for this. If I had to slide an ice-cold dagger through all their throats and leave them to bleed out, I would do it without blinking.

To take me from my apartment was one thing. But to involve my family? I had already lost one sister. I was not going to lose my mother.

My choice was set in stone as I delightfully welcomed my intrusive, murderous thoughts.

My mother was my priority now. She trembled and held back.

"Mom, we have to go this way. Trust me," I said confidently, trying to stay strong for her.

"Alluna, dear, that way is dangerous." Her voice shook with fright. "That's where the scary men are…they chased me here."

My throat tightened. I would never put her in any danger. The Phantos must have made their way into this forest. They could have gotten my mother…

"Where do we go?" I asked her, all my confidence leaving me

like the air from a balloon.

"This way, dear, come on," she led me over the small river and never let go of my hand as we hopped from one rock to the next. "It's safe here."

Leading me to a smooth azure lake as still as death, she dipped a foot in.

"Come on," she beckoned me to join her, but I held back.

"This is a lake," I said doubtfully. She nodded and gestured for me again.

"Yes, we have to swim underneath, there is a safe opening on the other side." She took another step in and took my hand, leading me behind her.

"How do you know that if you're completely dry?" Drawing back, I eyed her suspiciously.

This could not be my mother. My mother would not act this way.

She dropped her beckoning hand and sighed.

I was right. This wasn't my mother.

My mother's warm brown eyes swirled into an onyx pool as her entire sclera turned black. All the expression left her face as a blue tint covered her skin and the wrinkles smoothed out.

Just as I suspected. A Syren.

I had to play it cool. "Stay away from me, Syren," I said, false confidence ringing through my ears.

My mother was transforming into a blue creature before my very eyes. Any hint of my mother's warmth was gone.

Zura stood in her place, her legs still intact. The smooth planes of her body caught the light as the shadows from the trees illuminated her perfect form. Her sharp cheekbones jutted out from starvation, her sunken eyes drawing me in with a piercing look that shivered down my spine into my toes.

"You're alive and made it back?" I was surprised, thinking Sage had killed her back in Central Park.

"Made it back where? We've never met." She held out her hand again, her aura wholly mesmerizing me. I lost my ability to look away from the black ocean in her eyes and forgot my train of thought.

"Come," she said, her voice alluring. My legs betrayed me as I stumbled closer and closer to her entrancing idea of death.

Hazy calmness washed the nerves right out of my body into the soil. This might all be part of the bigger plan. Better to die here, rather than at the hands of the dirty pirates.

She started sinking lower into the water, her impaling stare not leaving mine. Her arm remained poised, waiting to take mine and take me down to my watery death.

My fingertips were mere centimeters from hers when a familiar voice interrupted the spell.

"Not this one, Zura," Echo appeared beside her in the water, materializing above the inky surface.

She drew her hand back and stared at him in boredom. "I'm hungry."

"I know, but they'll sever our tails if they find out." His calm voice matched hers in boredom, a slight lace of warning tracing the edge.

My mouth dried at the image that popped in my head.

Zura sank deeper beside him. "Then take care of it," she said before disappearing underwater.

Echo left the water, his tail shifting into long blue legs as he towered over me.

"What are you doing here?" He asked me without a single variation in pitch.

"I was…I was…" My mind felt blank from the whiplash. Zura was about to drown me. I was recovering.

"Doesn't matter," Echo said. "You can't stay here."

Echo neared me, the scent of saltwater and moss rolling off him like a wave. His scent sparked me into my normal range of consciousness and I remembered where I was.

He was so tall I had to strain my neck to look at his lush face.

Echo gazed back at me blankly.

"There's another entrance to the caves. I will take you there," his soft voice sensually massaged my ears. The allure of a Syren was truly a force to be reckoned with.

"Where?" I asked carefully.

"In the water," he responded euphoniously.

There was no way he could trick me into getting into that water. Shaking my head, I said, "I prefer to go on foot."

He yawned in response.

"Let me show you the way," he said eventually, drawing out

the words monotonously.

Nodding, I started walking beside him.

Better to die on foot with him than drown in those murky waters.

THIRTY-THREE

s I fell into step with Echo's long legs and had to speed up my usual walk, I figured this trek would be the perfect time for small talk and hopefully take my mind off everything. With this in mind, I got the ball rolling.

"Why is it called the Pit of Poison Tears?" I ventured, stepping over a loose branch.

Echo stared ahead as he answered, "We survive on the tears of souls who come to us. Each tear holds a memory of the pain that caused the tear. In order to digest it, we must consume the pain within."

I believed him. Echo had no reason to lie about this. I couldn't imagine a life like that.

"That must be why Syrens sound bored all the time," I said

carefully, not trying to step on his toes too much.

His blue lips cracked the slightest smile. "We are immune to pain," he simply said.

Turning to me with his black eyes possibly sweeping my face, he paused before adding, "We welcome happy things."

His words shook me to the core far deeper than I expected. A life of pain and sorrow, and they were all numb, drugged by their desensitization. They wanted to be happy and peaceful, just like the Faeries. All of them just wanted to be happy again.

It hit dangerously close to home. I knew what it felt like to be numb from my own pain and want my happiness back. It was all I ever felt following Vita's disappearance. Day after day, the numbness took over my mind and clouded anything positive.

That is, until I met Reid. He was the closest thing I got to feeling alive again. His flirts with danger, the way he pushed my boundaries further and further…he showed me there was more to life than the small perspective I saw from the ground. And he would probably kill me himself for sneaking off.

"Reid is very lucky to have found you," Echo's voice interrupted my train of thought.

"Excuse me?"

"Very few find their one true other," he vaguely stated.

One true other? Never in a million light-years would I think Reid would feel that way about me.

I presumed, "What happened to yours?"

Echo stopped in his tracks. "Raine was killed."

Was Raine his one true other? The Syren that Reid slayed? He clearly didn't know what happened to her, but I had to find out what he knew.

Testing my luck, I asked, "What happened?"

"We joined the caves together a century ago with her brother Pine," He said, referring to the Anti-Keeper Society but careful not to say those words aloud, especially in a non-protected area in the forest. Better to act like every leaf on every tree had ears.

"We were reckless. We thought we could help a soul escape from the Trial. Pine tried to stupefy the Council and take the soul underwater, but the Keeper magic was too strong. They put him on trial for his dual crime: soul theft and being in the presence of the Keeper without a place on the Council. He was found guilty for both charges and executed on the spot. After that, Raine changed. She stopped believing in the cause and thought we could escape to the human realm instead. She left and I never saw her again, but I know she's dead. I can feel it."

No matter how much Echo pretended to look bored, I knew that look in his dark eyes. It was all a mask. He still felt that jolt of pain shooting through every vein in his body. I know he did.

"What about Zura? How did she come back?"

"Come back where?"

I truly wondered if any of the Syrens told each other anything.

"You couldn't help the souls escape after that," I continued for him.

He nodded.

"Yes. We had to hope a soul could escape independently." Echo looked at me expectantly.

I was the soul they prayed for. I was the only one who could help them. In an entire century, I was the only soul who managed to escape the clutches of the Council.

"Do you miss her?"

"Every waking moment."

My heart clamored for him regardless of my wariness. Pain was pain. Anyone could feel it. The bad guys could feel pain just as much as the good guys - though the line between the two was starting to blur in my vision. Not too long before, I was erratically imagining slitting dozens of throats. Was I even the good guy anymore?

Was Naerin changing me? Or did I always have this darkness inside of me?

I had my purpose. I was willing to kill for my mother, that wasn't enough of an indicator of my goodness. Plenty of others would have reacted the same way in my place.

We neared the familiar part of the forest when Echo said, "I must leave you here, the others will wonder where I am. Keep heading north and you will find it."

"Sure," I said, waving to him. "Good talk."

Echo disappeared through the trees quieter than a mouse.

His story replayed in my thoughts. I never expected to get to know Echo on a personal level, nor did I think he would ever open up to me out of all people. He was vague for a reason; all Syrens were. They were used to the pain they swam and drowned in again and again—

A wailing noise caught me off guard. Jumping behind the nearest tree, I fused with the bark, not a single breath escaping my lips.

Someone was screaming in pain. Too afraid to leave my spot, I hardly budged, my limited vantage point providing no indication of the events on the other side.

The screaming sounded young, like a young boy. A child, yowling thunderously.

The boy was thrown onto his back beside me, and I shimmied slightly out of his peripheral view. My nails dug into the tree as I pressed my stomach against it and watched the battle unfold.

The boy was bleeding. A deep gash in his arm gushed crimson waves as he snarled in pain. The sharp fangs and irregular canines jutting from his gums raised the hairs on my arms and legs. He was wearing the skin of an older man covered in wrinkles. Scraps, as Moone had said. I shuddered.

A Pheraboy. Another wild child lost in the woods, like the one that attacked me a few days ago. This one was small in stature and looked to be no older than five years old, similar to the other one.

Keeping my maternal instincts at bay, I reminded myself that this little boy would tear me to shreds, especially if he got in contact with my blood.

I couldn't do anything but stare.

The child's attacker silently stalked toward him, hardly visible as his attire matched that of the environment. Covered in leaves and dirt, the male form stood tall. His long brown hair was woven in a tight braid that reached below his shoulders, though his features were difficult to make out underneath the dirt that was smeared far too carefully to be an accident. He was one with nature.

He raised a long, sharpened piece of wood - a stake - and waited. The child sprung from the ground clumsily and charged toward the male, who waited until the child was about to claw him and pierced the child through the eye.

The other end of the stake jutted from the back of the boy's head as he hung limply, his brain punctured. The male kicked the boy from the stick and the boy fell to the ground in a heap, all light gone from his unseeing eyes.

The man started to turn until he paused and looked me directly in the eye. Time stood still for the second that felt like an eternity as he watched me, knowing exactly who I was, what I was worth.

He raised a finger to his lips, signaling a shush, before turning and skulking into the shadows of the forest.

Full of adrenaline and breathing heavily, I sank to the ground, unable to look at the murdered child. He may have been a creature of the island, a monster, but the Pheraboy still had every look of an abandoned child who was left to the will of nature and the predators within.

I wept for the lost life, unable to hold back the tears. I wasn't only weeping for the boy's lost life, but my own as well. I was reminded of the life that I lost in New York City the moment I was damned by the Keeper who viewed me as nothing more than the power to reign over the poor citizens of Naerin.

I was no chosen one, but I had the capability to fight for the creatures who needed me, and I couldn't walk away from them. I had to fight. I had to—

I had to have faith in myself. I had to trust myself.

I also had to rest, as I was completely wiped out, exhausted past my limit, drained physically and mentally. I should've gone back to the caves, where it was safe.

But I didn't have the strength to keep my eyes open. There was only so much I could take in one day. I didn't need long, just enough time to gather my strength.

I didn't bother fighting the urge to open my eyes again.

"There yew are." Two voices cackled in front of me...the same ones from the ship.

As I met the source of the voices, my face blanched. I'd escaped from them once, but who knew what lengths they'd go to this time to keep me from running away? My breathing quickened as my eyes grew wet.

Their cackles rattled my ears and sent a tremble down my spine.

The pirates - Dell and Hill. They found me.

For the first time, I saw the pirates in their full glory, or lack thereof. They were just as ghastly as I'd pictured in my mind, if not worse. Not knowing which was which, my mind combined both of them into one massive monster. They had every look of a pirate - tattered clothes, dirtied hair, disheveled appearance, drunken gait. The terrifying part was not the leer in their cruel eyes as they ogled me.

It was their transparent skin, which was beyond transparent - I could see right through them. They were grey as death - walking corpses with their gruesome appearance and cadaverous skin. It was like looking through a dirtied screen covered in filth but still see-through enough to make out blurry shapes and shadows within.

The tall one on the left was wearing an eye patch covered in mold, or moss, I didn't want to find out. The one on the right was shorter, stouter, with a peg leg to accompany his swaying stance and a beard on his rotten face.

"Keep running, human," the tall one sneered. He must be Hill, considering his lanky height and the pirate knack for their telltale nicknames.

I was stuck, unable to run toward the hatch and risk discovery of the caves and unable to run forward right into their vicious grasp.

"Aye, yew've nowhere to go," the other one, Dell, added while advancing toward me.

"Come with us and yew won't get hurt." Hill matched Dell's step as they came closer. The lie couldn't have been any more obvious and failed to act as a formality.

"If you leave me be, I promise not to hurt *you*." Astounded by my own boldness, I fisted my hands and stood tall, hoping to intimidate them.

The Phantos did not hesitate as they continued advancing toward me, completely ignoring my threat. My boldness washed away along with my confidence as the panic settled in my throat instead.

Hill was undressing me with his eyes and I was so disgusted by his stare that I wanted to cover myself up. He must have been well over a head taller than me, his menacing height creating fear within me. His wrinkled eyes flashed as he stared at my breasts and licked his lips.

Dell was missing from his side and I didn't even notice where he had gone. I was glued to the ground, completely shaking from fear, powerless to stop.

Hill was towering over me.

"This game is over." His singular eye glared at me. "Time to go."

It was now or never. I had to run, I had to try something.

As I was about to move, I felt two cold hands grasp my wrists and bind them behind me with some tight rope that dug right into my skin. Wincing from the burn, I turned my head.

There was no one behind me.

But the feeling of the cold hands was certain.

Dell's face came into view as he appeared out of thin air behind me, blowing me a kiss as he finished tying up my hands.

Disgusted by his face full of welts and rotting teeth, I swallowed the bile that rose into my throat.

Dell pushed me forward, forcing me to walk behind Hill as he stayed behind me, his hands on the rope.

Treading silently, I assessed the trees around me and tried to hatch an escape plan as we walked further and further from the caves. Dell reminded me of his strength every now and then as he roughly pushed me forward faster. I doubted I could carry his weight and escape while he was holding my arms.

There was one other option since we were still somewhat near the entrance to the cave.

"HELP!" I bellowed, willing my lungs to expand past their capability. "HELP ME!"

Someone was bound to hear me.

Echo, Nova, Moone, Sage, Reid…someone.

Anyone.

Please, someone, hear me.

Reid…please…help me…

"HELP—"

I was interrupted by a blow to my jaw, cutting off my air and sending me into a state of confusion and disorientation. That is, until the unspeakable pain started. I couldn't fully close my mouth from the stabbing torment as blood pooled in my mouth.

Blood trickled from my lips and down my chin, dripping onto my shirt and jeans. Spitting a mouthful of blood onto the ground, I fought back the tears that flooded my eyes.

Hill grabbed me by the collar and pulled me so close that the smell of rum went straight to my head.

"No one will help yew, *human*. Now shut up and keep moving unless yew really wanna feel pain," Hill snarled, his transparent eyes darkening.

Dell swiped a grubby finger under my bloody chin and sucked it off his fingertip.

He shivered in pleasure and licked his lips. "It's delicious, Hill. Have a taste."

Hill followed suit and ingested a drop of my blood, tilting his head back and groaning slightly.

I wanted to die. I would truly rather have my life end than be at the mercy of these two. The two pirates salivated as they gave me a hungry look. Dell eyed my ripped jeans and torn shirt that was nowhere near the pink it used to be, but now browned. He rubbed at his transparent crotch through his dirty pants.

"Would make a nice change from the Syren's," Dell said to Hill, who agreed. "It can't grow a tail and swim away."

"I'll make you suck on this," Hill snickered and removed his eye patch, exposing his rotted eye socket. Nauseated beyond belief, I was barely able to keep myself from retching.

Dell sucked his grubby finger again and swiped at my chin. Ducking awkwardly, I ended up with Dell holding a fistful of my hair. He pulled my head close to his and yanked my hair back, snapping my head up to the sky. The tension on my neck strained my aching jaw.

Crying out from the pain, I prayed silently to the sky, not knowing nor caring who was listening.

Dell's rough tongue took a big lick up my neck and into my chin as he savored my blood. At this point, I couldn't stop my tears as they spilled over. Wrangling my wrists against the burning rope, I sought any way to get my hands free.

His filthy hand roughly squeezed my breasts as he yanked my face right in front of his and gave me a bloody smile, his blackened teeth covered in my blood. Shaking harder than a leaf caught in a tornado, I started hyperventilating as my anxiety took over.

Reid couldn't save me. He was too late.

Anything that happened next was completely up to me. I was no heroine in an epic novel. I was also not a damsel in distress. I had to make do with the unfair hand I was dealt and save myself from these filthy animals. I had to be the hero in my own story.

Deep breaths and meditative thoughts wouldn't save me. A therapist I briefly had shortly after Vita's death, until my mother found out and told me she could've be my therapist instead and not to waste money, once told me to download an app on my phone that would play soothing ocean sounds to help me accept the bad thoughts and allow them to wash away. Clearly, that therapist had no idea what they were talking about.

Ocean sounds couldn't save me now.

Only I could.

My body felt numb. I wasn't really here. A phantom pirate wasn't really molesting me. I wasn't humiliated by his touch. I wasn't about to suffocate from my own air. I wasn't experiencing gut-wrenching violent thoughts and relishing in the idea of bleeding the pirates dry so they could hang transparently forever.

What would Vita do? She would be brave and cunning.

I was at my wit's end and couldn't rely on a clever escape. All I had was the brute force of adrenaline driving me past my panic into an impulsive, and hopefully successful, action.

Using this thought as fuel to my whim, I smashed my skull against Dell, knocking him backward onto the ground.

"Bitch!" He bellowed, but I didn't turn back.

I was running.

The rope was getting looser as I wrangled my hands. Leaping over a branch, I ran back toward the cave, hoping I could hide from the pirates until I ran into an ally. At this point, I'd even welcome Nova and her gloriously insulting remarks.

All I had to do was pull my wrists out of the—

A blow to the back of my head sent me sprawling to the ground. I was seeing double on the ground as the ringing in my ears drowned out my thoughts. I thought I was going to vomit, then pass out. But I laid there, unmoving, as my head felt like it was being stomped on.

Muscles in my scalp and neck grew tight as my migraine consumed me and I could hardly fight the black spots appearing in my vision.

"Feisty bitch." Feeling him spit on me, I could hardly feel the wetness on my arm as the peg leg blurred.

I knew I'd lost when I succumbed to the darkness and let them drag me away.

THIRTY-FOUR

The agony in the back of my head and my jaw had faded into a dull throb, infrequently reminding me of its presence. Every few rocks and branches that snapped into my face as the pirates dragged me away reawakened the pounding in my head, the control I was giving up, the life I was going to lose.

But fear was not overtaking me. Fear was the farthest thing from my mind.

I knew from the bottom of my heart that Reid would save me. If he hadn't heard me yelling by the caves, someone surely did, and someone surely told him. He must be on his way. He wouldn't let anyone hurt me. He said so himself; he would protect me. His protection was all I needed. Dell and Hill wouldn't stand a chance against him.

He'd already saved my life back home, and without a doubt, he would do it again. And again. And again. I just had to wait for Reid. No matter what happened, he was my bottom line, and he always would be, whether I liked it or not.

I was in and out of consciousness, hardly aware of where I was being taken. The pirates definitely didn't make it a smooth process - they hauled me by my arms or legs as roughly as they could. Even though I wasn't fully conscious, I still felt every scrape and laceration along the way.

The forest was getting farther and farther away. We were heading up a few stairs that reached a short cliff when Hill slung me over his shoulder and gripped my ass the entire way. But I was too far gone to care. His stench was enough to knock me out again. Didn't they ever shower?

Past the stairs was a flat road to the edge of the cliff. A large dome made of rock provided an entry to a large space inside, which we entered through the jaggedly cut door.

The eerily white circular room had a dais at the outermost edge, closest to the cliff outside. The throne was three steps above the ground, in the center of the four other seats, two on each side, which were far more common by comparison, only one step above the ground.

The dais was adorned with a lavish quilt, providing comfort and style. The other four seats were plain and uncomfortable. The whiteness made it difficult to distinguish the common seats, as they were washed out by the bland lack of color. They disappeared into the background, the walls, as the dais was front and center, the pride and glory of the dull quarters.

The pirates dropped me in the center and stood guard by the door as I examined the room further.

This must be where the Council of the Five commenced their inhumane trials.

The dais was fit for a king. Or in this case, the Keeper.

I envisioned a magnificent master in a large black cloak sprawled across the throne, his skeletal hands resting on the armrests, ruling over his subjects, the creatures of Naerin, the Council. His glowing eyes subjecting each soul to their final breath. His scythe leaning against his throne, within arms reach.

I pictured the Keeper as the Grim Reaper of this world and my world. The taker of life. The giver of death. The collector of souls. The undertaker of torture. It was only natural to imagine him as the scary monster with his scary scythe.

Little did he know, I had an advantage that was bound to drive me from his skeletal clutches.

I had Reid on my side, and the Anti-Keepers helping him. He would save me. I was just as valuable to them as they were to me now. We needed each other. And I knew, the moment he saved me, I would march right into the Keeper Society. Condemn them to the fiery pits of hell they deserved to be in. Rewrite the esoteric laws they created to send this world into damnation. Emerge into a new world with the citizens.

So fear was not something that was crossing my mind. I had to be careful and stall the Council as much as I could.

At this rate, no one else was here besides Dell, Hill, and I. All I had to do was bide my time wisely.

The pirates leered at me from the entrance, taunting the only exit I had access to. They laughed in my face. Dell even decided to grace me with his full moon, shaking his see-through ass at me, further humiliating me.

"You like that?" He sneered, Hill chuckling beside him. "How about I give you some of this while we wait." His hands were on his crotch again.

Hill leaned over to Dell and loudly whispered, "You get the back. I'll get the front."

The white space was already soiled, droplets of my blood trailing all the way from the threshold. My vomit was soon to follow.

But I could see right through the pirates, and I didn't mean that literally. I knew they were bluffing. They couldn't risk my escape. So I had to match their play.

"Then come here and show me what you got," I sputtered hoarsely through the pool of blood in my mouth, daring them to give up their upper hand.

They hmphed together, not budging from the entrance.

Sighing in triumph, I knew I was safe in the middle of the white room, at least from them. Future horrors may have remained unknown at the hands of the impending arrival of the Council, but the pirates were becoming the least of my worries.

I might even get some information from them.

"How does the Council know to come?" I tried, half-heartedly, not expecting them to answer.

"It dares speak to us," Hill sputtered, sending a spit in my direction.

Yeah, right back at you, bud.

Trying again, I asked, "Is there a communication system?"

Hill briefly left Dell alone by the entrance as he sauntered over and backhanded my face so hard my healing blisters split open in my mouth. Spitting a gulp of blood, I glared at him, baring my bloody teeth.

"Stay on the ground where you belong, *human*." Hill rejoined Dell, daring me to test him. "Say any more and you won't wake up next time we knock you out."

The agony reopened in my jaw, and I settled in the center. I may win in the end, but it wasn't worth the extra blows.

I had to be as stealthy as Echo, no matter how innocent he seemed. His silent presence prompted trust and an underestimation of a threat. I had to channel him, his energy, his monotone.

I had to reject my timid nature. Throw it off the cliff I was standing on. Replace it with a poker face so unnerving it would throw them off their tracks.

I could've been dead already, but I wasn't. I could've been captured before, but I wasn't. I managed to evade those who hunted me for days, which was apparently record-breaking. I set the first record and broke it with each passing second that I escaped.

If this land had a Guinness World Records book, I'd be on the front page. I'd make headlines.

The only human to have escaped the Keeper this long

The pirates' muttering voices faded out as I focused on self-determination and perseverance. Hope was not lost, I made sure of it. I was clinging onto it with every cell in my body.

The voices ceased abruptly, and I forced my stinging head upward, sensing a change in the air. Dell and Hill had their backs to me, facing the doorway, their shoulders tense. Standing in the doorway was a human.

No - she couldn't be human. She had wings every bit as translucent as those of Moone and Nova.

But she was tall and graceful, at least six feet tall, a slender gazelle who glided rather than walked. Her aristocratic stance was dignified as she looked down her sharp nose at the Phantos. Adorned with a vividly teal bodice and a flowing skirt that moved with the air, she truly looked like a queen.

She must be the Faerie Head of the Council. Her majesty has arrived…arrived at her plain seat by the dais. She may have been royalty to anyone underneath her status, but she still bowed to the mysterious Keeper, even if it was hard to believe, with her grace.

The way the pirates were trembling in her very presence indicated her position on the totem pole, clearly miles above that of the dirty pirate scum, the bottom feeders of Naerin.

Her honey-colored hair flowed past her slim waist, her big

amber eyes as golden as honeycombs fixated on the lowly pirates dropping to their knees before her.

"Kuna," they both chanted as they bent forward to the goddess before them. "Kuna…" To see these threatening pirates drop their act and completely bow before this woman was empowering, though her unblinking gaze was starting to terrify me too.

"You went onto the human land." Her low voice was alarmingly calm.

"Yes, Kuna, we went to bring the s—"

"And you lost…the soul." She didn't bother letting them finish.

"Yes, Kuna, but we found—"

"And you dared to enter the Council territory without a warrant." She lifted her chin, revealing the golden markings that descended from her bottom lip and ears, joining together at her neck, forming a Y into her chest with a line through the center.

"Yes, Kuna, we wanted to make sure it didn't esc—"

"That's three laws you broke." It didn't matter what they said, she was already on her course. "And almost a fourth. Being in the presence of a Keeper is forbidden to anyone but a Council member."

"Kuna, Kuna, please forgive us."

"By Avis," she paused, not sparing me a single glance. "I've killed for less."

And with that, her Faerie dust flowed from her fingers. She harnessed it like a whip and smacked it against the ground until it broke in two flying leashes.

Drawing back her slender arms, the leashes formed two nooses that fell onto the pirate's heads as they remained bowed to her. Before they had time to pick their heads up and plead for her forgiveness, she snapped up the ropes of dust, and the pirate's neck's cracked together.

She hung the ropes to an invisible thread in the ceiling and the pirates hung there limply.

"Idiots," she said to herself.

For the first time, her eyes landed on me and she assessed my tattered and bloodied state.

Flying gracefully into the room, she gave me a look.

"All this fuss over you," she pondered as her hands shimmered with the glowing ball of energy.

"You insignificant little *human*." The flow of dust rained around her, a show of power, her eyes narrowing on me.

Clamping my eyes tighter than a vise, I braced myself for the blow that never came. Opening them slightly, Kuna was gliding to her seat to the left of the dais.

The Keeper's left-hand queen.

Though her back was to me, she was hardly bothered. Her shimmering wings fluttered softly as she took her sweet time gracefully adorning her seat. She couldn't be bothered by turning her back to me and creating an opening for me to strike, she was that confident in her strength. She didn't even deem me an opponent at all, considering how strong her power was. She was right, I never would've struck her after seeing what just unfolded.

Her elegant presence completely dazed and slightly scared me.

The way Kuna regally executed Dell and Hill, who hung by the entrance, their necks mangled, without blinking an eye. She was capable of anything in the name of the Keeper. Within her scope, she didn't bother waiting for them to go on trial. She took it upon herself to rid Naerin of these two pirates who were impervious to the strict abstruse laws.

Or perhaps it was the darkness that seeped into her heart from the new reign of cruelty that plagued anyone who set foot in Naerin.

Kuna crossed her long legs as she observed me. I remained on the ground, looking up at her, too terrified to utter a single word, afraid of the pain that would come from her hand. My face was throbbing enough as it were.

She broke the silence first. "What is it…about…you?" Her tone was so low I had to double-check my hearing to make sure I didn't imagine her voice. Surely enough, her perplexed stare spoke volumes.

The culmination of the shit that I'd been dragged through to get to this point caused my fear to step into another room for a second and make way for boldness I didn't know I possessed. Speaking impulsively through the pain of moving my jaw, I said, "It's about what you're not," not caring about the consequences to follow from speaking back to her.

Her response was faster than the crack of a whip. "Silence," she hissed, a warning to my sharp tongue.

Duly noted. All statements from Kuna would be considered rhetorical.

Pursing her lips, she smoothed out a crease from her tulle gown, closed her eyes, and relaxed against her seat.

She was waiting for the others to come.

I barely moved a muscle. I knew that if I tried to run away, she would send a vein of dust to hook me in and keep me locked inside the room forever. I had to remain calm and disappear into the floor. Make my presence unknown, and prevent any impending rage.

Besides, it would be loads easier for Reid to swoop in and fly me away if my body wasn't held hostage by her unyielding dusted grip.

I just had to wait this out. Reid had to be coming for me. I knew he was…

This was all my fault. If I didn't run away to find Vita, I would still be in the caves. How could I think I was accomplishing something by shedding the protection of the Anti-Keepers and venturing into a deadly land? I severely overestimated my ability to overcome the allure or danger of my enemies. I could have just told Reid. I could have communicated what I wanted and had him safely escort me. Why did I have to be so stupid and reckless?

Zura would have drowned me in a second if Echo hadn't shown up. I was stupid enough to fall for her half-assed cosplay as my mother.

And the braided man who murdered the Pheraboy in the forest. Instead of running, I just gawked at him like a deer caught in headlights, allowing him to get a full picture of me, the fugitive on the run.

And the Phantos. I could have run to the caves faster. I could have tried to escape harder. I could have tried more. I could have—

"You're not trying to run," Kuna observed me like a feline cornering her prey.

I wasn't sure what she was expecting. She made it clear speaking was out of the question. If she wanted to entertain herself to pass the time, that was her prerogative. But I would not participate in any twisted mind game she was trying to trick me into.

Keeping my eyes on the ground, I didn't bother reacting or responding.

Her sly mouth grimaced downward, as if she didn't like my silence. She wanted me to say something so she would have an excuse to hurt me. To punish me. To rule over me. To establish a level of control she knew she didn't have, though we both knew she wasn't the true ruler of Naerin.

The Keeper was.

She could pretend all she liked with everyone else, but not me.

Because soon enough, I would be rescued and travel far, far away from this godforsaken domain. I would set her world on fire and dance along the flames as the new world of love and peace was reborn from the chaos and disorder that Kuna was an accomplice to.

I'd ended her mind game before she had the chance to roll the dice. The silent song was playing far too long, and she didn't like it. Hearing her stand from the chair, I held my breath and braced myself.

"Look at me when I'm speaking to you," she said, her calm voice somehow piercing louder than a scream.

This was a small victory for me. Let her get mad and throw her tantrum. I wouldn't bow down to her. My gaze remained on the ground.

A white-hot bolt of electricity whipped my back as she lashed a vicious flame of dust. Screaming, I fell to my stomach, feeling the deep welt form on my back and tear into my insides. Too weak to move, I sank below the ground, still not looking at her.

Another scourging lash on my back. It hurt to scream but I did it anyway. I was being ripped in half. Every inch of my skin was on fire. I was going to erupt in flames and burn to a crisp. The electric whips singed my skin with a heat I've never felt before. The burnt smell of flesh tickled my nose and I was horrified to imagine what my back looked like.

"Stupid humans," she hissed. "Willing to die to never sacrifice their stubborn idiocy."

All I wanted was Reid to hold me, to heal me, to save me, to rejoin our souls…her words meant nothing to me. She could whip me to death if she pleased, but my heart was forever bound to Reid.

According to Echo, my one true other.

Nothing else really mattered anymore. Everything else would fall into place, whether it be my death or reuniting with Reid. I could hardly focus on what I wanted anymore, I was buried in agony.

The pain was too much. I was hardly awake. Hearing the crackle from her vein of flame getting louder as it emerged for another lash, I closed my eyes, accepting the pain to come—

"Enough," a new voice sounded from the door.

THIRTY-FIVE

The Syren Head was here. Another unmistakably powerful figure. He stood by the door, his blue legs covered by a pelt of scales.

Once he stepped through, his gaze fell on Dell and Hill, hanging by the door. The lack of expression on his face was unnerving. He proceeded forward without a stop.

Another monotone monster. His boredom filled the room, though it was a different tone from Kuna.

Kuna's calmness had a cruel edge to it, something to persistently prove.

The Syren wore a deadly calm, unfazed by anything.

Both of them scared me. And these were only the first two members of the Council.

No matter how scary the Heads were, the Keeper scared me the most. These creatures were bound to serve the Keeper, perhaps at no fault of their own, though that didn't excuse the part they played in this woven disaster that beseeched Naerin.

"Ozul," Kuna greeted him curtly, barely giving him a second glance. He nodded in acknowledgment before his black eyes fell to me.

Without a single ounce of pity at the sight of my barely conscious mangled body bleeding on the ground, he took small steps to his chair. Recalling what Echo had told me previously, walking on legs felt like walking on glass. I never would've known. The serene look on the Syren's face was deceiving. He delicately took his place on the seat right of the dais.

The right-hand man of the Keeper.

"Kuna." He reeked of boredom. "You've nearly killed the soul." His statement was more of an observation than an accusation. Why should he care, if he's not the one affected by my death?

Two sides of the same coin, Kuna's cruel calmness responded to his soulless calmness, "It deserved punishment for its actions."

"Calm down, Kuna." How ironic. "That is not your decision to make," Ozul reminded her.

Her huff strayed from her alleged tranquility. He'd hit a sore spot, indeed. But her response was nothing short of calm.

"Where is Voss?" Her pretense of boredom fooled nobody.

"On his way," Ozul said softly.

Voss must be another Head. Another creature I was dying to meet.

Ozul inspected his blue cuticles. "The last one went to the Faeries." He was referring to the last soul taken to Naerin. He was referring to Sage. He was referring to her body, mind, and soul being stolen and devoured by these savage laws.

"Mmm," Kuna flexed the Faerie dust that dropped off her, spinning a small circle of dust between her fingers, a show of her power. As a Faerie, her magic had been renewed by the last cycle, and she had no problem showing it off to the starving Syren.

"Seems you have to wait until the following cycle," Kuna's red lips curved into a cruel smile. "The Phantos will get this one."

"Indeed."

They spoke as if they worked together in a corporate office job in which they were forced to tolerate each other despite their blatant disdain for one another. Forced interactions, trite exchanges, vapid remarks. They were currently waiting for their colleague to join the work meeting to discuss corporate rules and equity stock exchanges.

I had to diminish the situation to a mere work meeting. I had to minimize the danger and fear within my heart, or else I would fall apart. I was only hanging on by a bare thread at this point.

Regardless of my petty metaphor, the few drops of blood that remained in my face drained. There was no chance for me if Reid failed. I'd face no salvation at the hands of the Phantos. Only death and even worse - humiliation by those perverted savages.

My hope was waning by the second. With each passing moment, the clear path to freedom was fading. The more Heads there were present, the harder it would be for Reid to save me.

He had to come…

"He's here," Kuna said blandly.

My ears perked up. Could it be? Could Reid have really found me already? Could he—

"Voss," Kuna and Ozul greeted him in the same lackluster color.

My heart sank into the ground below the bottom of the cliff.

Of course it wasn't Reid. Kuna would've had a polar opposite reaction if he showed up just now. Reid was a fugitive on the run too.

But Reid was smart. He would find a way to save both of us without getting himself caught in the process. Of that, I was certain.

My burst of adrenaline at the thought of seeing Reid vanished. Slumping against the ground, I didn't bother to watch the next Head walk in and exchange pleasantries.

But the moment I heard the bootstraps clacking on the ground, my breath hitched in my throat.

As I slowly raised my head to analyze Voss, a smooth "Hmm," was heard from the towering man.

He wasn't looking at me. He was looking at Dell and Hill.

Even the back of his head was intimidating. His long black locks of curled hair hung below his shoulders, and it was far from transparent. His clothes were fully opaque as well. Within my limited view of his exposed hand on his cocked hip, his skin was not transparent as Dell and Hill either. But a slight translucency was there, evident to the eye. If he walked down the street in my world, one might think his pallor was diseased and he owed a visit to the doctor.

"This was clearly signed by Kuna," his deep voice rumbled as he observed his dead men.

"Of course it was," Kuna responded as if it would be an insult to think she did not murder them. But unless someone else had Faerie dust pouring out of every crevice and a lust for vengeance, the scene had Kuna written all over it. Shocked by her brazenness in addressing the Keeper in such a tone, I wondered what their relations truly were.

Kuna had no regard for the lives she'd taken. She hardly addressed the Phantos with respect, nor did she acknowledge Ozul with respect. The Heads clearly wanted nothing to do with each other. This was all just a power game to see who could climb to the highest point on the totem pole. Who knew if they even wanted to be here, be a part of this?

Based on their formal interactions and forced calmness, I could tell their distaste for one another. But they all had their parts to play in this twisted show.

"You didn't deem it necessary to ask me before slaying them?" Voss finally turned, revealing his face, looking through me at Kuna as if I were invisible.

His piercing blue eyes sent the first chill down my hemorrhaging spine. Bluer than forget-me-nots, they reminded me of a never-ending storm, the ice within unwavering and steely. His handlebar mustache twitched.

"They were found guilty of their crimes," Kuna responded smoothly as if she didn't break any rules.

"By you?" His condescending tone was condemning.

Ozul stifled a laugh. This interaction must've been entertaining to him if it stripped him from his boredom.

I wonder if Kuna and Voss seldom bickered. But in this world where everyone sought more power, it wasn't surprising that they picked at each other.

Kuna coolly said, "Yes," and nothing more.

Straightening the lapel on his velvet overcoat, he narrowed his eyes and approached his seat, stepping right over me as if I were roadkill on the road, unimportant, insignificant.

It was better this way. I could hardly form words at this point. My jaw was swelling, my throat tightening, my head pounding, my back bleeding, my appendages bruising. I was a breathing carcass at this point. Death seemed so romantic now. A sweet escape from this painful, painful world that continued to torment me.

But I had to hold on for Reid. Hope was not lost. At least, not yet…

Voss raised a cunning eye at Kuna.

"You'll face judgement from the Keeper." Voss crossed his legs.

Kuna released a small gasp, her amber eyes widening. Even Ozul in the corner had flinched.

"By Avis, Voss, you fool. It is within my right." Kuna was either extremely brave or extremely stupid for speaking to Voss like that.

The colleagues were bickering again. They weren't pleased with the PowerPoint group project. They needed to figure out a different sales pitch to their boss.

"It is also within your right to delude yourself, Kuna," Voss responded, his long fingers curling against the armrest. He was enjoying himself. His curved mustache was a vessel for cruelty and taunting, constantly driving into Kuna's need to prove herself.

Kuna had fallen for the bait and shot back instantly, "Watch your tone, Voss."

He smirked. "Or else, what?"

Straightening her long neck, she looked down her nose at him and said, "Or else I'll have to make a report to the elder Keeper. You wouldn't want that, now would you?"

Voss was silent for a moment. His smirk never faltered, and he scoffed at Kuna, but didn't respond.

Clearly, a report to the elder Keeper was enough to force subordination out of anyone. I wondered if Kuna was truly the advisor to the Keeper and what that entailed. Did they have meetings in private? Was she his eyes and ears? Or was she all bark and no bite, considering the way they all trembled at the mention of the elder Keeper.

At that moment, all their heads shot up instantaneously in the direction of the door, all their eyes wide, and their mouths set in hard lines.

Struggling to turn my head to the door, I twisted through the aches and throbs.

My blood ran cold, chilling every fiber in my being.

The same man with the braid who'd spared me in the forest stood tall, his broad shoulders taking up most of the doorway.

But that begged the question…who was the man in the braid? Why had he spared me in the forest? Was he the Keeper?

He was smeared in dirt and leaves, his long braid thrown over his shoulder, with a few loose strands of his dark hair framing his angular face. He was silent and watchful, and his eyes eventually met mine.

A small smile pulled at his lips. I recalled when I saw him in the forest, how he raised his finger to his lips to shush me, before disappearing into the shadows and allowing me to walk free when he could have easily taken me.

Could he secretly be an Anti-Keeper? Did he team up with Reid to save me?

Maybe they were allies. Perhaps they'd hatched some plan on the way to the Council headquarters on this cliff. Reid could be playing along with his captor. If that were the case, I had to do the same. I had to give Reid every chance to execute his escape plan as smoothly as possible.

A shuffling sound snapped my head to the Heads, and I watched

Ozul get to his feet, his head lowered. Kuna and Voss's heads were lowered too.

"Let us pray," Ozul said softly, keeping his gaze locked on the ground. Kuna and Voss got to their feet as well as they all clasped their hands together.

Did he really say pray? Why would they pray?

Before I could orient myself, I felt Kuna's unforgiving force of dust restrain my head to the ground. Staring at the floor, I was unable to look up, for each time I tried to raise my head, her claim on my head pushed down harder.

There was no point to continue fighting. I had to play my part anyway. Complying with her forceful dust, I kept my head to the ground, hyper-aware of the sounds around me.

They all began their prayer together, chanting the same verse, their voices blending together into one dull mantra.

"By the solvable Keeper,

Let us stand in prayer,

Rejoice over the salvation he provides,

The nurturing he supplies,

The food he yields.

We come from the wicked old way,

The Keeper is here to show us light on a new day.

Let us stand in prayer,

Be thankful in our worship,

To the solvable Keeper."

Once the chant concluded, they all took their seats quietly and the hold on my head was released. Slowly raising my chin, I tested my mobility. All clear. I could freely look around again.

Still confused about the purpose of the prayer, I waited for the cartoon light bulb to go off in my head, but nothing was clicking. Perhaps the Council of the Five had a ritual in a certain order and had to pray before the Keeper.

At first, I thought they got their prayer wrong. The phrase I've been hearing in Naerin was "by the unsolvable Avis", whatever that meant. Yet they all said, "by the solvable Keeper" instead.

Either way, the prayer itself was ludicrous - how could anyone praise the Keeper for the current state of Naerin? The Keeper didn't "solve" a single thing - if anything, the Keeper was to blame for the state of ruin and starvation that tormented every single creature living in Naerin. How could they all say that prayer with a straight face? Were they brainwashed?

Yet the way they all said it without a single beat - they must have been so accustomed to that joke of a prayer that they could say it in their sleep. It must be ingrained in their brains by now.

I wondered if all the citizens of Naerin were forced to chant such a prayer or face repercussions.

How it must feel to pray to someone you hate…I could never do such a thing. I would rather die.

Kuna cleared her throat nervously and spoke, "The time for the trial is now."

My heart sank.

I was going to die.

"Bring the defendant forward," Kuna said as she waved her hand in allowance to whomever she was ordering.

A small sound of bells filled my ears. Was I hallucinating, or did I just spontaneously develop tinnitus?

The bells grew louder and louder until Moone was tossed right in front of the dais, right out of my arms reach, her shoulders violently trembling. She mouthed *I'm sorry,* a single tear sliding down her face. Her lips quivered as she tried to contain herself.

Completely confused, I looked from her to the braided man, who remained by the door, his face unreadable.

Kuna whipped a dusty lash at Moone and bound her mid-air by the wings so she was unable to move. Moone flinched as the binding drew her wings taut, undoubtedly hurting her.

"The trial will now begin."

Wait—

This wasn't my trial.

It was Moone's.

THIRTY-SIX

No. No. What? I didn't understand. When did Moone even get here? Why was she the one on trial?

Moone's back was reddened, and her wings stretched past their limit. I couldn't imagine how much it hurt her, and my heart broke for her. She did not deserve this. She was the last person who should be here right now. She has only ever been kind-hearted and good-spirited.

"Let her go," I croaked hoarsely, my voice raw, speaking for the first time in ages. My voice had come out weaker than intended, but still, I was completely ignored.

Kuna yanked on her grip, and the wail that came from Moone was enough to tear me to shreds. I couldn't stand to see her in so much pain. Feeling completely helpless, I tried to regain my strength.

"Enough!" My voice came out louder and bolder. Kuna paid me no mind as she slowly tightened her grip further.

"As the Keeper's *advisor*," Kuna shot a quick look at an uninterested Voss, "I declare the beginning of the trial."

"You were seen in the forest assisting this soul five days ago. The soul hasn't been seen again until today, which leads us to believe you were hiding the soul. Do you deny this?"

Despite her wings being pulled so tight that they'd lost their shine and splendor, Moone was somehow composed. "I do not deny this."

What was she doing?

"No!" I called out again. "I was hiding by myself!" I was desperate to say anything to protect her and clear her name.

"Silence," Kuna snapped at me and thrust a gag of dust in my mouth, which felt like hot ice. Any attempt of speech was quickly numbed and rejected by the stronghold. Even a small sound was easily muffled.

"So you confirm five days were spent hiding the soul from the Council, thus leading the citizens of Naerin into starvation." Kuna wrapped a long finger around her armrest, her eyes full of glee. She wasn't leaving a single stone unturned.

"Yes." Moone's voice didn't have a single ounce of fight left.

"Did anyone else help you hide the soul?"

"No," Moone breathed smoothly and easily. Even I believed it for a second. She would never give up her friends. Even Reid, someone she had just met. Moone's heart would never stray from those who stood with her. As terrified as I was for her, I held admiration for her bravery.

"In the history of Naerin, such heinous crimes have never been committed. Faerie, you will be the first to bestow an example for future citizens." Bile rose to my throat. Kuna didn't even name her. Moone was nothing but a toy for her to torture. She wasn't even worthy of a name.

Moone was not there anymore. I could see it on her face. Her mind was a million miles away. I hoped she was somewhere nice. Somewhere with nice beaches and peaceful rays of light.

Kuna raised her sharp chin in the direction of the braided man by the door, but my neck was too sore to follow her gaze. She gave a small nod, a gesture that had to mean something.

His silent step made his way toward Kuna. He never met her eyes. He just accepted the blade encrusted with jewels she offered him.

Oblivious to the daggers I was shooting with my eyes, he ignored me as I squirmed against my chains. Unable to speak, some muffled sounds escaped my mouth as I gagged on the dust which crumbled down my throat and dried out my tonsils with each attempt. Nonetheless, I let out more strangled sounds, desperate to do something—anything.

My heart was breaking for Moone.

As the braided man approached Moone while raising the blade, it dawned on me what he was bound to do. It was as clear as day, as Moone and Nova's previous conversation from a few days prior collided with my thoughts.

Our wings will be clipped for this

Oh, God.

No. No. No…

My shirt was already soaking wet with the tears that couldn't stop flowing from my eyes but I couldn't stop…I couldn't stop envisioning what was about to happen.

The braided man was barely giving Moone a second glance, and her head was hanging low. He couldn't see the face of the Faerie he was about to mutilate, maim even. He was about to take away the very element that made her who she was.

Moone hardly noticed he was there, she was a million miles away - and for that, I was glad. However her small body decided to cope with the tremendous pain larger than life that was about to follow…the natural anesthetic flowing from her neurotransmitters better do their job.

But it was the slight tremble of her lip that completely set me loose. No matter how hard she was trying to mentally space out, she knew exactly what was to come.

It was that slightest action that caused me to leap forward, despite the pain that surged through my back, to protect her from the braided man. Harnessing the energy of my adrenaline, an animalistic cry escaped me as I lept to my feet, determined to get in between him and Moone.

It was the adrenaline that blinded me to the consequences, deleting the inhibitions that would have told me Kuna's wrath was not something to be messed with, especially when her buttons were being pushed.

It was the adrenaline that distracted me from her lash of dusty air that swept around me, lifting me into the air and crashing me to the ground at an unnatural angle.

My bleeding body shattered into a million pieces as my weight collapsed downward.

For a single second, I forgot where I was.

That was until my wrist was twisted in the other direction and snapped.

The dusty gag did little to qualm the million needles that shot up my arm with each movement of my bent wrist. Overtaken with surprise and excruciating pain, I was unable to coherently get a grip on myself.

No one was looking at me. No one cared.

Only I could help myself, even if just by a little. Avoiding pressure on my wrist, I gently cradled it against myself, keeping it suspended.

But all I could do now was watch. Watch the dagger come down. Watch it slice cleanly through Moone's taut wings, watch as the wings withered to Faerie dust and dissipated into the air, watch as Moone let out an animalistic scream that could split hairs.

The entirety of the present Council barely batted an eyelash as her bloodcurdling wails filled the entire room.

But I had to focus on holding on to my sanity, which was slipping away with each passing second. If I could shut it all off right now, I would. If I could toss myself over the cliff and be lost to the murky waters, free of the pain that raged through my heart and soul, I would.

I didn't know what I was capable of anymore. If I got ahold of Reid's dagger, I would slay the entire Council for putting Moone through this psychological and physical torture. If I were to drown now, at least I would do myself the courtesy of not dying a murderer.

Moone's screams entered a permanent pocket of my brain. For the rest of my pathetic life, I would never forget them.

There were two gaping holes in her small back, bleeding bright red blood and dripping onto the ground. Kuna's grip around Moone's waist kept her afloat, eye level to the braided man.

The sight of Moone's back was too much for me to bear. I had to look away. I could only imagine how she must have felt, though I wasn't exactly cream and sugar myself.

As if to remind me, my wrist throbbed from the fall and sent repeated shocks up my arm.

"The Faerie's punishment for breaking the law has been delivered." The braided man spoke for the first time. He was so…clinical. Distant. Removed. Only then did I realize he was another Council Head, a species foreign to my knowledge. There was so much that Reid never got to tell me.

Kuna nodded, her eyes hungrily drinking in the disastrous sight of Moone's back.

"Thank you, Suldor," she murmured in delight. "And now the punishment for hiding the soul."

Was Kuna out of her mind? Was Moone not punished enough? What else could Kuna take from Moone?

Suldor wrapped his large hand around Moone, breaking through Kuna's dust grip. She winced tremendously at the contact of his fingers on her bleeding back. Moone was no bigger than his hand, her neck and waist locked behind his fingers. Holding her up, he squeezed his fist, tightening his grip, the veins on his arm bulging out.

His hand was Moone's cage, getting tighter and tighter. Once Moone started coughing, it was clear her neck was pinched and she was running out of air.

Once Moone's cough became silent, she gave me one last look, with so many words written all over her, yet none to be said ever again.

Her face was turning red from the blood forced to her head. Shutting her eyes tight, she squirmed in his grasp, unable to fight back with her hands locked in his cage.

I couldn't watch. I had to look down.

Her bones cracked altogether in one quiet snap. Her neck, her spine, who knew what else. Flinching with the crack, I cried for Moone's soul.

I had to see her one last time. She was as delicate as a flower, limp in Suldor's grasp, her pretty head and slender legs untouched.

I didn't want to imagine how the rest of her body looked inside Suldor's hand.

Moone was gone forever. A small part of me died with her.

He loosened his grip on Moone but did not open his fist.

Kuna giggled. Kuna actually giggled.

The sorrow in the air must have escaped her and Ozul and Voss and Suldor as they watched the scene without a flicker of humanity.

They must be accustomed to this inhumane behavior. Even if none of them were human, surely they had compassion in their hearts. Surely compassion wasn't limited to humans.

This was sick. I was sick. These animals had a sickness inside of them. They've allowed the sickness to take root and are sowing it.

But it was far from over.

Especially when Kuna finally acknowledged me, a devilish smile crossing her face, and saying, "Your turn."

My turn? By all means. Kuna could tear my soul, debase my body, abuse my mind all she wants. I already felt dead inside.

My cheeks were stiff from the mixture of dried blood and tears staining them. I'd given up on trying to speak with the crumbles of dust slowly choking my dried throat.

Kuna snapped her finger and the dust gag disappeared. I'm sure she wanted to hear any pleading or screaming or surrendering or breaking or—

Suldor was still holding Moone, his grip loosened to a soft cage now. If Moone were alive, she could have slipped right out, flown back to the caves, flown back to the realm of Tesek Glen that she told me about, rejoining her Faerie community.

Tesek Glen would never see Moone again. I'd never see Moone again.

I should've been used to death by now.

But having someone vanish inexplicably from my life is one thing. Seeing someone murdered up close was a whole different playing field.

The familiar numbness - my dear old friend - was paying me a visit. Like Medusa, my entire self was being covered in numb stone.

"What's there to discuss?" Voss spoke, ending his S's with a whisper. "This soul belongs to the Phantos this rotation." His condescending tone wasn't as apparent, yet the matter-of-fact intonation yielded superiority regardless.

A small sigh from Ozul reminded me he was there. He must be beyond frustrated with the animosity between his coworkers.

Extra effort was needed for me to listen to them. Their words meant nothing to me. My vision kept blurring as my mind took me to the living void in my brain. The safe space with no thoughts, no emotions, no pain.

"Have you forgotten the process, Voss?" Kuna's sharp voice pulled me out of my mind's living void. There was a hint of a whisper at the end of Voss's name, her sleight of hand way of inserting almost indistinguishable taunting.

"Of course not," Voss's whisper had a tang of disgust. "Have at thee," he said, which I assumed meant for her to proceed.

"Alluna Day." Kuna announced my name for the first and definitely last time. I wasn't worthy to be anything more than "it" or "soul" in these waters. "You were brought here for a reason."

No shit, Sherlock. But sure, let Kuna go through the whole process like any other marking that wasn't riddled with escape and defiance.

"The treasoned Faerie fed you nothing but lies. You were chosen with great honor to become a part of Naerin forever." Kuna's mighty chin lifted, her amber markings in full view. "It is with great honor that I bestow upon thee the choice of staying with us or agreeing to be the sacrificial lamb of our harvest."

Voss cleared his throat loudly enough to indicate he was intruding. Kuna sharply jerked her chin at him.

"Something to say, Voss?"

"Indeed. I don't blame you for forgetting the intricate fine print, my dear. Allow me to remind you that this soul belongs to the *Phantos*." His emphasis on *Phantos* explained it all. What choice could I possibly have to join the Phantos, and why would I take it even if I did?

"Feel free to continue," Kuna said through gritted teeth before taking her seat.

Voss rose quickly and didn't hesitate. He addressed me plainly, "Alluna." My eyebrow rose at his mention of my name and the pang of familiarity struck me again, though I couldn't place it.

"Unfortunately, you are not a descendant of the great pirates before your time and alas, cannot join the crew."

What a pity.

"We can proceed one of two ways and the choice is yours, my dear." Voss held up his elongated index finger. "One, you can surrender your soul before the harvest - you'll feel no pain." Up went his middle finger to keep the first finger company. "Two, you retain the very core to your soul until the end, and can deliver the fatal strike to yourself - after the harvest."

Gathering his words into a bundle and throwing them out of my mind, I wasn't able to internalize what he was saying.

"To clarify-," my voice was raspy and raw, "I die painlessly before my soul is eaten or I kill myself painfully after my soul is eaten."

Voss shook his head and tsked. "The human concept of death is so...narrow-minded. So sheltered. So...uneducated." He narrowed his icy eyes at me, and suddenly I was frozen to the spot. "It is not about 'killing' or 'dying' here, you are missing the point, we are not animals."

I begged to differ.

"It is about the life you give to all of Naerin, the contribution you make to the livelihood of thousands of citizens. You will always have that glory that no one else does. We are forever in your debt and cherish your sacrifice always." Voss made it sound so poetic and seductive, even tempting. If I hadn't known any better, if I were just a random soul plucked from my life with no prior knowledge, I'd have easily believed him. I could see why he was chosen as the Keeper – he could seduce anyone with the flirts of death.

But I had the advantage of seeing right through his shameless lies.

Fixed on the storm threatening to brew within his glacial eyes, I knew now was not the time for snark or cleverness. Humility was key.

And so I went with my gut. "You've articulated the meaning of my sacrifice very well, Voss." Matching his smile, I knew I was on the right track. Better to butter him up so that when I sliced right through him, it would be clean and easy.

"It would be my honor to participate in the process," I lied easily, feeling giddy with the upcoming spontaneity of killing him.

"Excellent. I'm glad you see it my way," Voss cocked his head, looking down his nose at me in a way that somehow isolated everyone else and pulled me in closer to him, just us two. He was a master manipulator.

My returning smile was one of feigned naïveté. Of course, I'll feed into anything he tells me. Of course, I'll believe him and agree with him.

"My beauty, which path are you to go down?" Voss purred.

"I wish to gift my soul before." I knew I was speaking his language and looked down shyly. "For the sake of pain." I looked up at him through my eyelashes, humbling myself beyond belief.

"As you wish." His voice ended in a sensual whisper and I

almost fell into his spell. Voss jerked his head toward Suldor. "Go on and prepare the soul." Suldor moved with stealth as he neared me. The silent worker of the Keeper.

Suldor coasted toward me, his braid swinging behind him, his muscles bulging out to the point they may pop. Bracing myself, I held my broken wrist closer to my heart, shielding it from any potential harm that would come from this man driven by the Keeper, the devil who created the plague to spread for centuries in Naerin.

He smelled like the earth. Soil, grass, and saltwater. He must've known how to stealthily move across the land unseen, unheard. He held up a hand that was larger than my head straight up to my face and moved it in circular motions, touching base with my surrounding air.

The throbs and aches and scrapes and bruises and blood were seeping out of me as he continued his trajectory. I could feel each wound leave my body and condense into blackened energy in front of me, before disappearing into thin air.

He was healing me.

My wrist painlessly cracked back into its normal position on my arm, the same as cracking a knuckle. Moving it around incredulously, the pain was absent.

Even my bleary and puffy red eyes settled down. I was becoming the picture of perfect health.

How could I be surprised? If the Phantos entered a metaphorical grocery store and were dependent upon a single fruit that would provide sustenance, why would they pick the bruised one?

I had to be a prim and proper pretty soul before they ravaged and devoured me. I'm sure I would taste better too.

It was evident on Voss's face too. Where he'd previously regarded me as roadkill he had to step over, he was now eyeing me in a new light - a light that I would never want to step into.

Even my clothes were becoming less tattered by the second. The rips in my shirt were sewn up, and the dirt on my jeans disappeared.

Catching a glimpse of myself in Suldor's reflective armor on his chest, I couldn't believe how healthy I looked. My hair had a new shine to it, untangled, unknotted, sitting prettily on my head. My lashes were darker and my eyes were brighter. My cheeks had a healthy rosy tint to them that matched my lips, which looked soft. As if I had just awoken on a plain day back home, ready to venture to Kaffeine and spend my day being perfectly human.

Voss was practically salivating. At that moment, it occurred to me that Suldor was bringing my body beyond the point of restoration, past the point of perfection.

My rosy face paled when I recalled the sick things Dell and Hill did to me. They were all sick. They couldn't just heal me, they had to emphasize the alluring parts of me, as a human woman. Would Voss have his fill on my soul and body before tossing me to the Phantos? I wondered if he did this with every human. He could pretend to feel something that humans had on my earth – pleasure. Feed his hungry stomach a pretty young thing?

For once, I felt disgusted with my pretty body. I wanted to be ugly and bruised again, hoping it would deter Voss.

I only wanted my body to belong to Reid.

Voss was moving closer to me as if my pull was gravitational. He wanted me. Especially after the way I'd buttered him up, he might've even thought I wanted him too.

What I really wanted was to vomit.

"It is done," Suldor spoke, his deep gravelly voice filling the room. He must've been proud of the monster he created in me, luring all this unwanted attention. Even Kuna seemed to back down since the attention wasn't on her and slumped into her seat, though I saw her eyeing Voss every now and then. She probably liked it when they had their spats since it meant he cared enough to induce reactions out of her.

But the spotlight was on me now.

"You've made the right choice," Voss whispered in my ear, and I flinched, not realizing how close he'd gotten. His hand trailed down my arm, and goosebumps rose from his cold touch. Hearing his exhale, I wanted to run as far away as I could, before he could soil my new perfect self and bruise my soul.

How was I supposed to die with dignity and painlessly before the harvest if he were to rape me before it happened? My soul would have a forever stain on it, and I could never pass peacefully, knowing the last man to touch me was this manipulating narcissist rather than my one true other.

It was too late. Voss was already touching me. My arm would

lead to my waist, which would lead to my hips, which would lead to—

"Let us start the harvest with a prayer." Ozul's voice snapped me out of my trance and reminded me of his presence again. What was his job, the prayer announcer?

"The Keeper may enter now."

The final moment. Unveiling the beast that was the reason for all this chaos. The puppeteer orchestrating these foul creatures that called themselves the Council.

Turning, I was ready to face the beast for the first time, ready to give them a piece of my mind.

But when I saw who entered, I was ready to throw myself off the cliff and send myself to a watery death, for the pain would've hurt far less.

It was Reid.

THIRTY-SEVEN

*T*he moment my eyes collided with Reid's, I felt a rush of emotions that brought tears to my eyes, and I couldn't name a single feeling.

"It was…you?" My newly healed voice croaked. Reid's face was completely blank as he stared at me vacantly.

"It dares to speak to the Keeper," Kuna snarled as she prepared to whip me with her dust. Voss's arm shot out over my chest as if to block the impact.

"The soul is not yours to degrade, Kuna." Voss snaked closer to me, putting his arm around my waist, a lot lower than I'd have preferred. "You're all mine to degrade later," he purred in my ear as if any part of that statement would sound appetizing to me.

I didn't care about the consequences. Everything that led up to this moment was finally starting to make sense. All the missing cracks in the picture were slowly filling my head. The more I understood, the more I felt like my heart was getting pushed through a meat pulverizer. Suldor may have physically healed me past perfection, but he couldn't touch the illness in my mind. The pain that raged through my skin, the tears in my eyes, the lightheadedness from the fear, the anger from the revelation, the faint whiff of copper from the puddle of semi-dried blood by my legs from the beating I received, the beating from the creatures that served Reid. The grim reaper. The man who brought me so close to death, while making me feel more alive than ever.

The man who was the commander of them all. The Faerie who damned me to fall in love with him, despite it all.

"You used me," I stated quietly, knowing he could hear me perfectly. "Was any of it true?"

"Now, now," Voss brushed my hair behind my shoulder as his finger trailed my collarbone. "You needn't worry about the Keeper anymore, my beauty. You're mine now."

Ignoring him, I moved away from his creeping touch. "Was any of it real?" I repeated, my eyes trained on Reid. He owed me that truth, at least.

But the Reid I saw wasn't the same one I woke up next to. This Reid was foreign. This one wasn't being witty or sarcastic. He was a stone statue, his face permanently marked with an aura of don't-speak-to-me authority.

Voss yanked me back next to him and hissed in my ear, "That's enough from you." No longer playing nice with him, I glared at Voss, a silent indication of where my loyalties were. A black curl fell over his face as he cocked his head and smiled darkly. "Feel free to fight as hard as you want later. The whole crew can watch, then take turns."

I spat at his feet, and his smile deepened.

"Looks like you can't keep your precious soul in check," Kuna scoffed. Reid shot her a look and she cowered in her seat, muttering an array of apologies under her breath.

"Start the prayer already." The moment Reid's impatient tone rang through the room, each of the Heads sat up straighter and diligently followed his command in unison.

By the solvable Keeper, let us stand in prayer…

Voss's voice rose above the others against my throat before he kissed my neck. His long black curls spilled over my shoulder, tainting my skin.

The food he yields…

I was sick to my stomach. Voss was treating me like his plaything, something to play with before corrupting and consuming forever.

I couldn't go through with this. I couldn't—

We come from the wicked old way…

Voss was a part of the wicked way, and it was far from old. I fidgeted against his touch, uncomfortable with any part of my skin that touched his lifeless skin.

The prayer would be over soon, and any hope of seeing my

sister again would be gone forever. Everything that I did, everything that I sacrificed, was for nothing.

My life was ending before the harvest began.

I wanted to scream. I wanted to die. I wanted—

Be thankful in our worship, to the solvable Keeper.

The prayer was over. Why was it already over? It just started a moment ago, and their voices moved so slowly through it, yet it was already over.

My life was already over.

It was done. Done. No going back.

"Let us bow to the Keeper and begin harvesting the soul," Ozul's voice sounded miles away, even though he was standing just a few feet from me. He bent his head low, as did the others, with Kuna forcing my head down with her dust, while Voss dropped his hand dangerously low on the small of my back in the process.

"Before we progress, I want my one true other to be a part of this before she becomes my queen." Reid's mighty tone bred a silent bow from each of the Council Heads.

Was this Reid's final play before he saved me, or was I truly losing the few marbles I had left?

"Of course, our savior," sounded through the room by the members of the Council.

His voice was firm. "For many moons, we were apart. And now, we can finally rule over Naerin. We will breed the next heir who will continue my reign." His fist shot out into the air, and the entirety of the room echoed behind him. "Long live the Keepers!"

"We will use the soul to bond us together forever." He finally looked at me, really looked at me, and his eyes were darker than I'd ever seen as if darkness had taken over them. Holding his arm out toward the entrance, he bellowed, "Come in, my one true other, my future queen."

A female figure wearing a long veil over her face came into the room. A Syren. Her smooth blue skin was as clear as water as she glided over as if she barely touched the ground. She drifted toward him as he welcomed her, grasping her hand tightly.

So this was his long-lost love. The girlfriend lost to Naerin, the reason he used me, the person I could never hold a candle to.

Briefly, I wondered why Echo said I was Reid's one true other, and I finally understood what he meant. We weren't destined mates or anything. I just fell in love with Reid harder and faster than I ever should've. He might've been my one true other, but I wasn't his. I was never meant for him. It was finally time to face the music, the consequences of living in the moment and casting my fear of emotions aside to be with him along the journey to Naerin.

It didn't matter how real it felt. Maybe it really was real in the moment. He was still a male, at the end of the day. But his heart did not belong to me. It was with her. The veiled Syren about to be his queen.

At this point, I no longer cared what happened to me. I didn't care what Voss and his vile crew would do to me. I was already dead inside. There was only one real question left before I could depart into the dark hole in my brain and walk out unresponsive and catatonic, the same place Moone went before her wings were clipped and she was murdered.

Who was the Syren?

Watching Reid tenderly brushing her arm with affection, I felt another stab to my weak heart. Without taking his eyes off her, Reid gestured to Voss. "Bring the soul over."

Voss blew out some air that was imperceptible to anyone but me and grabbed my arm, pushing his new toy forward.

Every step closer to Reid and his love felt like walking on glass, but I didn't fight it. There was no point now. My fight had already ended.

While Reid's hand never left the Syren's, he gave me one last, final glance. "You got what you wished for, Alluna."

I looked at him with dead eyes, not having enough soul within me to gather any emotions. "What wish would that be, Reid?"

"You saved her without caring if you died in the process, just like you always wanted."

Reid lifted the Syren's veil, revealing my sister underneath.

Vita was staring back at him with enigmatic eyes while she shapeshifted back to her human form. Her black eyes faded away, rosy skin replacing blue. She was the same, beautiful sister I'd risk my life for time and time again.

"Hey, Sis." She grinned at me, and I considered if I was hallucinating again.

"Vita? You're alive?" Happiness surged through me as I

launched myself at her, hugging her tighter than ever, tears streaming down my face. She hugged me back, her favorite spring lavender scent wafting in the air and taking me back to a time when life wasn't so complicated. "You're alive," I cried into her hair.

"Yes, I'm alive," she said. "You saved me by sacrificing yourself. Now I can be with Reid forever." She squeezed tighter until I couldn't breathe and her words sunk beneath my skin, seeping into my bones.

From Me to You

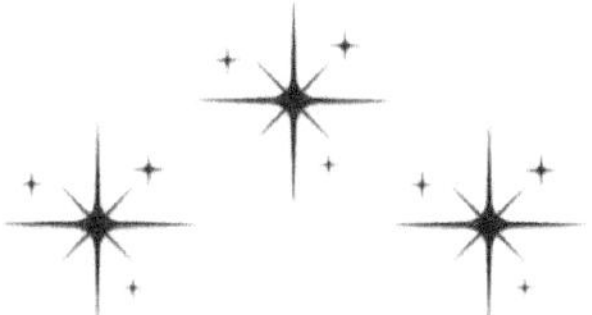

Thank you for deciding to step into the magical world I've created and staying along for the ride. I hope you've enjoyed reading my novel as much as I've enjoyed writing it. If you did, I would really appreciate a review on Amazon or Goodreads. Each review makes a huge difference.

See you next time!

ABOUT THE AUTHOR

NZ Khotimsky is a new adult author based in New York City. She graduated from nursing school and currently works as a registered nurse, while spending her free time reading and writing.